ONCE THERE WAS

KIYASH MONSEF

Simon & Schuster Books for Young Readers
NEW YORK · LONDON · TORONTO · SYDNEY · NEW DELHI

SIMON & SCHUSTER BOOKS FOR YOUNG READERS
An imprint of Simon & Schuster Children's Publishing Division
1230 Avenue of the Americas, New York, New York 10020
This book is a work of fiction. Any references to historical events, real people,
or real places are used fictitiously. Other names, characters, places, and events are products
of the author's imagination, and any resemblance to actual events or places or persons,
living or dead, is entirely coincidental.
Text © 2023 by Kiyash Monsef
Jacket illustration © 2023 by Mike Heath
Jacket design by Krista Vossen © 2023 by Simon & Schuster, Inc.
All rights reserved, including the right of reproduction in whole or in part in any form.
SIMON & SCHUSTER BOOKS FOR YOUNG READER
S and related marks are trademarks of Simon & Schuster, Inc.
For information about special discounts for bulk purchases, please contact Simon & Schuster
Special Sales at 1-866-506-1949 or business@simonandschuster.com.
The Simon & Schuster Speakers Bureau can bring authors to your live event. For more
information or to book an event, contact the Simon & Schuster Speakers Bureau at 1-866-
248-3049 or visit our website at www.simonspeakers.com.
Interior design by by Krista Vossen
The text for this book was set in Adobe Garamond Pro.
Manufactured in the United States of America
0223 FFG
First Edition
2 4 6 8 10 9 7 5 3 1
CIP data for this book is available from the Library of Congress.
ISBN 9781665928502
ISBN 9781665928526 (ebook)

SIMON & SCHUSTER CHILDREN'S PUBLISHING
ADVANCE READER'S COPY

TITLE: Once There Was

AUTHOR: Kiyash Monsef

IMPRINT: Simon & Schuster Books for Young Readers

ON-SALE DATE: 4/4/23

ISBN: 978-1-6659-2850-2

FORMAT: hardcover

PRICE: $18.99 US/$25.99 Can.

AGES: 10 up

PAGES: 416

Please send a URL for any online coverage related to this book to:
childrenspublicity@simonandschuster.com.
Please send two copies of any review or mention of this book to:
Simon & Schuster Children's Publicity Department
1230 Avenue of the Americas, 4th Floor
New York, NY 10020
212/698-2808

Aladdin • Atheneum Books for Young Readers
Beach Lane Books • Beyond Words • Denene Millner Books
Libros para niños • Little Simon • Margaret K. McElderry Books
Paula Wiseman Books • Salaam Reads
Simon & Schuster Books for Young Readers
Simon Pulse • Simon Spotlight

To Jane McGonigal

ONCE THERE WAS

CHAPTER ONE

THE GIRL WHO SAVED A UNICORN

Once was, once wasn't.

A long time ago, in that forest that lies between the Alborz Mountains and the Caspian Sea, a girl went foraging for mushrooms.

It had rained the day before. The ground was soft and damp, and the air smelled of loam and moss. It was a good day for mushrooms, and the girl had nearly filled her basket with lion's mane and hen-of-the-woods when she heard a sound away off in the trees. It sounded like an animal crying out in pain.

There were leopards in the forest, and jackals, and brown bears. But this girl didn't like to think of any creature suffering. So she set out into the forest in the direction of the sound, to see if she could help. A little ways off the path, in a clearing in the deep woods, she found the source of the cries.

The unicorn was bleeding and scared, its leg caught in a hunter's snare. It was a huge beast, and very wild. The girl had never seen such an animal before, and she knew at once that it was special. She also knew that as soon as the hunter returned to check on his snare, the unicorn would be no more. So she swallowed her fear and crept up on it, as gently and as carefully as she could. To calm it down, she offered it some of the mushrooms she'd picked. And when she felt it was safe to approach, the girl bent down and opened up the trap.

The beast seemed to fill up the entire clearing with its long legs and its sharp, treacherous horn. The girl stood there frozen, too awed and frightened to move. The unicorn looked at its savior for a long time. Then it took a cautious step toward the girl on its injured leg, lowered its massive head, and plunged its horn into her chest, right above her heart.

The girl fell to the ground, and as she did, a piece of the unicorn's horn broke off inside her. The unicorn watched her for another moment, then turned and loped off into the woods, favoring its wounded leg, and was not seen again for a hundred years.

The girl, bleeding and in shock, managed to gather enough strength to return to the village at the edge of the woods, where she lived. There she collapsed and was carried to her bed. She lay there for many days. At first no one thought she would survive. But after a day, the bleeding stopped. And after three days, the pain began to subside. Slowly the wound grew smaller and smaller, until all that remained was a crescent-shaped scar, just above her heart, and a little piece of unicorn horn, lodged between her ribs.

Time passed, and the girl became a woman. She married, and had children, and when they were born, some of them had crescent birthmarks above their hearts too. And so did some of their children, and their children's children, and so on. It's said, though no one can be sure, that some of the girl's descendants are still alive today, and that a few of them still carry that mark on their skin, where the unicorn first touched her.

And it's whispered that maybe, just maybe, there's still a little of the unicorn inside them.

CHAPTER TWO

THE WORK

I shouldn't have been working reception.

A veterinary clinic is no place for an impatient person, and I was furious with everything and everyone in the universe. But Dominic needed a lunch break, and the techs were all busy, and as my dad would have said, *The world does not stop for our feelings, Marjan.* Which left me as the friendly face of our practice. So there I was, praying the phone wouldn't ring, and that the lobby would remain empty for the next half hour, so that I could be angry at the world in peace.

Mainly I was angry about two things. The first thing was the clinic itself. As of three weeks ago, the West Berkeley Animal Clinic belonged to me. I'd never asked for it, and the first week of my sophomore year in high school wasn't exactly the best time to suddenly become the owner of a debt-saddled veterinary clinic. In addition to school, homework, and what passed for a social life, I now had payroll, rent, utilities, insurance, and a bunch of other responsibilities I didn't want. Including covering the reception desk so Dominic could take lunch.

And then there was the way it had happened.

This was my dad's clinic. He was a veterinarian, and he'd owned the place for as long as I could remember. Dads don't normally just hand over their businesses to their teenaged daughters. But my dad wasn't normal. Anyway, he hadn't had much of a choice.

The police weren't sure exactly how he'd been killed. There was no murder weapon, but no one could figure out how a person could have done *that* with just their bare hands. I heard one of the first responders say that it looked like he'd been hit by a truck. But even that didn't explain the burns.

There were no suspects. There were no fingerprints, no footprints. There was no DNA, no hair samples or skin flakes or anything else you see in the TV shows. There was no security camera footage. There wasn't even a motive that anyone could guess. Nothing had been stolen from our house. Nothing had been disturbed, except in the room where my dad had died.

So that was the second thing I was angry about.

I'd been coming to the clinic for the past week. Mostly I kept to my dad's old office, which was quiet and small and felt safe in a way nowhere else did. Or I hung out in the procedure room, where I could put on a face mask and disappear, and all I had to do was pet the animals and keep them calm. The lobby felt exposed. I felt like a puppy in a pet shop window, only instead of a puppy, I was a wolverine, and rabid.

But there was no one else to do it, so I'd sat down in Dominic's chair, and dug my fingernails into my palms to distract myself, and told myself I'd be okay—not fine, not by a long shot—but okay, as long as I didn't have to talk to anyone.

I was telling myself that when the door opened.

She came right up to the desk, no hesitation, a heat-seeking missile with a happy face drawn on. I guessed she was in her early twenties. Brown hair, delicate wire-frame glasses, brown eyes that locked on mine the second she saw me. A smile that made me feel a bit like a friend, and a bit like prey.

She didn't have an animal with her. Never a good sign, in a veterinary clinic.

"You must be Marjan," she said. "I'm sorry about your dad."

And she knew my name. Even worse.

"Who are you?" The edge in my voice could have cut bone, but her smile never even flinched.

"We've never met," she said.

"Did he owe you money?" I asked. "Because you'll have to talk to his accountant, and I can pretty much guarantee . . ."

She waved the question away, then reached into her canvas bag, drew out a business card, and set it on the reception desk in front of me. There were no words on it, just a symbol foil-stamped in bronze—a teakettle with a serpentine shape coiled inside it. I waited to see if she would explain what I was looking at, until it became clear that she was waiting for me to recognize it.

"No?" she said at last. I shook my head. She smiled again, a sad smile. "He didn't tell you. Is there somewhere we can talk?"

"About what?" I asked.

"Lots of things," she said. "Your dad. What happened to him." She paused. "The work."

The work.

The way she said those words stirred something warm and alien in my chest. Maybe it was just more anger—a nice vintage anger I'd been holding on to for a long time. Or maybe it was something else. Maybe it was curiosity.

Maybe it was hope.

• • •

Sometimes, when they called his cell phone, I'd pick it up. My dad hated that.

"Is Jim Dastani there?" they'd say, which always sounded weird to me. My dad's name was Jamsheed. "Jim" felt like an especially pathetic kind of cultural surrender, because aside from being aggressively ordinary, it didn't even work. He was so obviously not a "Jim."

I'd make sure whoever was calling heard me shouting "DAAAAAD! It's for YOOOUUUU!" because that seemed about the most unprofessional first impression you could make on a client. My dad would come thumping down the stairs, two at a time. Whenever he was annoyed, he made a face that was kind of like a smile, if a smile were physically painful. To be fair, though, a lot of things looked physically painful when my dad did them—eating, laughing, sleeping. Which is probably why he didn't do any of those things as much as he should have.

Snatching the phone from my hands, he'd give me a stern look, like I was about to be in trouble. But I never was. What was he going to do? Ground me? You can't ground someone if you're not there to enforce it.

He'd take the call into his room, not a word to me. He'd shut the door, and no matter how hard I pressed my ear to it, all I'd hear would be murmurs.

The calls never lasted very long. He'd open the door as soon as they were over, hand the phone back to me, not mad or even annoyed anymore. In his head, he was already packing, already leaving, already heading to the airport or the train station or wherever the hell he went.

"So, where to this time?" I'd ask when I really felt like being a brat.

If I was lucky, he might say something like "Somewhere

warm," or "It's a quiet little town." That's about all I'd get. Whether he was actually talking to me, or just reminding himself so that he packed the right things, was never exactly clear. And he might ignore me completely until the bag was packed.

Our ritual, the real ritual, happened at the door. He'd stop at the doorway, like he'd just remembered something, and he'd turn around. Always, I'd be there, waiting for that moment.

"Marjan," he'd say, "everything you need is—"

"I know." There was no need to go over it—credit card in the kitchen drawer, cash in an envelope next to the sink. Emergency phone numbers—fire, police—taped up next to a business card for a local taxi service, and the number for the pizza place that delivered. Everything I needed was where it always was.

Then the promise. "I'll be home soon."

"Soon" could mean a day, or it could mean a week. I wouldn't know until it was over.

Then he'd put the bag down and hug me. I guess I used to hug back, when I was younger. Hard to remember. He'd hold me like that a few seconds, and then the apology.

"I'm sorry. One day . . ."

Right. One day this would make sense.

When I was younger, I thought all veterinarians had clients like this. After Mom died, I started to figure out how weird it was. I used to get angry at him for leaving. Then, later, I got mean. I accused him of being all kinds of things. Drug smuggler. Spy. Had another secret family, somewhere across the country. Or maybe I was the secret family.

"It's just people who need my help," was always his explanation. And because I'd never seen him care about anything more than he cared about his work, I believed him.

Then he'd say, "I love you."

Never really sure what he meant by that. He was always leaving when he said it.

Finally, the last look. The one where I felt like an animal on the table in the procedure room, like he was trying to spot the tumor, or the infection, or the worm in my eye. And then the little sigh of defeat, like whatever it was he'd seen was beyond his power to fix.

That's how he'd leave me, ever since I was ten years old— completely on my own, wondering what was wrong with me.

And in the end, that's how he left me, forever.

That was the work.

I convinced Dr. Paulson to lend me her tech for a few minutes to watch the lobby. Then I led the woman back to my dad's office and shut the door behind us.

The office wasn't really designed for meetings. The walls were too tight, and the desk was too big. You could fit two people comfortably enough, if one of them sat on the floor, which was what I usually did when my dad was alive. But this wasn't that kind of meeting, and so we both bumbled around the desk, shuffling the chairs so that we could sit, see each other, and not be too cramped against a wall or a bookshelf. I had the odd feeling that my dad was somehow standing between us, shouldering this way and that, making things even harder. But of course, that was impossible.

Finally we figured out how to both sit without bumping knees. The woman placed one hand on the desk, palm up, and smiled at me.

"Can I see your hand?" she asked.

I don't know what I thought she wanted my hand for, but

the confidence with which she asked for it was enough for me to place it on top of hers, palm up. Before I could say anything, she had jabbed a needle into the tip of my index finger, and squeezed up a tiny red pearl of blood.

"Ow!" I said. "What the hell?"

It wasn't until I tried to pull my hand back that I noticed how tight her grip had become.

"Just a minute," she said calmly. "There's nothing to be worried about."

She dabbed up the blood with a thin strip of paper, which she then set on the desk between us. As I watched the blood spread up the paper, she let my hand go.

"Have you ever heard of the Hyrcanian Line?" she asked.

"Um, have you ever heard of asking before you stick someone with a sharp object? What was that?"

"A sterile needle," she said. "Promise."

She picked up the test strip and held it to the light. It was hard to say for sure, but it seemed like some kind of pattern was emerging in the places where my blood had bloomed. The woman smiled to herself, a smile of relief and satisfaction.

"I'm sorry about that," she said. "It won't happen again. Now, the Hyrcanian Line: Have you heard of it?"

I had not heard of the Hyrcanian Line.

"I'm going to assume, then, that you don't know anything at all," said the woman, "and that what I'm going to tell you will come as a surprise."

She opened her bag and took out a brown envelope, then slid it across the desk to me.

"I need you to go to England," she said. "Tonight."

"Excuse me?" I said.

"Everything's paid for," she continued. "It's all there. The only ticket available was first class. I figured you wouldn't mind."

"Are you joking?" She didn't look like she was joking. "Who are you? What's the Hyrcanian Line?"

She ignored my questions. "A man named Simon Stoddard will pick you up at the airport and take you to an estate in the Midlands. Does this make sense so far?"

"Sure," I said. "I fly to the other side of the world, where some guy I don't know takes me somewhere I've never heard of. Then what happens?"

"Then you'll meet a griffon," she said. "It's sick. You'll help it."

"A griffon," I said. "You mean, like a dog? A Brussels griffon? You know I'm not a vet, right? You know I'm fifteen."

"I know," she said. "And no, nothing like a dog."

I kept checking her face for signs that this was some kind of elaborate prank, but all she gave me was a half-hidden smile that seemed like it had been baked into her face. Finally I took the envelope and opened it. Inside was an airplane ticket—first class, as promised—and a stack of candy-colored English currency. All of it looked very real.

"A griffon," I said again. "What am I supposed to do with a griffon?"

"Meet it, examine it, make a recommendation," she said. "That's all. And then you'll come back."

"A recommendation?"

"You'll understand," she said.

"Who are you?" I asked. "What is this?"

She took off her glasses, folded them, and set them on the desk.

"This," she said, "is the work."

"Why should I believe you?" I asked. "Why should I believe any of this?"

"Because if you trust me, maybe I can help you find out who killed your dad."

Her face, playful a moment before, became suddenly serious.

"I don't know who it was," she said, in answer to the question my face must have been asking. "But I'd like to know. I'd like to help. We'd like to help."

"Who's we?"

She sat forward, resting her hands on the table. "Did he ever mention Ithaca?"

"Ithaca?"

"I know this is a hard time. And I know you have questions. Right now, it's better this way. We can talk more when you get back."

"Who says I'm going? I have the clinic. I have school."

"Of course you do," she said. She stood up to go, a movement that would have been dramatic if not for the tight quarters. She nodded at the envelope, its contents fanned out on the desk in front of me. "Well, hang on to all that, in case you change your mind."

Then she turned and walked out the door.

Technically I *did* have the clinic. But I was pretty sure we would be out of business within months. When I looked at the numbers, I couldn't for the life of me see how they had ever worked. Even Dominic, who had managed the office with unwavering confidence for the last two years, was starting to remind me of an old shelter dog who'd given up all hope of ever being adopted.

And school, well. I hadn't been there since Dad died. I wasn't really looking forward to going back. I didn't need my whole class looking at me and trying to figure out what to say.

Still, I collected the things the woman had left behind and put them back into the envelope. It was easier to be reasonable with myself when I wasn't looking at a stack of money and a first-class ticket to somewhere else. I stood up and walked back out to the lobby.

There was a picture of my dad on the wall. Dr. Paulson had put it up after he died, after checking with me that it was okay. It was the same picture that he'd used for everything—the website, all the brochures that the medicine companies printed for us for free. I'd seen it a million times. He was wearing his white jacket, with a light blue button-down shirt underneath. His face was long and thin and the color of chestnut. He had a serious expression, like someone in a picture from a hundred years ago who's never had their picture taken before. Eyebrows clenched together, mouth tight, thick black hair swept away from his face, his dark glaring eyes softened by long, delicate lashes. Jamsheed Dastani—a man of education and wisdom, a man of compassion, a man you'd trust with your pet.

It was a convincing illusion. If you really looked, though, the eyes broke it. They were heavy and haunted, the eyes of a lost soul. The picture's secret—the one you'd only figure out if you studied it a million times, like I had—was that he wasn't really looking at the camera. His face was tilted the right way, and the eyeline was close enough to fool almost anyone. But his gaze was really fixed on something far away and sad, just like it had been when he was alive.

I looked at the picture then. It was demanding my attention, like it had just cleared its throat, like it had something to say. But it didn't say anything. My dad's eyes gazed out of the frame, looked past me toward things in the distance, things he never talked about.

It would, of course, be incredibly reckless to get on an international flight, bound for a mysterious destination, to administer care I was unqualified to give to a creature that didn't exist. No thinking person would ever do something so dangerously stupid.

I looked at my dad's picture until I couldn't stand it any longer. This was his fault. All of it. This clinic, this waste of time and money that was now legally my responsibility: his fault. This strange woman and her unreasonable requests: his fault. The fact that I was even considering them: his fault.

Someone had murdered him one afternoon, in his own home: his fault.

I walked back to Exam One, where Dr. Paulson was just finishing with her patient. I knocked gently on the door, then opened it a crack.

"Something wrong?" asked Dr. Paulson.

I'd always liked Dr. Paulson. She was blunt, but in a way that felt compassionate. Our resident avian specialist, she loved all animals, but birds in particular. She had a pair of lovebirds named Tristan and Iseult, and an African gray named Hemingway that recited T. S. Eliot and Emily Dickinson with manic glee whenever she brought him into the office. She kept a copy of *The Sibley Guide to Birds* on her desk, and two framed prints from *Audubon's Birds of North America* hung on her wall. She even reminded me a bit of a bird sometimes—something still and patient and precise, a heron maybe. She was tall and slender and serious, but it wasn't that. It was the stillness—the way certain kinds of hunting birds can freeze and become part of the landscape. That's how she seemed to me in that moment. Poised and alert, scanning for information.

"I think I'm going to go home, Dr. P," I said.

That was it—I would go home and think about things in a rational way, and having done that, I'd see that getting on a plane to England with no idea who or what awaited me there was reckless and irresponsible.

"I'm sure we'll manage," said Dr. P. "Everything okay?"

"Yep," I lied. "All good. I think I just need to rest a bit."

And stop thinking crazy thoughts about flying halfway across the world to administer veterinary care I wasn't qualified to give, to an animal that didn't exist outside of fairy tales.

"You have to take care of yourself," said Dr. Paulson.

"Oh, and I might take a couple days off."

Wait, what? Had I just said that?

"Of course," she said. "Whatever you need to do."

"Thanks, Dr. P," I said.

I must have been making a weird face. It felt like too much work to be a normal face.

"Marjan?" she asked. "Are you okay?"

"Fine," I said. "I'm fine." I don't think I sounded fine.

"If you ever want to talk," she said, "I'm here."

She looked like she wanted to talk, which made me want to talk even less. The last thing I needed to hear was how someone else was handling the death of my father.

"Thanks," I said. "I'm good."

Before she could say another word, I drew back out of the room and shut the door behind me. I stopped one last time in front of the picture of my dad, and tried to stand so that he was actually looking me in the eye. But everywhere I tilted and cocked my head, he was still looking past me.

"If I die," I said to the picture, "it's your fault."

• • •

I did go home, so that wasn't a lie.

Home was a fifty-year-old stucco house in the north Berkeley flatlands. From the street, it was a simple gray wall with two windows, a cement porch, and a door, beneath a streetlight on a telephone pole and a maple tree that grew from a square of dirt in the sidewalk. My dad's Civic sat in the driveway, gathering leaves at the base of the windshield. It hadn't been started since he died.

I was walking my bike up the steps from the street to the porch when I heard my name from behind me.

"Marjan, how are you, sweetie?" asked a warm voice, filled with care.

My next-door neighbor, a bustling woman named Francesca Wix, was now my legal guardian. She lived in a little old house that she'd inherited from her grandfather, with a revolving cast of foster dogs that my dad had treated for free, a year-round garden of fruits and vegetables, and an impressive collection of romance novels. She was three inches shorter than me, but her voice, toughened by years of peaceful protest, more than made up the difference. She wore bright, chunky ponchos with African designs, and big round glasses that made her eyes look like they were about to pop delightfully out of her head. When she wasn't phone banking or making protest signs, Francesca worked at an anarchist bookstore. I'd never been there, but I often wondered if they had a romance section.

She'd volunteered to be my guardian partly because she felt like she owed my dad for all the years of free vet care, and partly because she was the kind of person who volunteered for things. On the day the approval came back from the courts, she brought us empanadas and Mexican Coca-Cola, and laid out her rules.

"Grief's weird," she said. "Do whatever you need to. You don't need to tell me or ask permission. But"—and here she paused, wiped a crumb from her cheek, and became serious— "no drugs."

Mostly she was too consumed with her dogs, her plants, and her anarchy to do much legal guarding. Still, she signed all the documents that needed signing, and occasionally she left food on my doorstep. Other than that, she stayed out of my life except to make sure, every time she saw me, that I was holding up okay, and not doing drugs.

"I'm fine," I said.

"You're home early," she said, pushing her glasses up so they rested atop her close-cropped Afro.

"I'm tired." Yep, that was it. Tired. Definitely not on my way to do something incredibly stupid.

"Do you need anything?"

I shrugged and shook my head. There were many things I needed, but I wasn't going to get them from Francesca Wix. With a wave and a forced smile, I left her at the bottom of the steps and carried the bike into the house.

The inside of my house was as dreary as the outside. A little kitchen with a tired old electric range and a noisy refrigerator that was probably in violation of the Paris Accords; a living room where very little living had ever happened; and a dark upper floor with two bedrooms, one bathroom, and an extra room full of boxed-up stuff that we never used for anything.

Just a girl, coming home early. The fact that I was emptying out my backpack, and then filling it up again—some clothes, toiletries, a passport (never used)—didn't mean anything. Nothing to see here.

They'd found my dad in his bedroom. Someone had called

911 and then hung up. The front door had been open. The first day, the whole house had been taped off, and detectives had come and gone, gathering and cataloguing evidence. Then they'd packed up their stuff, handed me a receipt for the things they'd taken, shut his bedroom door, and disappeared. I hadn't opened it since.

I paused outside it. Right then it felt like that door was everything my dad had been in life. Closed. Silent. Full of dark and probably unpleasant secrets I'd so far managed to avoid.

I wanted it to stay closed forever. And I wanted to kick it down.

My ears were ringing and my heart was pounding. My feet itched to move. It felt like my whole body was vibrating with electricity, with questions, with hunger. I had a bag in one hand and an airplane ticket in the other. What was I doing?

Nothing about the next few hours felt real.

From the car ride to the airport—I sat in the back of a shuttle van in quiet, stunned disbelief that I'd even come this far—to the fact that the airline was willing to honor the piece of paper I handed them as if it were in fact a ticket, and a first-class one at that, I felt like I was walking deeper and deeper into a slow-moving fever dream, until I was actually on a plane, watching as the doors closed and the world I thought I knew fell away out the window.

I had no idea where I was going, and what would be expected of me when I got there. I had no idea how to prepare—or even if any preparation would help. When I thought back to my conversation with the woman, I wished I'd asked more questions, or asked the same questions over and over until she had answered them. A *griffon*? Was that really what she'd said? Had

I heard her wrong? And anyway, why me? What good would I be to anyone, least of all a griffon?

But for all the questions I wished I could ask her, there were a million more I wished I could ask my dad. They were buzzing and whispering in my ears and in my head and in my heart, all the time, every day. They made me angry, and the anger made me exhausted. And if I didn't at least try to answer them, they'd probably keep buzzing and whispering for the rest of my life. I'd probably be angry forever.

Somewhere over Hudson Bay, the exhaustion overrode the anger and strangeness, and I fell asleep and dreamed about a story my dad had told me, when I was very young.

| CHAPTER THREE |

THE SHIRDAL'S FEATHER

Once was, once wasn't.

On the great steppes of old Scythia, in the time of year when the grass dies and the wind howls across the plains, a young nomad discovered a strange and pitiful beast curled up beneath an outcropping of rocks.

The little creature was unlike anything the youth had ever seen before. It had the dusky body of a cat, but the beak and talons and wings of a raptor. It was weak and shivering from the cold. Its ribs showed through its fur. Had the youth not found it then, it would surely have died. But the young man took it, and wrapped it in a blanket and carried it to the warm fires of his camp.

This youth came from a poor, wandering tribe. They kept a small herd of sheep, and from their wool they wove carpets that they brought south to the great merchant caravans to trade. They lived at the mercy of the wolves and the weather, and neither was merciful. Their lives were hard, and they never had enough. They could ill afford another mouth to feed, and so when the youth brought the creature to the warm hearth, the elders of the tribe told him he would have to leave it behind.

But the youth wouldn't listen. Instead he fed the creature his own share of food, and made a place for it to sleep in his family tent.

That night, the creature, its belly full, slept on a carpet of warm wool. The next day, the elders again ordered the youth to dispose of the creature, and again he responded by offering the beast his own share of food, and making it a bed on the carpet of his tent.

By the third day, the creature was strong enough to spread its wings and fly. The youth, weak from hunger, was powerless to stop it as it took to the sky and disappeared, leaving behind only a single feather.

Every day, the youth watched the sky for some sign of the creature, and every day he was disappointed. The season turned, and the ground froze, and soon it was time for the tribe to depart for the warmer lands to the south. The youth mourned that he would never see the little creature again.

The winter was harsh that year. The merchant caravans were few and far between, and the carpets never brought enough in trade. The rivers and creeks were barely flowing. There was little for the sheep to graze on, and little for the people of the tribe to eat.

But one day, the youth saw a familiar shape soaring through the sky, and followed it. It led him to a bubbling spring and a sheltered oasis of green surrounding it. And for the rest of that season, the youth and his tribe had enough water, and their sheep had ample grass and scrub to graze, and even though the merchant trade was slow, they were comfortable enough.

When the seasons turned again, the tribe headed north to the high steppes. Their herd grew fat on the rich grasses that sprang up that year. One night, wolves struck, and took ten sheep.

The next night, the men and boys of the tribe stood watch over the herd, staring out into the vast darkness in search of predators. But no wolves came. Instead the tribespeople heard a terrible sound from somewhere deep in the night. In the morning, they discovered five wolves, torn to pieces. After that, no wolves ever troubled their herd.

It was late in that northern season when the tribe's food stores ran out. Having lost so many sheep to the wolves, they couldn't afford to slaughter another. And though they'd set snares for rabbits and game birds, their traps had come up empty. Desperate, the tribe sent hunting parties out into the steppes, but they all came back empty-handed.

The tribespeople found themselves dreading the southward journey. Without food, some of them would surely starve along the way. But if they stayed where they were, the winter would be just as cruel. There was no choice but to try to reach the southern lands.

On the eve of their departure, they were startled by the sound of great wings in the air above them.

There could be no doubt that the creature that descended out of the sky was a griffon—a shirdal, as the old Persians called them. Clutched in each talon was a freshly killed antelope. The griffon landed in the midst of the nomads' camp. It laid its gifts at the feet of the youth who had saved it.

The nomads survived that winter, and many others after. The youth went on to become the chief of his tribe, and though life was never easy for them under his leadership, it was perhaps a little less hard. Many seasons later, when he passed his rule on to the next chief, he also gave her the feather of the shirdal.

And she, in her turn, passed it again to the next leader, and then it was passed to the next, until no one could say for sure whether it was an eagle's feather, or a vulture's feather, or perhaps a shirdal's feather, or whether the story of the youth was true, or just a tale to be told around a fire when the nights grew long. But the people of the tribe understood that some things can be true and not true at once, and that a story is a thread that can be woven into the world, until it is as solid as a carpet beneath one's feet. And so they guarded the feather and the story that went with it, and passed them both down through the generations.

And among the patterns of the carpets they wove, the shirdal could always be found, just at the edges, invisible to all but the keenest eye.

CHAPTER FOUR

KIPLING

We landed at London Heathrow airport on a gray morning, under a ceiling of low, flat clouds. I pulled my jacket tighter against the September chill, and shivered my way to passport control, where, despite my pitiful attempt to explain the reason for my trip (family friends, last name "Griffon"), the border agent stamped my passport and handed it back to me.

The arrivals area was full of people, all rushing: rushing to greet their families, rushing for taxis, rushing to catch trains and buses. It felt like a river flowing around me, and I'd stepped right into the deepest part. My heart began to race. What was I doing here? It seemed impossible that I could be an ocean and a continent away from everything I'd ever known. Anything could happen to me, and no one would know. I could disappear forever, and no one would even think to look for me here.

I glanced back at the security doors I'd just come through, and wondered if there were a way I could squeeze back through them, back onto the plane, back home.

"You must be Marjan."

The man looked to be about my dad's age. He had small

features, a slim build, bright blue eyes, and skin that looked like it might burn under anything brighter than candlelight. His tweed jacket and brown slacks would have looked fusty if they hadn't been so perfectly tailored.

I hesitated. Maybe I should lie? *Nope, definitely not me. Wrong completely-out-of-her-depth girl.*

But even though I felt lost and alone, even though I had no reason to trust this stranger standing in front of me, I saw something in his eyes that I recognized: worry, gathered in the creases of his narrow face. The same kind of worry I saw in my dad's face, when he looked at me before saying goodbye. And somehow, I felt like I could trust this man. He needed help, and for some reason, he thought I could provide it.

All of a sudden, the walls of silence my dad had built around his life felt thinner than ever. I could almost hear the years of secrets clawing for daylight. I had to know. I had to know what it all meant.

"That's me," I said.

"My name is Simon Stoddard," said the man. "I'm glad you've come."

We were met at the curb by a black Mercedes. A driver got out and opened the door for us, and waited.

Instinct kicked in. A strange car, strange men, a strange country, all because of a strange woman and her strange envelope—I stopped, so quickly that Simon almost bumped into me.

"I'm sorry," I said to Simon. "I don't know you. I don't know him. I don't know where we're going. I just . . ."

Simon looked so embarrassed, I started to feel bad for him.

"Oh dear," he said. "This is all wrong, isn't it? I'll send the driver on. We'll hail a taxi instead, and we'll have him wait for you, as long as necessary. Would that be better?"

He waved his driver off, flagged down a black cab. Simon gestured for me to go first, then slid into the seat across from mine. Inside the cab, a button controlled a two-way speaker to the driver. Simon gave the driver an address, and then, as we pulled away from the curb, politely switched the speaker off.

"I understand you haven't been told much," he said in a reassuring tone. We merged onto a smooth, straight highway heading north. As the edges of London blurred past the windows, Simon began to tell me a story.

The griffon had been in his family for three hundred years. Simon's ancestor, a merchant sailor named Aloysius Stoddard, had rescued it from an abandoned nest near the city of Aleppo, in Ottoman Syria, when it was just a whelp. "He must have been the runt," said Simon.

From that day onward, no Stoddard childhood had been without the gentle presence of the griffon. Aloysius, a man of humble roots, had been knighted by the king of England himself. The family wealth had grown at a steady, respectable pace. His descendants were blessed with beauty, intelligence, and compassion.

We left the highway and joined a smaller road. Green hedges streaked by on both sides. Farther away, sheep dotted low slopes. Stone walls that must have been hundreds of years old marked property lines. Farmhouses and manors sat away from the road. Horses tottered in muddy paddocks.

Was this what it was like for my dad? Did he sit in the backs of strange cars, watching strange landscapes float past? For a second, as the countryside unspooled outside the windows, I felt closer to him. If he hadn't died, he'd have been the one sitting here. The image of my dad riding in this car, instead of me, stirred up an unexpected surge of resentment. If he'd been here, I would have been at home, all alone, eating peanut butter sandwiches three meals a day, and pretending to everyone I met that everything was fine.

I looked over at Simon, who was himself gazing out the window.

"How did you find me?" I asked.

"It's a very old method," he said. "When Kipling is ill, we raise a certain flag over the house."

"Kipling's the griffon?" Simon nodded. "So you raise a flag, and then what?"

He looked at me like I was joking.

"Why, and then you come," he said. "There are some messages passed. Intermediaries. No names, of course. I don't know who arranges these things. I don't care to know. I care about Kipling."

"I don't know what you expect me to do for you," I said.

"Kipling is unwell," said Simon. "I'm aware of your lack of experience, but from what I understand, you might still be a help to him." He switched on the two-way long enough to say, "Turn left here."

We veered onto an even narrower road shaded by a canopy of arching birch trees. I could feel the crunch of the country lane beneath the tires.

"This is the beginning of the grounds," said Simon.

The road wound around a corner, then across a wooden bridge that crossed a rippling creek. The forest seemed to grow thicker as we went. An undergrowth of ferns and blackberry brambles sprouted at the edges of the creek, and continued on either side beneath the slender birches. The air smelled like autumn and rain.

"This is all your land?" I asked.

"There are about a hundred acres of wild forests here," said Simon. "They used to be for fox and grouse hunting. But we don't hunt anymore, except for Kipling, who does what he pleases."

With a grand flourish, the trees fell away to reveal a gabled brownstone manor bigger than any house I'd ever seen before, crawling with woodbine and flanked by manicured gardens on one side, and a large pond flecked with tiny green lily pads on the other. The driver brought us around to the main entrance, a giant door of varnished oak with a huge brass knocker in the center, and let us out.

"You . . . live here?" I asked Simon, shivering a bit in the chill of the gray afternoon.

Simon laughed to himself. "I feel the same way, at times. We have been very, very lucky."

He walked up the steps, grasped the doorknob with both hands, and twisted. A heavy latch slid out with a muffled thud. He swung the door open and motioned for me to enter.

At the end of a long hall, the great chamber of the Stoddard mansion glowed with a cavernous warmth. The walls were paneled mahogany set with cozy yellow sconces of frosted glass. A paisley rug of cream and burgundy stretched the length of the massive room. Several large windows striped one wall, letting in the weak daylight. On the opposite wall, a fireplace of rough stone was flanked by family portraits from generations past. A blazing fire whispered and snapped on the hearth.

In the center of the room was a griffon.

"Kipling?" said Simon into the flickering gloom. "Will you say hello?"

Kipling's huge wings were half-furled over his body. His rear haunches, tucked in tight against his ribs, were the paws of a lion, and had the dusty color of lion's fur. His forelegs were graceful talons, folded upon themselves at the wrists. As Simon approached, Kipling's head raised ever so slightly up from the floor. He clicked his beak once as Simon drew near, then gently nuzzled his feathered scalp against Simon's outstretched hand. His feline tail tapped against the carpeted floor. Simon knelt at Kipling's side and whispered something into his plumage. Then he scratched the griffon's head and stood again.

"Ms. Dastani," he said, "meet Kipling."

For a second, my brain shut down completely. I wasn't scared. I wasn't in awe. I wasn't anything at all. I had exactly one thought, and it was all my head could hold.

Griffons exist.

Slowly I rebuilt the world in my head. I was still Marjan Dastani. I was still in high school. My friends were still Carrie Finch and Grace Yee. My dad was still dead, and I was still in England. Everything else was the same, only now there were griffons.

And apparently I was supposed to examine this one.

Kipling's eyes narrowed to wary slits. His wings fumbled open, nearly filling the room from one end to the other. With great effort, he drew his body up to standing. His head, plumed and beaked like an eagle, wreathed in a magnificent mane like a lion, dipped low between the blades of his shoulders. His talons grasped at the carpet, claws cutting into the intricate patterns. *Maybe there were shirdals hidden there, too.*

Those claws could have easily ripped me apart. There was nowhere to run. I was at Kipling's mercy. So, without even thinking about it, I did what my dad did whenever he approached unfamiliar animals. I held out my empty palms to show that I had nothing to hide, and I looked down to let Kipling assert his dominance.

After a moment, Kipling snuffed at me through his beak, unimpressed. Then he seemed to collapse inward. His eyes shut, his chest expanded, his neck shrank, his wings curled up. Everything gathered up into a tight, clenched ball, until all of a sudden a retching cough exploded out of him, rattling his ribs and echoing lung-deep. His wings flailed out, bumping against the ceiling and the floor. His chest heaved. His whole body contorted and shook.

When the spell had passed, Kipling's legs were quivering. He slumped back down to the floor, unable to hold up his own weight, and lay there, exhausted.

Suddenly, I didn't see an impossible creature anymore. What I saw was an animal like any we would have treated at the clinic. An animal that needed help.

Slowly, one step at a time, I approached. Kipling watched me with weary, halfhearted interest. He had the dander-y smell that parakeets have, but it was mingled with the smell of tree sap and green pine needles, and something more muscular and intense that I couldn't exactly place.

I glanced back at Simon. His face was sober with concern. I recognized this moment. This was where I was supposed to start talking. I pictured my dad standing here, confident and assured, saying wise things, or even just asking smart questions.

But what was *I* supposed to say? I had no idea how a griffon worked. I wasn't my dad. I wasn't even a veterinarian. I shouldn't have come here.

Kipling seemed skeptical too. He watched me with bored resignation, even as another micro-spasm of coughs rippled in his chest. His doubt was oddly comforting. Simon was hoping for results, for answers, but Kipling expected nothing from me. It would be impossible to disappoint him.

Up close, I could see that his feathers were molted off in places. His fur was patchy like an old carpet. His eyes were filmy and crusted at their edges. I reached out my hand and stroked the feathers of his neck, following their smooth grain down to the withers, where they became fur.

I felt it first as a tingling in my fingertips. It felt the way you'd imagine TV static would feel, if it were a feeling. The tingle shot up my arm like lightning. It swelled in my chest and radiated out into the rest of my body until it was all I could feel. The sensation got stronger. A rushing sound filled my ears. I stood riveted where I was. I couldn't have moved if I'd tried.

Then, like a bubble popping, the tingling sensation was gone. In its place was a whole host of other feelings, all coming at me at once. I struggled to make sense of them.

There was, first of all, a fierce, stubborn will that felt like I was leaning against a strong wind. There was a melancholy longing that made me search for a view of the sky through one of the windows. There was a bitter and unfocused frustration, like the whole world had too many bumps and corners, and all the spaces in it were suddenly too small.

Mostly, though, there was pain.

My body boiled with foul poison. I felt it in my lungs, in my stomach, in every beat of my heart. Something thick and strangling gathered against my ribs and snaked around my spine. A corrosive taste burned in my mouth. Every sensation, every sound, every breath, every touch, brought pain.

I pulled my hand back, and all the feelings evaporated. For a moment, I was in a bright, close room—too bright, too close—and all was still, and everything was breaking.

And then I felt nothing, and the world turned on its side.

Simon caught me before I fell, and eased me down to the floor. A moment later, gentle hands pressed a glass of water into mine. Beneath a tangle of brown curls, a pair of blue eyes much younger than Simon's looked down at me with concern and care.

"Sebastian?" said Simon, somewhere in the floaty space behind me. "What are you doing here?" The eyes glanced up over my shoulder for a second, then back down to me.

"Aunt Chelsea said he was ill," said Sebastian.

"Of course she did," said Simon.

"And is he?"

"That's what we're trying to determine."

"How are you?"

It took a moment for me to realize that the voice called Sebastian was now speaking to me. I tried to answer, but my throat had gone dry. I drank the water in the glass too fast, like I was trying to fill up some newly empty space inside me, and choked.

"Easy," he said. He started to say something else, but that was when I passed out.

We had a fight one morning, Dad and I. He'd just come back from somewhere, and he was in a bad mood. I guess the trip hadn't gone well. I was thirteen.

It started with toaster waffles that were still cold.

"Gross," I said, and pushed them away.

"You can make your own, then," he said, before swigging a big gulp of coffee from his mug. "Or you can have some of my breakfast."

He had a plate of feta cheese, radishes, and flatbread, and I think he already knew what my answer would be.

"Eww," I said. "No one eats radishes for breakfast." I could have left it there, but I was mad. "Why don't you ever make any real food?" I asked.

"This is real food," he said. He paused, then added, "This is your culture, Marjan."

My mom, an American, had been more enthusiastic about Iranian culture than my dad ever was. Since she'd died, he almost never brought it up. When he talked about it now, it never felt like he was actually talking to me. There was another conversation going on in his head. I think it had been going on since the day she'd died. I think it was always going on. Usually he kept it to himself, but sometimes it snuck out.

When it did, his voice changed just slightly, in a way that made something twist in my chest. Like I shouldn't be there. Like I was eavesdropping on an uncomfortable grown-up talk, but like I was being forced to do it, not given any choice. And it always made me angry.

"My culture is waffles," I said. "Toasted. Not cold. And *that*"—I nodded at his breakfast—"is barely even *your* culture, *Jim*."

My dad didn't get angry, exactly. He didn't shout or lose his temper. Instead his voice got sharp and cold and hollow, the bevel of a hypodermic needle piercing skin, looking for a vein to tap. It hurt, and it made me feel sorry for him at the same time. When he got that way, I could see right through him, see how broken he was.

"The world does not stop for our feelings, Marjan," he said. His English was perfect except for the accent, which turned "world" into "verold," and rolled "our" into a long two-syllable word. "It owes you nothing. Least of all an explanation."

Then he went back to his coffee and didn't say another word. I toasted that waffle myself and burned it. It tasted terrible, and I was angry all day.

After school, I stomped the pedals of my bike all the way to the clinic, which was where I always went after school, angry or not. Even if I was mad at my dad, I still liked the animals. When I got there, the lobby was full, the exam rooms were empty, and the procedure room was humming with chaotic activity.

"Boxer ate some rat poison," said one of the techs as she brushed past me carrying a stack of freshly sanitized towels.

I shut myself away in my dad's empty office to start my homework. He came in after a little while, dressed in his white coat. His hair was a little wilder than usual, and he looked just a bit more exhausted than he normally did.

"Come with me," he said.

He led me down the hall to Exam Three.

"Open it slowly," he said, his voice low. "And shut it behind us."

Inside, the lights were dim. A *whuff* sounded from the exam table. A moment later, another. On the table lay the boxer, eyes half-closed, tongue hanging from one side of her mouth. She was hooked up to an IV drip.

My dad pulled out a chair and set it down next to the table, careful not to make a sound. He sat gently in the seat, then nodded for me to bring another chair to join him.

"Strychnine," he said, in a whisper, after I'd sat down next to him. He looked at me to make sure I was paying attention. "We induced vomiting. We gave her activated charcoal. We sedated her. So"—he paused, his eyes on the sleeping dog— "what are we doing now?"

He was testing me.

I thought for a second. Strychnine poisoning in dogs causes violent convulsions that lead to death if not treated immediately. My dad had done everything he could for it—everything you'd do for a poisoned dog. Now we were—

"We're watching," I said. "We're watching for spasms."

"Good," said my dad. "And if she starts to have seizures?"

I had to think a minute. "More sedative?" I said. It was kind of a guess.

"Very good," he said. "And why the dark room and the whispering?"

"Because . . . ," I said, hoping the answer would come to me. When it didn't, my dad finished the thought.

"Because bright lights and loud noises can trigger seizures."

"Is it . . . ," I said.

"We got there in time," he answered, and I heard something like relief in his voice.

And then we sat, listening to the boxer's breath, watching her chest rise and fall.

Whuff.

Whuff.

Whuff.

"The world doesn't owe you an explanation," he said. "But I do. When you're ready, I'll tell you."

"Maybe it's just something that takes practice."

We were in a study down the hall from the great chamber. I was lying on a narrow couch, my consciousness, strength, and balance returning. The boy named Sebastian—he looked just about my age—was standing by the window, hands in his pockets, looking out onto the grounds. I guessed he'd helped move me here, but I was too embarrassed to ask. Simon was nowhere to be seen.

"I might agree with you," I said, "if I knew what 'it' even was."

"Are you feeling any better?"

"Mildly. Where's Simon?"

"I think he's talking to my school right now. Hopefully, corroborating my story."

"Simon's your . . ."

"Uncle," he said. "I was away at boarding school, but when I heard Kipling was sick, I . . . Well, here I am."

He looked like he'd just remembered something, then walked quickly across the room to a table with a pitcher of water on it. He poured a glass and handed it to me. I drank it slowly this time, and once I'd finished, I found I had the strength to sit up.

My nerves were still jangling from surprise and shock and pain. The actual sensations were gone, but I felt a hollow echo of them in my bones. When I stopped and paid attention, I realized that I was breathing gingerly, anticipating the clenching burn I'd felt before.

Sebastian sat down across from me. He was tall, a little too tall for the chair he'd chosen. His legs were too long, and so his knees came up just high enough that they took up real estate where his arms might have naturally come to rest. The end result was a halfhearted pretzel with a freckled face and a scruffy ginger prep-school haircut. He was probably just a bit awkward everywhere he went, but it was a charming kind of awkward. Elbows and knees, and despite them, a face so perfectly intense that it grabbed you like a spotlight. That was my first real impression of him.

"What exactly *did* happen in there?" he asked. "If you don't mind me asking."

"I'm not sure," I said. It seemed too silly to say out loud. *I felt Kipling.*

At that moment, Simon came in.

"Ah, you're awake," he said. "And you're acquainted with my wayward nephew." He gave Sebastian a scolding glance.

"I'd do it again too," said Sebastian, standing up in defiance. "For Kipling."

"I'm sure you would," said Simon. "But you'll need a better excuse next time. Sick grandmothers invite too many questions. We must be careful not to draw that kind of attention."

"What did you tell them?" asked Sebastian.

"Only that you were lying through your teeth," said Simon. "That you're a very naughty boy who will be back at school tomorrow, and that the whole family, including your perfectly healthy grandmother, is mortified at your behavior."

"Tomorrow?" said Sebastian with dismay.

"Be grateful I'm not shipping you back tonight." He turned to me, and his expression went from stern to pleading and hopeful. "Now, about Kipling. Tell me."

I took a deep breath, savoring the absence of pain in my lungs. *Was this what my dad did? Was this the work?*

"He's suffering," I said.

Simon's face fell. I tried to imagine what my father would have done with all that pain. I pictured him going to Kipling, a needle in his hand, whispering to the griffon not to worry, that the next few moments would be strange, but that after that, the agony, the corruption, all of it would be gone forever.

And then—

No, that wasn't right.

"He needs painkillers," I was saying. "He needs nutrients. Put him on an IV drip if he doesn't eat. Take X-rays, MRIs, blood panels, stool samples. Treat whatever you find."

The words felt shallow and squirmy, like they were eels in my stomach, and I had to spit them out as fast as I could before they bit me. I didn't even look at Simon or Sebastian until I was done, until I'd spilled every last slithering syllable onto the carpet. When I did finally look at them, I half expected to see disgust.

When I saw relief, I felt relieved too.

"So it is treatable," said Simon. "He can be helped, after all."

"He could get better," I said. *Eels.*

"Can you help?" said Simon. "With . . . what you're suggesting?"

"I'm still in high school," I said.

Simon was quiet a moment. "Of course," he said. "I'll have to find another doctor, then." He nodded, satisfied. "I suppose I have some work to do." He turned and left the room.

Sebastian, still standing, looked at me a moment longer, then stalked after his uncle. I heard their voices from the hall, speaking in hushed tones. With great effort, I pulled myself up and crept to the open door to listen.

"At least let me stay another night," said Sebastian. "To be with him."

"He needs rest," said Simon. "When he's better, you can have all the time you want. Perhaps we'll gather the whole family together to celebrate."

"But—"

"No buts," said Simon. "You've already raised enough suspicion with your actions. A sick grandmother . . . honestly."

I peeked out into the hall. Sebastian was hanging his head.

He looked like he was about to walk away, but something stopped him.

"What if she's wrong?" he asked. "What if he doesn't get better?"

Eels, eels, eels.

"You mustn't think such thoughts," said Simon, a little too quickly. "He's strong. He'll get better. And in the meantime, we must proceed with our lives. It's the only way to keep him safe."

"We could protect him better if we didn't have to do it in secret," said Sebastian, his voice sharp with frustration.

"You're upset," said Simon. "Kipling means a lot to all of us. We'll see he gets whatever he needs."

Sebastian glared at his uncle a moment longer, then began to stalk back to the room where they'd left me. I crept back to my couch and lay down again. The fierceness was still in his eyes when he returned, but after he'd taken a breath, he calmed himself and sat down in the chair.

"He's not a pet, you know," said Sebastian. "He doesn't *belong* to us. He could leave anytime, but he's chosen us. For hundreds of years, he's trusted us. Will he be okay?" he asked.

I didn't feel like another round of eels, so I just nodded helplessly, and hoped that was enough to convince him.

"What about you?" he said, after a moment. "Are you okay?"

When I looked at those blue eyes and saw nothing but sympathy, something broke inside me.

I hadn't cried when my dad died. Or at the memorial, or any day since. It just never came. But now, here, in this unfamiliar place, face-folding sobs surged up out of nowhere. There was no stopping them, nothing to do but sit there and cry and feel stupid and embarrassed and small. I couldn't even say exactly what I was crying about: my dad, the strange and beautiful animal in the next room, the unfairness of it all, the endless echoing *why, why, why.*

"I've been better," I said, wiping my eyes after the worst wave had passed. Sebastian was still looking at me, and to my surprise, he didn't seem completely disgusted by the blubbering mess before him.

"Maybe some fresh air?" asked Sebastian.

There were walking paths all around the manor. Sebastian led me through a rose garden and a grass field designed for a lawn game I'd never heard of. As we walked, he rattled off bits of history—this wing was completed in 1836, this fountain was a gift from King George, those stained-glass windows were made in Flanders using chemicals that drove people insane.

"Why do you know all this?" I asked.

"My family takes its history very seriously," he said. "I guess it's partly because one of us has lived through all of it."

"I heard what you said before," I said. "In the hall."

He looked embarrassed. "I didn't mean . . ."

"It's okay," I said. "I don't know how any of this works. You should talk to someone else."

"He won't do it," said Sebastian. "He believes in . . . something. Looking after Kipling—he thinks things must be done a certain way, or the covenant is broken."

"What covenant?"

Sebastian laughed. "Some think Kipling's given us everything we have, that he chose us because we were somehow deserving, and that we must continue to live as we always have, or else he'll leave, and take all our good luck with him."

"But you don't think so."

"For me," said Sebastian, "Kipling is family. We feed him, we give him shelter, because he's one of us. Nothing else matters."

At the end of the playing field was an old stone wall like the ones I'd seen as we'd driven up. On the other side of it, the land opened up into a gentle green slope, and beyond that, a low, thick forest. We walked down the slope until it ended at a murmuring creek. In a shallow pool, tiny fish darted in and out of the light.

For the last three weeks, time had felt heavier, like gravity on another, much bigger planet. A minute on this alien world where I now lived weighed as much as ten minutes in normal time, and when I looked too far ahead, the weight of all that super-dense time made my bones ache. So I'd kept my eyes on the ground, looked where I was putting my next step, and hadn't worried much about what came after that.

But here in the cool gray afternoon outside the Stoddard manor, far away from anything familiar, time felt lighter again. I could see further, see more clearly. And it didn't hurt so much to look ahead. I should probably, I realized, get back to school. I should sell the clinic before it ran completely out of money. Maybe someone else would know what to do with it.

"There must be others out there," he said. "Like Kipling. I assume we're not your only clients."

"I wouldn't know," I said.

"You probably couldn't tell me, even if you did," he said.

"My dad never talked about any of it."

"Of course he didn't," said Sebastian. He paused. "I'm sorry. I didn't know your father. I only know my family. All the sneaking around, the lying, I just hate it. Maybe he was sparing you."

"Sparing me?"

"We Stoddards grow up learning how to lie, how to keep secrets. Some days, I just want to tell everyone. Kipling is such a wonder—why keep him to ourselves? But it's probably not that simple, is it?" Sebastian sighed. "Anyway, Uncle's right. I should have been more careful. I do wish he'd bought me another day or two, though."

He picked up a small stone and flicked it into the water. The fish scattered in all directions in a tiny iridescent firework. The sweet, soothing trickle of the creek filled the chilly air.

"Kipling's woods," said Sebastian, nodding at the trees. I tried to imagine the griffon roaming that forest. Sebastian as a little boy, roaming alongside him. The image made me smile.

"What's it like?" I asked. "Growing up with a griffon?"

"I don't know any other way to grow up," said Sebastian, "He's always here. You know you'll see him, every time you come back. It's hard having a secret like him, but it keeps our family close."

"I know a little about that," I said.

"I imagine you do," he said.

Whatever he meant, whatever he thought, he was probably wrong. But I didn't feel like correcting him just then. Because even if he thought the secret I'd shared within my tiny two-person family was the same wondrous one his family had treasured for so long, and not the small, chaotic, frustrating secret of an erratic and unreliable single father who maybe loved me but who also disappeared for days on end with no contact and no explanation—even if Sebastian thought that, he still understood me better than any of my friends.

And maybe I understood him pretty well too.

"Sebastian?" I said. His name, when I spoke it for the first time, sounded like a tiny castle on a hill somewhere, safe and secure and warm.

"What is it?" He was looking at me, face bright and unguarded.

Something familiar and ragged and true hovered just in front of me, a brilliant tear in the fabric of the universe, begging to be seen, to be spoken. I'd seen it before, when I'd felt Kipling. I wanted Sebastian to see it, to know. But whatever it was I was trying to see, it was too close, and too bright, and too fractured. And whatever it was I was trying to say just turned into eels in my stomach.

I shrugged. "I'm tired."

He looked at me oddly, trying to tease out with his eyes the thing I hadn't said. I gave him a weak smile and looked away. After a long moment, he gave up and went back to looking out at the trees.

"You're welcome to stay here," he said. "Plenty of rooms."

I wanted to keep talking with him. I wanted it desperately. Someone who understood, who wasn't speaking in mysteries. I needed it.

But I didn't want to stay. The thought of going back into the manor, of seeing Kipling again, made the world quiver like pond ripples. I wanted to be far away. I wanted to be home.

"Maybe another time," I said. "This is all really weird to me."

Sebastian smiled an understanding smile, but I could see that he was a little disappointed.

"I hope you'll keep in touch," he said. "It's not often I can be brutally honest with someone I'm not related to."

"So far, you're the only person I know that I could even talk to about this," I said. "Sign me up for brutal honesty."

He smiled at me. It looked like he wanted to say more, but he didn't.

When we returned to the manor, Simon presented me with a

check that seemed much larger than I deserved. He insisted it was the negotiated rate, and finally I accepted. A car took me to an airport hotel, where I spent most of the night pacing the floor of my room as rain guttered against the window.

I'd felt all kinds of things since I'd come home that day three weeks ago and found out about my dad. Shock, disbelief, guilt, anger—so much anger. None of it had been as simple and pure as the tears that had erupted out of me at the Stoddard manor. And now that the tears were gone, I felt empty.

Something in me was hungry and broken. I could feel it in my chest, beneath my ribs, beneath the crescent-shaped birthmark just above my heart. It felt *right* to just be sad. It felt natural and honest and comforting, in a way that nothing else had, these last three weeks. But I couldn't find that feeling anymore. When I tried, I just felt angry and lost.

CHAPTER FIVE

ZORRO

The night I returned home, I stood outside my dad's bedroom door for a long time, wondering what secrets might be behind it. Were there other animals like Kipling? Other people like the Stoddards? How many? Where? Which animals? Could I connect with them, the same way I had with Kipling? My dad had filled my head with stories when I was young. How many of them were true? And the biggest question—the one that made my stomach drop every time:

Why did he never tell me?

Hands shaking, I reached once for the doorknob, but stopped myself before my fingers touched the brass.

Did he really think I couldn't keep one more secret?

I willed my angry questions at the door, through it, as if the door were my father's ghost, as if it might open up of its own free will and answer them. But of course, it didn't.

Fine, I thought. *I'll show you. I'll show you how I keep secrets.*

Two days after I got back from England, I rode my bike to school and snuck in late to first period. My best friend Carrie glanced back from her seat in the front of the classroom and gave me the universal expression for *What the hell, Marjan,* which I sort of deserved, since I'd been basically a ghost since my dad died. I did my best nonverbal *I'm sorry,* and Carrie gave me a short withering glare, followed immediately by a sincere and heartfelt *Are you okay?* I gave her a thumbs-up that then became a fifty-fifty, and we agreed via hand signs to meet up after class.

Carrie Finch had been my first friend in middle school. Day one of sixth grade, when everyone was trying to figure out where they fit in, Carrie and I ended up seated next to each other in Mrs. Ascherman's homeroom. My first impression of her was of careful neatness. Everything, from the tight braid in her blond hair to the golden tan she'd brought back from summer vacation, to the way she slid her backpack under her seat, seemed to land in exactly the right place. She began taking notes as soon as homeroom started. Her handwriting was small and swift and clean, and she'd filled a whole page before first period was done. I'd never taken notes in class before. I'd never seen someone my age work so hard at simply listening. And it was only *homeroom.* I was fascinated.

Her dad was a tenured professor at UC Berkeley, her mom was a hospital administrator, and her brother, Kyle, was a gawky sixth grader in Mrs. Ascherman's homeroom. The Finches lived in a big, bright house near the university, took family vacations to Yosemite and Hawaii, and invited people over for dinner parties, all of which seemed incredibly exotic to me.

After first period was over, Carrie gave me a big hug. Her arms were freakishly long. It was one of the few things about her that wasn't annoyingly perfect, but she made the best of them. She'd been swimming for the varsity team since freshman year. And her hugs were always big.

"I was so worried about you, Marjan," she said. "I thought you might get shipped off to somewhere and we'd never see you again." Carrie could conjure up worst-case scenarios with shocking ease.

"Sorry, Care Bear," I said. "It's been a weird few weeks."

A moment later, we were joined by Grace Yee, who came rushing up from the far end of the hall and nearly tackled me.

Even with the pompadour undercut she'd debuted on the first day of school, Grace was the shortest of the three of us. But somehow she was always the one people noticed first. She had a loud, raspy voice that cut through background noise like a finely honed scalpel, and a way of walking—and even just standing still—that seemed to create a kind of electrical charge around her. And she always wore bright colors—today it was a green zip-up hoodie with matching Chuck Taylors.

"We missed you, you stupid," she said, punching me in the arm. "Why don't you ever write back?"

"Just needed some time, G," I said.

Grace was the reason we'd all become friends. During Advisory that first day of sixth grade, she'd maneuvered herself into the same reading group as Carrie and me, mainly because she, like me, was achingly curious about how and why Carrie had managed to write down so much when so little had actually happened. But unlike me, she wasn't afraid to ask.

And when Carrie explained how she couldn't help it because she felt physically ill if she didn't take detailed notes, Grace immediately declared that we three were now a study team. "You," she said to Carrie, "are going to make sure we don't miss anything." That day, we all learned two things. One, that beautiful, perfect Carrie was actually a nervous wreck on the inside. And two, it was impossible to argue with Grace Yee.

The bell rang for the start of our next classes, and a flock of chattering freshman boys scurried past us.

"Hang on," said Grace before we could all split off in different directions. "Where are you going?"

"Chem," said Carrie.

I had to think about it. It had been three weeks since I'd had to remember. "Spanish, I think."

Grace looked around. The hall was starting to clear out.

"Congratulations," she said. "You're both wrong. The next class is boba. Let's go."

Carrie made a whimper of worry. I'm pretty sure skipping a class would have made her break out in hives. I'm also pretty sure she would have done it, in this case.

"Can't, G," I said. "Not today. I gotta figure things out with admin. Can't be cutting class while I'm trying to convince them not to hold me back a grade."

Carrie let out a sigh of relief, and Grace scrunched up her face.

"You're no fun, either of you," she said. Then she did a haughty spin on her heel and stomped off in an exaggerated huff. Over her shoulder, she called out, "Lunch, outside." It wasn't a suggestion.

At lunchtime, Carrie, Grace, and I sat in the campus quad. It was a sunny day, and a lot of kids were out, bunched up in groups, laughing, shouting, looking at their phones. A cluster of theater kids huddled around a girl playing a ukulele and singing Halsey. A few boys, including one Grace had had a crush on since freshman year, juggled a soccer ball back and forth with their feet. It felt almost like an ordinary day.

Carrie had chicken breast cut in thick slices, and a can of iced espresso. Grace had cold spicy noodles and vegetables her mom had made the night before. My lunch was peanut butter on white bread. At least that's what it was until Grace saw it.

"Absolutely not," she said. And then my lunch was cold spicy noodles and vegetables Grace's mom had made the night before.

"Where have you been, anyway?" said Grace as she studied my smooshed sandwich with fascinated disgust.

"Home," I said. "And then at the clinic. Which, by the way, I own now. Yay." It wasn't enough of an answer, and I could feel it. "I'm putting things back together. I wasn't trying to shut you guys out. I just wasn't ready for this"—I nodded out at the school and the grassy field— "until now."

"I can't believe what you've been through," said Carrie. She shook her head and looked at the grass. I thought I saw tears coming to her eyes.

"For real, you guys," I said, "I'm actually doing okay."

"Do they know who did it?" asked Grace. I had a feeling she would be asking me that question every few days until I could answer yes.

"Not yet," I said. *And they're nowhere close.*

I tried to remember if either of them had ever met my dad. Maybe Grace had stopped by the clinic once or twice? Maybe he'd picked me up from a school dance one time? I'd always tried to keep him separate from the rest of my life. I was afraid he'd mess things up by being too serious, or too sad, or just too strange.

"Do you want to talk about him?" Carrie ventured. "I mean, if it helps?"

I did want to talk about him. But I'd never be able to say the things I needed to, not to Carrie and Grace.

I held a story in my head, and didn't say anything. Grace rested a compassionate hand on my arm. At that moment the soccer ball came bouncing through our picnic, and Grace's crush came running through after it, apologizing to all of us, and to Grace in particular, and she turned bright red. We all laughed, and the conversation moved on, but the story stayed where it was.

It was a summer morning, and I was eleven years old. My dad had been away and then come back. A short trip, I think, but they all felt the same to me: angry, lonely, and terrifying.

We'd spent the night before playing cards. When I was little, my dad had taught me a Persian card game called Pasur. We didn't play often, but every now and then, one of us would bring out the deck and we'd go through a few hands. It was just an ordinary deck of cards, but my dad would call out the suits and the face cards by their Persian names, and count score in Farsi, and somehow that made the cards all seem different.

My dad seemed different too. He went somewhere else when we played. I don't know if it was Iran, or my childhood, or someplace he never told me about. Wherever it was, it was happier and more hopeful than the place where he spent the rest of his life.

I went to bed that night feeling safe and secure. I wasn't alone anymore. The next day, I woke up to a note on my chair in my dad's sharp, precise handwriting:

"*Went to work early. Didn't want to wake you.*

—Dad"

My chest tightened. Everything I'd been feeling while he'd been gone came rushing right back, only now it was worse. I was even angrier, even more lonely, even more scared. That was the day I realized that this would never end. It would always be this way, and it would never get better.

I tore up the note, kicked my chair over, slammed the door of my room, and went downstairs.

I stood in the kitchen, feeling chaotic and dangerous, and underneath it all, empty, like there was a black hole somewhere at the center of my heart that was hungry to be filled. Something deep down was missing—something I needed.

That's when I started making the sandwiches.

I used a whole loaf of white bread, and as much peanut butter as I could fit on each one. I didn't know how to make anything else. I stacked them, smooshed them down, stuffed them back into the bread bag, and then put the bag into the backpack. The backpack went onto my shoulders, and I left. I didn't know where I was going.

When someone found me the next day, I had walked twenty miles. My legs were stiff and aching. I'd eaten all the sandwiches, and I felt sick to my stomach. I was cold and confused and frightened, and I was no closer to the thing I'd been looking for.

My dad picked me up and drove me home.

"I'm glad you're okay," he said, and that was all.

When we got home, he looked at me the same way he did whenever he left. Like there was something wrong with me that no doctor in the world would ever be able to fix. I don't even think he was angry.

I think he was ashamed.

Grace caught me at the end of school, putting her arm through mine as I walked toward the exit.

"We're going to Care Bear's," she said. "You're coming."

The family room at Carrie's house was our default hangout. It was warm and clean and had lots of cozy places to sit.

You could flop down anywhere, open your backpack any-where, plug in a laptop pretty much anywhere, and get on the TeamFinch Wi-Fi (password Fringilla216). Plus there were snacks, and the fridge was stocked with cans of fruit-flavored seltzer. And everyone was always welcome for dinner. It was the exact opposite of my house.

"I don't know, G," I said. "I was going to go to the clinic."

"Come on," said Grace. "Anyway, you gotta meet the Blue Whale."

I'd been hearing about the Blue Whale for weeks before my dad died—an old Subaru wagon with two hundred thousand miles on it that Grace's parents had acquired, to give her on the occasion of her sixteenth birthday, which—

"Oh no!" I said, stopping in my tracks. "I missed your birthday!"

"You missed a little dinner thing," she said. "Don't worry. But now I'm gonna guilt you into coming, because, oh my God, Mar, I can't believe you missed my birthday."

The Blue Whale was somehow round and boxy at the same time, with headlights that looked like they were squinting, and a grille making a frowny face. It was long and low, like it was trying to sneak underneath a bigger car. The inside felt low too, and the gray upholstery was worn and cracked. But it was a car, and Grace was the only one of the three of us who had a license.

Just to be safe, I called the clinic. Dominic assured me that things would run just fine without me.

"Go see your friends," he said. "The techs will sweep up the lobby, and I'll stock the meds and turn out the lights. You're good."

There was enough room in the back of the Whale for my bike. Carrie volunteered to sit in the back seat, even though her legs were longer and the back seats were cramped. When we were all buckled in, Grace backed out of the parking spot—a little too fast, but in a fun way—and we all laughed. Then we cranked down the windows because the inside of the Blue Whale had a musty smell, and because it felt good to drive with all the windows down and only your best friends in the car with you, and in a few minutes, we were pulling up outside Carrie's house.

"Welcome back, Marjan," said Carrie's dad when he saw me. "It's good to see you again."

I waited for him to ask me about my dad, or to say he was sorry to hear. It was a relief when he didn't. Just a knowing nod, and that was it. Carrie's parents were easygoing and friendly, and never asked any uncomfortable questions.

I got a can of raspberry seltzer from the fridge, snuggled into a beanbag chair, and laid out the homework I'd accumulated in my absence. It was a lot. The school claimed they'd forgiven my weeks away, but now I was beginning to wonder if I was really forgiven after all.

Carrie sat in her normal spot on a big floor pillow under the window, studying her Kiswahili grammar book. She'd gone to a Chinese immersion school for six years before we'd all met, and she still liked to practice her Mandarin with Grace every now and then. Counting the French her parents sometimes spoke at home, she knew four languages.

Grace was doing chemical equations in a workbook with headphones on and a look of grim determination on her face. She lay on the couch, shoes kicked off, tapping her toes as she gritted through pages of molecular diagrams. Once, she took off her headphones to say, "This is just pretend chemistry," before putting the music back in and going back to work.

We could sit like this for hours, the three of us lost in our own projects and assignments. And sitting here like this, the world seemed almost normal. I could almost pretend that I hadn't just been on the other side of the world, face-to-face with a sick griffon, feeling what it felt.

Almost, but not quite.

That night, after Grace drove me home, I sat on my bed and typed Sebastian's number into my phone. When I thought of Kipling, sick and weak in that dark room, something wobbled inside me. But when Sebastian had sat with me while I'd been sobbing, when we'd walked through the grounds, when we'd looked out onto the woods, the world had felt a bit less confusing. A bit warmer.

I wanted less confusion. I wanted more warmth. And more than anything, I wanted someone I could really talk to.

Hey, I wrote. It's that American girl who was crying all over your fancy furniture.

I stared at the words I'd just sent across the ocean, and waited.

The phone blooped at me. A little bubble appeared below mine.

I hope you've managed to pull yourself together.

I smiled.

Still a hot mess, I wrote.

Be grateful you're not scrubbing two hundred dishes every night for the next week.

?

School punishment for skiving off. They're not allowed to beat us anymore, so instead they try to kill us with repetitive stress injury.

A pause. Then another bloop. Can a bloop feel meaningful? This one did.

How are you doing?

I've been back two days, and it's already exhausting.

It gets easier, he wrote. You get used to it.

I didn't need to explain anything to Sebastian. He understood exactly what I was talking about.

How long does that take? I blooped.

About seventeen years.

Not at all helpful, thanks.

Lucky for you, he blooped, you now have a direct line to a certified expert on the subject of Keeping Big Secrets.

Yay lucky me.

There was a long pause, long enough for me to wonder if I'd been too sarcastic. Had I made him mad? Had I hurt his feelings? Would he decide I wasn't worth the effort? Was that what I really wanted, after all? It would be less complicated, less wobbly, if I could just put Kipling and everyone connected to him behind me.

Bloop.

I'm serious, he wrote. You can always talk to me. You can tell me anything.

I started to type. I wrote two words, looked at them, and didn't hit send. They sat there on the screen, the truest truth I'd ever written anywhere.

I'm scared.

I looked at those words a long time, my thumb hovering over the send button. Could I tell him? Could I trust him?

Bloop. From Sebastian.

Anyway, I've got to go wash the breakfast dishes.

I deleted what I'd written.

They'd better be spotless, I blooped. And thank you.

· · ·

After a few days, school fell into a rhythm. People stopped noticing me in the halls. I somehow managed to make up most of my missed assignments. Some days, I studied with Grace and Carrie in the Finch family room until it was dark. Other days, I was at the clinic, dealing with dusty, grown-up responsibilities I'd never asked for. Vendor invoices, payroll, rent, utilities. There was an X-ray machine that was dying. There were two mortgages. Something was always due. Something was always late. And nobody cared that the only reason I had to worry about all this stuff was because my dad had just been murdered.

Sometimes, when the clinic was quiet, I took out the card the strange woman had left behind—the teakettle with the curling serpent inside—and studied it for clues. A hidden phone number, an email address I'd missed, some secret message encoded in the blocky design. But there was nothing, and the more I stared at it, the more meaningless it seemed.

Sometimes it seemed like none of it had happened at all.

Once a week, Carrie, Grace, and I went to the boba place near school, and talked about ordinary things. School, music, boys. The biggest topic was Grace's soccer-ball crush, a boy named Howie.

"He was totally smiling at you at all-school today," said Carrie one afternoon.

"He smiles like that at everyone," said Grace. "It doesn't mean anything! Marjan, tell her one smile doesn't mean anything."

To which I smiled, and sipped my tea.

"What's so funny?" demanded Grace.

What was funny was watching Grace, who was normally so

composed and confident, act like Carrie before an exam. This had gone on for weeks, and I was starting to think Grace was secretly enjoying the drama and attention.

It felt almost the way it had been before my dad died. But there were things I couldn't say. There were stories that were burning to get out, but I couldn't tell them. Sometimes I wanted to just shout, *There are griffons! Real, live griffons!* I felt like the three of us were small, and only I could see it.

Fortunately, there was also Sebastian.

We chatted every day. Sometimes on video, sometimes just in silly little texts. It was crazy how much I looked forward to seeing his name pop up in my notifications. Crazy how comforting it was to not have to be careful, to not feel like I was hiding half of my life every time I talked to him.

"I get angry at people for not knowing the things we know," I said. "Like it's somehow their fault that I can't tell them anything. Do you ever get that?"

"All the time," he said. "You have to be able to be two different people. The one who knows, and the one who doesn't."

"I kind of hate the one who doesn't know," I said.

"Me too," said Sebastian.

We were on video. I was in the back office at the clinic, and he was in an empty study hall at his posh boarding school. Beneath the scruff of his hair, Sebastian's face, a little bleached out by the camera, a little distorted by the lens, and a little sleepy, still had the same intensity I remembered from when I'd first met him. There was something about his features and the way they fit together that I could never quite hold in my head, that I was always trying to grasp and keep up with, like they were some kind of unsolved mystery. On video, I could study his face more closely without being weird, without looking like

I was staring at him. I did it all the time, and I was still no closer to understanding why I couldn't get myself to look away.

"So what do you do?" I asked. "When you get angry."

"I find Kipling," he said. "I sit with him. Remind myself why it's worth it."

"What if I don't have a Kipling handy?"

"You're welcome back anytime," said Sebastian.

"Are you asking me out?" I asked.

"Are you free?"

He smiled. He was joking, of course, and so was I.

"Sebastian?" I said. "Do you think I'm allowed to be doing this?"

"Doing what?"

"Talking to you."

"Why wouldn't you?"

"I don't know. It just seems like there might be some rules or something. Maybe not for you, but for me. Like, I don't think my dad ever talked to clients like this."

"Did you want to stop?" said Sebastian. "Should I not text you anymore?"

"No," I said. "I think I would literally explode if I couldn't talk to anyone. Anyway, it's kind of cool. Not knowing. It makes it more fun."

Sebastian smiled.

"What?" I said. "Did I say something?"

"You said this is fun," he said. "I feel the same way."

When I left the clinic that evening, I could still see Sebastian's face, that smile, those eyes, that *thing* about it that I couldn't ever quite get to hold still. I could hear his voice crackling through the speaker. And I felt good. I felt hopeful. As I biked home, a tiny and confusing warmth flickered in my chest.

There was a pizza waiting on my doorstep when I arrived, along with a Post-it note with a smiley face drawn on it.

I called out a loud "Thank you" in the direction of Francesca's house, which started up a chorus of dogs. I brought the pizza inside, intending to take it up to my room to eat.

As I walked along the upstairs hallway, the carpet felt softer than usual. It felt like I was waking up from something, coming back to life. Then I saw the door to my dad's room—closed, as always—and anger rose up and drowned out every good feeling.

Weeks went by. Everyone—my friends, the guidance counselor I'd seen a few times, Dr. P and the techs at the clinic—assumed I was going to sell my dad's business. I hadn't tried yet.

I couldn't say why, exactly, it was so hard to part with the clinic. I wasn't a veterinarian. Plus business sucked. David Ginn, my dad's accountant—and now mine—confirmed this to me one evening.

"Not looking good," David confided over the phone.

"What should I do?" I asked.

"Dump it, the first chance you get," said David.

David had started working with my dad in the strange, radioactive months after my mom died. There weren't many people who willingly waded into the cloud of confusion that was our lives that year. David was the only one who stayed.

I knew he was right. He was usually right. But also, I think I was waiting, hoping, for the phone to ring, for the strange woman who'd brought me to Kipling to peek into the door of my office again. I wanted to be useful. I wanted another chance.

But it wasn't her the next time.

. . .

"The first thing you should know about me is that I'm a witch."

Those were Malloryn Martell's first words to me, after introducing herself. The lobby was empty except for the two of us and Dominic, who had just answered a phone call. It was three days after Halloween, and almost two months since I'd met Kipling, and in that time, nothing remotely unusual had happened. And then, one afternoon, I went to the clinic after school and found her waiting for me in the lobby, sneaking leftover trick-or-treat candy from the bowl on the reception desk.

Malloryn Martell looked like someone had transformed an eager puppy into an emo teenager. She was wearing a Totoro T-shirt, a faded denim jacket, black leggings, and green Doc Martens boots. An old backpack covered in patches and witchy-looking symbols drawn in faded Sharpie hung wearily from one shoulder. She had curly dirty-blond hair in a bouncy bang cut, and warm hazel eyes that refused, despite a lot of smoky eye shadow, to do anything other than sparkle brightly.

A cardboard cat carrier rested at her feet, silent and still. My breath caught in my throat. *Is this it? Is she the one? Is this my chance?* Without another word, I motioned for her to follow me back to the office.

Once we were in the office, she set the cat carrier on the floor. From inside, I heard the brief shuffle of something furry reorganizing itself in the narrow space, then settling. But I couldn't see anything through the little breathing holes in the cardboard.

"A witch," I said after I had shut the door behind us.

"Not an evil one, though," she replied with a laugh. "Don't worry."

I tried to laugh too, but I wasn't sure I understood the joke. Were there evil witches? Should I be worried?

Either I was talking to a witch, or a crazy person. Whichever one she was, there was still something in that cat carrier. And I still wanted to know what it was.

"So, uh, is that your black cat in there?" I asked.

It was the wrong question.

Her face fell. The smile went away. Her eyes went dull with weariness. I could have sworn she groaned with disappointment.

"Right," she said, "because *all* witches have black cats."

"I mean, don't they?"

"No." She glared at me. "We don't all have black cats. We don't all ride broomsticks. And we don't float in water, either. Does that clear up your default assumptions?"

I got the feeling this wasn't her first time having this conversation. Before I could say anything, her expression softened.

"I'm sorry," she said. "That was rude of me. It's been a hard week. For me and Zorro both."

"Zorro is . . ."

"My familiar," she said. I must have looked confused, because she gave an understanding nod and continued in a patient tone. "You can't do magic alone. It's way too powerful. You need a spirit medium to connect with the aether."

"A spirit medium," I said.

"Yep, and so you summon a familiar. It's the first big spell you cast, and it's sort of like an initiation, or . . . or a final exam. It's an all-or-nothing kind of deal. Pass-fail. You get one chance, and if you mess it up, it's all over. If you can't summon a familiar, then the doors are closed and you'll never do magic. But if the spell works, then you know you're a witch. You've been chosen."

When she talked, everything about her sort of danced. Her

hands moved. Her blond ringlets bobbed just above her glimmering eyes. Tiny dimples appeared and disappeared on her pink cheeks.

"Chosen," I said. "Chosen by whom?"

"Well, your familiar, for one. But also the bigger powers, the spirits, the ones behind the veil of the world, in the aether. They have to accept you, and if they don't accept you, then no familiar, and no more magic."

"But you were accepted."

"I was," she said with pride. Her hand rested gently on the carrier.

"Where'd you learn all this?" I asked.

She grinned, slid her backpack off her shoulder, unzipped it, and dumped out a pile of dog-eared bargain-bin paperbacks with names like *The Call of the Witch* and *The Sisterhood of Midnight*, printed in curvy, blocky 1970s fonts. The covers were psychedelic designs and New Age photographs of crystals and naked bodies silhouetted against the moon. I flipped through a couple of them, and wasn't convinced.

"So you used these books to summon—" I said.

"Not a cat," said Malloryn.

She reached down and opened the pet carrier. Inside was dark and close and crowded with blankets, but I could see something furry and sleek uncurl itself. Pointy ears pricked up. A slender paw reached out and gently padded at the wall of the carrier. A long, elegant snout inched into the open air.

Zorro was a gray fox.

"He's the best-trained fox you'll ever meet," Malloryn said. "He's even housebroken. Bet you weren't expecting that."

I glanced up at her.

She was looking at me, and she wasn't smiling. "I'm not

stupid, you know. I can tell when someone doesn't believe me."

Zorro blinked at the sudden brightness. He rested two dainty paws against the lip of the carrier, then leaned his weight against it until it tipped over. He crawled out, seeming quite proud of his little trick, and scampered up Malloryn's leg to curl up in her arms, then rested his snout in the crook of her shoulder. With one hand, she scratched at the tuft of orange-silver fur between his ears.

"How did you find me?" I asked.

"Rubashkin," she said.

"Uh, gesundheit?" I said.

"Rubashkin's *Selection Spell*?" Like she was reminding me, like I should have known. I shook my head, and she sighed. "I put the names of all the vets in town into a bag, and yours—well, your dad's, anyway—is the one I pulled out. And since he's gone, I figured you were the one I was supposed to find."

"That's called Rubashkin's Selection Spell?"

Another sigh, a twinge of agitation. "I know, I know, Rubashkin was debunked in the eighties," she said. "It's not *technically* a spell. But it still worked, right?" She smiled brightly, hopefully.

All of a sudden a panic-laced thought occurred to me.

"When you brought him in, did anyone see him?"

"I was careful, jeez," said Malloryn. "It's not like I haven't ever had to take him somewhere before. I know the law. I know I'm not supposed to have him."

"Your parents let you keep him?"

She was quiet a moment. "They don't know," she said. "And they won't know."

Her eyes told me there was more to the story, but they also told me I wouldn't be getting the rest right then.

"How did you even get him? How did you train him? Aren't foxes supposed to be, like, impossible to tame?"

"If you have to tame your familiar, you're doing something wrong," said Malloryn. "And I didn't *get* him. I *summoned* him."

"You summoned him. Like, out of thin air?"

"I don't know where he came from," said Malloryn. "Do I, Budgins? One day you were at my door, weren't you?" She gave the fox a squeeze, and he made a kind of clucking, purring noise. "I summoned him, and he came, and I love him. That's right." She wasn't talking to me anymore, really. You wouldn't talk to another human in that kind of voice, unless they were very small.

"He's not an ordinary fox, you know," she said. "He's special."

"I'm sure he is," I said.

Malloryn bristled. "You don't believe me," she said. "You'll see. You can believe whatever you want. We're used to it."

She held Zorro in a tight and protective embrace, and gave me a look that dared me to question her devotion to him.

"So what's wrong with him?" I asked.

Malloryn's expression softened. She looked at Zorro with loving eyes. "We don't know, do we?" she said, stroking his ears. She leaned in toward me, like she was about to confide a secret. "I have a theory, though."

"What is it?" I asked.

She lowered her voice. "I think he was hexed."

"Hexed?"

"As in, cursed," said Malloryn.

"Who would do that?"

"Minor demons, outer spirits, a jealous warlock," said Malloryn. "Could be anyone."

Zorro opened his snout and began to pant. It's hard to read

expressions on canid faces, but if you see enough of them—for example, if you grow up hanging around a veterinary clinic— you start to notice where they show their feelings. I could see how the corners of his eyes seemed to droop where you would expect them to be sharp, how his brow seemed heavy and weary. I could see that his mouth, though open, wasn't smiling. Instead it drew back flat and slack, an expression that could indicate pain or discomfort.

Something was troubling him. I seriously doubted it was "minor demons." But there was only one way I knew I could be sure.

"Can I pet him?" I asked.

Malloryn shifted her arms so that Zorro was pointed toward me. When I reached out a hand, he closed his eyes and bowed his snout for me to touch. I ran my knuckles up the bridge of his nose, between his ears, and at first I didn't feel anything. Then, in the thick, wiry fur at the base of his skull, I began to feel the tingle in my fingers. Malloryn started to say something. I shushed her with my free hand, and closed my eyes as the feeling spread.

There was a tightness in my chest, like there was nowhere for the air to go, no matter how deeply I inhaled. My heart thumped against my ribs, a nauseating feeling, too slow and too strong. Malloryn might not have been any kind of witch, but she was right about at least two things. There was something special about Zorro. And there was something very wrong with him.

"What is it?" asked Malloryn. "Is it demons?"

"He's sick," I said. "It could be serious."

"So what do we do?"

I didn't know how to turn the sensations I'd felt a moment

ago into any sort of proper diagnosis. For all I knew, Zorro did have a demon hex. And whatever it was, I was almost certainly violating a few state wildlife codes just by having him here in the office. But I could see the fear in Malloryn's eyes. It wasn't just fear for Zorro's safety. It was the fear that I would turn them away. And I knew that if I didn't help her, no one would.

"I can't do anything for him right now," I said. It was almost four o'clock, and I wasn't going to risk any sort of thorough exam until the clinic had cleared out for the evening. "He'll need to stay overnight."

We closed at five. Soon after, I heard Dr. Paulson's bicycle roll down the hall. The vet techs clattered around for the next thirty minutes or so, wiping down surfaces, sweeping floors, organizing files, and stocking inventory for the next day. Then, one by one, they left too, locking the front door behind themselves.

Malloryn and I had decided it would be less suspicious if she left with the carrier everyone had seen her walk in with, even if it meant Zorro would be free to roam. So she hugged him and whispered goodbye to him, and then assured me again that he wouldn't do anything stupid. Fortunately, she was right. Zorro curled up in the corner behind my desk and stayed there, and didn't make a sound.

Once it was quiet, I peeked my head out and glanced up and down the hall. Zorro and I were alone in the clinic. I opened the door all the way and motioned for Zorro to follow. Together we walked quickly across the hallway to the procedure room. The sound of fox claws clacking on the linoleum in the empty clinic was oddly comforting.

I knew how to operate the new X-ray machine because I'd been there last month when the sales rep had explained it. But

I didn't really know how to read an X-ray, or what I should be looking for. All I knew was that something was making it hard for Zorro to breathe. And something was making his heartbeat heavy in his chest. Maybe an X-ray would tell me what that something was.

The new machine was a gleaming white system consisting of an X-ray gun, a receptor plate on an adjustable armature, and a monitor to display the images. Zorro was more cooperative than most animals. In just a few minutes, I had three angles on his chest. I lifted Zorro off the procedure table and set him gently on the floor. He sat at my heel and watched as I pulled up the images on the screen and clicked through them one by one, and tried to make sense of what I was seeing.

Beneath the zebra stripes of his rib cage, Zorro's heart was a dark, translucent presence suspended in a pale, milky cloud of organ mass. From another angle, blood vessels and alveoli branched out against the angel-wing backdrop of his lungs. Through the segments of his spinal cord, I could trace the path of nerves, rising up to his brain. Whatever Malloryn thought him to be, on the inside, Zorro was pretty much the same as any other small mammal.

Zorro's amber eyes met mine. He didn't care that I still had no idea what I was doing running a clinic. He didn't care that I was angry most of the time. He didn't care about debts or mortgages. He didn't care about the things I hid from the people closest to me. When animals look at you, they don't see all the complexities of your life. They only see you as you are in that exact moment, and they're not ashamed, and they're not afraid.

I didn't know a lot about X-rays, but a few things stood out. A bright spot that probably shouldn't have been there. A thin, dark, wavy line that seemed suspect. A general state of affairs in his chest cavity that didn't look quite right. I was pretty sure they were all important. But I didn't know any more than that. We'd reached the end of my veterinary expertise. I looked at the X-rays, one after another, again and again, hoping something would click. It didn't.

"Sorry, Zorro," I said. "I don't know what it is."

Zorro looked up at me, asking for nothing at all. And at that moment, I knew I had to fix him.

I took pictures of the X-rays and texted them to Dr. P. A moment later, my phone rang, so loud in the empty procedure room that my heart jumped.

"What are these?" she asked.

"My friend brought in her, uh, dog," I said. "I just wanted to help her out. Does anything look wrong to you?"

There was silence on the other end of the line.

"Are you still at the office?" said Dr. P.

"Yeah," I said, trying my best to keep the waver of panic out of my voice. "It's, uh, no big deal. I just . . . My friend came by, so I . . ."

Another long silence.

"Maybe I should come see for myself," said Dr. Paulson.

I froze up for a second. I felt the walls closing in around me. She would come back to the office and find me taking pictures of a restricted animal. She'd call Animal Welfare, because that was the responsible thing to do. Zorro would be taken away, and poor Malloryn Martell would never forgive me.

"You don't have to," I said. "That's why I sent you the pictures. So you don't have to come. Does everything look okay? Does anything look wrong? I can take more pictures if you want. I . . ."

Silence crackled on the other end of the phone line.

"There's fluid in the chest cavity," said Dr. Paulson at last. "You can see it."

"Oh," I said, trying to contain my relief. "What does that mean?"

"That'll make it hard to breathe."

"It does," I affirmed, then quickly corrected my intonation. "I mean, it does?"

"Marjan," she said, "this really would be a lot easier if I could examine the dog myself."

"It's not a client, Dr. P.," I said. *Or a dog.* "Just . . . tell me what to do."

She must have recognized the desperation in my voice. I could almost hear her deciding what to do next. Even Zorro was paying attention now, as if he sensed that something important was hanging in the balance. Finally Dr. Paulson spoke.

"Do you know how to do a blood draw?" she asked.

My dad had in fact shown me how to take blood from both dogs and cats.

"And you know where the antigen test kits are?"

I had stocked them myself, just three days earlier.

"Okay," said Dr. P. "Then we're going to take a little blood, and we're going to do a test."

A minute later, I was swabbing Zorro's foreleg with alcohol, and sliding a needle into his cephalic vein. Zorro winced, and then relaxed. Blood climbed up the hose, and when it reached the nozzle, I snapped on a collection vial. When I had enough, I twisted the vial free and removed the needle.

A drop of blood went onto the test kit, where it bloomed slowly toward the antigen strip. The last time I'd watched something like this, the woman who'd sent me to see Kipling had been asking me about the Hyrcanian Line.

"The test takes ten minutes," said Dr. P.

I set a timer, then sat down to wait. Zorro paced lazily around the procedure room, his magnificent tail switching this way and that. Dr. P shuffled gently on the other end of the line, making dinner, maybe, or cleaning up a messy room, or maybe just sitting down and breathing.

"You know," said Dr. P, after a few minutes had passed, "this is pretty unusual—bringing a friend's dog in after hours and running diagnostics on it all by yourself."

"I just thought it would be easier this way," I replied.

"Maybe it is." I could tell she had a lot more to say about it, but whatever she was thinking, she kept it to herself, and instead she changed the subject. "How are you doing, anyway? How's school?"

"It's fine," I said.

"Just fine?" asked Dr. P. *A stalking bird, patient and precise.*

"Getting back to normal, I guess," I said. I had to say something, and also it was true. "I mean, normal's completely different than it used to be, but I guess I'm starting to recognize what it looks like."

"I think we're all doing that," said Dr. P. She was quiet for a minute. Then she said, "We miss him a lot. Everyone does."

"I do too," I said, and wished that my feelings could be that simple.

We sat quietly until the timer beeped. I picked up the test kit and studied the results. The blood had faded, and in its place were two bright blue dots.

"Just what I thought," said Dr. P when I told her what I saw. "Heartworm."

"So you're saying it's not a hex?"

Neither the shock of the news nor the cackle of an iffy cell phone connection did anything to dampen the natural sing-song cadence of Malloryn's voice. I was back in my office, preparing the course of treatment Dr. P had recommended. Zorro was curled up in the corner.

"No minor demons were involved," I said. "Just a mosquito. And some worms."

"Oh." She sounded almost disappointed. "So . . . what do we do?"

I told Malloryn what Dr. P had told me: It would take months of medication and rest for Zorro's arteries to be clear. First, a round of antibiotics. Then a lumbar shot of arsenic, a month of quiet time, and then another two shots.

"Months? Arsenic? Are you sure we need to do all this?"

I told Malloryn all the wonderful things I knew about heartworms—how they can grow to be a foot long, how there could be hundreds of them living in his arteries and lungs and heart, how after the medicine kills them, their decomposing bodies break up into pieces, and if the animal is too active, those pieces can block blood vessels and cause sudden death.

"You can't let him die," said Malloryn. "He's all I have. And he's special."

"Nobody's going to let him die," I said. "Come back tomorrow. We'll work out the treatment plan then."

Zorro, curled up under a table, looked at me as I put the phone down, his head cocked sideways as if asking a question.

"You heard me, Zorro," I said. "I'm not going to let you die."

I walked over to him and stroked his fur. He stretched his neck out under my palm, and I felt all the sensations coursing through me—the heaviness of breath; the slow, nauseating beat of his heart; and somewhere else, the twinkling brightness of his wild little fox mind, bouncing and darting, scurrying in low grass, hunting for crickets and mice.

He stood and arched his back. His fur, a mottle of red and gray that favored the gray, shimmered where it caught the light. His tail hooked and twitched, to his right, to his left, rose up over his body like a curving wave, slithered between his delicate black paws. It seemed to be everywhere around him. It seemed to have its own mind, its own restless will. It was as graceful as a wisp of smoke.

And then, like smoke, it began to separate. It split first into two, then three, then four, each strand unbraiding itself, coming free with an elegant whorl. They flicked and flowed to their own special rhythms—this one swaying as smoothly and evenly as a river, that one twitching like it was surging with electrical current—until the space around Zorro's wiry little body was alive with movement and color.

I stepped back and sat down on the floor.

Zorro had nine tails.

| CHAPTER SIX |

THE FOX WITH NINE TAILS

Once was, once wasn't.

Long ago, there lived a witch who made her home in a bamboo hut on a mountainside.

No one dared venture anywhere near her hut, for fear she would bedazzle them, or turn them into toads, or wither their rice paddies, or cook them in a stew and eat them. They needn't have worried—she didn't mean them or their crops or their livestock any harm. Nonetheless, they stayed well clear.

So this witch never saw another soul, except for the animals that lived on that mountainside—the deer, the rabbits, and the foxes. But the silence gave her the peace she needed to focus on her work, and so she was grateful. She spent her days reading the great old books of magic, and her nights inventing and perfecting new and potent spells. For many years, she lived thus, until she was an old woman.

One morning, she felt a strange sensation. Though the day was warm and sunny, a darkness crept in at the edges of her vision. A chill touched her bones. She knew the feeling instantly, as would any witch.

It was Death, coming for her.

All at once, a great sorrow filled her heart. She had committed her life to a purpose—the pursuit of great magic. She had invented new spells, found new ways to harness magic. For all of this, she was very proud.

And yet, there was no one to share any of her knowledge with. She had no children, no students, no lover, no apprentices. She was all alone. When she died, all her wisdom would vanish from the world. Her work would be erased from history. It would be as if she had never lived at all.

With Death approaching on swift hooves, she walked out to a meadow on the mountainside, and she called out in the language of the beasts. A young fox in a field of chrysanthemums heard her call and came to her side, and she scooped him up and held him tight.

Then she whispered a spell into his ear. The witch's whispered words traveled down the fox's spine and wrapped themselves around his tail. She whispered another, and his tail split in two. Each new spell peeled off a bit of the fox's tail, until there were nine tails, and nine spells. With her dying breath, the witch commanded him to carry her wisdom to the ends of the earth if necessary, until he found someone worthy of learning them.

This was many years ago, and no one can be sure, but it's said he is still looking.

| CHAPTER SEVEN |

SECRET SMILE

I sat for a moment in silent awe, as Zorro's tails swished and flicked. He looked right back at me, his gaze as even and still as it had been when I was taking X-rays. Carefully, because I didn't want to alarm him, I reached out a hand, so that his tails brushed against my fingertips. Each time they touched me, I felt the bracing rush of something powerful run through me, heard the muffled and indistinct whisper of a word in my ears.

"She doesn't know," I said, as if Zorro might respond. He didn't, of course, but he didn't have to. I already understood: Zorro was far more special than Malloryn Martell could possibly imagine. And more than anything, I wanted to cure him.

The want was an electrical current arcing through my bones, sizzling in my fingertips, burning in my chest. I wanted him to be free from the worms that were choking his arteries and filling his lungs. Everything in the world would be a little better, if only I could do this right. If only I could help this one animal.

We had a couple of dog crates lying around. I took one of them and moved it into my office, then lined it with fresh blankets and set a bowl of water inside. I led Zorro out of the procedure room, and once he saw the crate, he seemed to grasp the idea, and padded in without a fuss. Then he curled up and closed his eyes. He was tired too.

Malloryn would come for him in the morning. I'd meet her at the back door, and I'd bring Zorro to her when the coast was clear.

I sat down on the floor next to Zorro and watched him sleep for a minute. His breath was soft and shallow, and when he did breathe deep, he made a sort of strangled snoring noise that didn't sound peaceful or comfortable in the least.

"Don't worry, Zorro," I whispered. "I'm going to fix you."

He didn't stir. I stood up, looked him over one more time to make sure he'd have everything he needed until morning. Then I walked out of the office and locked the door behind me.

From the outside, the West Berkeley Animal Clinic wasn't much to look at. It was painted an unassuming shade of beige and marked with a vinyl sign backlit by flickering neon tubes. There were cobwebs under the eaves, and clots of dust in the corners of the sign. On one side of the clinic was an Indian restaurant. On the other was a copy shop. On a good day, the street outside smelled like vindaloo and tandoor ovens. On a bad day, toner.

Something rustled in the low bushes near the door, sudden enough to make me jump. A moment later, a slinking shadow emerged from the foliage and padded down the sidewalk on shaky, scrawny legs. As it entered a pool of light from a streetlamp, it stopped and turned to look at me.

He was feral—a gray, mangy coat; white socks; and ribs that showed through his skin. He'd been prowling this neighborhood since I was a little girl, always hungry, always wary of anyone who tried to get near. He must have been ten years old at least—ancient in feral cat time. It was a wonder that he was even still alive. I hadn't seen him since my dad died.

I've never liked cats, but this one always felt different to me, which I guess is how people end up with cats in their lives. Sometimes I left a bowl of cat food out on the front steps of the clinic in the evenings. If the sidewalks were empty, he would approach and eat in greedy, crunching little bites, until something startled him and he darted to safety. He never let me get close enough to touch him. But I'd never gotten the sense he was afraid of me either, and eventually I'd come to respect his need for space and freedom. We had a quiet sort of understanding. We could watch each other from a distance, without fear or distrust. Occasionally a dead sparrow would show up on the doorstep—one of those inscrutable cat gifts that are at once both horrifying and touching.

"Hey," I said. "How's life?"

The cat regarded me a moment longer, then slunk back into the shadows. That was our relationship, boiled down, and I wasn't sure what either of us got out of it. But it was comforting to know that it was still there.

That night, the house felt huge and empty. I wandered from room to room, too wired to sleep. There was an earlier, simpler version of myself here, in the walls, the mirrors, the shag flooring. You could see her in the old pictures that hung on the walls, the ones with my mom in them. She was always smiling, that girl, always laughing.

I wondered sometimes if I would have still been that way, if Mom hadn't died, if Dad hadn't retreated into himself and his work. But at some point I'd splintered off from that little girl and left something irreplaceable behind. Sometimes I could feel that she was close. I could almost feel the person I'd started to be. I could almost make out the shape of what it was I'd lost.

I found myself standing in my bedroom, taking in all the ordinary, familiar details: The desk where I did my homework. The straight-backed wooden chair I sat in. The vanity where I kept my clothes and put on makeup when I was trying to be fancy. The stool my dad had sat on, beside my bed, night after night, all through my early years, telling me stories about fantastic creatures, stories about unicorn scars and nine-tailed foxes and griffons and a hundred other impossible animals. Stories that always began with the old Persian refrain "Yeki bood, yeki nabood." I never learned much Farsi, but I did learn what those words meant.

Once was, once wasn't.

When my dad said those words, he created a place that was real and not real, at the same time. The world that came after those words was bigger and older that the one I lived in. It had more light and deeper shadows, and there was room for things to be strange and wonderful. And somehow, even when the stories ended, that world never quite went away.

The stories were still clear, still vivid, still ringing in my ears in my dad's old voice, the confident, curious one that disappeared after Mom died. So much around them had washed away, but those stories held. They were pillars, the only pillars I had. Maybe he'd been trying to tell me about all this. Maybe he'd been preparing me to understand.

My mom grew up in a small farm town in rural Montana, an only child of Norwegian heritage. Her parents both died before she was twenty. After her dad died—aneurysm, out of nowhere—she sold their farm and moved to Oakland, where she found work as a vet tech. When a job opened up at the UC

Davis veterinary hospital, she took it, thinking that she might become a vet herself. That's where she met my dad.

Mostly I knew my mom from photos. She had dark eyes that always seemed to hold a spark in their centers. She had a smile that went wider on one side of her face than the other. In her pictures, it looked like there was a mystery just behind it, something wondrous and wise and a little mischievous. Maybe she knew about the work, the griffons and foxes and whatever else there might be. Maybe it felt different to know, back then, when my dad was the person that he used to be.

I had that same smile. You could see it in the pictures from when I was little—a lazy crescent with a dimpled little twist at one end. I remember that my mom was proud of it, proud that she'd passed it on. She called it our secret smile. But since she died, it always felt more like a smirk. The same shape, but no joy in it. I definitely didn't feel wise or wondrous.

I was seven years old when they found the cancer in her bones. It had spread to her lungs by then, and in a couple of months, she was gone. It was still hard for me to wrap my head around that time in my life. I knew things had happened in a certain order—my mom was tired a lot, then she went into the hospital, and then she came home—and I could roughly imagine what those moments had been like, but I couldn't actually *remember* any of those things happening. When I tried to picture them, when I tried to see how my mother looked when she couldn't get out of bed anymore, I got these badly drawn images that didn't look like anyone. I couldn't even remember the day she died.

In the weeks and months after, I saw my father come apart, over and over again. I saw him struggle for English words, and then lapse into Farsi—not just with me, but at the grocery store, or with clients. People stared at him, baffled and embarrassed. I saw him get frustrated with tiny things—a stuck door, a car driving too slowly on the highway. I saw grief strike him like lightning, leaving him speechless and sobbing at the kitchen table, in his bedroom, in the doorway of our house. I didn't know how to comfort him. His sadness was a different language. I didn't speak it.

His stories stopped then. He was tired, always. And the world felt too small and cruel for benevolent shirdals and wild unicorns. I don't know if I even bothered to stop believing in them. I just stopped caring. They didn't matter.

Once was, once wasn't.

CHAPTER EIGHT

ALL OF THEM, ALL AT ONCE

Before school, I met Malloryn at the clinic, and brought her back to the office. Zorro, curled in his crate, raised his head when she entered. His tails—now tightly braided together—flapped against the walls of the crate. Malloryn knelt down and shugged his cheeks, then came around the desk and gave me a tight hug.

"Thank you," she said.

Malloryn shuffled her feet and bowed her head. In his crate, Zorro darted his little snout from Malloryn to me, and then back again.

"There, um, there's something I need to tell you," she said.

"Okay . . ."

"I can't afford to pay very much," she said. "Actually, I can't really afford to pay anything. I'm sorry. I should have told you that before I left him. I don't know what this normally costs, but . . ." Her words trailed off, and she avoided looking me in the eye.

"Honestly, I don't know what it costs either," I said. Malloryn seemed ashamed, and I felt bad for her. "It's fine," I added. But she still wouldn't look at me.

"There's something else," she said. "The reason I brought him—the reason I thought to find him some help—Zorro put some scratches on my wall. He never does that—I think he was trying to tell me he was sick. Anyway, my parents, they're super religious, and they've been talking about this school, like, threatening me with this school, because of the witch stuff, and—they don't know about Zorro. Anyway, this school, it's in the middle of the desert, and the people come get you with a van in the middle of the night and— Anyway, I knew when they saw the scratches . . ." She paused, and when she spoke again, her voice was quiet and fragile. "Is there anywhere we can crash, around here? Just until he gets better? I can't pay anything right now, but I can cook and clean, and I won't take up much space."

I did not know of anywhere that would accept a runaway teenaged witch and her pet fox, free of charge.

"I'm sorry," I said.

She nodded like it was no big deal. "No problem," she said. "Thanks anyway."

A proud, brittle smile forced its way across her face. She picked up Zorro from the crate and set him gently into his cardboard box. Then, holding her head high, she started to walk quickly out of the office. I wished I could do more for her.

At that moment, an idea occurred to me.

You can't do that, was my first thought. *Dad won't let you.*

It was a surprising thought, and it came out of nowhere. I hadn't needed my dad's permission for anything in months, and all of a sudden he was telling me what I could and couldn't do. Anger flared up in my chest. He had no right to tell me how to live my life.

Suddenly I felt a great freedom, like something had been

lifted off me. I didn't have to listen to my dad anymore. I didn't have to do things the way he did. I could make my own rules now. I ran after Malloryn, caught her at the end of the hall, and pulled her back to my office by the arm.

There was no reason I should have trusted her. I knew almost nothing about her. But I did trust Zorro. And if *he'd* chosen Malloryn, then maybe she was okay.

More than anything, I didn't want to be alone in my house any longer.

"You can stay with me," I said.

"Oh, no . . . ," she sputtered. "I didn't mean to . . ."

"It's fine," I said. "As long as you don't mind being in a house where someone died."

"I know some rituals for that," she said. "If you want to clear out the dark energy."

"Okay," I said. "Why not?"

"Are you sure?" she asked. "I mean, about all of it? I don't want to impose, especially after what you've done for Zorro. You're really sure?"

"Yeah," I said. "It'll be nice to have some company. And clear out the dark energy."

Immediately her face brightened. "You won't regret this," she exclaimed. And just as quickly, a thoughtful look came over her. "There's something I want to do for you . . . to thank you. I want to remove the hex on you." She paused. "Or try, anyway. No guarantees."

"Um," I said. "What hex?"

"*The* hex, silly," she said with a laugh. "The one that's, like, all over you? Don't tell me you don't know about it."

I shook my head.

Malloryn's eyes were wide with disbelief. "Hoo boy," she said.

"I noticed it the second I met you, but I didn't want to say anything because, well, sometimes they can be embarrassing. If you want me to, I'll try to break it. If it works, you'll feel better, I promise. If it doesn't, no loss. My gift to you. Mine and Zorro's."

At the sound of his name, Zorro wagged his tail and let out a proud little yip.

"Um, thank you?" I said.

"No, thank *you*," she said. "You have no idea how much this means to me."

I walked with them back down the hallway, and to the front door.

"The hex," she said. "No rush. You have to be ready. In the meantime, leave the cooking to me. And the energy clearing."

I gave her the address, told her when I'd be home, and watched her set Zorro into the oversized front basket of an old bicycle. A black feather and a string of beads hung from one handlebar. She smiled and waved as she got on. Then she whispered something into the box to Zorro, and the two of them pedaled off together. I wondered what I'd just let into my life.

That afternoon, I got a call from David Ginn. When I saw his number come up, my stomach tightened. When David called, it was usually about money, and how there wasn't enough of it.

"Don't worry," he said. "You're not in trouble. I just thought we should meet. See how everything's going."

David's office was in a small complex that always smelled like fresh paint. David was on the third floor, behind a frosted glass door with an antique brass knob and the letters *D. Ginn* printed in gold leaf at eye level. It felt a bit like walking into a private detective's office in a noir story, but as soon as you were inside, the illusion vanished.

The office was a single, shallow room, cramped with wall-to-wall filing cabinets and a desk that took up most of the remaining space. A drop ceiling hung down just a few inches too low. Fluorescent tubes lit the room in a stark, flat wash.

When I got there, David greeted me with a weary wave. His face was pale and round and tired. His clothes were a bit rumpled, his sleeves rolled up. The moment I walked in, he smoothed at the wrinkles in his shirt with the palm of his hand and stood up straight to welcome me.

David never looked exactly happy. He always seemed exhausted. His beard was just a bit ragged, his eyes always just a little dark and sunken. His office felt tired and worn-out. Everything was stacked on top of everything else—desktop computer; piles of client folders; pictures of his wife, Elizabeth, and their kids, Cole and Ramsey; trinkets from a Grand Canyon trip. It all seemed like it might collapse at any second.

"How are you doing, Marjan?" he asked, in that way that people asked me that question now.

"Seriously, David," I said, "I'm fine. I'm totally fine. It's been almost three months. I'm good."

He gave me a long, funny look, and finally accepted my answer with a nod, then motioned for us both to sit. He pulled up a spreadsheet and scanned it.

"So," he said. "X-ray machine. It's working out for you?"

Just diagnosed heartworm in a nine-tailed fox, so . . .

"Yeah, pretty good so far," I said.

"Then let's make sure you can keep it," he said. He squinted at the spreadsheet. "A bit tight this month, but you should just squeeze by."

"Well, that was easy," I said.

David turned the monitor away and clasped his hands on the table.

"You must be busy these days," he said. "The clinic. School. What else is there in your life?"

"Um . . ." A griffon. A witch. Normal stuff.

"Marjan," he said. "Can I say something? And you won't take it the wrong way?"

"Shoot."

"You don't need to do all this."

"What do you mean?"

"I mean the clinic," he said. "This is . . . and don't get me wrong, it's always great to see you . . . but this is your dad's. Was your dad's. It doesn't have to be yours."

"I know," I said. Except, maybe it did? It was hard to tell.

"Trust me," said David. "Life happens real fast. Before you know it, three, five years have gone by." He paused to look around the room. "You're still a kid, Marjan. You don't have to be a grown-up yet."

"I don't feel like a kid," I said.

"You've been through a lot," he said. "More than any kid should ever have to go through. But look, this is golden time. This is when the world is yours, so make sure you're paying attention. Don't miss it. One day, you wake up and you're an accountant in a little office, doing the best you can for your family, and that's it. Do you get what I'm saying?"

"The world doesn't stop for our feelings," I said.

"Now you sound like your dad," said David. "I get it. It's hard to let go. But it'll only get messier, the longer you wait." He paused, a wistful look on his face. Then he smiled. "Take things slowly, if you want. But not too slowly, or you'll miss out on all the—whoops!"

He swung an arm out toward whatever it was I was going to miss out on, and bumped his monitor, almost knocking it off his desk. He sprung up to catch it, and we both laughed.

"See what I mean?" he said. "That's what happens when you're not paying attention. Anyway, don't listen to me. I'm just a nobody."

"Hey, David," I said. "Do I look . . . I don't know . . . hexed?"

He cocked his head to the side. "You look a little tired," he said.

"Maybe that's all it is."

Then he stood up.

"You should come by our place for dinner sometime, after things settle down," he said. "Elizabeth's been bugging me to ask, and the kids would love to see you. They miss their favorite babysitter."

"Babysitter" was a generous description. After Mom died, I sometimes spent nights at David's house when my dad went on trips. David and Elizabeth would have grown-up dinners downstairs, while I hung out with Cole and Ramsey upstairs. They were sweet, curious kids who loved making things and inventing worlds. When I was building marble runs and Lego castles with them in the evening quiet of the Ginn house, the strangeness of my dad's absences always felt a little further away, a little less real. And then one day, David asked my dad why he traveled so much. That was the last time I stayed there.

"Dinner sounds great," I said. "And thanks for the advice."

"Ahh," he said, waving it off. "It's only worth what you paid for it."

I stood up too. As I reached for the door, David spoke again.

"Any news on what happened to Jim?" he asked. "Any leads?"

"Nothing." I hadn't heard from the police in weeks.

"I don't know how you do it, Marjan," he said. "I don't know how you're so strong in the face of this."

The truth was that I didn't know either. And I wasn't even sure I was being strong at all. I talked to doors now, and let random strangers move into my house because I trusted their pets. Neither seemed like a sign of strength.

I met Malloryn at the house just as Francesca was returning from a walk with her newest foster—a pit mix named Buster with short, stubby legs and a goofy grin.

"Who's your friend?" asked Francesca, looking for once like an actual legal guardian.

Malloryn maneuvered herself to block Zorro's box, still in the bike basket.

"This is Francesca," I said to Malloryn. "She's my legal guardian. Francesca, this is Malloryn. She's going to be staying with me for a while."

Francesca looked Malloryn up and down with suspicion. "You in trouble or something?" she asked. Buster sniffed at the air, caught a scent of Zorro, and whined.

"Kinda," said Malloryn.

"Your parents know you're here?"

"It's complicated," said Malloryn.

Francesca's eyes narrowed. "You on drugs?"

Malloryn grimaced. "No," she said. Then, "Ew." When Francesca still didn't seem convinced, she added brightly, "I'm a witch."

"Ah," said Francesca, clearly relieved to hear this. "Well, that's fine, then." She turned to me. "Samosas. I left some for you." She nodded toward my front door. Then she turned and began tugging Buster back to her cabin. Over her shoulder, she called out, "No curses!"

Watching Malloryn Martell carry a box of Zorro and a bag of samosas through the front door of the house I grew up in was like watching someone take my life and fold it in half like a piece of paper, so that the two farthest points were suddenly touching. I don't think a patient or a client, or even another doctor, had ever come into our home, in all the years my dad was practicing.

But it wasn't just clients. I never invited anyone over. I couldn't predict what might happen, and I didn't want someone there if, say, my dad had to pull one of his disappearing acts. Or if there was nothing in the fridge except ketchup. Too much to explain, too many questions.

And now here was Malloryn, a client who belonged at the clinic, and Zorro, who, as he tipped himself out of the box, reminded me how much I still didn't know or understand about my father's life and work. They were standing inside the doorway of my home, and every important part of my life felt smushed together in that one moment, so tight that for a second it was hard to breathe.

"I don't normally have guests," I said.

"Nothing like having to explain your weird family to new people, right?" said Malloryn.

She laughed, an easy, knowing laugh, and patted Zorro on the head. I felt the tightness inside me relax a bit. Maybe she really was a witch.

Just then, her phone rang. She looked down at it, and her expression darkened. She took a deep breath, then answered the call.

"Hi," she said. "I'm alive and I'm safe. Don't call me. Don't look for me. I'll call you when I'm ready." She hung up and looked at the phone for a long time. "My weird family," she said at last. She smiled again, put the phone away, and knelt down to stroke the fur of her pet fox. "I can't go home right now. Probably not for a while. If you ever need me to leave, for a day, or forever, I understand."

Now that she was here, though, I didn't want her gone. Just hearing another voice inside these walls, after weeks of silence, was comforting.

"You can stay as long as you need to," I said.

"Thank you," said Malloryn. She stood up straight and proud, and her eyes glimmered. "I have a plan, you know. There's this occult shop in Oakland. They don't know it yet, but they're going to hire me. When I get some money, I'll start paying rent, and whatever I owe you for helping Zorro. And I'm going back to school, so my parents don't get in trouble. Probably whatever school you go to—I'll figure it out. Don't worry, you won't even notice me. I'm good at being invisible. In the meantime, let me handle dinner."

And that was that. Malloryn Martell was now my roommate.

The spare room upstairs had always just been a place to put things and forget about them. Clothes no one wore. Boxes of useless paperwork. Old school assignments. I hadn't been in the room for years. Never needed anything we kept there. Now, as Malloryn and I pushed boxes out of the way, I felt a vague uneasiness, like some distant part of me was getting turned inside out.

"I'd give you the other bedroom," I said. "But it was my dad's. It's kind of still his."

"I understand. We'll be totally fine here," she said. Zorro purred with what sounded like agreement.

We rolled out a sleeping bag, and I found Malloryn a pillow. Zorro curled up in a corner and wrapped his tail under his chin, his eyes weary and watchful.

"Now," said Malloryn, "dinner."

I showed her the kitchen, put the samosas in the fridge, and walked upstairs to my dad's door. It didn't seem quite so impenetrable anymore. It was a regular door, just like all the others in the house. One that anybody could open or close, whenever they felt like it.

It was a relief, not feeling the dark gravity of the room behind it. The house felt a bit bigger. But somewhere in that gravity was my dad, and if it wasn't as strong now, then he was a little farther away, a little more dead.

The scent of something delicious wafted up from the kitchen. The last time the kitchen had smelled like real food was the spring after Mom died.

We went to a Noruz party that year.

We hadn't celebrated Persian New Year the year before. Maybe no one had invited us. We used to go to them every year before Mom died. She liked them—I remember that.

My dad knew a bunch of the East Bay Persians, but he wasn't really close with any of them. I think he just liked to be able to speak Farsi, to be the person he could be if he wasn't using so much energy trying to remember the English words for things. Anyway, someone invited us that year, and we went.

My dad wore a suit, and he got me a new dress to wear. I remember it was at a big house, full of music and noise and laughing and smells of all kinds—saffron, rose water, perfume, cigars. The grown-ups were dressed up in suits and fancy dresses, dancing and drinking vodka cocktails. The older ones sat on couches, gossiping, eating sweets, and smoking cigarettes.

The kids wore blazers and dresses and watched *Big Hero 6* on a gigantic TV screen and ate heaping plates of rice, kabobs, and a rich, sweet stew made from pomegranates and walnuts. Later some of the older kids snuck out behind the swimming pool and set off bottle rockets until they got yelled at. Everyone seemed to know one another. The kids talked about other kids they all knew, kids I'd never heard of. They sang along to songs I didn't know. They slipped in and out of Farsi without any visible effort. A word here, there, a joke, a punch line. I realized that night that I had no idea what it meant to be Iranian. It was half of me, and I didn't understand the first thing about it.

When we left, I felt dizzy and overwhelmed. My dad drove us home, and I rested my head on the window of the passenger side while the party's echoes drummed in my ears.

"Did you have fun?" he asked me.

"The food was good," I said.

Two days later, he was cooking.

"You should know your culture," he explained. I hadn't asked to know my culture. But, of course, he wasn't really talking to me. I just didn't know it yet.

He made rice with saffron and butter. He sliced potatoes and lined the bottom of the pot with them, so that they would get crispy and the rice wouldn't burn. He chopped up fistfuls of herbs until his hands were flecked with bits of green, and mixed them into a stew of red beans. That day, the kitchen smelled of fenugreek and black limes and saffron and sumac. And that night, he served us a traditional Persian dinner.

And it tasted terrible.

He knew it was bad the second he tried it. Too much salt, and too much heat. The potatoes were scorched, the rice was dry, and the stew was bitter.

My dad threw out the food and took me to a Persian restaurant. The waiter greeted us in Farsi. My dad answered in English, and the waiter took the hint and switched to English himself. The food was better, but my dad still grumbled that it didn't taste right.

That was the last time my dad cooked anything that didn't come out of a can or the freezer.

I think he was trying to be a version of himself that didn't exist anymore, a version that had ended when Mom had died. I think he was realizing that he was different, that he would be different forever. I don't think he ever figured out what to do with the part that was left over.

I turned around to head downstairs. As I did, I saw Zorro watching me from the gloom at the end of the hall. I wondered who he saw—who I was in that exact moment. Was it the brave, confident girl who'd invited a witch into her home? Was it the girl with the unicorn scar, ninety-nine parts human and one part magic? Was it the lost and confused kid who talked to doors that she was still too afraid to open? Or the girl in the corner at the Noruz party, dazed and dazzled and unable to understand how she could possibly belong there, or anywhere? Maybe it was the little girl I'd once been, the one who still haunted these halls, whole and happy. I felt all of them, all at once, and something else, too. Something I couldn't name.

Maybe it didn't have a name.

CHAPTER NINE

TWO WORLDS SIDE BY SIDE

"You look different, Marjan."

Carrie had her head cocked sideways, eyes narrow. Grace was standing next to her, trying to see whatever it was Carrie saw. It was morning, by the lockers, our usual pre-class meetup. Nothing weird about it, except that the night before, I'd invited a witch and her fox to stay at my house.

They were both looking at me. I wondered what they could see. I wanted to explain, but I didn't know where to start. The truth didn't seem like an option.

So I shrugged, and after a second, Carrie shrugged too.

"Where were you last night?" asked Grace. "I thought we were gonna study."

"I got caught up with some stuff at work," I said. "Boring stuff."

"When are you going to sell that place, anyway?" said Grace.

"Soon, maybe?" I said.

"Get that money, girl," she said.

"Yeah, yeah."

They both knew about the clinic. Every now and then,

they'd ask about it, and I'd tell them a little bit and watch their eyes glaze over. I tried not to bring it up anymore.

"Seriously, what are you waiting for?"

At that moment, Howie walked by with a couple of his soccer buddies. He smiled at Grace, and she smiled back.

"Hi, Grace," he said.

"Hi, Howie."

It was the perfect chance to change the subject.

"Are you kidding?" I said after he was gone. "Why aren't you dating him yet?"

"Shut up," she said, giving me a shove. "I'm taking my time, okay?"

"I'm gonna tell him you like him," said Carrie.

"Do not," she said. "I swear I will not be your friend."

"Finch! We're going to first period."

Three swimmers were heading past on their way to class. Everybody on the swim team called each other by last names, which always sounded strange and fake to me. The swimmers weren't friends with us. They were only friends with Carrie.

"Coming," said Carrie. She waved goodbye to us and then drifted off to join her teammates.

Grace looked at me. "You really like that place, don't you?" she asked.

I could have made something up, but Grace wasn't easy to fool.

"I never really understood my dad," I said, "and I feel like I'm supposed to. The clinic was this huge piece of him. And it's only just starting to make sense to me. So I can't walk away, G. Not yet."

"I get it," she said. "Just promise me you won't make yourself crazy."

"Promise," I said.

"And if you need help with anything . . ." She smiled and waved and pointed to herself.

Grace and I had something in common that Carrie didn't understand. Grace's parents had come here from Taiwan. She spoke Mandarin at home, went to the Chinese church on Sundays, and disappeared for a week every lunar New Year. She shared some of her culture with us—the amazing food her mom always made too much of, the occasional snippet of Mandarin with Carrie, playlists of syrupy Taiwanese pop songs that I'd find myself inexplicably humming a week later—but there were parts of it that we never saw. Maybe we weren't welcome, or maybe she just didn't know how to invite us in. If anyone could have understood how I was holding two worlds side by side, and trying to be a complete person in both of them, it was Grace.

"Okay, G," I said. "You'll be my first call. Now go talk to soccer boy."

She glared at me. Her eyes got tight. "Fine," she said in a defiant voice. "I will." She took a deep breath, smoothed her hair with her hands, spun on her heel, and raced off after Howie and his soccer friends.

I stood there for a moment, feeling off-balance and exposed. My friends both had other friends, other places to be. Maybe I did too.

Later that morning, I ducked into a study room in the library and pulled out my phone. I texted Sebastian, and when he blooped me back, I opened a video chat. He was in his dorm room, a bunk bed visible behind him.

"How are you?" he asked.

"Lonely," I said. "Misunderstood. How about you?" It was

true. And also, I was smiling. It felt so good to be honest.

"Yeah, pretty much the same," he said with a laugh.

"What'cha doing?" I said.

"Maths," he said with a twirl of his finger.

"Ah yes, the completely unnecessary plural."

"Math," he said in a fake American accent. "It just sounds easy."

"I've got a roommate now," I said. "She's a *W-I-T-C-H*."

"That sounds awkward," said Sebastian. "Why?"

"She needed a place," I said. "And I guess I needed company. Anyway, I think she's fine, but if I suddenly start turning into a frog, you know why."

Sebastian was quiet a moment.

"Wait," he said in a small voice, "can she really do that?"

I'd forgotten who I was talking to. Sebastian had better reason to believe in magic than most people.

"It was a joke, Sebastian," I said. "Even if she wanted to, I don't think she could. I don't think she could do anything."

"Well, that's a relief," he said. "Because I don't know how to turn a frog back into a girl."

Was he worried about me?

"You think I'm making a mistake?"

"I have no idea," he said. "Your life is now officially stranger than mine, and that's saying something."

"Great," I said with a laugh. "Thanks a lot. That's exactly what I wanted from this call—to feel like a weirdo."

It was easy to joke with Sebastian.

"You know you can tell me anything, Marjan," he said. "I'll always believe you."

The way he said it, the way he looked at me, even through the phone, it felt like he meant something more. The room got smaller around me, like the words took up all the space. Suddenly I was thinking about Kipling, his wings filling the great chamber, the awful corruption filling his body. I had the feeling of looking around a corner at something terrible, something I couldn't make out because it was brighter than the sun, and it burned. A hole in the universe, and behind it, nothing made sense.

That's one thing I can't tell you.

The eels started swimming again, the way they always did whenever the subject of Kipling felt too close. Out of the corner of my eye, I saw Grace wandering through the library, looking for an empty seat.

"I gotta go, Sebastian," I said. "Catch you tonight?"

"Always," he said with a smile and a wave. I waved back as I ended the call.

A moment later, Grace was slipping into the room, spiral-bound World History reader tucked under her arm, and I was slipping the phone away into my pocket.

"Who were you talking to, Mar?" she asked.

"No one," I replied.

She gave me a skeptical look.

"Um, I'm pretty sure you were just talking to someone."

"Oh," I said, "uh, yeah. It was"—I flailed for a second—"my accountant."

"Uh-huh?" She didn't believe me.

"Serious," I said.

"Marjan Dastani," said Grace with a wicked grin. "I do believe you're crushing."

"I swear," I said, "I am *not* crushing on anyone." And then, because it's so much easier to lie by telling the truth about something else, I said, "Least of all my accountant. Ugh."

"Who is it, then?" she said.

"It's no one, okay?" I said, my voice getting sharp.

Grace's smile vanished.

"Okay," she said. "Forget I said anything. Jeez." She sat down across the table from me and started taking out books. "Anyway, I did it," she said, a sly grin spreading across her face.

"Soccer boy?"

She nodded.

"And?"

"He's sweet," she said. "We'll see." She smiled and shrugged, and I was proud of her.

"I wasn't always a witch, you know."

We were finishing dinner—her second home-cooked meal for us in two nights. Malloryn was almost always eager to talk, and I was eager to fill the house with something other than silence, doubt, and anger. She'd burned sage the night before, to drive out the bad energy. I couldn't tell if the bad energy was gone, but the house felt more welcoming with her in it.

"What were you?" I asked.

"Just a girl," said Malloryn. "An ordinary girl named 'Mallory.'"

Mallory Martell had grown up in a small, depressed town in northern California with one big church, a high school football team, a shuttered sawmill, and a meth problem that nobody wanted to talk about.

"There are two kinds of people in a church," she said. "There are the people who go to be closer to what they love, and there are the people who go to hide from the things that scare them. My town was mostly the second kind. It was okay for a while, because I had my own church."

Her church was the old-growth redwood forest that sloped up the hillside from the town. She could get lost in it for hours, lie on the forest floor, look up through the branches at the shifting slivers of sky, hear the wind passing through the ancient boughs, the rustle of deer and coyotes, the softly churning sounds of life. There in the woods, she first felt the stirrings of a force she came to know as magic.

"Who knows, though," she said with a shrug, "maybe I was hiding too."

When she wasn't in the woods, she never felt like she fit in. She was always asking the wrong questions—("If God had to rest on the seventh day, how do we know He doesn't still take breaks every now and then, and how do we know He's not taking one now?"; "Do aliens on other planets believe in alien Jesus, or do they all go to alien Hell?"; "If the Devil can take any shape, then he could take the shape of a youth pastor, so how do we know you aren't the Devil, Pastor Chris?")—questions that made youth pastors take her parents aside for gentle but serious conversations. Questions that made other kids look at her funny. Questions that made adults shake their heads in disapproval.

When she was young, the forest was refuge enough—a place where she felt free and alive. But by the time she'd turned fourteen, even that was too small, and too close to everything else, to feel safe. The town, her parents, her school, the youth pastors, everyone was trying to mold her into a person she didn't want to be, to force her to believe things she didn't believe. There seemed to be no way out, and no point in fighting back, because no one wanted the person she was trying to be.

Then one day she discovered witchcraft in the pages of a garage-sale paperback, and suddenly she saw a way to give her life purpose. A witch, the book told her, could harness the hidden power that flowed through all things. A witch could see the strings that held the world together, could twist them into new shapes, untie old knots, weave new connections. A witch had power. A witch had freedom.

She spent a year devouring every book she could get her hands on. She hoarded them in the back of her closet, where she hoped her parents wouldn't find them. At night, when her house was asleep, she read them by flashlight and candlelight, absorbing every detail. She was learning, or she was sleeping. Every free moment, she devoted to her craft.

One moonless night five months ago, she stood at the top of a hill and called to the spirits for the first time. She introduced herself by her witch name—a name similar to the one she'd been born with, but also transformed. That night, Mallory became Malloryn, and her first act was to send a plea out into the dark sky for a companion and a connection to the world behind the veil.

A day passed. Then another. She waited for some answer, some kind of sign that the spell had worked. And with each passing day, she grew less and less hopeful. A week went by. But she never lost faith. She'd done the spell correctly, as correctly as it could be done. It had to work.

It was at midnight, ten days after she'd cast the spell, that she was awakened by a scratching at her window. When she went to investigate, she found a fox, weary and dirty and hungry, but seemingly friendly. She took him in and made him a secret bed in the corner of her closet, next to her collection of forbidden books.

The spirits had accepted her, and they'd sealed their bond by sending her Zorrocious Budgins McCrazypants. Malloryn Martell was now a witch.

"When Budgins came along, I thought my problems were over," said Malloryn. Then she laughed. "Turns out witches have the same problems as everyone else."

Being a witch wasn't much different from her old life. In some ways, it was even harder. She was still stuck in her little town. She still didn't fit in. All the things she'd hoped to change with magic stayed exactly the same. Only now, she also had a fox familiar to keep fed and hidden from her parents.

"So magic doesn't work?" I asked.

"Oh, it works," she said. "It's always working. It's just really, really hard to get it to work the way you want it to."

She and Zorro cast spells for luck, for love, and for prosperity. They performed rites to the spirits and to the seasons and to the earth. They worked charms for health, and hexes against disease and evil.

"But we never cursed anyone," said Malloryn, looking at me with grave emphasis over a plate of lasagna stuffed with zucchini and ricotta cheese. "I can't say I wasn't tempted, though."

Even if they had tried to lay a curse, though, it probably wouldn't have made any difference. None of their spells had worked. Not a single one. Her proportions were always a little off, or she missed a word of the incantations, or she did a step out of order. However hard she tried, however carefully she prepared, the spirits were silent.

It didn't matter, though. Not to Malloryn.

"Most witches spend their whole lives trying to get it right, even once," she said. "So I'm already doing better than average."

Even if she never cast another proper spell in her life, she'd summoned Zorro, and that was enough.

Of course, she had no idea how special Zorro really was.

· · ·

A padded envelope arrived by messenger at the clinic a week after Malloryn moved in. It wasn't addressed to anyone, but it was stamped with the kettle-and-serpent logo. I signed for it, then took it back to my office. No sooner had I shut the door than it began to vibrate in my hand. I tore it open and removed its sole contents—a clamshell cell phone. Ringing.

"Hello?" I said.

"There's a car coming for you," said a voice that sounded mechanically altered. "The driver's name is Sam. He knows nothing. Your client is Horatio Prendergast. He has a house gnome." A pause. Maybe, just maybe, a mechanically altered sigh. "It's incontinent."

"Who is this?" I said. "Are you the lady who was here before?"

Silence.

"Is this how this works? You just call me, and I go? Just, drop everything else?"

Silence.

"What am I supposed to do for it?" I asked.

Silence.

"Just, what, make a recommendation?"

Silence.

"Hello?"

"I'm still here," said the voice.

"What do I do? What do I do for an incontinent"—I lowered my voice to a whisper—"gnome?"

The voice was quiet for a long time. I was about to ask again, when it spoke. "Whatever you can."

Then the line went dead.

A car horn sounded from outside.

CHAPTER TEN

THE LONELIEST MAN IN THE WORLD

Sam had a friendly, sun-baked face and warm eyes. He drove with a dutiful calm, alternating between breezy small talk and polite silence. He told me his family was from Mexico. He'd moved up from San Diego a month ago to take this job. The pay was good, and drivers here were less aggro. And Horatio Prendergast was a decent, if sometimes distant, boss.

"But who is he?" I asked.

"Ever hear of Menagerie?" I shook my head. "You wouldn't know about it unless you needed it, and then you would definitely know about it. It's a software framework that's designed for processing really big sets of data. Oil companies use it. Military, banking, heavy-duty research facilities, that kind of thing. Anyway, Horatio created it and made a ton of money off it."

A quick search put him right in the middle of those World's Richest Person lists. The few photos that were floating around on the internet showed a striking face with sharp, hungry angles; wild gray hair; a close-trimmed beard; and eyes that disappeared beneath a powerful brow. "That's Horatio," said

Sam when I showed him one of the pictures.

For some reason, I felt safer than I had the first time I'd gone to meet an animal. Maybe because it wasn't so far away. Maybe because my client had a name and a reputation. Or maybe I was just getting used to this work.

We crossed the Carquinez Strait and headed east past the oil refineries until we caught the interstate. We drove through Fairfield, Vacaville, and Davis, then skirted the edge of Sacramento, pushing even farther east, until finally we peeled off the highway into a suburb with low, flat houses and green lawns. A fine place to live, I'm sure, but hardly billionaire territory.

"Where are we going?" I asked.

"Not too much farther," said Sam.

The houses got more patchy, and the spaces between them opened up wider and wider. There were oaks and cottonwoods, and big empty spreads of dry grass. We soon found ourselves on a country road with open land on both sides, dotted with stands of dark trees. Up ahead, a narrow, unmarked strip of pavement veered off to the right, into a rough wall of willows. Sam slowed down, then turned.

"There's nothing here," I said.

"You can't see it from the road," said Sam.

We crossed a little bridge made of wooden beams. On the other side stood a high fence, with a tall metal gate that swung inward as we approached. Beyond the fence, there were buildings—bland, square apartment buildings that all looked pretty much the same. There were people here, walking, or sitting under trees and staring into laptop screens, or standing in little knots of conversation. Sam waved at a small group of them as we passed, and they smiled and waved back and called out his name. They had sunburnt faces and dirt on their jeans.

"Welcome to Menagerie," said Sam with a proud smile.

In the distance, on a little hill, I could see a building that stood out from the rest. It wasn't square, and it wasn't bland. It was a shimmering palace of glass and steel, with pure white walls and a thrusting roof that rose over the top of the hill like a big ship riding up a wave. Two wings wrapped away on either side, so that it looked like it was holding the entire hilltop in a big metal-and-glass hug.

"What is this place?" I asked.

"Used to be a military base," said Sam. "He fixed it up, though. It's got apartments, cafeterias, work spaces, everything."

"You live here?"

"Came with the job," he said. "Apartment, meals, everything's taken care of. There's a gym, a pool. The apartments aren't fancy, but they're clean, and the food's good. And it's free."

"What happens here?" I said. "Who are all these people?"

"Everyone here works for Horatio," said Sam. "For Menagerie. There's a corporate office. Servers. There's also a farm, some cattle, some sheep. Lots of different stuff."

I'd never seen anything like it. In a way, it reminded me of school, the way groups and cliques just sort of naturally found each other. But school was messy. Everyone was following their own plan, even in a tight group. Your friends could float off in the middle of a conversation, chasing after something or someone completely different, and all you could do was watch them go. But Menagerie already felt like a place where everyone was working on the same thing. The farmers, the cooks, the engineers, the drivers, all on the same page, or at least, all reading the same book.

"Does Horatio live here too?" I asked.

"Lives, works, all of it," said Sam.

As we pulled up outside the main entrance to the palace on the hill, the metal front door swung open on silent hinges, and a woman with dark skin; high, gleaming cheekbones; and a soldier's face stepped out to greet us. She wore glasses and a stern suit, and carried a tablet under one arm. She motioned me in with a quick, almost frantic gesture, so that I felt both late and important at the same time.

Inside, the ceilings were high, and every surface shimmered in the sunlight that flooded in through huge windows and skylights. There was some furniture—clean, precise couches and settees and tables—but it was hard to imagine being comfortable anywhere in this room. Every angle seemed sharp enough to draw blood. Hallways branched off in either direction, continuing out of sight.

"Come on," said the woman, starting off down one of the long hallways. "He doesn't have all day."

Horatio's office was a wide room with broad windows. A massive canvas on one wall was splattered with a single spurt of red paint, like a giant artery had been opened up onto it. In the center of the room was a long black desk. As we entered, a leather chair behind that desk swiveled slowly around to face me. In it was the face from the pictures I'd just been looking at.

Horatio Prendergast stood up to greet me. He was tall and thin, and as angular as any piece of furniture I'd seen in the lobby. His gray hair was swept back from his furrowed forehead, showing a vampiric widow's peak, and it ended in a wild cloud of round curls at the base of his neck. His beard traced the line of a strong jaw. He wore a light gray suit with no tie and the top two buttons of his shirt open. A pair of thick black glasses reflected the blue light of his computer screens—the only hint of color anywhere on him. A smile rested comfortably on his broad mouth. He glanced back at the painting behind him.

"Be careful," he said. "It's hypnotic. Thank you, Ava." The woman left the room with a curt nod, and shut the door behind her.

"I was sorry to hear about your father," he said.

"Thank you," I replied.

He pointed to a chair across the desk from him, then watched as I crossed the floor to sit in it.

"I was also disturbed by the news," he said. "The manner of his . . . Well. I'd like to help you. We'll come to that."

"She said you're busy," I said.

He chuckled. "It's a persistent state. The world won't fix itself."

There was a joke somewhere in his words. I saw it light up his dark eyes. But I didn't understand it.

"They told me there was a gnome," I said.

Horatio laughed again. He made an abrupt, severe motion with his hand that ended in him removing his glasses and resting them gently on the desk.

"There is," he said. "But that's not who you're here for."

"I don't understand," I said.

"You're familiar with the work?"

"A bit," I said. "I'm learning."

"We're all learning, I think," said Horatio.

He leaned back in his chair and said nothing for what felt like ages. Then he looked at me, his eyes wide and glimmering with wonder.

"In the jungles of the Amazon," he said, "there's a creature with a giant ruby growing in the center of its forehead. They call this animal the carbuncle. Do you know of the carbuncle, Marjan?"

"Carbuncle?" Had my father ever told me a story like that? I couldn't remember.

"That's fine," said Horatio. "Very few people do. The carbuncle is shy and mistrustful. Almost nothing is known of their habits in the wild. What we do know is that once a year, the carbuncle molts. It sheds its stone and begins to grow a new one.

"You'd think by now that the jungle would be littered with gems," he continued. "But something tragic happens to the old ruby during the shedding process. It is destroyed. A priceless gemstone turns to worthless dust within moments of being molted." He made a gesture with his hand, a gentle flinging open of his fist, as if a sudden wind had spread his fingers and opened his palm toward me. "If the stone is forcibly removed, or if the carbuncle dies, the same." He looked down at his open palm.

"It's said that the only way to procure a carbuncle ruby is for the carbuncle itself to willingly give it to you. And the carbuncle will only give its stone to an honest soul."

He rested both hands upon the desk and fixed a meaningful gaze on me.

"So," I said, "you want me to go to South America, find a carbuncle, and convince it to give me its ruby?" The idea that I might somehow qualify as an "honest soul" made me smile.

His eyes widened in delight. "Well," he said. "You're eager for a challenge, aren't you. I'm almost tempted to say yes, just to see what you would find." He chuckled. "But no. You won't need to go quite so far."

Then he stood up and motioned for me to follow him.

He led me out of his office, down the long hallway. At the end of the hallway was an elevator. Horatio pushed a button, and the doors slid open. He gestured for me to enter, and then followed. The door shut behind us. With one long finger, he pushed the down button. We began to descend.

"Where are we going?" I asked.

"Do you ever wonder how they choose us?" said Horatio. "The creatures? I wonder all the time. I've had the privilege of meeting others like me, others who were chosen. No one's ever certain. They're not a reward, though they can be rewarding. And they're not a punishment, either, though they can be punishing. They're not here to save us or damn us. They don't explain themselves. They just enter our lives one day, and then there they are—full and complete and unequivocal."

As we descended, the air became cold, dry, and flinty. It was like breathing stone.

"We few who find them in our lives, we aren't the smartest people in the world," he continued. "Nor are we necessarily the bravest, or the kindest, or even the wickedest. We're just people. And yet, these animals make us something more. It's hard not to see some element of destiny at work, to feel you've been selected for an important purpose. It's hard not to imagine yourself exceptional in some way."

"You're rich," I said. "Doesn't that make you a little bit exceptional?"

Horatio smiled. "It's been suggested to me," he said, "that the common denominator is loneliness." The elevator began to slow down, and Horatio's eyes twinkled with mischievous delight. "If that's true," he continued, "I must be the loneliest man in the world. Perhaps that's an exceptional quality too."

The elevator finally came to a lurching halt. We were deep

underground. The door opened to reveal a long, broad hallway. A high ceiling of rough rock arched overhead. The floor was smooth, cold marble tile.

Most of the light in the hallway seemed to emanate from the walls, and as I stepped out of the elevator, I began to see why. The hallway was lined on both sides with floor-to-ceiling glass panels. Light—all different kinds of light—shone through the glass, creating a kind of patchwork of soft colors, orange, blue, green.

"What is this place?" I asked, and my voice echoed down the long chamber.

"In an earlier life, this was part of a missile silo," he said. "Now it's . . . something else."

He turned and began to walk down the hall.

Behind the glass panels were rooms of different sizes and shapes. Some were small and shallow, while others stretched away into darkness. The whole place reminded me of those African Savanna halls that you see in big natural history museums—the ones with the taxidermy lions and wildebeests set in fake grasslands with painted skies in the background.

As we walked, I became aware of shapes gliding and shambling and lurking among the rocks and trees of their enclosures. At first they were too timid or too quick for me to make out clearly. I wasn't even sure I was seeing them at all. Then, in one of the cases, a tiny glimmer danced up to the glass and hovered at eye level, unafraid. I stopped. It seemed to be beckoning me toward it.

I came closer. And then closer. And closer still, until my face was pressed right up against the glass. Until there could be no doubt of what was on the other side.

It hovered on dragonfly wings that hummed ever so softly

through the glass. It was naked and bald from head to toe. Its body looked almost like a human in miniature, but its arms and legs were longer than they should have been, and its genitals—what I assumed were its genitals—were unfamiliar to me. Its pale limbs hung, limp and relaxed, swaying gently in the air. Its eyes twinkled like curious black diamonds in its round, lily-white face.

"It's a faerie," said Horatio, and the world seemed to unfold around me.

I stepped back from the glass, and felt the weight of strange, wondrous eyes gathering on me.

In one case, birds with wings of pure sunlight flitted from the branches of a plaster tree, chittering excitedly to one another. "Alicanto birds," whispered Horatio, "from Chile."

In another, a white stag with golden antlers looked up from a patch of heather. "Goldhorn, originally from Slovenia," said Horatio.

Farther down, a creature with silver scales and a dark mane glided beneath the surface of a crystal-clear pool. "A makara, from a lake in the Annapurna mountains," said Horatio.

On and on. Every story my dad had ever told me, living and breathing, watching me.

"What do you think?" asked Horatio.

"How . . . ," I said.

"It's taken years," said Horatio. "A lot of patience, a lot of investigation. But that's part of the fun of it too. Combing through satellite photos, employment records, death certificates. Looking for that little detail that just doesn't sit quite right." He looked up the long hall, at the rows of enclosures teeming with strange and impossible creatures. "They all take up space somewhere in peoples' lives, if you know how to find it."

Each case was a box of pure wonder. A salamander, black and sleek, slithered among the burning embers of a stone fire-pit, its skin shimmering with an amphibious sheen. At the edge of a dark cavern, a pair of huge, knobby, four-fingered hands drew slowly into fists. ("Stone giant," whispered Horatio, "very fierce.") A large cat watched us from a high stone perch, flicked its tail, and grinned.

"Did my father know?" I asked.

"Of course," said Horatio. "He's cared for several of them."

"How many?" I asked. "How many are there here?"

"One hundred forty-five," said Horatio.

Off to my left, a slender serpent with sapphire-blue eyes uncoiled itself from a tree branch and took to the air as if it were slipping into water. Horatio watched as the serpent glided gracefully around the tree's trunk, its tongue flashing silver from between its exquisite jaws.

"Do you know why they exist?" Horatio asked. I shook my head. "I don't think anyone does. But I have a theory. I think they're more than they seem. They're not just flesh and blood—though, as your family's work proves, they *are* flesh and blood. But there's more to them. I think . . ."

A quiet look came over him. He watched the serpent undulate across the enclosure, several inches above its leafy floor. Then he turned to me.

"Well," he said. "They remind me that anything is possible, and that's a treasure greater than any wealth." It wasn't what he'd been about to say a moment before.

He turned and continued walking until we reached an enclosure larger than most of the others, and completely dark. Then he stopped. I took a breath, and the air felt thick and rotten in my chest. My legs felt weak. I thought I might pass out.

"You feel it, don't you," said Horatio. "You look pale."

I steadied myself. The darkness on the other side of the glass seemed to pulse with evil. I wanted to be as far away from it as I could. But I couldn't stop looking. The shadows seethed with invisible horrors.

"What the hell is in there?" I said.

"That," said Horatio, "is the manticore."

I thought I saw something move, a flank, maybe, long and sinuous and predatory. The faintest hint of a face, emerging for just a moment from the darkness. But if any of it was ever there to begin with, it was gone before I could see anything more.

A change had come over Horatio, too. He seemed to stand taller, like the shifting darkness behind the glass fed something inside him.

"It's horrible, isn't it," he said. But he made no motion to leave. "Sometimes when I'm feeling especially brave, I like to stand here, to see if she'll show herself."

"Why would you do that?"

"We must face our fears, if we hope to grow. She's the sum of many fears, the nightmare from which no one wakes." He paused, like he was facing his own fears in the darkness for a moment.

The clacking of soles on the hard floor echoed from down the hall. Two people were approaching—a short man with olive skin, and a tall woman. The man wore a white doctor's coat and walked with a proud, shuffling gait, like a small king surveying his lands.

The woman was hard and cold-eyed and shimmering with intelligence. There was merciless grace in her strides, in her posture, in the cut of her hair. She wore a leather jacket in a shade of purple at the very edge of the visible spectrum. Her skin was a bloodless, icy white. Under one arm, she carried a leather document portfolio.

"Ah," said Horatio. "Dr. Batiste, Ezra. Thank you for joining us. This is Marjan Dastani. She's here about the carbuncle."

The man, Dr. Batiste, came to stand alongside Horatio. He glanced over and looked me up and down with obvious disdain. The woman—Ezra—hung back, away from the manticore's enclosure. She nodded in my direction, and maybe smirked, but it was hard to tell because of the shadows.

"Dr. Batiste is the chief of our medical team," said Horatio. "He looks after all these animals."

"Even that one?" I asked, pointing into the dark.

Dr. Batiste gave me a dismissive look. I think he was about to make a snide comment, but before he could speak, something whipped through the air inside the enclosure and smacked the glass, hard, just below my face. I jumped and cried out. Dr. Batiste jumped too. I thought I heard Ezra laughing—whether at me or the doctor, it was hard to tell. Horatio stood still, unfazed, as a black, segmented scorpion tail came to rest on the sandy floor of the paddock, then drew back into the darkness.

"We removed the venom sacs," said the doctor, recovering his composure. "But the barb can still puncture an artery."

I took a step toward the glass. What I had thought was darkness was actually a grim shade of orange. I put my face to the thick pane and peered into the dim light. A dry heat radiated from within. At first I could see nothing. Then the darkness shifted, and a face appeared.

Legend says that the manticore has a scorpion's tail, a lion's body, and a human face. I'd say that's roughly true, except for the face. It has skin, two eyes, one nose, and one mouth, more or less in all the places you'd expect. But there's nothing human about it.

Whoever put it there had no idea what a face is really for, or how people use them. You don't notice how much a human face moves, and how much humanity lives in those little tics and twitches, until you've seen one that doesn't. The manticore's brow was as smooth as a river stone. The eyelids didn't blink. The nostrils didn't flare, not even a little bit. There was the tiniest curl at the edges of its lips, but otherwise the manticore's face was completely blank, a creamy death mask of pale skin. And even that hint of a smile seemed frozen in place. The manticore's face had no hint of emotion, no life.

Except for its eyes—red, catlike things that locked on me and tracked my every move. For a long moment, we just watched each other, tried to understand each other. Then, very slowly, the manticore slid out of the darkness. Its lion's body caught the light for the first time. Thick muscles rippled beneath its dusky fur. It steadied itself on broad, flat paws, its eyes never leaving mine.

A sick terror shot through me. I didn't want to get anywhere near that animal. I didn't want to feel what it felt, or know the things it knew. I didn't want it inside my head.

As its paw came to rest on the floor, the manticore let out a high, soft mewling sound. The muscles of its leg twitched. It took another step, and again it uttered a quiet wail. Its face showed no emotion.

"What's that?" I asked. "That sound."

"She's like this whenever she moves," said the doctor.

Another paw came down. Another whistling moan of pain.

"When she walks," I said.

"That's what I said," said the doctor.

"No, you said, 'when she moves.' It's when she walks."

Another paw, gingerly. Another whimper, coming just as the paw splayed out onto the floor. I felt a giddy flutter of triumph, almost enough to drown out the horror. I knew exactly what was wrong with it. I turned to the doctor.

"Has she been de-clawed, Dr. Batiste?"

The doctor stiffened. "I hope you're not questioning our capabilities. We have the most advanced surgical equipment in the world, the best facility, and the most accomplished staff in any private facility anywhere."

"Did you de-claw her?" I persisted.

"We performed a standard, minimally invasive procedure."

I could have let him off there. It probably would have been better for all of us if I had. But I couldn't resist.

"You performed a tendonectomy." Horatio gave me a questioning look. I explained. "He cut the tendons that let her extend her claws. Isn't that right, Doctor?"

Looking closer at the manticore's paws, I could see tiny triangles of black keratin extending from each toe.

"You set the claws where they could be seen but couldn't shred, and then you cut the tendons. Is that right?"

The doctor was silent.

"The nails are growing into her skin," I said. It was obvious. Couldn't be more clear. Our clinic had treated at least a dozen house cats with the same affliction over the years, and it always made my dad angry. "They might be growing into muscle or bone. You have to treat this, or she'll be in pain for the rest of her life."

The doctor looked from me to Horatio. "This is ridiculous," he said. "This girl is what—twelve? She shouldn't even be here."

"I'm fifteen, you condescending ass," I said. "And you know

I'm right."

Horatio said nothing for a minute. He looked at the manticore, which was still watching us with placid malice. He looked at the doctor. He looked at me.

"You're certain."

"You can take an X-ray and see for yourself," I said. "But I'm sure."

Horatio pondered, Dr. Batiste glared, and Ezra, somewhere in the gloom, was probably enjoying the popcorn.

"Interesting," said Horatio at last. "We'll talk about this later."

Then he shrugged and led us onward. The sick feeling stayed, long after the manticore's black box was out of sight.

We stopped at last at a pane of glass that looked in on a dense, humid forest. Creepers hung from the branches of thick fig trees, and smaller shoots reached up toward the canopy and the manufactured sunlight beyond. A fog of moisture over the glass gave the whole display a kind of soft, smeared look.

"The carbuncle," said Horatio. "She's usually in the back."

"What am I supposed to do?" I asked.

"Get her to give you the stone," he said. "She has to give it freely to you, or it's no good."

"What makes you think she'll do that?" I asked.

"Your honest soul," said Horatio with a smile.

"You must not know me very well," I said.

"Well, that and your unique talents." Horatio was about to say something else, but his breath caught in his throat. "There she is," he whispered.

He pointed to a disturbance in a patch of ferns. A shape, about as big as a medium-sized dog, revealed itself in the deep recesses of the enclosure. A shaft of light caught on something round and red, and it blazed as bright as fire. Then the creature bounded into another thicket and disappeared.

"Can you do it?" asked Horatio.

"I guess I can try," I said.

A small door in the space between two of the animal enclosures led to a tight corridor with access doors leading into the paddocks. Dr. Batiste followed me down the corridor and unlatched the door into the carbuncle's enclosure.

"Good luck," he said. He handed me a pair of surgical gloves. Then he opened the door and I stepped into a rain forest.

The air was steamy and syrupy and fragrant. Water dripped from the broad fronds of prehistoric-looking plants. Overhead, banks of radiant lights gave the illusion of sunshine, and a leaf-studded mesh canopy cast a dappled shadow on the ground. My shoes sank into the damp earth.

Far across the enclosure, the red gem flashed again. The carbuncle darted behind the wall of a fig root, through a bramble of underbrush, and finally into a little clearing, where she stopped, sat back on her haunches, and watched me warily.

The carbuncle looked and moved like a large hare. She had dusky fur; long ears; and big, round eyes as black as pitch. Her body was long and sleek. In the center of her head, right below where her ears began, was a smooth red bump that looked like a wound, until it caught the light with a brilliant crimson flash. Best of all, she wasn't a manticore.

"Hi, girl," I said.

The carbuncle sniffed at the air.

"I'm Marjan," I said. "Marjan Dastani, in case that means anything to you."

The carbuncle appeared unmoved.

"I don't blame you," I said. "It doesn't mean much to me, either. Not as much as it means to them, anyway."

I gestured toward the window, and the carbuncle sat up on her hind legs, alert, ready to bolt. I froze, and the two of us stood there for a long moment, wary and watchful and completely still.

"I'm going to move now," I said. "But I'm going to move very slowly, and I promise I'm not going to do anything to hurt you."

I took a single step—sideways, not toward the animal. The carbuncle flinched, but didn't bolt. I tried to let the tension in my muscles relax and drain away. It wasn't too hard to do in the sweltering rain forest heat—everything felt loose and limber.

I took another step, this time closing a bit of ground between me and the animal. Her black, button eyes tracked me. The stone in her skull flashed again.

"I don't blame you for not trusting me," I said. "You're probably used to being hunted."

The carbuncle held her ground, so I took another step. I glanced over at the glass. Horatio looked like a spectator at a sports game, his hands in his pockets, an expression of rapt attention on his face. When I made eye contact, he gave me an encouraging nod. Beside him, Dr. Batiste frowned, unimpressed. Ezra was watching me too, but her expression was harder to read.

Another step. The carbuncle cocked her head to one side, watched me closely with one tar-black eye. Another step. The space between us was closing. I could feel my heart quickening in my chest. I spoke to the carbuncle in as soothing a voice as I could muster.

"I don't want to hurt you," I said. "If this hurts, I'm not going to do it. I promise. I'll just tell them I couldn't. But if there's a way to take that stone from you without hurting you, if there's a way you'll let me take it, I'd like your permission."

Another step. The air felt thick in my lungs. Sweat or condensation—I couldn't tell which—was beading on my forehead, and I wiped it away with the back of my hand.

Suddenly the carbuncle bolted. In three great leaping strides, she put ten feet between us and vanished into a thicket of ferns. A moment later, she popped up again on her hind feet, chest heaving, the ruby in her forehead blazing.

I glanced back at the glass in time to see Dr. Batiste mutter something over his shoulder to Ezra. The doctor shook his head and walked away from the glass, but Ezra stayed right where she was. I thought maybe she nodded at me, so I nodded back.

The carbuncle was on high alert, her ears tense, her body ready to dart away at a moment's notice. I didn't move. I didn't even make eye contact with her. Something I'd done had set her off, and I was determined not to do it again. I worked back over the last few seconds in my mind. I'd been standing still, between steps. I hadn't made any unusual faces. I'd been talking to the carbuncle, but my tone hadn't changed.

I looked down at my hands and saw the gloves. Then I looked back over my shoulder at Horatio and Dr. Batiste— now grudgingly watching me again—seeing them for the first time the way these animals saw them—through the thick glass wall of their enclosure. Something squirmed in my guts. The carbuncle watched me.

"I get it," I said. "I'm not like them."

I reached down and peeled the gloves off, then shoved them

into my pockets. Then, very slowly, I showed the carbuncle my hands. Showed her that they were empty. Showed her that they were made of flesh, and not blue latex. The carbuncle watched, and didn't run.

I took a step toward her, and then another, and when she stayed put, another. I knelt down so that she and I were almost at eye level and I was staring into the blackness of her beady pearl eyes and wondering what rabbity thoughts were racing through her head.

She lifted her chin and pushed out her chest, and if she'd been a human being, you would have said she looked proud and defiant. I showed her my hands again, and then very slowly extended one toward her. Her eyes rolled down and strained at the edges of their sockets, tracking my tiny movements until my palm was open just beneath her nose, and I could feel her breath coming in short staccato huffs on my skin.

"I only want it if you want to give it up," I said. "They tell me you'll grow another one."

She turned her head away from me, as if she knew what I wanted, and was withholding it. Still, she watched me with one eye, and waited.

"To tell the truth," I said, "if you're really looking for an honest soul, I probably don't fit the bill."

The carbuncle kept watching.

"I tell my friends that I'm fine," I said, "which I'm not. I haven't told Malloryn about her weird fox. And I think maybe I'm lying to Sebastian and his family about Kipling, but I'm not sure why, and now I'm too afraid to tell them. You have no idea what I'm talking about."

She took a step back, putting space between us. But she didn't bolt. She leveled both eyes at me, and watched.

"And I'm not really sure what I'm doing here, with you, with any of this," I said. "I think I'm trying to prove something to my dad. I think I'm trying to prove that he could have trusted me. That he should have trusted me. But it doesn't even matter what he thinks, because he's dead."

The carbuncle's eyes narrowed, but she didn't run.

"And I'm not even sad about that," I said. "I know I should be, but I'm not. I'm angry, and confused, but not sad. So in addition to not being the most honest person, I'm probably not even a very good person at all."

The carbuncle pawed a shallow trench out of the soft soil. Her nose twitched. Her ears raised, then lowered. Light rippled over the smooth, rounded surface of the stone. Her eyes never left me.

I looked back at Horatio, at Ezra, at Dr. Batiste, who'd returned to the glass. I felt foolish, but I couldn't say why. I felt like something intimate and private was taking place, like the carbuncle was confessing some personal secret, just by giving me her attention. Even if they couldn't hear a word, it seemed wrong that they were watching. It seemed unfair—to me, and to the carbuncle—but I couldn't quite say why. Suddenly I didn't want the ruby anymore.

"Keep it," I said to the creature. "Keep it another year. I don't deserve it."

I stood up, looked over at the surprised faces in the glass, and shook my head. Horatio started to grimace, and Dr. Batiste smiled with secret glee, but then all three pairs of eyes on the other side of the glass went wide.

Something hit the earth beside me with a soft *plink*.

Something round and smooth and warm rolled up against my foot, and stayed there, and didn't turn to dust.

I looked back down to the carbuncle. She was watching me with a serene gaze. Where the stone had been, there was a pale, hairless indentation, and in the center, a tiny red bump—the next stone beginning to form.

The carbuncle watched me for a moment longer, then ducked low into the underbrush and bounded away to the far side of the paddock. I turned back to the glass and held up the ruby. Horatio applauded silently. Dr. Batiste scowled. The look on Ezra's face appeared to be wonder.

CHAPTER ELEVEN

WOLF WORK

Dr. Batiste took the ruby from me without a word and placed it in a plastic bag.

"Clean it, then bring it to my office," said Horatio. Dr. Batiste nodded, gave me another scowling glare, and then spun on one heel and stalked away down the hall.

"He'll be fine," said Horatio. "Come, I want to show you one more." He turned away from the carbuncle's case and continued down the hall. Ezra peeled her shoulder from the wall as we passed, and followed, a few steps behind. Definitely smirking.

"I don't understand why you need all of them," I said.

"Because each one is unique," he said as we walked.

He stopped in front of a case that appeared to contain a somewhat outdated-looking boy's bedroom. A garret window looked out on a fake sky. A faded poster of a skier was pinned to the wall over a twin bed. A dusky-colored globe sat on top of a wooden dresser. A desk with a reading lamp sat in a corner. There was an algebra textbook on it.

"What's this?" I asked.

Horatio smiled. "This was my bedroom," he said.

"Why is it here?"

"Watch," he said. And he pointed to a shadow, hunched over and skulking under the bed. Horatio knocked at the glass and grinned like a little boy. Then he waved at the shape. "Sturges!" he called out. "Sturges, come out and say hello!"

The shape waddled out from under the bed. It looked like a small, oddly formed person. Its legs were short and bent forward and backward like frog's legs. Its arms were long and thin. Its skin was the color and texture of old paper. Its face was round, with big, round, sad eyes. It shuffled up to the window and waved with a weary, defeated expression on its face.

"This is Sturges," said Horatio, "and he was my very first. I discovered him living under my bed when I was twelve years old."

"The house gnome," I said.

Horatio smiled.

"Is he really incontinent?" I asked.

Horatio shook his head. "I had to tell them something," he said.

"Who are 'they,' anyway?" I asked.

"You don't know?" Horatio chuckled. "They're called the Fells. They fancy themselves protectors of these amazing animals. Protection racket is closer to the truth. They know about Sturges, of course. Nothing to be done about that. And they watch your family, I'm sure of it. So when I need your father's help, I simply tell them Sturges is sick again. He's been my cover for all the others, all these years. My poor, dear, incontinent cover."

A realization dawned on me.

"They don't know," I said. "They don't know about the

manticore, or the carbuncle." A smile of expectant pride crossed Horatio's face, and I understood. "They don't know about any of them," I said.

"And why should they?" said Horatio. "What business is it of theirs?"

I looked at Sturges. He stood at the glass, shoulders hunched, face cast down. He didn't once look up to meet my gaze.

"He doesn't look very happy to be here," I said.

"He's always been this way," said Horatio. "For a long time, he was my only friend. I didn't even know that others existed. It was your father who opened my eyes to this world."

Horatio turned and began the long walk back down the hall. I followed, but I couldn't help glancing back at Sturges. He was still standing at the glass, watching us go, his eyes empty of all hope.

Horatio led the way to the elevator, where Ezra finally caught up to us. I thought she might say something. Instead she entered the elevator without a word and stood in the corner, hands in the pockets of her jacket, silent, but clearly watching and listening.

"I first met your father twelve years ago," said Horatio as the elevator lurched up the column. "It was just Sturges then, and he had a skin ailment. I made discreet inquiries, and Jim— your father—was recommended. I'm sure the Fells had a hand. They're everywhere—you'll see. Anyway, I liked Jim. A little scattered, maybe, a little overwhelmed, but always warm. You were just a little girl, I suppose. I called on his services several times over the next few years. I enjoyed his company, and I think he enjoyed mine." He paused, and for the first time, he turned to face me. "Then your mother died."

The elevator slid to a halt, and the doors opened. Horatio stepped out, then held the door for me. He led us down the hall, past his office, and into a small conference room with a view of the barracks at the bottom of the hill.

"The next time I saw Jim," he continued, "it was soon after. The wonder and the joy were gone. He was confused, lost, afraid. I offered to help him. He refused, at first. And then one day, he came to me."

"For what?" I asked.

Horatio smiled at me. "I was as surprised as you," he said. Ezra slid quietly into the room and leaned against the wall. "He wanted a loan. He wanted to expand, to hire another doctor for his clinic, to be able to do more to help the people who really needed it. And then he told me something that would change the course of the rest of my life. He told me there were other animals like Sturges."

He was quiet for a moment, letting that sink in.

"Of course, the thought had occurred to me that Sturges was not alone in the world," he said. "But I never imagined I might get to meet another like him. I helped your father in his mission, and in the process, I found mine."

"What is your mission?" I asked.

"I want them to be free," he said. "These animals deserve a world that will accept them and honor them. They deserve to be protected, to walk in the sun without fear of poachers or collectors or scientists who want to take them apart."

"They don't look very free."

"Not yet," said Horatio. "It's not safe yet. But it will be. In any case, I owe your father a great debt of gratitude. And that's why Ezra's here."

As he looked up over my shoulder, Ezra stepped forward

and held out a hand.

"I'm with you," she said, looking me square in the eye. "Dr. Batiste is a condescending ass."

"Ezra Danzig, my private investigator," said Horatio. "As we say in the boardroom, she does the wolf work."

"Grr," said Ezra halfheartedly.

"Well," said Horatio, "I'll leave you two. Jim was someone I considered a colleague at least. Ezra's time is my gift to you, and to him." And with a final nod, he left and shut the door behind him, leaving me and Ezra alone in the room, which somehow felt smaller than it had a moment before.

In the light of day, Ezra was older than she'd seemed underground. Old enough to be my mother, at least. Her face was drawn and hollow. Her skin was an unhealthy-looking pale hue. But electricity sizzled beneath the surface, lighting up every feature. Her eyes locked on me with the intensity of roadside flares, crackling with heat.

"So," she said. Her voice had the rasp of hunger. "Let's figure out who killed your dad."

She sat down in the seat opposite mine, opened the leather portfolio, and removed a thin manila folder from within. She slid it to the center of the table.

"What's that?" I asked.

"Police report," she said. "You're welcome to look. There's nothing to see, though."

"What do you mean?"

"No prints, no DNA, no clues. They don't know anything. And they never will. But, it's there. In case you want to look."

"Great," I said. "If there's no evidence, then how are we going to solve it?"

"First we're going to forget this exists." She picked up the folder, considered it briefly, then tossed it aside. "We're going to start over." She leaned across the table, and a little thrill of excitement went up my spine, like she and I were about to plan a jewel heist. "I've been doing some background."

"Background?"

"The only way we solve this case is by understanding the motive. And we start with what we know. Which in this case is the victim. So, background." She stopped for a moment. "Now, Marjan, would you like to know about your dad?"

Her eyes pinned me like a butterfly. I was frozen in my seat. I wanted to punch her, but my body wouldn't move. So I glared back, feeling mean, and a little scared.

Without warning, she kicked up out of the chair and swung her jacket up over one shoulder. "Let's take a walk," she said.

We left the mansion and walked down the hill. It was late afternoon, and the sun was starting to dip toward the willows that marked the edge of Horatio's land. The barracks and the grounds hummed with life. The smell of food and the sounds of conversation and clinking silverware wafted from what looked like a dining hall. Electric golf carts loaded with gardening tools or boxes of bulk foods trundled down worn side paths that led off the main road. A herd of sheep grazed a low knoll behind a wire fence. We passed a few solitary people hunched over laptops, earbuds in, squinting over lines of rainbow-colored code. Menagerie programmers. They sat on slabs of broken stone in the sun, or in the shade at the bases of the broad oak trees that popped up here and there.

"Jamsheed Dastani. Did I say that right?" asked Ezra, breaking a silence that felt like it had been engineered to be broken. I gave her a nod, and she smiled in satisfaction. "Born in Rasht,

Iran, a couple years before the revolution. Youngest of four children. Father was a structural engineer. Mother raised the kids. One brother's a teacher, the other's an architect. Sister's a librarian. Managed to dodge military service, thanks to a well-placed uncle, and instead came to America on a student visa, to study medicine. And then, six months in, switched to veterinary science." She paused and looked at me. "Family loved that, I'm sure."

For most of my life, I knew my dad's family as pixelated people who waved at me on Skype a few times a year. The first time I met any of them in person was after he died. One of his brothers came—Hamid, the teacher. He looked a lot like my dad, but a bit shorter, with a bit more warmth in his eyes. He stayed in an airport motel for four days. He was kind to me, but he was also constantly flustered—by English, by jet lag, by grief. Everything seemed just a bit harder when he was around. By the time he left, I think we were both more confused than when he'd arrived.

"I never really talk to them," I said.

Ezra smiled. It was a charming smile, and for a second it softened the cold, hollow fires behind her eyes. But there was something rough about it too. It was the smile of someone who was daring you to tell her not to smile. It was the smile of someone who was daring you to tell her not to do anything.

I didn't know much about my dad's family. I knew he sent them money. I had the sense that it wasn't enough. It wasn't doctor money. The Skype calls always turned serious after I left the room. My dad would speak in dark, sour tones, his Farsi coming out rough and spiteful. He always seemed to be trying to justify something to them. He always seemed frustrated. I think they wanted something from him that he couldn't give them. I think he resented them.

Ezra thrust her hands back into her pockets, and the smile slid off her face. She was all hunger again. "Anyway," she said, "I'm pretty sure we can rule them out as suspects."

"You get paid for these blazing insights?" I said.

She shot me a steely glare that softened after a moment into a chuckle. Then she turned and continued speaking, as if I hadn't said a word.

"Married in vet school. Sophie. Vet tech. Hard worker. Resourceful. By all accounts, they were very much in love. Two years later, a child. Daughter, obviously. Happy family, I'm assuming." She flicked a little glance over at me. I didn't give her anything, and she shrugged.

"How's any of this going to help solve the murder?"

"It's background," said Ezra. I could feel her looking at me, but I kept my gaze forward.

"Jamsheed—he goes by 'Jim' now," she continued, "does a couple of years as a relief vet, and then opens up his own clinic. The daughter's about three, four, at this point. Sophie helps out—answers phones, does the books, everything. It's a big risk. They're already in debt. Mortgage, student loans. Now he's in more. Business isn't great. But, happy family." She paused, an actually respectful pause. "And then, three years later. Osteosarcoma. Untreatable. Rapid decline. I'm sorry. It must have been difficult."

There was sympathy in her eyes, I could sense it. But there was also something more calculating and keen. She was watching me, studying me. Maybe it was morbid curiosity. A lot of people become morbidly curious when they find out your mom's dead. It's like this one thing changes everything else about you, makes everything you do or say mean something slightly different. Sometimes I've felt like people were talking to me in code, trying to unlock some secret emotional wisdom they thought I must have earned. I'm sure there's a way to be graceful in these moments.

But grace has never been my strong suit.

I don't like to talk about those months. I don't care who you are. You can't ask me about my mom without it feeling like you've just stuck a needle into me, and are trying to draw all the blood out of my veins with a stoppered syringe.

"I guess we can rule her out too," I said.

If I'd rattled her at all, Ezra didn't show it. She looked at me a moment longer. A thoughtful expression came over her, and she didn't say another word for a long time.

I didn't say anything either. It felt like I'd already said too much.

Ezra didn't bring up my dad again for a while. She walked with a quick, fierce pace, but her expression was quiet and patient. After a few minutes, she spoke.

"You're angry," she said, and it wasn't a question. "It's okay to be angry. You've got the right to be angry."

I was waiting for some bit of useless advice to follow her observation, to give me a reason to start hating her.

Nobody wants you to be angry. Sad, sure. But no one wants to see your anger. Anger is ugly and scary. It makes you a different person, something harder to predict. Most people try to talk you out of anger. But Ezra left the words hanging there, a cold knot of truth that couldn't be untangled with easy greeting-card sentiments. I kind of liked that.

"Where are we going?" I asked.

"I like to walk," said Ezra. "It helps me think. We can stop anytime." The way she said it, it sounded like a peace offering.

The barracks were busy with movement and life. A family

caught my eye—a little boy and girl, a mom, and a dad, playing soccer on a patch of green grass outside one of the buildings. As we passed by, I watched the children play, and wondered, *Do they know what's down there?* Did they know about the manticore, stalking its box of darkness on wounded paws? Did they know about the carbuncle, or any of the others?

Ezra followed my eyes, and chuckled. "Menagerie's a funny company," she said. "People who come here to work don't usually leave. He's never had layoffs. Most of these folks have probably been here a long time. They know. Even if they haven't seen them." Here she nodded at the ground, and the impossible creatures beneath. "They know there's something special about this place."

I looked around at all the faces. Laughing, smiling, or screwed up in concentration. They didn't look any different from anyone else you'd see on the street. There was no special glow in their eyes, or secret curl to their smiles.

"It takes some getting used to," said Ezra, "Horatio's way of doing things."

"What is he trying to do, exactly?" I asked.

"He wants to make the world a better place."

"How does that *thing* down there make the world a better place?"

"You mean Dead-face?" asked Ezra. "You'd have to ask Horatio about that. I don't like her either."

I stopped walking. "Why are you here?"

She stopped a few paces ahead of me and considered my question, her back to me.

"Because," she said, "I like finding things that have been hidden." She turned to face me, and for a second, I saw something other than hunger in her eyes. I saw hope. "And the world could stand to be a better place."

She was quiet until we looped our way back around to the dining hall. It was about half-full, a mix of programmers quietly coding, salespeople unspooling hard pitches and generous compliments into their phones, and families in various states of casual chaos. A few minutes later, we were settled into a couple of seats by a window that looked out on the rolling golden hills of Horatio's land, a bowl of vegetarian chili and a thick square of steaming corn bread in front of each of us.

"Well," said Ezra, "shall we get back to our story?"

She glanced at me for approval or disapproval. I was determined to give her neither, to give her nothing at all as she pried into my past. She continued.

"I don't think Jamsheed ever recovers completely from his wife's death. But he goes back to work. He manages to keep the clinic open."

Ezra paused again, took a sip of Coke from a straw.

"Family life, I'd say, suffers," she said.

A group of farmers a few tables over clinked bottles of beer together, shared a hearty laugh at a joke that I couldn't hear. A kid ran by, maybe nine or ten, chased by what looked like his older brother.

"The girl—Sophie and Jamsheed's daughter"—here Ezra gave me a conspiratorial smile—"has some troubles. Smart kid, very smart—everyone thinks so—but she struggles. Age eleven, she runs away from home with nothing but a backpack full of peanut butter sandwiches. They find her the next day, sleeping alone in a park twenty miles away. Never says why she left, never says how she got there, or where she was going. Child Services gets involved briefly, declines to take action. It's a sad situation, but there's nothing criminal going on."

Ezra stopped and looked at me, waiting to see if I'd say anything.

But what was there to say, really? How to explain? I was looking for something. Something was *missing*, and I had to find it. I needed to find it so badly that I was willing to walk out the door, and keep walking until the thing that was wrong felt right again. I thought I could outrun the hunger in my guts.

"Back to our hero," Ezra continued. "He doesn't date. He travels for work, but he doesn't take vacations. He drifts away from his few friends. Seems to pretty much live for work and nothing else. Doesn't seem to go anywhere except home and the clinic. And of course to his out-of-town clients. Must be hard, a dad like that. Maybe you feel invisible sometimes?" Another pause, another piercing stare. "He's hired another vet, but business is still slow. Somehow, though, it all balances out, just barely, year after year."

She stopped and leveled a cool, hard gaze at me. I didn't give her anything, and after a moment she gave up.

"Except that in the end," she said, "it doesn't, and he's dead, and we're sitting here talking about it."

"Great story," I said.

"Here's the part where I ask you if you know anything about what happened to him. Anything that might not be in the police report. Anything that might have slipped through the cracks."

I couldn't tell if I liked Ezra or not, and I wasn't sure if I could trust her. But she'd done her homework, and she was the first person I'd talked to who seemed both interested in solving my dad's murder and possibly up to the task.

"Ithaca," I said. "The woman from the Fells, she asked me about it. That's all I know."

"Anything else?"

I shook my head.

"Ithaca," said Ezra, feeling out the word, balancing it in her head. "That's new."

She turned her face to look out the window, and didn't say another word.

"So is that all?" I asked.

"For now," she said. She stood up, taking her tray with her.

"Where are you going?" I asked.

"I have a lead to follow," she replied, and for a second it looked like there was hot plasma sizzling under her skin.

As terrifying as it was, her eagerness was contagious. And suddenly I wanted what she had, more than anything. I felt it like a fever: I wanted to follow leads too, until all the questions were answered, all the secrets revealed, all the hidden things found.

"Can I help?" I asked.

My voice felt naked and small, like somehow I'd just told her every single thing about me in just three words.

Ezra smiled sadly. "You already did," she said.

"But . . ."

"This is wolf work," said Ezra. "And I don't think you're a wolf."

And with that, she turned and strode away, leaving me with a hunger that no amount of food would fix, and a view of gentle slopes covered in dry grass and filled with secrets.

That's exactly how Ava found me, a few minutes later.

"Horatio wants to see you," she said.

When we got to his office, Horatio Prendergast was holding up the ruby between two fingers. Sunlight refracted red through it, painting a crimson orb over one squinting eye.

"Magnificent," he whispered.

He set the ruby down on his desk.

"It's rare," he said, "even in my life, to encounter true perfection. When you can have anything you want, you begin to realize that everything is flawed. But this . . ." He ran his fingers along its pristine contours. "Not a single blemish," he said.

He sat back in his chair. "You were uncertain, going into her paddock," he said. "But you knew exactly what to do. Perhaps they understand you better than they do the rest of us."

"I'm not really sure," I said. "It just kind of happened."

Horatio nodded. "Your father once suggested that there was a kind of bond between your family and them. I don't think he quite understood it either. But he knew how to use it, and apparently so do you."

"I guess," I said.

"There's a job here for you, Marjan, if you want it. We could use you, and I believe you could use us, too. You have a connection with these animals that no amount of veterinary training can match. Come work with us, help us care for them, and we'll help you hone that skill. I'm sure Dr. Batiste would be honored to mentor you."

"Ha," I said.

"He's proud, but at the end of the day, he's also fair. There's housing here on the estate, free of charge. Meals included. Full benefits. And not to be crass"—he smiled—"but I pay well."

He flicked the ruby with one finger, and it spun gently on its axis. In the hungriest corner of my heart, a spark flickered.

"I have the clinic now," I said. "I have school. I can't just walk away."

"People do it all the time," said Horatio.

He took out a checkbook and a pen, and filled in the top

check. Then he tore it from the book and slid it across the desk to me. When I saw it, my mouth went dry. It was more money than I'd ever seen in my life. It was more money than I had any right to deserve.

"Why?" I whispered.

"Because I want you here," he said. "Because I had great respect for Jim in all the years I knew him. Because I always wanted to do more for him, and for your family, than I could. He was a good man, but stubborn, and I always felt he suffered for that."

"I—I have to think about it," I stammered.

"Take all the time you need," said Horatio Prendergast.

CHAPTER TWELVE

DEAD-FACE. WITH THE CLAWS

It was night when Sam dropped me at my house. Malloryn was out—as promised, two days earlier she'd marched into the occult shop and asked for a job. Today was her first training shift. She'd already texted that she was staying late.

Zorro was curled up just inside the front door, and when I came in, his head popped up eagerly. When he saw it was me, he gave a disappointed little yip and settled his chin back onto his flank.

"She'll be home soon, Zorro," I said. The fox snorted, skeptical, but he allowed me to scratch the top of his head one time before shaking me off. My fingers tingled at the touch of his skin. Impatience, frustration, and boredom traced antsy spirals up my hand. He was getting better, though—I could feel it. I could feel his eagerness to run, to stalk prey, to slink through dark brambles. I wondered if he could ever be happy, living in one of Horatio's cages.

I took the check from Horatio and laid it out on the kitchen table. It felt heavy, and when I looked at it by the light of the old overhead lamp that had hung there all my life, it looked as strange and improbable as the carbuncle's ruby, and as undeserved. I didn't want it, any more than I wanted that gemstone.

Take all the time you need, he'd said, with the confidence of someone who could afford to look at the world as a series of equations; who could, with the right math, turn any no into a yes.

Ezra was right. I was angry. Angry at Horatio for putting this terrible treasure into my hands, for thinking I would want it, for trying to make me want it, for making me feel like an idiot for not wanting it. I was angry at the check, at the numbers on it, for simply existing. I was angry at my dad, for getting himself killed before he could explain any of this to me. I was even angry at Zorro, for glancing up at me. For seeing me like this.

"Leave me alone," I said to the fox. I crumpled up the check and stormed upstairs.

I stopped outside the door to my dad's room. For just a second, I hesitated. Then I threw it open, hard enough that it slammed against the wall.

The silence inside the room stopped me. Behind that door, my father's absence had been trapped, preserved. Anger dissolved into something quiet and small, something I didn't have a good name for. I stepped out of my shoes, and walked for the first time into the room where he'd died.

The room had a stillness that felt thicker than the rest of the house, like it had been gathering mass these past months behind the closed door. I sat down at the foot of the bed and curled my toes into the carpet, the way I used to do when I was younger.

It was seventh grade, and my dad was getting dressed for work . . . It was the first day of high school, and he was packing a bag, getting ready to disappear again . . . I was a little girl, and

Mom—a dim, shadowy idea of Mom—was sitting on the side of the bed that used to be hers, looking up from a book, smiling through the halo of a bedside lamp that was suddenly impossibly bright.

I blinked the memories away.

"What am I supposed to do?" I asked.

In the closet, ten invisible versions of my dad, one in each hanging shirt, stood in a line like soldiers. Some part of me thought—wished, hoped—that one of them might be watching, might be present enough to see his daughter in this room, be able to send some kind of message, some kind of answer.

But the only answer was silence and stillness, which made me even angrier than the check still balled in my fist. I stood up and grabbed at the bedsheets, ripping them from the bed until it was stripped down to the mattress. I grabbed at the mattress and tried to pull it to the floor, but it only came halfway, which made the rage inside me burn hotter. I stalked over to the closet and pulled out his shirts, threw them onto the floor and stomped on them.

Wordless, breathless sounds came out of me. I snatched up a shoe and threw it against the wall as hard as I could. It hit with a loud thwack, and I responded with a louder yell, followed by more shoes, more thwacks, more yells. I grasped the back of the nightstand and tipped it forward so that it rattled down, drawers falling open and spilling their contents. I grabbed one side of the narrow bookshelf that took up one corner of the room, and pulled. Particle board cracked. Books landed everywhere. I found a belt and began lashing at the walls. When the buckle hit the mirror, the glass split, and I saw my reflection in it, fractured, wild-eyed, red-faced.

For a long moment, I stood there, chest heaving, belt hanging loose in my hand. Then I looked around. The mattress, half on, half off. The bed frame askew. Sheets, pillows, clothes, and shoes, everywhere. The nightstand, lying on its side, its drawers awkwardly opened. One last surge of rage coursed through me, and I threw the belt down on top of the pile like it was a poisonous snake, and then stalked out of the room, disgusted with myself and everything else in the world.

Stalked out, and then stalked right back in.

Because the least, the very least, that I could do was clean up the mess I'd just made.

I started wrestling the mattress back up onto the frame. then looked up to see Zorro watching me from the doorway with curious eyes.

I wasn't angry at him anymore.

"Sorry I snapped at you," I said.

Turning back to the mattress, it occurred to me that Malloryn might prefer a bed to a sleeping bag on the floor, and that maybe I could actually turn my act of senseless destruction into something helpful. With great effort, I dragged the mattress down the hall, then found a fresh set of sheets and pillows.

Once I had Malloryn's bed set up, I began to feel like a human being again. I went back to my dad's bedroom and pushed the nightstand into place against the wall, then took one of the drawers and began to fill it back up. Earplugs, a cell phone charger, a tiny reading light, a pair of sunglasses, pens, a blank notepad from a budget hotel chain.

And something else. An envelope. It seemed to have been wedged behind the drawers of the nightstand. As I picked it up, I felt a hungry little charge in my fingertips, and understood what Ezra had meant about finding things that had been hidden.

The envelope was crisp and new. There were a couple of folded pieces of paper inside, but it wasn't sealed, which made it feel almost casual—something my dad had grabbed for convenience. I slipped the papers out and unfolded them.

They were plane tickets. Oakland to Ithaca, with a layover in St. Louis. They were dated two days after my dad had died. One was for my dad, which I'd expected. The other one made my heart stop.

The other one was for me.

Something important had happened in Ithaca. Something that meant enough to the Fells that they had asked me about it. Something that had meant enough to my dad that he'd been ready to take me along.

Maybe something important enough that my dad had been killed for it.

Why didn't you say anything, Dad? Why didn't you tell me?

I couldn't take this information to the police. They would ask all the wrong questions. They wouldn't see the clues. Another thing Ezra had been right about—they wouldn't be any help to me. Still, for the first time since it had happened, I felt closer to understanding why he was dead. And I wanted people to know.

Sebastian would understand. I wouldn't even have to tell him much. But it was the middle of the night in England. He was asleep, probably. Any sane person would have been asleep.

Still.

I texted, **hey**.

Then I waited. Crickets chirped outside. I went to my room and sat on my bed. Downstairs, Zorro shifted his body in his corner. The phone screen remained still, my little word hanging at the very end of our conversation, a tiny blip perched at the edge of an endless pit.

No response.

I sighed and put the phone down, and as I did, it blooped.

hey

At the sight of a single word from a boy I had met in person exactly once, my heart skipped.

you awake? I wrote.

Yeah. Can't sleep. You?

It's not that late over here, I said. So yeah. Awake.

What's up?

Let me tell you, Sebastian, about my dad and all his secrets. Let me tell you how angry I am, now, and all the time. Let me tell you about this thing I found, and these people that I met today.

It didn't feel right. Not even with him. It didn't feel safe to tell him the things I'd seen.

Talk to me, I wrote, about something normal.

A moment later, he videoed. I checked my look quickly in the vanity, framed the room in a way that wasn't too embarrassing, and accepted the call.

He didn't ask me any questions. Instead he told me about the best curry in London, and I found myself telling him about the most excellent burrito in Berkeley, and the correct way to drink boba (always chew the pearls, or you'll get a stomachache), and for a little while I felt almost like a normal kid with a crush, until I heard Malloryn coming home, and remembered that I had a witch staying at my house and a billionaire trying to hire me. Then I was filled with a warm and humbling gratitude that there was someone with whom I could be ordinary, who understood in the same way that I did how strange ordinary was.

"I have to go," I said. "I'm glad you were around tonight."

"You can always talk to me," he said. We both smiled and waved, and the call ended.

"Hello, Budgins," said Malloryn downstairs. "It's good to see you, yes it is."

I heard her bustling up the stairs, Zorro trotting along behind her. She seemed to hesitate outside my dad's room, as if she could sense some change in the energy there. Then she continued on, and when she got to my room, she stopped, cocked her head in my direction, and waved.

"How was day one at the magic shop?" I asked.

She paused, gathering her words and only barely containing the glow in her eyes.

"There are," she said in a voice soft with reverence and awe, "*other witches.*"

"I mean, it's a store for witches, right?" I said.

"You don't understand," said Malloryn. "I've never *met* another witch. And today I met, like, ten of them. They were *nice* to me."

"Congratulations?" I said.

"Thank you," said Malloryn.

"So, now what?" I asked. "Do you, like, form a squad or . . ."

"A *squad*?" said Malloryn, a patient smile crossing her face. "Do you mean a coven?"

"I don't know anything about witches, Malloryn. I'm sorry."

"A group of witches that practices together is called a coven," said Malloryn. "And no. You do not just *form* a coven. And you can't sign up, either. It's not like joining the robotics team—by the way, how cool is it that our school has a robotics team?" Malloryn had also apparently enrolled at my school, and was already attending classes, though I hadn't seen her once. Invisible, as promised.

"So, what is it like?" I asked.

"A coven is a powerful force," she said. "If it's going to happen, it happens on its own. You don't plan it. You don't organize it. If it needs to be, it'll be. A true coven finds itself. That's where its power comes from."

Then a puzzled expression crossed her face, like she'd just noticed something.

"Your aura seems different," she said. "It's cloudy. Are you confused about something?"

I laughed out loud. "More like 'everything.'"

"It could be your hex," she said.

I seriously doubted it was my hex. I was pretty sure an unhexed teenager in my situation would also be confused. On the other hand, maybe an unhexed teenager wouldn't find herself in my situation to begin with. It was hard to say when it came to Malloryn's interpretation of magic. It was always vague enough that it just might be true.

She started to head to her room.

"Malloryn," I said, and she stopped. "I have a question for you."

"Sure," she said.

"How are you so confident about everything?" I asked. "How do you do that?"

She thought for a moment. "Maybe it's magic." She smiled and shrugged, and then bounced off down the hall, Zorro padding along behind her. A moment later, she called out, "Wow, nice bed!"

I smiled, then laid the plane tickets out on my bed.

What did they mean? Had he really planned on taking me? Why? Had I really been that close to knowing all the answers?

And what was in Ithaca?

For a moment, I listened, eyes closed, deep into the silence, as deep as my ears could draw. Grass rustled in a faint night breeze. An airplane passed by overhead. I heard the muddled murmur of humanity, the grumble of nighttime traffic. I thought about Zorro, and Kipling, and the hundred creatures behind glass and under the earth. I thought about my father, driving me home after picking me up from the park where I'd finally given up running, him glancing over at me in silence like he didn't recognize me. Would he have looked at me like that on the plane to Ithaca? Was I still that girl? Had he still been afraid of what he saw? I tried to think of my mother, but the pictures wouldn't hold their shapes, and her face kept becoming the blank, cold face of the manticore.

Something was missing.

It was Dr. Batiste who called me, early the next week, during a break between classes. I ducked into the music room, which was empty and quiet.

"You were right," he said. His tone was gruff. "About the . . . We're not supposed to say their names over the phone. But you know which one."

"Dead-face," I said. "With the claws."

"When she arrived, I made a decision, for the safety of my team," he said. "We're going to do a corrective procedure, and I want you to be there." He paused. "Well, Horatio wants you to be there."

"I can't do school days," I said.

"That's exactly what I told Horatio," said Dr. Batiste. "We're going on Saturday. Sam'll pick you up Friday night."

I didn't want to be anywhere near the manticore—not Friday, not Saturday, not ever. If I never saw those eyes or that face again, my life would be better for it. But before I'd realized what I was doing, I agreed to be in the room while Dr. Batiste and his team operated on her.

At least she'll be asleep, I thought. But I couldn't imagine that monster sleeping. I couldn't imagine her doing anything other than hunting or eating, which were two things I didn't really want to imagine at all.

I must have looked shaken when I came out of the music room, because Carrie was passing by on her way to class, and she stopped.

"Are you feeling okay?" she asked. "You look like a ghost."

"I'm just stressed," I said.

"Take a night off," she said. "You know about Friday, right?"

"What's Friday?" I asked, hoping the answer would make it easy to say no.

"Party," she said. "One of Howie's friends. Grace is going. We should go too."

I didn't know Howie's friends. I didn't really know Howie. But his world, whatever it was—sports, smiles, a reasonable taste in music—had crept up alongside us as he and Grace had gotten closer.

A good friend probably would have gone to Howie's friend's party, just to look after her girls.

"I can't," I said. "There's a thing I have to do." When Carrie looked at me funny, I added, "It's for my dad."

It was a get-out-of-jail-free card, and I felt rotten for playing it. But I knew it would work.

Carrie nodded, apologetic, sympathetic. "I'll go with Grace," she said. Her eyes offered me all the support in the world.

She wouldn't have been so eager to help if she'd had any idea what I was about to face.

CHAPTER THIRTEEN

THE MANTICORE'S APPETITE

Once was, once wasn't.

A young man lived with his father and his mother and several sisters and brothers in a village at the edge of the desert that lies across the province of Kerman. They were poor, and life was hard, but they all worked together, and the people of the village took care of one another, and so they survived and were happy, year after year.

One fateful day, a band of marauders rode out of the desert and attacked the town. They set fire to homes and stole all the villagers' livestock and food. They slaughtered anyone who stood in their way, and also slaughtered many who didn't. And then they rode away, leaving the village in ruins.

Of his entire family, only the young man survived. His father, his mother, and all his brothers and sisters were killed. Their home was a smoldering pile of ash. Their food was gone. The well where the villagers drew their water was poisoned by corpses.

The few other survivors wept and mourned and wailed at their lot. But the young man could feel no sorrow. Instead he felt only a burning rage inside him, and vowed a dark vow that the marauders would pay for their atrocities. He left the village that very day, and ventured alone into the desert in search of vengeance.

All day long, he followed the marauders' trail through the dunes, and though the sun blazed and the sand and rocks radiated with heat, he craved neither food nor water. His rage fed him and fueled him. And when the sun went down and the desert became cold, he kept walking for hours, and his rage burned within him like a furnace, and kept him warm. Finally, when the moon was high in the sky, and the heavens were deep with stars, sleep took him, and he collapsed amid the shifting sands.

In the morning when he woke, a manticore stood before him, watching him.

The young man had heard stories of the manticores that prowled this desert. He'd heard that they were creatures of insatiable appetite, that they devoured men and women and even children whole, that they delighted in the terror of their victims. Until that moment, the young man had himself been terrified of them. But now he felt nothing, nothing but his rage, and so he faced the manticore without fear, and held out his hand to it.

The manticore approached. It lowered its great bald head and sniffed at the young man's open palm. And when the young man looked into the manticore's eyes, he saw there a hunger older than the world itself, and he knew that it was the same hunger he felt within his own heart.

"You and I are very much alike," said the young man, his hand still outstretched to the monster. "Join me, and let us spill the blood of murderers together."

The manticore regarded the fearless, wrathful young man for a long time. At last, after much consideration, it opened its mouth. The young man, believing this to be his end, roared at the manticore with all his rage and fury, and refused to run. But the manticore did not devour him. Instead, with the most delicate of bites, it removed only the littlest finger from the young man's outstretched hand, and ate it. Then it bowed down before him, and allowed him to climb onto its back, and together they rode out in search of the marauders.

With the manticore as his steed, the young man made much better time than any horse, and by and by, they came across a small encampment of men roasting one of the village's sheep whole on a spit. The young man saw among them one who had butchered his brothers. He cried out for the manticore to attack. The manticore set upon the men, tore them to pieces one by one, and ate them.

That night, the young man slept among the bones of his enemies, and in the morning when he awoke, the manticore was standing over him.

"Come," the young man said. "We have much more work to do." He held out his hand—the one with the missing finger—and the manticore promptly bit it clean off. Then it bowed down before him, and together they rode off in search of the rest of the marauders.

By and by, they came across another encampment. Here men wore clothes taken from the backs of the people of the young man's village. The young man saw among them one who had slaughtered his sisters. He cried out for the manticore to attack. Once again, the manticore set upon them, tore them to pieces one by one, and ate them.

That night, the young man wrapped the stump of his missing

hand in rags and cloth, and lay down among the bones of his enemies. The wound throbbed and ached. He lay awake for many sleepless hours until finally he drifted off into a dream.

In the morning, the manticore stood over him.

"Come," whispered the young man. "There is still more to be done."

He held out the stump of his hand, and the manticore took his arm off at the shoulder. Then it bowed down, and with great difficulty, the young man climbed onto its back. Together they rode off in search of the marauders.

By and by, they came across another encampment. Here the men had adorned themselves with the jewelry of the villagers. The young man saw among these men one who had murdered his mother. He cried out for the manticore to attack. The manticore set upon the men of the camp, tore them to pieces one by one, and ate them.

That night, the young man lay down among the bones of his enemies and, clutching at the stump of his arm, tried to sleep. But the pain was too great, and he lay awake all night. And when the sun began to rise, the manticore rose too, and came to stand over him.

The young man struggled to his feet.

"Come," he said, in a feeble, halting voice. "There is still more to be done."

He held out his one remaining arm, and the manticore bit it off at the shoulder, and ate it. Then it knelt down before him, so that he could climb onto its back, and when the young man had found a way with no arms to balance himself there, the manticore rose again. Together they rode off in search of the marauders.

By and by, they came across another encampment. This one

was finer than the others. Its tents were more grand, and its men better fed and better clothed. Among them, the young man saw the warlord who had led the marauders in their massacre, and who had by his own hand slain the young man's father and set fire to the young man's home. The young man howled in rage, and cried out for the manticore to attack.

Once again, the manticore set upon the encampment. It tore the men to pieces one by one, and ate them, until only the warlord himself remained, wounded and unable to defend himself. The young man approached him and sat down beside him and listened to the injured man whimper in pain and terror, and plead for his life.

But the manticore came for the warlord, too, and all the while, the young man watched. Every cry of pain, every cracking bone, fed his rage.

When the warlord was dead and eaten, the young man lay down among the bones of his enemies, and was not satisfied. He wished he could kill them again and again, a hundred times, a thousand. But they were already dead, and they would not die again, and anyway, the young man was too weak and weary to move.

He turned away from the bones to see the manticore looming over him. He saw in its eyes a hunger older than the world itself, and he knew it to be the hunger that still burned within his own heart.

"You and I are very much alike," said the young man.

But if the manticore understood him, it did not care. It ate him, too, what was left of him. Then it left the silent camp and its lonely bones to bleach in the sun, and padded away into the desert in search of other prey, for it was still hungry.

| CHAPTER FOURTEEN |

THE PROCEDURE

Sam picked me up on Friday afternoon. When I arrived at Horatio's compound, the grounds were bustling with Menagerie employees and their families. Dinner was being served in the cafeteria, but I didn't feel hungry.

I found Ava in the lobby of the main house.

With a couple of brisk swipes at her tablet, she found me a place to sleep, and directed me to one of the barracks at the bottom of the hill.

"Tomorrow, eight a.m.," she said. "That's when they'll be starting prep."

I glanced down the hall for Horatio.

"You're on his calendar," said Ava, without looking up. "After the procedure."

"Marjan." The voice came from behind me, close enough that it made me jump. Ezra. She'd come from out of nowhere, so quiet that I hadn't even heard her approach.

She brought me to a meeting room with a window overlooking the sprawling Menagerie campus. "I found something on Ithaca," she said. "It's the kind of thing we like to pay attention to."

She opened her briefcase and slid a folder over to me.

"Park ranger took these," she said. "Just outside Ithaca."

"What is it?"

"It was"—she paused—"a pack of coyotes." I opened the folder. There were several pictures inside. "Officially, this was the work of either a grizzly bear or people. But grizzlies don't live here."

"When were these taken?" I asked.

"June," she replied.

Not long before the trip my dad had apparently been planning to surprise me with—a fact that I didn't feel like sharing with Ezra.

"Is there another manticore on the loose?" I asked.

"She wouldn't have left so much behind," said Ezra. "It's probably nothing. But we'll keep an eye on it, just in case. There's something else, though." She took the pictures back and handed me another folder. "Does the name Vance Cogland mean anything to you?"

"No," I said. I opened the folder. A bald, angry face glared back at me in front of a wall of beige bricks. Tattoos under his mean little eyes. A sneer on his lips.

"Consider yourself lucky," said Ezra. "He was a punk. Drugs, theft, assault. Interestingly, never convicted. He's been dead for years. He was found in the back room of the pawnshop in Lubbock, Texas, where he fenced stolen property. He'd been . . . Well, whatever you call what happened to your dad, that's what he'd been."

"You think he has something to do with my dad?" I asked.

"Maybe."

"So who killed this Cogland guy?"

"Cogland was a scumbag with no living family." Ezra smiled

a dry smile. "Not much incentive to pursue a serious inquiry. I don't know who killed him. But I'd like to know. So if you happen to see his name pop up anywhere, or if you find any connection to Lubbock, we should talk."

I couldn't shake the feeling that Ezra was still sizing me up, reading me with every word she spoke.

"I'll, uh, yeah. I'll let you know."

"And Ithaca," she said. For a second, it seemed like she could see through my eyes right into my bedroom, to the expired plane tickets stuffed under my bed. "Anything else you can find out about Ithaca."

She smiled, a cold, cruel smile. The smile of an animal on the hunt. Then, just as quickly, the smile vanished from her face, and she stood up to go.

"Tomorrow," she said, "I hope it all goes well." She paused. "And if it doesn't, I hope she's the only casualty."

Night was falling as I made my way down to the living quarters. Pale footlights marked the paths that crisscrossed the grounds. The people I passed along the way greeted me with easy smiles. I tried to smile back, but inside I felt heavy.

At the barrack, a friendly, matronly woman led me to a simple, clean bedroom on the second floor. Horatio wanted everyone to feel at home here, she explained. When we got to the room, she gave me a key.

"You're Horatio's guest, aren't you?" she asked.

"Uh, yeah," I said.

She smiled, her eyes twinkling with eager delight. "Has he shown them to you?"

"Them?"

She glanced at the floor. "Down there?"

"Oh," I said. "Uh, yeah. Are we allowed . . . ?"

"To talk about them?" she said. "No. But I could tell. You can always tell when someone's seen them. What did you think?"

"I'm not sure," I said. "I don't know what to think."

"I've been invited down to see them three times now. It doesn't get old." She puffed up a bit in pride.

"What do you . . ." I wasn't sure what to ask. "What do you think of them?"

"I think they're the greatest glory of the world, of course," she said, as if there were no other conceivable answer. "The seeds of the future, isn't that right?" She laughed, a warm little chuckle that lit up her cheeks. "My favorites are the faeries. Did you know they sing to each other, every night? It's true. Sometimes, even from all the way up here, if you listen really hard, you can hear them."

Her eyes went to someplace off to the right, like she was hearing them then, or trying to. After a moment, she looked back at me, smiled, warm and polite, and said, "Well, I hope you have a good night."

The door shut gently behind her, and I was alone. The quiet was sudden and deep.

The next day we were going to cut a manticore's toes off at the knuckles. My stomach tightened at the thought of all that could go wrong. I felt like I'd somehow lost control of something important, like I shouldn't be here.

Still, I lay down on the bed, closed my eyes, and tried to listen for faerie songs. But if they were singing that night, it wasn't a song for human ears.

• • •

They wheeled the manticore into the operating theater on a gurney the size of a formal dining table. She was sedated, and her legs were pinioned to the gurney with leather straps, all her toes exposed and shaved clean of fur. Her tail was looped around her body, and strapped down in several places. Its pointed barb rested near her placid, unchanging face.

The theater was a huge, white room, lit from above by a halo of halogen. A bramble of surgical lamps on jointed armatures hung down from the lighting apparatus, a giant spider made of steel and light. The table was wheeled to the center of the room, beneath the halo, and locked into place.

Dr. Batiste commanded the room with gruff calmness. He wore green scrubs and a surgical mask and cap, and he stood at the head of the table as several other masked and scrubbed men and women bustled around him, moving machinery into place, fussing over surgical tools, responding to the doctor's succinct orders in hushed voices. Dr. Batiste was almost comically short compared to his assistants, but their constant movement combined with his assured stillness made them seem almost invisible, while he seemed nearly as powerful and imposing as the thing on the table.

At one end of the operating theater, Horatio Prendergast was donning a surgical mask. With him were several large men with blank, ready stares, and rifles of various sizes. Behind them was Ezra. Horatio watched the proceedings in respectful silence. The men with him were silent too, but it was a different kind of quiet.

I knew I didn't belong with their group, but there was no place for me in the swirl of activity around the manticore's gurney. Instead I found myself standing in a corner, sandwiched

between a shelving unit of surgical supplies and an unused respirator. No one had asked me to do anything. Other than a brief glare from Dr. Batiste, and a nod from Horatio, no one had even acknowledged my presence.

Which was fine with me. I had no idea what I was doing there either.

The flurry of activity around the table reached a crescendo, and then grew quiet.

"Ladies and gentlemen," said Dr. Batiste, his voice soft and oddly formal. He was speaking to his team only, not to Horatio, and certainly not to me. "Today we'll be performing amputations of the first through the fifth distal phalanges on each of the patient's paws. After the initial incision, we will cauterize the wound, remove the bone, and then close the wound with stitches. The patient will remain fully sedated throughout the procedure. Speak only as necessary, say as little as possible. Thank you all, and good luck."

Then, with a curt nod to his team, he picked up a scalpel from the tray beside him, and the operation began.

They worked in near-silence. Tools passed from one to another, and back again. The breaths of the manticore kept rhythm, and soon Dr. Batiste and his team were moving in time with her cadences.

They murmured to each other, a word here, a word there, sometimes a question, rarely a complete sentence. Their feet shuffled on the floor. A pulse oximeter beeped. One by one, the distal bones of the manticore dropped into a metal pan. I picked one up and examined it, wiped away the blood. I brought it over and showed it to Horatio, pointing wordlessly to the place where the claw had grown back, twisted and gnarled, into the bone. He nodded, understanding and maybe a bit impressed. Dr. Batiste ignored us.

Asleep, the manticore didn't look so terrible. She was just mass, a bulk of fur and chitin and skin, lumped on the table. The sick dread that had radiated out from her paddock the first time we'd met was gone. The air around her was as blank and empty as her face.

The first time she moved, it was barely a twitch. A paw curled, ever so slightly, then released, and she was still again. Dr. Batiste and his staff froze, set their instruments down slowly, and stepped back from the table. The doctor looked over to the anesthesiologist, who motioned to the pulse-ox—which was still emitting even, regular beeps—shook her head, and shrugged.

"Muscle tremor," said Dr. Batiste after the manticore had been still another minute. He didn't sound entirely convinced, but he nodded himself into conviction and stepped up to the gurney again. His team followed suit, and they resumed the procedure.

She twitched again a moment later. This time, the movement was fiercer, more powerful. It rattled the table, and caused one of the assistants to jump back in alarm. Again Dr. Batiste lifted his hands from his work and stepped back, never taking his eyes from the patient.

"Dr. Laghari?" he said. "Should we be concerned?"

The anesthesiologist shook her head. "Her vitals are stable," she said. "They haven't moved. She's out."

Dr. Batiste glared at her, asking a hundred angry questions with his eyes. She pointed again to the sine waves on her screen. They came in regular, even pulses, one after the next. No disturbances, not even a flutter.

But I felt something flutter, just for a second, dark-winged and hungry, against the inside of my ribs.

"She's not," I said. Every eye in the room was on me. Horatio. Ezra. Dr. Batiste looked from Dr. Laghari to me, then back.

"Do tell," he said.

"I felt . . . ," I began.

And right then, all the confidence left me. Yes, I'd felt *something*. But what was it? What did it mean? Maybe it was just breakfast settling.

"Yes?" said Dr. Batiste.

"I . . ." I couldn't be certain. "Maybe it was nothing."

Dr. Batiste glanced at Horatio, a micro-expression of gloating triumph that made my stomach churn. Then he turned back to his team.

"Marjan," said a voice from the dark. Horatio. "Perhaps you should lay a hand on her. It couldn't hurt."

"Is that necessary?" asked Dr. Batiste.

"It's only a suggestion," said Horatio. But it was clear that it was more than a suggestion.

I approached the table. She smelled like a butcher shop, like fat and blood and cold, naked muscle. The atmosphere around her felt empty and airless. I'd never wanted to be this close to her, but in this condition, there was no horror in her. She felt sterile, helpless, inanimate, dead. Not even her deep, purring breaths gave her the illusion of life. I steeled myself for the flood of nightmares I imagined churning behind her placid face, then took one of my vinyl gloves off and laid a hand gingerly on her cool, smooth scalp.

And felt nothing.

"Stay out of our way," hissed Dr. Batiste, quiet enough that only I could hear. Then he addressed the assistants. "Give her some space."

The work continued. The manticore twitched twice more. Each time, I felt that flutter, faint but insistent. Each time, the work stopped, the team set down their tools and stepped back, tense and silent.

Dr. Laghari became my silent ally. I could feel the fluttering the moment before the twitches came, just long enough to warn her with a nod, so that she could watch the animal's levels for any observable fluctuations. There were none. The manticore's vitals were as pure and even as a metronome.

Dr. Batiste had removed the last of the manticore's outer toe knuckles. One of his assistants was suturing the flaps of skin folded around the stump. A hush of relief had descended on the room. I could see it in every eye. Shoulders that had been held tight were softening. Nervous, shallow breaths were cautiously deepening. The work was done. The assistant drew the final stitch, tied off the string with a neat trick of his fingers, and stood, pulling his gloves off, a smile practically glowing through the fibers of his surgical mask.

Then, the flutter again, but instead of disappearing, it unfurled inside me like vomit, exploded into every nerve, faster than I could speak. The sound of splitting bones echoed inside my skull. I tasted raw blood and wet marrow in my mouth. I felt flesh pop and cartilage crumple between my teeth. Hunger, pure and endless, devoured me.

She was awake.

Restraints snapped. Her tail slammed against the lighting apparatus. The armatures swung wildly. Glass shattered. Sparks rained down everywhere. Dr. Batiste and his team scattered for cover, while Horatio and Ezra and the bodyguards ducked behind a doorway. Reeling away, sick, I staggered to a corner of the room, out of her immediate line of sight.

She crouched atop the gurney, muscles taut and rippling beneath her skin, her eyes scanning the flickering room, her face still blank, placid, unreadable. I knew what was in her heart, though. I'd felt it.

I only saw what happened next in snapshot moments that strobed through the darkness. The manticore stood up, shrugging off her bindings. Dr. Batiste cowered behind a silver instrument tray. The tail shot out. The tray clattered to the floor, and the doctor cried out in terror. The barb drew back slowly and deliberately, sliding gently over the doctor's shoulder, passing within inches of his exposed throat.

As she prepared to strike again, the manticore's mouth began to open in a terrible, flat slash that split her face in two. That blank face hinged up, and the lower jaw stretched wide, exposing three concentric rows of jagged, sharp teeth. A giant tongue curled against the pink, vaulted ceiling of its cavernous maw. Almost like a smile. Dr. Batiste sobbed and pleaded.

"Shoot it!" someone cried. "Somebody shoot it!" The oily clatter of guns finding their mark. The manticore rose up. It was ancient and unafraid. Its eyes blazed in the dark, daring the gunmen to take their shot.

"WAIT!"

The voice was loud and piercing. It rattled off the walls, and brought the screaming, shifting room to a dead halt.

I was surprised to discover in the silence that followed that it was my own voice, and that I did not, in fact, want this horrible creature to die. Not here, not like this.

Very slowly I stood up, just as emergency lights painted the room a gloomy shade of green. The manticore had left

Dr. Batiste, and her focus was now on me. Her awful smile drifted away. Her teeth vanished beneath the smooth veneer of her mask. She regarded me with a drowsy stare. Her tail, still poised to strike, flicked and twitched in the air. My mouth went dry.

"Hi," I said.

The manticore did not respond, but she also did not impale me, so I continued.

"No one here wants to hurt you, but if you try to hurt the doctor or anyone else, something bad is going to happen."

Her red eyes narrowed. Her tail made a shape almost like a question mark in the air. Was she listening, I wondered, or calculating range? The barb dangled from the end of it, swinging lazily between life and death, hers and mine. I felt that same sick feeling wash over me again. I gritted my teeth against a wave of nausea and felt my body swaying.

I wondered if human hands would be fast enough to put the manticore down before it killed me. I decided they probably wouldn't. I closed my eyes, held my breath, and waited.

Nothing happened.

The sick feeling passed. I opened my eyes, and the manticore was still looking at me, her face perfectly unreadable. Then she shrugged her shoulders inward, folded her legs beneath her, and lowered her tail, one segment at a time, to the ground.

"Good," I said. Over the manticore's shoulder, Dr. Laghari was preparing a syringe. "We're going to take you back to your room now. But we need you to sleep a little bit longer, so you don't hurt anyone. Is that okay?"

Nothing.

Dr. Laghari took a step toward her. The manticore's eyes darted sideways, and the doctor froze.

"It'll be fine," I said. "Just one more little sleep, and then you'll be better."

The manticore turned back to me. I nodded to Dr. Laghari and took a step toward the manticore, just as the doctor reached her and drove the needle into her flank.

I put my hand on the manticore's nearest paw as she tensed in surprise. For a moment, I felt her hunger again, sharp and clear, saw the ravages of meals past in a shifting slideshow of bones and gore. Then, as the sedative spread, it all became gummy, soft and vanishing like tallow being poured down a drain, until all I felt was a swimming gray nothingness. The manticore's breath came in slow, hot bursts that reverberated inside my skull. Beneath my fingers, I felt nothing. Behind my eyes, I saw nothing.

When I woke up, there was sunlight shining through my eyelids. My head was pounding, and my limbs felt heavy. I opened my eyes.

I was lying on a couch beside a window, in what looked like a sitting room of Horatio's mansion. It was early afternoon. I sat up slowly and looked around.

"Welcome back," said Horatio. He was sitting in a chair opposite the couch. He held out a glass of water. I took it and drank it all. There was an awful taste in my mouth, and I felt an immense gratitude as the water washed it away.

"How long . . . ?" I asked.

"Only a little while," said Horatio. "I'm not entirely sure how it works, you and them. My best guess is you got a dose of ketamine."

"Huh," I said. My thoughts were still muggy.

"She's safe, in case you're wondering. Not happy, but safe. Thanks to you. In fact, I'd say there are a few people today who owe you a good deal for what you did. Myself not the least of them." He laughed. "I'd say you've earned Dr. Batiste's respect, should you have any use for it."

I looked around, half expecting to see the doctor glaring at me. But Horatio and I were alone.

"You haven't taken me up on my offer," said Horatio. "I thought it was generous. Perhaps you're holding out for a better one?"

"I don't think I want to work here," I said.

"No?" he said. "Your dad never took my offer either. He was stubborn too. But we found common ground eventually. Maybe you and I will come to an understanding too, if not a formal agreement."

"Why do you have that thing? It shouldn't even exist. None of them should."

"And yet," he said with a grim smile. "And yet. They aren't perfect, Marjan. But they *are* real. And each one of them tells us the truth."

"Then maybe some truths aren't worth telling," I said. "Maybe some truths don't do anyone any good."

"I would argue that those truths in particular are the most important," said Horatio. "The world is full of darkness, and the darkness is terrifying. But if you give the darkness a face, then maybe you can speak to it. And if you can speak to it, then maybe you can control it. And after all, isn't that why we invented monsters?"

"Did we invent them?" I asked.

"It's quite a puzzle, isn't it," said Horatio with a smile.

"This isn't right," I said. "That place, down there. It isn't right."

"No," said Horatio. "It's not."

"Then why?"

"Because," he said, "they're not safe. Up here, out there." He gestured out the window. "The world isn't ready for them. It was, once, I think. A long time ago. But it's not safe anymore. They're in danger, every second. And they're too precious to lose. I know you can feel that."

"So you're just going to keep them all down in your cellar forever?"

Horatio laughed. "When you say it like that, *I* sound like the monster," he said. "I don't plan on keeping them forever. When the time is right . . . I was thinking Wyoming."

"Like a ranch?"

Horatio smiled. "No," he said. "I mean, the whole state of Wyoming. You're surprised? It sounds like a crazy idea, I know. But we must not limit the scope of our dreams. Do you know how I became who I am?"

"Menagerie?" I asked.

He chuckled. "That's one answer," he said. "I'll tell you another: order."

"Order?"

"The world is a chaotic place," he said. "War—chaos. The spread of diseases—chaos. The uneven distribution of resources . . . We have enough food to fill every belly on this planet, and yet . . . ." He shook his head. "And that's just the human chaos. There are hurricanes spinning up in the Atlantic, typhoons in the Pacific. There are tectonic plates grinding against each other. There are methane deposits under arctic ice, volcanoes building up pressure. All of them unpredictable, uncontrollable. Any one of them could disrupt the fragile bonds that hold society together. Any one of them could break us apart, at any moment.

"I've always abhorred chaos, ever since I was young. A messy bedroom, a class full of unruly students. At best, these things made me uncomfortable. At worst, they terrified me. Maybe it's instinctive in some of us, the need to bring order to our environments. Computers fascinated me. A system that only does exactly as it's programmed! There's nothing more seductive for a mind craving order in the universe.

"I created Menagerie for the same reason. What greater service than to gather in the disorder, to quantify it, to control it? We'd be a better world, I thought, if only we had better tools for understanding the chaos that was all around us. I was young and idealistic. I thought everyone wanted the same things I did. I thought I was building a tool that would help scientists make the world a better place. That's what Menagerie was supposed to be. Do you know who bought it?"

He paused, a bitter, rueful smile on his face. I shook my head.

"Oil and mineral companies," he said. "Looking for new reserves, new fields to drill and mine. Banks and trading shops looking to sharpen their market algorithms. Defense contractors." He paused, and his expression grew dark. "All of them assured me that they shared my vision. I believed them, because I wanted it to be true. But they used my technology to build missile navigation systems. I made something to try to save us from destroying ourselves, and they weaponized it. I became rich. I made"—he gestured around—"this. But I also learned a valuable lesson. You're a fool if you don't take advantage of opportunity when it presents itself. But you can never rely on others to share your dreams."

Ava came into the room, took my empty water glass, and handed me a full one. I drank it in one long, dribbling gulp. I tasted, for a second, blood. I began to feel woozy again.

"You're welcome to stay here as long as you like," said Horatio.

"I should go." I stood and made my wobbly way back down the hall. Ava nodded as I exited into the bright sunlight of a Saturday afternoon. My head was still throbbing, but just then, I didn't want to spend a moment longer at Horatio's compound.

Sam drove me home. I tried to make small talk, but couldn't. In my head, I kept replaying the flash-bang clatter of the manticore's sudden awakening. Sometimes it felt like it was happening again, in the car, her tail suddenly filling up the back seat, her eyes glowing out of every shadow and dark corner, her body rising up across the windshield.

When I got home, Malloryn was positioning a number of small, smooth stones on the floor to match a diagram in one of her witchy books.

"It's nothing bad, don't worry," she said. "Scrying spell. I'm just practicing. You have to—" She stopped talking when she saw my face, then scooped up the rocks and put them into a little leather satchel. "You don't look good," she said. "Let me make you some tea."

"I'm fine," I said, but it wasn't true, and when she walked me to a chair and sat me in it, I went without a struggle.

She set a teakettle on the stove to warm up.

"Did something bad happen?"

"No . . . ," I said. "Yes? I don't know. No one was hurt. Everyone's fine. I guess nothing bad happened. I think maybe I saved somebody's life today."

"That sounds like a good thing," said Malloryn. "You should lead with that next time."

I didn't say anything for a while, and neither did Malloryn. The kettle started to whistle, and she poured the steaming water into a cup with a ball of loose-leaf tea. She watched it steep for a minute, then pressed the cup into my hands.

"It's oolong," she said. "Healing properties."

I took a sip. It warmed the inside of my face. I don't know if any actual healing properties were at work, but it felt good.

"I'm doing some things right now," I said, "that I don't feel good about. I don't know if they're right or wrong, and there's no one I can ask. There are people who want my help, and I don't know if they deserve it. But I don't know if I get to pick and choose. And if I do, I don't know how."

Malloryn had poured herself a cup of tea also, and as I spoke, she came to sit down across from me.

"And I've seen some things that I wish I hadn't seen," I continued. "I want them to go away. I want a lot of things to go away."

Malloryn's face was gentle, her expression soft and full of concern. "There's something special about you, Marjan," she said. "I don't know what it is or how it works, but it's powerful. And you're not even trying. I'm jealous. That's not gonna make you feel any better, but it's true."

"I don't want to be special," I said. "I didn't ask for any of this."

"Your gift—why you have it and what it means—is, like, way above my pay grade." said Malloryn. "So take this however you want. If there's a voice in your head telling you something doesn't feel right, you should listen. That's your heart talking. And when there's no code, your heart is the code. When there are no rules, your heart knows the rules."

"My heart's a big old mess," I said.

She reached across the table and put a hand on mine. "I know that," she said.

Then she was hugging me, a fierce, glowing hug that smelled like patchouli, and for just a second, I felt like I was five years old. "I know," she said over and over again. "I know, I know."

Malloryn might have been wrong about magic, but she was right about everything else.

"Malloryn," I said into her shoulder, "I don't know if I believe in hexes."

"That's okay," said Malloryn.

"And I don't know if I believe in witchcraft," I said.

"You don't have to," she said.

I pulled away, so she could see my face, and know that I was serious.

"Will you still try to take my hex away?" I asked.

Her eyes lit up.

"Will I ever," she said.

CHAPTER FIFTEEN

DISENTANGLEMENT

I spent most of Sunday sleeping. My nightmares were industrial-strength terror. I could see the manticore's eyes everywhere I looked. I was full of doubt about my part in keeping that monster alive.

When I told Sebastian about the hex removal, he was even more skeptical than I was.

"So is it like getting a tattoo removed?" he asked, only half-serious. "Because that's what it sounds like."

"I think it's a little less painful than that."

But I wasn't sure, and Malloryn hadn't told me much—only to be ready on Friday night.

All that week, I sat with Carrie and Grace at lunch, but it didn't feel like it used to. The three of us were in our own worlds. Carrie had just started two-a-days with the swim team. Grace was all moony for Howie, whom she was now officially dating—apparently I'd missed an eventful party. Meanwhile I was seeing manticores around every corner.

On Friday, after school and the clinic, Malloryn met me at the house door and walked me to the couch.

She brought me a steaming mug of something that tasted pleasantly like licorice. She poured a mug for herself too, sipped it once, and then sat down across from me.

"So," she said, "you want to know about your hex."

"What is it?"

"A hex is a binding spell," she said. "It keeps things in, or it keeps them out. Hexes can be friendly, but they can also be cruel. I put a few on my bedroom at home, to keep the most common evil spirits away, but I had to be really sneaky about it so my parents wouldn't notice. I'd never dream of putting one on another person. Way too dangerous." She laughed so that the word "way" took on a few extra syllables. Then she caught herself. "Sorry," she added sheepishly.

"So, what's mine do?" I asked.

"Do you really not know?" said Malloryn.

"I have no idea," I said. "I don't know who would have hexed me, and I don't know what it's doing. And honestly, I'm not even sure hexes are a real thing."

"Trust me, this one's real," said Malloryn. "And it's not doing you any favors. There's so much heavy energy around you. It can't be good."

"So what is it?"

Malloryn drew in a deep breath, like she was winding up to tell a story, then abruptly paused.

"Not a clue," she said flatly. "But I know it's there."

Her confidence was at least a little bit infectious. I was beginning to wonder if I *had* been hexed.

"The most common scenario is an ex with a grudge," she said.

"Can't have an ex if you've never dated anyone," I said.

"That's a relief," said Malloryn. "Exes and hexes are a nasty mix. Fortunately, even if we don't know who it was, we can still try to undo it."

"And how, exactly, do we do that?" I asked.

"I was thinking Gelsin's Disentanglement," said Malloryn.

"Who's what?"

Malloryn laughed out loud.

"Armand Gelsin was an Armenian witch in the early twentieth century," she said. She had begun to gather some things up from the kitchen, and she talked as she bustled. "His familiar was a hare named Oslo. Gelsin fled the Ottoman Empire as a young man, and ended up in London, where he learned enough English to make a living as a performing magician. He accidentally drowned himself while trying to develop a water-breathing spell, so there's some doubt about whether Gelsin's Disentanglement actually works."

Zorro sat at attention in his bed, watching her with bright, eager longing.

"You're not coming tonight, Budgins," she said. "I'm sorry. Doctor's orders." She glanced at me with a wink.

"Is this going to be safe?"

"Probably," said Malloryn. "Anyway, Gelsin wasn't very good with water, but he was really good with knots. Like, scary good. They say he could tie and untie five hundred different knots, without looking. You could blindfold him and hand him any knot you could imagine, and he'd know exactly what to do with it."

I caught glimpses as she worked. A pile of herbs, weighed out on a triple beam scale, then brushed into a hemp sachet. A crystal shard, held up to catch the sun's last rays in the window, then quickly wrapped in velvet. A kettle hissing, then being poured off. A smell like burnt lavender.

"What do knots have to do with the spell?" I asked.

"Hexes are a kind of binding. Bindings need knots, or they slip off. Obviously the knots that hold hexes in place are way weirder than any ordinary knot. But Gelsin could undo those, too. Or so they say. Anyway, there have been at least two reasonably verified successful castings of Gelsin's Disentanglement in the last fifty years."

"Is that a lot?"

"Yes," said Malloryn, "that's a lot."

"What happened to Oslo?" I asked.

"Hasenpfeffer," said Malloryn. "Also maybe earmuffs. Unconfirmed. It's a hard world for little things."

After a bit more fussing, Malloryn clapped her hands three times over a small pile of supplies that she'd set into a wicker picnic basket she'd dug out of one of our kitchen cabinets. She checked the time on an old pocket watch. Then she grasped the handle of the basket with both hands, turned, and walked past me to the front door.

Cell phones were forbidden. According to Malloryn, the radio waves interfered with magical energy, which was one reason why magic was so much harder today than in the old days. I did pack myself a flashlight and a little pocketknife. I had no idea what to expect, and I wanted to be prepared.

Our destination was a small, man-made lake nestled in the elbow crook of two intersecting highways. I'd come here sometimes when I was younger, with Mom. We would sit on the little beach area and build castles together with the trucked-in sand. It had been years since I'd been here. It wasn't ever that great. There were usually sketchy people hanging around, and half the time, you couldn't even go into the water because of algae blooms.

This time, though, we were the sketchy people, parking our bikes in the bushes, slinking around the edges of the park. It made me wonder if the people I remembered seeing here were just trying to unravel the strange knots in their own lives.

We walked up to the water's edge. It was starting to get dark. Malloryn led the way, following a worn footpath to a wooden fishing platform. She set the covered basket down gently on the boards, then sat down cross-legged beside it.

"What now?" I asked.

"We wait," said Malloryn.

I sat down too. I had the urge to take my shoes and socks off and let my feet dangle in the water. But I was worried it might screw up the spell, so I sat exactly as Malloryn had.

Twilight faded into night. Between the lampposts scattered throughout the park, the shadows lay deep. I was glad I'd brought my flashlight.

"What are we waiting for?" I asked Malloryn.

"Perigee," she said, motioning to the moon rising behind the hills.

Every so often, Malloryn checked the time. My knees had begun to ache, but Malloryn hadn't moved, so I stayed where I was too. The whoosh of traffic from the highways died down to a whisper. In its place came the gentle lapping of water against the platform, the sawing of crickets, the scurrying of mice and Norway rats, the cries of a lonely night bird.

At last, Malloryn stirred. She loosened the fold of her legs and opened the basket.

"Gelsin wanted to live forever," said Malloryn, "so he wrote himself into a spell. His spirit, anyway. That way, some part of him would never die—that was his theory."

She took out an old photograph in a frame. It was of a

dark-eyed young man with a thick mustache and his hair drawn back in a severe part. Malloryn set it on the platform. For some reason I'd pictured Gelsin as an old man, but he didn't look much older than us.

"Not sure how his spirit feels about untying knots until eternity, but that's not my problem, is it?" said Malloryn. She took out the sachet of herbs I'd seen her filling earlier, and set it down in front of the picture. Beside it, she laid the crystal shard still wrapped in velvet, a thermos, and a ragged-looking dog toy that must have belonged to Zorro. Then she removed a china teapot and three cups and saucers. She placed one in front of each of us, and the third at a spot between us.

She opened the teapot and set the lid beside it. Then she took the thermos, opened it, poured its steaming contents into the pot, and added the sachet.

"Armand Gelsin," she said, in a loud and awkwardly formal voice, "there is tea for drinking. Come sit beside us."

She glanced to one side, then to the other, as if expecting to see someone standing there. But nothing happened. She looked back at the picture, muttered something under her breath, then drew a cross with one finger over Armand Gelsin's dour face.

"Sweet tea," she said. She took the crystal and dropped it into the teapot, where it began to melt. Rock candy.

A plane rumbled overhead, its wing lights flashing.

"Armand Gelsin, we summon you," said Malloryn again. "We summon your spirit to sit with us and drink tea, and bless these hands with your skills."

The surface of the lake was smooth and dark. The full moon shone. A chill passed over us. It could have just been a night wind, but Malloryn took it as a sign of something, grasped the teapot by its delicate handle, and poured out three steaming cups.

Then she addressed the night once more. "Armand Gelsin," she said. "Your way is lit. By your own promises, sealed in your own blood, I call on your spirit to join us."

It might have just been the steam rising off my cup that sent a warm tingle over my skin, or it might have been the air around us getting colder, squeezing heat from my body. The smoky aroma of strong black tea reached my nose.

"If you're near," said Malloryn, "then show yourself and drink with us, that we might ask our favor of you."

She waited. It was definitely colder now. It was hard to tell if it was just the normal chilling of night, or something else. But it was easy, too easy, to imagine all manner of shapes moving in the darkness that surrounded us.

Malloryn held up the picture like she was trying to get someone's attention with it, then set it next to the third teacup. "Armand Gelsin, if you're near, give a sign."

She watched the third cup with great intent. A breeze must have passed over it, because the surface rippled for just a second.

"He's close," she said.

A wild delight had crept into the edges of her voice. I felt it too—a sensation of the world cracking open like an eggshell, revealing shimmering treasure inside.

Something in the bushes shifted. A raccoon, maybe. Or a deer. Or maybe a spirit from beyond the grave. Why not? We both jumped. I looked around, but saw nothing.

"It's okay," said Malloryn. "You can show yourself."

I reached for my flashlight, but Malloryn stopped me with a gentle hand on my arm.

"No," she whispered. "He has all the light he needs." She nodded to the moon.

Armand Gelsin stared out at us from the frame. He reminded me a bit of my dad—both of them immigrants, both of them carrying their secrets halfway across the world. Both of them dead in senseless ways.

The photographer had captured a rough fury in his eyes, in the sweep of his brows, in the angry perfection of his hair. For a moment, I was able to see him removed from history, as if he were still alive, still this age, today. He was young and proud and brash and full of mysteries and closer to his death than he realized.

The sound in the dark came again, closer.

Footfalls on the path. A shadow moved between shadows. A dark shape separated itself from the rest of the darkness, came in our direction. I heard Malloryn draw in a sharp breath.

"Here we are," she called out to the shadow, a look of triumph in her eyes. She patted the spot where his tea had been laid. "Here is your place."

The dark presence drew nearer. It was human-shaped. It picked its way up the path toward us. Malloryn was trembling with excitement and anticipation. But as the thing came closer, something in my gut went sour.

"Malloryn . . . ," I whispered.

"Shh," she said. "He's here. This is him."

The shape now stood at the end of the fishing platform, blocking our exit. We were trapped between the cold, algae-choked water and whatever it was in the dark there. It took a step forward. Then another. I remembered the knife in my backpack, and hoped I wouldn't need it.

"That's right," said Malloryn. "You can join us."

The boards creaked under its feet. The platform swayed.

"Malloryn, I don't think that's him," I said.

"It is," she said. "It has to be."

But I knew it wasn't. I could feel the strangeness of its energy, and it was a confused, human strangeness. It was someone venturing where they hadn't been invited, where they didn't belong.

"Malloryn, this is bad," I said as the shape took another step.

"You'll ruin the spell," she said.

The shape took another step.

"Screw the spell," I said. I reached into my backpack and brought out the knife and flashlight.

Malloryn cried out, an anguished cry of disappointment and heartbreak. I opened up the knife and trained the beam of light on the shape. It wasn't Armand Gelsin.

It was a dumb kid from my school named Eli Hatch.

There were a few things everyone knew about Eli Hatch. He was a junior. He drove a Land Rover and lived in a mansion. His mother was an heiress to a petroleum fortune, and his dad was a lobbyist. He had a straight D average, and would probably, through the magic of nepotism and money, still end up at an Ivy. And, predictably, he was a jerk.

And right now, he was squinting into the beam of my flashlight.

"The hell," he murmured.

"You're not Gelsin," said Malloryn, aghast.

Three other kids emerged from the darkness behind him—a boy and two girls. I didn't recognize any of them.

"Who's Gelsin?" asked Eli Hatch.

"Who are these freaks?" said one of the girls.

"Who are you?" I shot back.

"Hang on," said Eli. "I know you. You're the girl whose dad got killed."

"Oh yeah, I heard about that," said the other girl. "I heard they found him all—"

"All what?" I said.

The girls laughed.

"Let's get out of here," said Malloryn, head down, gathering up her things.

"What are you doing here, anyway?" said the first girl. "Is that tea? Are you having a tea party?"

Too late, Malloryn scooped up the dog toy and shoved it back into the basket.

"Aww," said the other girl. "They're playing with dolls."

"It's okay," Malloryn whispered—to me or to herself, I wasn't sure. Her voice cracked with tears. "It's gonna be okay."

The girls were giggling, and the boys were looking on with stupid grins. I hated them all. They couldn't see how hard Malloryn had worked, how much this meant to her. They couldn't see the care, the patience, the love. Instead they saw a dumb joke.

I felt the same electricity that I'd felt that night at the clinic when I'd looked at Zorro and known in my bones that I needed to fix him. Only now it was a dark, lashing current of anger.

"You leave her alone," I said, stepping up so that my eyes were inches from the first girl's. She smelled like green apple vape smoke.

"You don't have to . . . ," said Malloryn.

"Shut up," I said.

The girl laughed again, but it was a different kind of laugh. The anger in me wasn't afraid of her. It wasn't afraid of anything, and I think she could see that. I was serious, and she wasn't. None of them were serious, about anything.

"Freak," she said. Her voice was shallow, and there was nothing behind it. Malloryn picked up the last of our things and stuffed them into the basket.

"Let's go," she said. "We're going."

We rode back to the house in a gloomy silence. I could tell Malloryn was ashamed. And I felt a simmering darkness inside me that didn't go away.

When we got home, Malloryn unpacked the basket and put everything away. I offered to help, but she shook me off. Zorro watched with concern.

"I'm sorry, Malloryn," I said. I wasn't sure what I was sorry about. That some people were awful. That the spell had failed. That Malloryn had seen the anger I tried every day to keep locked up. I was sorry for all of it.

She paused in her work.

"No one ever stood up for me before," she said. "Thank you." She dumped the last of the tea that she'd brewed for Armand Gelsin into the sink. "In case you were wondering, it wouldn't have worked."

"The spell?"

Malloryn shook her head.

"Why not?" I asked.

"I was wrong," she said.

"About Gelsin?"

"About you." She looked at me. "It's not a hex."

"Okay?" I said. "What is it?"

"I don't know," she said. "There's nothing binding you. There's just . . ." She paused, searching for words.

"What?"

She looked baffled and defeated.

"Something's missing," she said at last.

| CHAPTER SIXTEEN |

A STRANGE LITTLE HEART

On Monday, I returned to school and a new rumor, which had me sacrificing puppies at midnight.

"Of course it's not true," said Grace. We were in the quad. Grace was sitting on Howie's lap, and Carrie was looking around nervously.

"Obviously," said Carrie, though when I looked at her, it didn't seem so obvious.

"But seriously, though," said Howie, a clueless smile on his face, "what did happen?"

"Well, first of all," I said, "they weren't puppies." Carrie's face fell. Howie's smile looked stuck on his face. I decided I didn't like him.

"Nothing happened. It's a stupid rumor, and Eli Hatch is a jerk," said Grace. "We got your back, girl. Don't worry." She gave Howie a withering glare, and he did one of those dumb *What?* shrugs.

The rest of the day, I felt like there was a bubble around me, made up of the curious, judging stares of people I didn't even know. Inside the bubble, it was hard to think. Sounds came through muffled and echoey. Maybe this was how Malloryn had felt, before she ran away. Maybe this was how my dad had felt every day of his life.

Carrie and Grace came and found me whenever they could. Grace made a point to glower at anyone who stared at us, which greatly reduced the number of people staring at us. I could tell that Carrie was uncomfortable. Still, she stayed close, and she didn't ask any questions. That's what friends are supposed to do.

When the last bell rang, I met the girls in the quad.

"I gotta swim," said Carrie. "But let's study after. I'll tell my dad to get us dan-dan."

Carrie's family room with all its coziness sounded inviting, and the Chinese place down the street made their dan-dan noodles from scratch, but once it was just the three of us, there would be questions to answer. Like, *Why is Eli Hatch spreading weird rumors? What actually happened?* I didn't want to have to explain. I didn't want to lie, and I definitely didn't want to tell the truth.

"I'm tired, Care Bear," I said. "I'm just gonna go home."

I didn't go home, though. And I wasn't tired. I got on my bike and rode down to the clinic. The pedals under my feet gave me a place to put my anger. I stomped at them until the wind rushed against my face, and the gawking, whispering nightmare of school seemed far away.

As I pulled up to the parking lot in back of the clinic, a graceful shadow moved at the corner of my vision. The old gray cat was slinking along the edge of the clinic's roof, stately and untroubled. He paused at the eave above the door and drew back on his haunches. His tail switched lazily in the air as he watched me for a moment longer, then padded along the rain gutter until he'd turned the corner of the roof and disappeared out of sight.

"Package for you," said Dominic, holding up an envelope as I entered. I didn't even have to look. I knew what it would be.

I brought it back to my dad's office, ripped it open, dumped the phone out onto my desk, and waited. A minute later, it began to buzz.

"Is it in good health?" asked the voice. "The incontinent one?"

"It's, uh, yeah. It's okay."

"Good," said the voice. "You'll receive a visit soon. Another client."

"What if I say no?"

Silence.

"Okay, fine. I say no. Not this time." Silence. I waited.

Finally the voice at the other end responded. "Why not?"

"Someone needs to explain all of this to me," I said. "I want to know who you people are. I want to know what you know about my dad."

A heavy, stewy silence filled the crackling connection, the stirring sound of options being considered. "Receive your visitor." Before I could protest, it continued, "Attend to the patient."

"And then what?" I asked. "I said I wasn't going to do it."

Quiet. A long, long quiet. I thought the line had gone dead.

"And then," said the voice, "I'll try to help you."

The phone clicked and went silent. I put it in a drawer and went out to the lobby.

"And here she is now," said Dominic to a stranger standing at the reception desk with a violin case in one hand and a birdcage covered with a towel in the other. As Dominic nodded in my direction, a pale, young face framed in wild black hair twisted over a narrow shoulder. A pair of sad, wary eyes met mine.

He was a boy, about my age, with fragile features, feather-thin arms, bird bones, and skin as pale and fine as frosted glass. A strong wind would have probably swirled him away, all except for his eyes. They were heavy with sorrow—and with something else that I recognized instantly.

Anger.

"Hi," I said. "Can I help you?"

He held up the violin case, and then the birdcage, as if that somehow was a logical answer to my question. Behind him, Dominic shook his head and shrugged.

"Yeah, okay," I said. "Come on back."

When we were in the office with the door closed behind us, the kid set both the case and the covered cage on my desk, side by side. Then he undid the latches of the case and opened it. I'm not sure what I'd been expecting, but an actual violin nestled in soft indigo padding wasn't my first guess.

The birdcage he left covered. It was, I had noticed, silent.

"I'm Kent Hayashi," he said.

"Do you play?" I asked.

"Since I was three," he said, without looking at me.

The violin looked like it had been well crafted and cared for. Its lines were clean and sinuous. Its color was a lush mahogany. A fine grain dappled the wood of its face. The strings were shiny and taut, and the wooden spiral at the head of the instrument curled with elegant precision.

Kent reached down and plucked a string. Even muffled by the case, the sound was bright and full. The note echoed in my ears for a long time, longer than it seemed should have been possible, like the sound had stuck there. It wasn't unpleasant, but it was strange.

As the note slowly decayed into silence, Kent watched the birdcage. He seemed as if he were waiting for something. But no sound emerged.

"Vivaldi is"—he paused, corrected himself—"was the sweetest, most gentle—" He stopped.

"Vivaldi?" I asked.

He sighed and removed the towel from the cage. It was empty.

"He could sing Schubert," he said. "He was so proud of himself."

"Did he escape?" I asked.

The boy shook his head.

A layer of yellow feathers rested atop the scatter of birdseed husks and droppings at the bottom of the cage. Too many feathers, and too fresh.

"I'm sorry," I said.

Kent's eyes were cold and fierce, his face pinched in helpless anger and sorrow. "Whatever it is," he said, "I don't want it. I want you to take it away."

"I don't understand," I said.

He rapped at the side of the violin case with the knuckle of a clenched fist. For a moment, nothing happened.

Then the violin took a deep breath and looked at me.

Her eyes—I knew without question that she was female—sat on either side of the spiral at the violin's head. They were curious things, round and wide and glistening with intensity. The whites of them were yellow and bloodshot. Her eyelids had no lashes. When they closed, their smoothness blended without a trace into the instrument's natural contours. If she shut them and held her breath, you wouldn't see any life there.

But now she was watching me, and she was breathing, inhaling and exhaling, her body expanding and contracting like a rib cage, the f-shaped slits on both sides of the strings working the air like gills. After a moment, she craned her neck up, revealing dark, lean sinews and veins behind the fingerboard, descending into a sort of clavicle where it met the body.

"It woke up a few days ago," said Kent. "Out of nowhere."

"She," I said. "She's a she."

"How would you know that?"

"I just do. Where did she come from?"

"It was a gift," said Kent. "I have a patron. Anonymous."

"She," I said. "Not 'it.'"

He scowled. "It was just a violin," he said. "Until a few days ago, that's all it was."

The violin blinked from one face to the other. Did she know we were talking about her?

A distant memory tumbled loose. Had my dad told a story, one long-ago night? I couldn't remember the details. Everyday objects—teapots, broomsticks, chairs—opening their eyes, coming to life after a hundred years of inanimate existence, full of wit and will and mischief. What were they called?

Yokai.

"Take it away," said Kent. "Sell it. Smash it. Burn it. I don't care. I don't want it."

I almost corrected his pronoun again.

The violin looked at me, innocent, oblivious.

"I should have known," said Kent, almost to himself. "I should have seen the way it—she—looked at him. I could have done something. I could have . . ."

He lapsed into silence and hung his head. I thought he might start to cry.

"What happened?" I asked.

"It . . ." I gave him a pointed look, and he sighed. "She. She ate him. She ate Vivaldi."

He fixed a pleading stare on the violin, like even now he was trying to undo the crime. Right on cue, the violin hiccuped. A single yellow feather discharged from one of the delicate slits in her belly.

We all watched it drift with slow, damning grace to the floor. My two guests looked at me, Kent first, and then the yokai. Kent's eyes were tight, smoldering nuggets of coal. The yokai's were wide and bright and free of guilt. In that moment, the two of them looked so much like an old vaudeville comedy duo, I almost expected them to launch into some kind of ventriloquist routine. But neither said a word.

"Vivaldi was . . . ," I began.

"A canary," said Kent. "He ate from my hand. He sat on my shoulder while I practiced. He knew how to sing ten different songs. He trusted me. And I let that . . . thing . . ."

He let out a cry of raw despair, and lunged for the violin. For a moment, I thought he would smash it, or strangle it, or rip it apart. The yokai flinched. Her strings loosened. One of them uncoiled from the nut and hovered in front of her spiral-shaped head, a slender tentacle tracing wary, defensive S-shapes in the air.

Kent hesitated, then relented. The yokai relaxed a moment later. Her string slid back into the nut and wound itself around—still loose, I noticed, but put away.

"I need help," said Kent. He sank to the floor, his back coming to rest heavily against the side of the desk. I came over and sat down next to him. After a few moments, the yokai joined us, climbing out of the case and lowering herself from the desktop with her strings, until her neck leaned with an easy curve against the side of the desk. And for a while, the three of us sat there like that, and no one spoke.

"My parents are both concert musicians," said Kent in a faraway voice. "They wanted me to follow in their footsteps. I grew up doing scales until my fingers bled. They said I had to work harder than everyone else. They said it was the only way." He shook his head. "They said I'd be grateful one day." He spat the words out.

"You must be pretty good," I said.

"I'm better at playing the violin," said Kent, "than most people will ever be at anything in their entire lives."

"That's a bold statement," I said.

"I've won national contests," he said. "Scholarships, fellowships. I've been invited to perform in London, in Moscow, in Beijing. I have patrons. I have fans." He paused. When he spoke again, his voice was low and bitter. "I hate it."

"Then why keep doing it?"

"I've been asking myself that same question for years," he said. "I've never been able to answer it. So I stopped."

"Stopped asking?"

"Stopped playing," he said. "Six months ago. I haven't played a note since. I thought it would feel better. It feels like I chopped my arm off."

He lapsed into silence. The violin, meanwhile, had begun exploring the office. She moved like an octopus, her four strings pulling her along with a whipping, watery grace. Her body still resembled a violin, more or less, but it had a softness to it, a heaviness that suggested guts beneath smooth, dark skin. When she wasn't examining my father's veterinary texts or pawing at a section of carpet, she hooked her neck around to watch us with her big eyes.

"I never asked for any of this myself," I said. "It got shoved onto me, without anyone bothering to check to see if I wanted it."

"How do you know what you're supposed to do?" he asked.

"I don't," I said. "Not really. I kind of have to figure it out every time. Sorry if you were expecting competent medical advice."

Kent laughed. An actual laugh.

"I do love music," he said. "I used to think that once I got good enough, I wouldn't feel sick to my stomach whenever I picked up a violin." His eyes were full of anger and anguish. "It's never good enough."

His delicate fingers curled into fists, then relaxed.

"My parents knew I was depressed," he continued. "They said it was normal, and they got me Vivaldi, to help me feel better. It worked. He sat on my shoulder while I played. He sang along. He made me enjoy playing, for the first time since I could remember."

The yokai returned to Kent's side and plopped down. She blinked from my face to his, attentive and curious.

"I don't think I can bring Vivaldi back, if that's what you were hoping for."

He shook his head like it wasn't, but I saw how his shoulders slumped a bit.

"I'll do the thing I can do," I said. "It might not help you, but it will help me understand your violin better. Would that be okay?"

Kent barely looked up to nod.

I reached my hand out to touch the violin's body. If the yokai had any fears or hesitations, she didn't show them. She watched with open curiosity. Her rare blinks made a soft clicking sound, like a camera shutter.

She had a dark, delicious radiance that warmed my knuckles when I touched her. I slid my hand along the edge of the body, along the rounded sweep of its expertly joined seam. It wasn't wood, though it looked like it. It was dry and firm, but it was a kind of skin. If I palpated, it gave. She didn't seem bothered by my touch. She just kept turning from one of us to the other, watching us with eyes as round and shiny as marbles.

She was confused. Overwhelmed. Restless. Hungry and impatient, full of desires. *What would a violin want?* I wondered to myself. *Why would it eat a canary?*

And what was I supposed to do for it?

I was sure Horatio would be happy to add a living violin to his collection. And I was sure Kent would be relieved to be rid of her, at least at first. But it didn't feel right to separate them. These two belonged with each other. Even if Kent couldn't see it yet, the yokai knew. They went together in a way I could feel in my guts.

"She's where she's supposed to be," I said. Kent's expression sank.

"That's it?" he said. "I'm just stuck with her?"

"And she's stuck with you," I said.

I lifted my hand away from the yokai's flank, and she and I looked at each other a moment longer before she flopped with a dramatic and oddly melodic sighing of air back against the desk. The warmth in my knuckles began to fade. Soon it was gone.

The hunger, though—that stayed.

Something's missing.

A thought occurred to me. "You should give her a name."

"I'm not naming that *thing*," said Kent.

"She's going to be with you awhile. She should have a name."

Kent scowled. After a moment, though, he became thoughtful.

"Fine," he said at last. "I'll call her after my grandma. The only person in my family who ever let me be a kid. Omi." He directed his attention to the violin. "Hey," he said. "Your name's Omi."

The violin, Omi, blinked, swallowed her new name with her eyes. It seemed to be acceptable.

The name was good. But it wasn't enough. Kent was still resentful of Omi. And Omi was still hungry. I could feel her hunger, a jagged, needy pit of hollowness at the center of my stomach.

How had this violin opened her eyes for this boy, at this particular moment? It *had* to have a purpose—otherwise, why had my dad told me all those stories when I was young? Why had he disappeared so many times? Why had he died? It *had* to mean something. If it didn't, then what was I doing getting into cars with strangers, and risking my life with manticores?

All of it had to mean something, including this bitter kid and his hungry yokai. But what?

A sliver of the note he'd plucked when he'd first opened the case still remained at the edge of my hearing, like a word on the tip of my tongue.

"When was the last time you played her?" I asked.

He looked at me like I was the one who'd eaten his canary.

Then he became thoughtful. "I have other violins. This one, I don't—I didn't play much. It's too nice for practice. But it's too temperamental for the stage."

"Temperamental?"

"It pops out of tune sometimes, no reason." He paused. "Well, maybe now we know why."

We both looked at Omi. She'd slid one string free and was scratching idly at the front of her spiral head. Watching the string, she had gone cross-eyed.

"You should play something," I said.

Kent glared at the violin. Omi gave up scratching. Her eyes refocused, found his, looked back at him and blinked.

"Why?" said Kent. "Why me?"

"She found you," I said. "There's a reason. Maybe it's good luck."

Or maybe she'll stab you in the chest when you try to help her, and wedge a splinter between your ribs, said a little voice in the back of my head. Under my shirt, my birthmark felt warm and tender.

The violin's bow was held in place on the inside of the case's lid by two straps of purple velvet. Kent undid the straps and slid the bow out, holding it gently in his fingers. Almost immediately something in him relaxed. The furrow between his eyes un-pinched. His arm, the one holding the bow, became languid, graceful.

He took Omi by the neck with his free hand, uncertain at first. The yokai closed her eyes, took a deep breath, and seemed to sink away. The violin came out of the case, its shape rigid in his grip. He slipped it under the stern jut of his chin. Then the bow came up and hovered for a moment in empty space, before slicing down and across the strings stretched over the yokai's mahogany belly.

The first note blazed like it had been amplified, electrified. It hung in the air long after the horsehair had left the string.

Kent paused as the lingering sound slowly decayed. Then he stabbed again at the strings, diving into one run, and then another. The music filled the room. Kent's fingers raced up and down the fingerboard. His posture transformed. His body, suddenly proud and stiff, found space in its sharpness to sway to the rhythm of the song.

It was a short, romping fragment that disintegrated after just a few measures, but the sound reverberated in the little back office. It seemed to me that the noise from outside had gotten quieter. People were listening.

Kent removed the violin from under his chin and chuckled to himself with baffled delight. Then his eyes fell onto the birdcage, and his expression clouded over. A darker confusion settled in, and he set the violin down and took a step away from it.

"It doesn't feel right," he said, in a quiet voice. "Except it doesn't feel wrong, either. I don't know what it feels."

The music was still ringing in my ears. A bright, brittle ghost tone sat on top of every note. It almost sounded like birdsong, like the joyful afternoon chirps of a canary.

I thought for a moment of Horatio's menagerie, of the faeries and their songs, and for some reason a chill ran up my spine.

"Who else knows about her?" I asked.

"My patron," he said. "That's how I found you. No one else."

I had a feeling I knew who his patron might be.

"Put her away," I said. "Don't let anyone see her. Don't tell anyone what she is. Ever."

I guided him back to the case, and helped him tuck Omi back into the velvet padding. As my fingers touched her whorled, wood-grain skin, I could feel something like blood racing just beneath the surface, a tiny stomach sated, a strange little heart flush with excitement.

"She's for you," I said. "No one else. Play her only when no one else can hear."

He said nothing, and after a moment, he wrapped an arm over the violin case and held it tight. He would keep her safe.

He glanced at the birdcage.

"If you don't want that anymore . . . ," I said.

He nodded. His eyes narrowed with resolve. Turning toward the door, he spoke. His voice was different: warm and wounded and shimmering with emotion.

"I never thought . . . ," he said. He looked at the floor and shook his head. "I never thought."

As he shuffled out of my office and down the hall, past the bewildered stares of the people in the waiting room and the techs in the hall, a curious space opened up in my chest with each breath. It was luminous and brave and tough, and as it swelled, I felt myself standing taller, seeing the world in sharp, clear lines. Something was missing. I was going to find it.

Inside the desk drawer, a phone was ringing.

CHAPTER SEVENTEEN

THE MERCHANDISE

The shopping mall was an aging fortress of concrete and glass, surrounded by two levels of near-empty parking structures. I stepped out of the bus and onto a sun-baked expanse of flat cement. There wasn't a soul in sight. Which made sense—there were newer, prettier shopping centers just up the road. This place was a relic.

The address I'd been given by the voice on the phone had guided me here, but there'd been no further instructions. I looked around the parking lot, half expecting a shady van to come rolling up. But nothing moved.

"Hello?" I called out, just in case my mystery rendezvous had fallen asleep in a nearby car. After waiting a few minutes— long enough to see exactly one person leave the mall, get into their car, and drive away—I decided I should go have a look inside.

A high skylight ran the length of the mall, letting in a slash of grimy sunshine. Fake plants swayed in untended islands, gathering dust on their plastic leaves. Cool, distant neon tubes hummed and crackled in bug-choked fixtures. More than half the retail spaces sat empty. The stores that remained were depressing: off-brand lifestyle and jewelry outlets, a perfume shop that smelled of roses and soap, a cell phone shop for a wireless carrier I'd never even heard of. Everything felt worn-out and cheap.

Shoppers trudged up and down the avenue like lost souls. Store attendants wandered away from their shops. Someone asked me halfheartedly if I wanted to try a sample of a new skin cream. They already knew the answer.

I wondered if I'd missed some crucial clue. I began looking more closely at the other shoppers as they passed me, trying to see if one of them would meet my gaze, give me a signal. None did, and soon I found myself joining their sullen death march from shop to shop.

I didn't see the teakettle sigil until after I'd walked past it three times. It was stuck in the corner of the narrow display window of the cell phone shop. If you didn't know, you might think it was some kind of business accreditation, or maybe a sticker left behind by the burglar alarm company.

My heart leapt in my chest. I took a breath and stepped into the shop.

The guy working at the cell phone store had close-cut salt-and-pepper hair; a carefully cropped goatee; and dark, sunken eyes. He was shorter than me, and dressed in a cheap shirt and slacks, with a cheap tie. He wore a brown rectangular name tag with the name "Glenn" printed on it. He looked like he was playing a game on his phone, which, I noticed, was not the cheap off-brand kind sold here. He glanced up at me with a weary nod.

"Help you find anything?" he offered, then went back to his game.

"Oddly enough," I said, "that is exactly what I'm hoping you can do."

His eyes darted back up to me, curious.

"What sort of phone are we in the market for today?" he asked.

"Not a phone," I said.

He set his phone down and glanced over my shoulder.

"Anyone else with you?" he asked.

I shook my head. He walked around the counter to the shop's entrance and pulled the rolling gate down. It slammed shut with a rattling clang. Whatever was about to happen, I was trapped.

"Who are you?" I asked.

He managed a weak smile that lasted a moment and then drifted away.

"Glenn," he said, pointing to his name tag. His look told me I wouldn't be getting a last name. "She said you were coming. Said to text her when you showed up." He made no move to do so.

Glenn looked to be somewhere between forty and forgotten. He was round from every angle, a man made of droopy circles. He had boredom the way old dogs have arthritis. It creaked in his joints as he shuffled back to the counter.

"What is this place?" I asked.

"Ha," said Glenn without laughing.

"Seriously," I said.

"You really don't know anything," he said.

I shook my head. He huffed a heavy sigh.

"Right," he said, pulling a stool out from behind the counter. "Sit down."

I sat, and Glenn leaned his bulk on the counter in front of me.

"This is a bidding room," he said, opening one arm out to

take in the empty store. "There are bidding rooms all over the world. They're all pretty much like this. Dumpy little places you wouldn't want to go. Bidding room agents know what's for sale, and we take bids. Some bids are huge. Some . . . aren't. We take all of them."

"Wait," I said, "you *sell* them?"

"We have field-workers," he continued, scoffing at my question. "They manage the merchandise."

"Merchandise," I said. "You mean the animals."

He rolled his eyes. "No, the cell phones," he said. "Of course the animals. We don't keep inventory. Too dangerous. We let the seller assume that risk. But we keep tabs on anything we're selling, make sure we can get to it when the sale's final. And when it is, the field-workers arrange the transfer of goods."

"So you auction them off?" I asked.

"Not me," said Glenn. "I just take the bids. Take 'em, hand 'em off. They go to a place called the Tea Shop, and someone wins." He shrugged. "Don't ask me how. Don't ask me where the Tea Shop is. I've never seen it. Don't even know if it's a real place."

"Who runs the Tea Shop?" I asked.

"The back-of-house people," said Glenn. "I don't know who they are. They're the ones calling the shots, though. They give you a charter, and that's your work. Me, they gave me this place. Thirty years ago."

"A cell phone shop?"

Glenn laughed. "It wasn't a cell phone shop back then. We sold computer games. But, you know, not good ones. We were always out of the good ones." He shook his head in wistful disappointment.

"That sounds . . ." I looked around the shop, at the flimsy

point-of-sale displays, and the sorry products they halfheartedly hawked.

"Depressing?" said Glenn. "You got that right."

"Then why are you still here?"

"You ever try leaving your family?" he asked.

"Once," I said.

"How far'd you get?" he said.

"Not far enough."

"Well." Glenn nodded, as if I'd just made his point for him.

"Wait a minute, so you're all related?"

"Somewhere, back up the tree," said Glenn. "I'm what they
call low-content. Means I'm a distant relative. Low-contents
get bidding room charters. Mid-contents are field ops. Back-
of-house are all high-content, that's what they say."

"That doesn't seem fair," I said.

"It's not," said Glenn. "But that's how it is. It's not so bad,
though. Pretty much, we get paid to sit around and do nothing all day. Once in a while, take a bid or two. Could be a lot
worse. Anyway, you get used to it."

He made a clicking noise that seemed to indicate that he'd
given up caring. He struck me as the kind of person who only
knew one way to be, and if he'd ever known another, it had
been beaten out of him years ago.

"Weren't you going to message somebody that I was here?"
I asked.

A sly, hungry look crossed Glenn's face.

"Fifty bucks," he said.

"What?"

"You heard me. Give me fifty bucks."

"Are you serious?"

He shrugged. "You gotta tip the doorman."

"No one told me that."

"That's too bad," said Glenn. "I guess she'll never know you came by."

I'd never been asked for a bribe before. It was shocking and pathetic. Glenn had no shame about it, no guilt. His face was smug and sad at the same time, and I wasn't sure if I was supposed to feel intimidated or embarrassed for him.

For a moment, we stared at each other. Finally I fished out my wallet and opened it up.

"I've only got forty," I said.

Glenn scowled in quiet disappointment, and I felt a petty surge of victorious joy. He snatched the bills out of my hand, pocketed the money, and tapped a brief message into his phone. Then he looked at me again and, failing to understand me, shook his head once more. He set the phone down on the counter, and it buzzed almost immediately.

"Someone will be here soon," he said.

I'd been robbed, and it was infuriating. But I couldn't help feeling sorry for him. He'd spent thirty years in this tiny shop. I'd been here fifteen minutes, and it already felt like too long.

"Can I ask you something?" I said. He looked up, a little too eager at first. "How do they find you?"

"Who?" he said.

"People," I said. "The people who bid. How do they know where to find you?"

He set the phone down again.

"Some people are invited," he said. "Usually very rich people. They're the worst. They don't even look at you. Like you're not even human." Glenn snarled at the thought of rich people. Then he became quiet and thoughtful. "The others, though," he said, "the real ones, they just know."

"Know what?"

A weary half smile creased his face. "They come in like they're lost. Like it's an accident they walked in here. And then they want to talk. About nothing. Anything. Cars. Their ex. Their parents. I keep them talking until the right time comes. Then I say something about pets. Their eyes light up." Glenn's eyes lit up too, acting out that moment. "It's like something just went off in their brain. *That's it*, they're thinking. I don't give them much of a sales pitch. You don't have to. The ones that know, they know."

"How many bids like that have you taken?" I asked.

"Maybe a dozen," he said. "In thirty years, maybe that. But I can spot 'em, the second they come in. They got that look in their eye." He pursed his lips and steeled his eyes, proud for the first time.

Glenn's phone buzzed again a few minutes later. Without a word, he held up the screen, showing me a message that directed me to the parking lot of the mall. As I read it, he opened the gate and gave a little half wave. Then he settled back onto his stool and hunched down over the game, his eyes slowly glazing over at the screen.

The car was idling out front—a boxy old black Buick with tinted windows. As I exited the building, a driver got out of the car and opened the rear door. He had a still face, a military-grade buzz cut, and a curious heaviness in his shoulders. When he saw me, he opened the door wider and motioned me in with one hand. The inside of the car was upholstered in dark leather. A very rational and reasonable voice in my head was screaming at the top of its lungs that I should get nowhere near that car, that I should in fact run very quickly in the opposite direction.

I didn't listen to it.

Instead I followed the other voice, the one that was very calmly reassuring me that everything would be fine, that the only place I needed to be at this moment was inside that car, and wherever it would take me. Just as I slid in and sat down, I noticed that the driver's hands were covered in tattoos. The door shut behind me, and then locked. The driver sat down in front and shut his door. There were tattoos up the back of his neck. Skeletons, fire, devils. Real happy stuff.

"Open the center armrest," he said.

The armrest hinged up from the back to reveal a compartment. Inside it was a black velvet bag, empty. I took it out.

"There's just an empty bag in here," I said. "Is there supposed to be something in it?"

"No," said the driver. "I need your phone too."

The driver glanced at me in the rearview. His hands were on the wheel, but he didn't make any move to put the car in gear. With a sinking feeling in my guts, I understood.

"I'm not putting a bag on my head," I said.

"There are other ways," he said. "But this one is the easiest."

The driver was watching me now. His hands had come off the wheel. I couldn't see them anymore. I tried the door, but of course it didn't open.

"Fine," I said. "I'll put it on."

The driver nodded his approval. I handed him my phone.

"You'll get it back," he said, powering it off and setting it in a metal case on the passenger seat.

Then I opened up the bag and looked into its dark depths. I took a breath and muttered something like a prayer, then slipped it over my head.

• • •

In the dark, it was hard to keep track of time. Maybe we drove for ten minutes. Maybe it was thirty. At last we came to a stop.

"Keep the bag on," said the driver, the first words he spoke to me since the drive had begun.

I didn't see that I had much choice.

The car door opened, and I felt my way out. A hand rested gently on my shoulder, guided me up several steps. It felt like I was indoors, walking on a hardwood floor. I heard a door shut behind me. The hand on my shoulder gave me a last guiding push, then lifted away. I stopped and stood where I was.

Several moments passed. Then I heard a familiar voice.

"You can take it off now," she said.

I was standing in the dining room of what appeared to be a well-appointed house. At the opposite end of a long dining table, a pair of hands perched on the back of a chair in a way that reminded me of a parrot on a branch. A small chandelier—an ornate glass bowl in warm colors—hung between us. Then the bright-faced woman who'd sent me to London peered around the side of the bowl, held up her hand in greeting, and smiled. We seemed to be alone in the room.

She was wearing a casual white blouse and pale jeans. Her hair was combed neatly to one side. Her smile had a reassuring sweetness about it, but behind a pair of oxblood-rimmed glasses, her eyes were doing something cold and methodical when they looked at me.

"Hi," I said. "Where am I?"

There were windows everywhere, but all the blinds had been drawn. I couldn't see even a hint of the outside world.

"Don't worry," she said. "You're safe. When we're done here, you'll be returned home."

"Is this the Tea Shop?" I asked.

She laughed. "No. This is just a house."

"Who are you?" I asked.

"You can call me Jane Glass," she said.

She sat down in the chair at the head of the table. In front of her was a small travel case made of hard plastic. She rested her forearms on either side of it and set her fingers against its edges. I sat down too, in the chair opposite her.

She smiled, the same reassuring smile, but something in her posture changed. Her back straightened, her shoulders drew broader. The slightest tic of unease and wariness crossed that pleasant face.

"You're here because I want to help you," she said. "But I need something from you, too."

"I already gave you something," I said. "I saw your musician friend."

"That's your job," she said.

"And I had to give your cousin Glenn forty bucks just to text you."

Jane made a sour face, but she didn't seem surprised. "I'm sorry. That shouldn't have happened. He'll be dealt with, and you'll get your money back. How was our musician friend?"

"Not happy," I said. "But I think he'll be fine. The violin's healthy."

"Good," said Jane.

"I'm sure that increases the resale value," I said.

Jane laughed. "You've got us all wrong," she said. "That violin's happy where it is. No one's going to be buying it any-time soon. But let's say our musician friend, many years from now, passes away peacefully in his sleep. Then, maybe, an estate liquidator might appear. She might, let's say, take a spe-cial interest in placing the violin with a good owner. With a *deserving* owner. That's a big part of what we do, Marjan."

"And what makes someone deserving?" I asked. "Money?"

"Money's never been a problem for us."

"Tell that to Glenn," I said.

Jane let the comment pass. "We have ways of vetting bidders," she said.

"Like what?"

"Another time, maybe," she said. "We have more important things to talk about today."

She tapped her fingers on the box in front of her, considered it, then seemed to change her mind.

"We don't know where the animals come from," she said. "They come and go, and we still don't understand where or how. But we know when they arrive."

"How?"

"There are signals," she said. "If you know how to watch the world, you might see a blip here and there. That's another part of what we do. When any new creature appears in the world, it's a significant event. When one appears that's especially powerful, we make sure it finds the right home."

She paused.

"Eight years ago," she said, "there was a signal. A very strong signal. Something appeared, and then vanished into thin air. We don't know what it was. But we think it was very powerful. And we think your dad might have been involved."

"What does that have to do with today?"

"Maybe nothing," said Jane. "But we have reasons to believe that the event and your dad's death might be connected."

"Are you going to tell me those reasons?"

"This isn't an official meeting. There are things I can't talk about. But I'm hoping we can still be friends." Her face was pleasant but serious. "I think we could both use a friend right now, Marjan."

"Why's that?"

"Because something bad is going on," replied Jane. She took off her glasses and set them down on the table beside the box. "We're losing them."

"Losing them?"

"They've been disappearing. One here, one there. They're being sold, without our knowledge. Sometimes they're being stolen. We've lost track of more than a hundred of them."

I realized with a sinking feeling that I knew exactly where they were.

"So you lose a few," I said. "They're not yours anyway. Why do you care?"

"I told you that money's never been our problem," she said. "That's because we invest well. We invest really well. And to do that, to invest as well as we do, we need information. Special information. It needs to be accurate, and it needs to be complete."

"Information about them," I said. "About the animals."

"They're part of everything," said Jane. "And everything is part of them. When they're well, good things happen. When they're sick, when they're hurt, bad things happen. We can make money either way, but only if we have accurate information."

"So this is about money after all," I said. I was starting to think Horatio might have been right about the Fells. They weren't to be trusted, even if one of them wanted to be my friend.

"Do you have any idea how much it costs to fund an operation like ours?" she asked. "Yes, it's about money. But it's about money as a tool for doing good. When their population falls, the world is a less pretty place to be. A small drop, and crime goes up. Marriages collapse. More suicides. More homicides. A big drop, and wars break out. Famine spreads. Civilization stumbles. People everywhere suffer. Chaos reigns. We don't just buy and sell. We watch. And when we start to see hints of trouble, we act." She paused and looked across the table at me. "Sometimes we need your help—your family's help. So you see, Marjan, this isn't just a business. What we do—what *you* do—affects people's lives everywhere."

"What's so special about me?" I said.

"You don't know?"

"I don't understand it," I said.

"You and your father are both expressions of the Hyrcanian Line."

"What the hell is the Hyrcanian Line?"

"Scientifically speaking," said Jane, "the Hyrcanian Line is a unique genetic mutation."

"So I'm a freak," I said.

"You're not a freak," said Jane. "You're a treasure."

"Lots of good that's done me," I said. "My dad's dead, and I'm a mess."

"Your dad's death was a tragedy," said Jane. "But this isn't just about you and him." She paused gravely. "Your family has been the carrier of the Hyrcanian Line for over a thousand years."

The room felt suddenly much bigger. Or maybe I felt smaller.

"A thousand?" I said.

"Maybe I should tell you a story," said Jane.

"Once was," I replied, "once wasn't."

CHAPTER EIGHTEEN

THE FALCONER AND THE SHAH

King Yazdegerd the Unjust, Shahanshah of the old Persian empire of Eranshahr, once received a royal visit from an emissary of the regent emperor of China. Accompanying the emissary were two majestic and ferocious lion-dogs—beasts with massive heads and powerful bodies, and whiskers that curled like waves, and manes like flames. They were unlike anything the shah had ever seen before, and he was captivated.

During the visit, one of the lion-dogs took ill. The shah, ever a good host, commanded his court do whatever was necessary to bring it back to health. One of his viziers had heard rumors of a certain falconer from the forests of Hyrcania, which lie between the Alborz Mountains and the Caspian Sea. This falconer was said to tend to animals of mysterious origin. So the vizier sought this man out and brought him to court.

True to the rumors, the falconer healed the lion-dog. The emissary concluded his business and returned to the East, grateful to the shah for his care. The falconer, his duty done, prepared to return home too. But the shah had questions for him.

"Are there more such creatures in the world?" he asked.

"Yes, Your Excellency," the falconer responded. It is best not to lie to a king.

"And you heal them?"

"I try, Your Excellency."

"Where do they come from?"

"Some are born here, Your Excellency. Some come here with the silk caravans of China. Some with the Romans, some with the Byzantines, some with the gold traders of Aksum, and the tea merchants of Hindustan. They come from everywhere that people can be found, Your Excellency, so surely they are found everywhere. But many find their way here, just as many peoples from all over the world find their ways here."

"Then it is fortunate that you are here, and not somewhere else."

"It is fortunate that our kingdom is blessed with such a richness of trade and passage," said the falconer. "It is fortunate that our borders touch so many others. It is fortunate that the greatest roads in the world run through the heart of our land. And it is fortunate that I am here, Your Excellency, where I can be of most service to those that need me."

A king will always appreciate well-wrought flattery.

"How did you come to possess this power?"

"My grandmother had it. And her father had it. It's said that the power was put in us by something older than man, in a time and a place that was, and was not; but that is only a story."

The shah was not interested in stories. He dealt in material things: gold, sapphires, silk. Thought the shah, *If the great emperors of China can have such creatures, and if the traders of Hindustan and the Khaganate of Mongolia can have such creatures, then surely the shah of shahs should have the greatest creature of all.*

And so he sent an expedition to Mount Damavand to capture the simurgh, the mighty bird whose feathers were said to heal wounds, and who could tell a king the secrets of his enemies. And when the expedition returned successful, King Yazdegerd ordered a walled garden built for the bird at his palace in Ctesiphon. There he kept it, and it was a source of great pride to him.

But the simurgh did not reveal any secrets to the king, and it did not heal any wounds. In fact, soon the simurgh began to weaken, and so the shah sent again for the falconer. This time, he ordered the falconer to bring whatever belongings he wished to keep with him, for he would henceforth live in the palace, to care for the shah's greatest treasure.

The falconer could not argue with the king. He and his daughter—his only living family—became guests of the shah, and were given rooms in the palace. The falconer set about examining the simurgh, and when he had completed his examination, he addressed the king.

"Leave me with the simurgh, Your Excellency," said the falconer, "for seven days and seven nights, and on the morning of the eighth day, the beast will be healed."

The king agreed, and saw to it that the simurgh's garden was left undisturbed for seven days and seven nights while the falconer performed his duties.

On the seventh night, the falconer's daughter awoke to find her father sitting across from her bed. He told her to dress in peasant clothes, wait until the palace gates were opened, and then slip out and leave the city of Ctesiphon forever. The falconer's daughter did as she was told.

That morning, the king came to the garden, and there found the falconer, alone. His prized simurgh was gone.

"Where is the beast?" demanded the king.

"I have set it free," said the falconer. "Its only ailment was captivity."

The falconer was swiftly executed. The king sent for the falconer's daughter as well, because one can never be too careful where summary execution is concerned. But she had escaped.

The king placed a bounty on her head, and commanded his men to search the entire kingdom until they found her, but their search did not last long. Soon after all of this, the king traveled north and east from Ctesiphon to Hyrcania on royal business, and while he was visiting a lake near the eastern city of Tus, a white horse came galloping out of the water, kicked him to death, and then disappeared back into the blue depths.

There followed a struggle for the throne. The bounty was abandoned, and the falconer's daughter was forgotten. And if, in the years that followed, people from all over the world sought out the particular skills of a certain woman from the land of Hyrcania, they did so quietly.

CHAPTER NINETEEN

THE SHARD

"Sucks to be a falconer," I said.

"Sometimes," said Jane.

"If it's genetic, then why me? Why not anyone else in my dad's family?"

"The gene doesn't always express," said Jane. "You're the lucky one."

"What if I don't like falcons?" I asked. "What if I don't want any of this?"

"It may be hard to believe," said Jane, "but I know what you're feeling right now. Things were decided for you a long time ago, Marjan, It's not fair. But this isn't something you can deny. It's inside you, and it always will be. So at least you should try to understand it."

"What is it, anyway?" I said. "What's the mutation?"

"Something in your blood connects you to the creatures," said Jane. "You're able to help them in a way that no one else can."

"That's why the nonconsensual needle stick," I said.

"I had to be sure."

"What about you?" I said. "Are you the Hyrcanian Line too?"

"I'm something else," she said. "But it's not so different."

"Why does it have to be a secret?" I said. "If it's so important, why not get some more help?"

"Because the world isn't ready to help," said Jane. "What do you think would happen, if tomorrow everyone woke up to learn that dragons are real? It doesn't matter that only a few people would be inspired to hunt them down, because that's all it would take to wipe them out. We have to be very careful. Have you ever seen what happens when someone meets one of them for the first time? Some people don't handle it well. It can be dangerous. The animals know that. They choose the people who are ready for them. We help them—the animals and the people. But mostly we watch the balance." She paused, rueful. "Or we used to, anyway."

"What would you do, if you found the ones you've lost?"

"Recirculate them," she said. "Reintegrate them into our models. Remove any threat to their safety."

"Remove."

"We're serious people, Marjan," she said. "I'm not going to deny that."

"Does this—the missing animals—does it have anything to do with my dad?"

"Maybe," said Jane.

"And Ithaca?"

"Yes," she said. "Ithaca."

She rested a hand on the box. Then she pushed it across the table to me.

"Open it," she said.

I took the lid with both hands and lifted it open. Resting

inside, on a bed of gray foam padding, was a small shard of a hard, shiny material that looked like obsidian. Jane had put her glasses back on and was watching me with great interest.

"What is this thing?" I asked.

The shard was maybe an inch long and half as wide, and sharp at all its edges. It had a funny way of catching the light, a kind of oily iridescence that seemed to happen somewhere just under the surface of its rough, broken facets. It gave me a strange feeling, a thrumming thickness right in the middle of my chest.

"It might be nothing," said Jane.

I didn't like it. I didn't like how it sat there, looking too heavy for the box. I didn't like how it sucked the light out of the room, and how that stolen light swam in its dark little core like a diver trapped under an ice floe. I didn't like how it looked back at me. I closed the box, and immediately felt better. I pushed it away, as far as my arms would reach.

"What do you want from me?" I asked.

"I want to know what it is," said Jane.

"How would I know?" I said. "A piece of rock. A chunk of resin."

"Or bone," said Jane with a helpful smile. She looked at the box, and looked at me. "Or horn." Then she raised her eyebrows and waited.

I didn't want to open the box again. I didn't want to go anywhere near the thing that was inside it.

"Why is this so important to you?" I asked.

"The world is always trying to tell us something," she said. "Ithaca's a signal. We're trying to figure out what it means."

The power of the shard radiated out from the box. I could almost feel it traveling in waves through the table itself. It might have even made a sound—the kind of super-low-frequency subsonic wave that makes people hallucinate angels. My thoughts felt jumbled.

"Take your time," said Jane.

The box's energy thrummed in my ears, daring me to walk away, and daring me to open it. I wished I could push a button and grind the shard to dust without ever again having to lay eyes on it. Whatever it was, it was something terrible. I wished I could walk away from all of this.

But I'd come too far to walk away.

"Fine," I said. "I'll try."

I reached out and took the box with both hands. The case seemed to shiver ever so slightly under my touch. I pulled it toward me and lifted the lid again. Inside, the shard sat heavy against the foam. I looked into it, forced myself to stare into its depths, in case I might see the answer I was looking for there. I started to feel sick to my stomach, but no answer came to me. I gritted my teeth against a trembling wave of nausea, and when it passed, I steeled myself for what I knew I had to do. And when I was as ready as I could make myself, I rested my palm against the shard's surface.

Running.

Hooves cleave dirt. The night sings arrows. Dusky flanks stream lather. Shouts rise like birds, filling the air. Cut left, right.

Lungs burn. Voices near. Woods embrace me, hide me. Tack again. Arrows whisper cold promises. Skin splits, blood flows. I keep running.

I keep running.

I pulled my hand away from the shard and slammed the box

shut. The scar on my chest blazed with a sudden and piercing pain that made me gasp. Across the table, Jane Glass sat up, her composure breaking for just a moment to reveal the eagerness beneath. I glared at her.

"What is it?" she asked.

I didn't know any more than I'd seen or felt. There'd been no helpful signs informing me of the breed of animal that had shed this shard. I'd been in its body for a moment, but not long enough to understand its form. I hadn't even seen what it looked like.

But I knew. The answer was in my blood, and it felt like it had always been there. Some part of me knew, the same way you know, before the doctor tells you, that the prognosis isn't going to be good.

Jane Glass reached across the table and pulled the box toward her.

"I was born into this," she said quietly. "I grew up in it. I've seen a lot, Marjan. I never thought I'd see this."

For just a second, I saw something in her that reminded me of myself—a shadow of myself, long gone, from when the world was still whole, and I was still capable of seeing wonder in the galaxy of glow-in-the-dark stars that my mom had stuck to my bedroom ceiling. I was six years old, and my father was sitting at the foot of my bed, his face aglow in lamplight. He was telling me about the animal that had come first. The one that had always been, even before there were people. The one that was all alone in the world. The one that had always been chased, everywhere it went, but had never been captured or tamed.

The one that had given me my birthmark.

"The unicorn," I said.

"The unicorn. The unicorn is in Ithaca."

"Did my dad know?" I asked. "Did he see that?" I nodded at the shard.

Jane looked at me sadly. "I wish I could tell you," she said. She stood up and scooped up the box. "I have to go." She headed toward a door on the opposite side of the room.

"Wait," I said. "Wait a second." She stopped. "Does this mean someone out there has the unicorn? Like, it was caught? Is that what this means? Is it alive? Is it okay?"

She looked at me, expressionless, and my questions bounced off her like grains of rice.

Finally, and very slowly, I asked her, "Are you going to sell the unicorn?"

"We might need your help again, very soon," she said.

And then she was gone, and someone was putting a bag over my head.

Sitting in the dark in the back of the sedan, all the little uncertainties of my life seemed suddenly insignificant. I'd felt for just a moment the presence of something massive beyond comprehension, like the entire ocean had risen up and crashed over me in a single endless wave.

The unicorn.

For a few seconds, I'd been in its skin. I'd felt the weight and wisdom of millions of years. It was older than anything. Its thoughts were thick with memories, a forest that stretched unbroken all the way back to the beginning of time. It was pure, raw, wild, and it didn't belong to anyone. If anything, it belonged to the earth, to the moonlight and the hundred ice ages it had survived.

If anything, we belonged to it.

It was the original. Everything else was a shadow.

In the dark of the bag, I had a vision. Hands, holding each other, reaching back through centuries. Fathers, sons, daughters, mothers. Falconers and veterinarians and who knew what else. The Hyrcanian Line, leading to a girl in a clearing, a basket of mushrooms spilled beside her, a piece of horn burning in the hole in her chest, becoming part of her, part of us all. A human chain of stories and struggle and wisdom, weaving through the fabric of history, and at the end of all that life, loose and waving crazily in the darkness of unwritten time: me.

I could feel all those lives that had come before me, just like I'd felt the unicorn itself. It was the same feeling, only it wasn't coming from outside of me. And for a second, I felt ready for whatever was coming next.

And then, just as suddenly, those lives were gone. My hand was empty. The past was as distant as the coldest star in the sky. There was me, and, somewhere, far away, there was the unicorn.

Once was, once wasn't.

Eight years ago, something woke up.

Eight years ago, Horatio began to assemble his menagerie.

Today the unicorn was somewhere in Ithaca.

And maybe my dad was dead because of it.

The driver dropped me at my house. It was night. I stood outside and watched him drive away, and I wondered what I was supposed to do with the things I'd learned.

Suddenly, in the quiet, cool air, I felt small and foolish. Clarity and nausea hit me at the same time. Before I'd touched the shard, it had been nothing more than a clue. Now it was proof—proof that the rarest and most precious creature to ever walk the earth was somewhere in upstate New York. And I'd just given that proof to the family that controlled the global market for mythical animals.

I'd made a terrible mistake.

Zorro gave me a questioning look as I sprinted past him and up to my room, phone in hand.

"It's quite late," said Sebastian after four agonizingly slow rings.

"I have to get to Ithaca," I said. "I can't explain why, but I have to get there now. Can you help me?"

CHAPTER TWENTY

A STORM OVER ITHACA

The next morning, I was boarding a private jet bound for Ithaca.

"My allowance is frankly embarrassing," said Sebastian as he was completing the reservation. He'd bought the ticket without question and without hesitation, in the middle of the night, from half a world away. It must have cost many thousands of dollars. I hoped it was worth it.

I had no idea what I'd do when I got there, no idea where the unicorn might be. Maybe it was long gone. June was months ago. I was missing school, and missing work. I had no plan, only a mission: keep the unicorn out of the hands of the Fells. Undo what I had just done. Exactly how I was going to accomplish that, I wasn't sure.

Anger made me restless in my seat. I was angry at the Fells and Horatio Prendergast and my dad. I was angry with myself; after all, I was the one who'd told the Fells where to find the unicorn. Now I was racing into the unknown, with no idea what might await me, and what I might be able to do.

Mostly, though, I was angry that I had to do this alone.

To make matters worse, I got a call from David Ginn soon after takeoff.

"Come to the office," he said. "We have a problem."

"What?" I snapped. Now I was angry with David, too.

"Payroll," he said. "You're not gonna make it."

Payroll was, to David, a sacred space. Everything else could slide, but payroll could not. And when it did, catastrophe was close behind.

"I can't come in today," I said. "Talk to Dominic."

"Dominic doesn't sign the checks," he said.

"We'll figure it out when I get back."

"Back? Back from where? Where are you?"

I didn't have a good answer, so I hung up, and I didn't answer when he tried to call me back.

I also didn't write back to a text from Carrie, wondering where I was, if I was okay. Was I okay? I wasn't sure.

As we got closer to Ithaca, I tried to come up with an actual plan. Find a taxi to take me to the center of town, find a local hangout, listen to conversations. Ask a barista about the coyotes. Keep an eye out for kettle-and-serpent logos. It wasn't much of a plan, and it hardly seemed like enough to justify flying all the way across the country.

But here I was, and now we were landing, and it was all I had to work with.

We touched down at the regional airport and taxied to the terminal. The pilot opened the door, and I stepped out into a bright, cold, blustering afternoon.

And there, across the tarmac, a big smile on his face, was Sebastian.

The jolt of surprise quickly passed, replaced by a sense of relief that I wasn't in this alone. Mostly, though, I felt something light and brilliant inside my chest, like a golden bubble filled with sunshine. It was wonder.

"What are you doing here?" I called out from the airplane door.

"Whatever's going on," he said, "I wasn't about to let you have all the fun."

The wind blew his words around, and I had to strain to hear him.

"It might not be fun," I called back.

"Then I'm sure an extra pair of hands will come in useful," he replied. "I've got lots of practice wrestling an animal twice my size."

"Only counts if the animal's actually trying to win."

Sebastian grinned.

"Also," he added, "I've got a car." He held up a set of rental car keys.

I did need a car. And the company wasn't too bad either.

Soon we were on the road, heading toward town. It was a country road, with trees on both sides, broken up by the occasional house. The wind was howling around us, so loud and fierce that it was hard to even think straight. All the windows were up, but the sound still echoed through the glass.

"If you felt like explaining," said Sebastian, "I'd love to know what we're doing here."

"I know what *I'm* doing here," I said. "I'm still trying to figure out what you're doing."

"You sounded like you could use a bit of help," he said. "Also, I was curious. I'd love to meet another animal like Kipling."

"Nothing's like Kipling," I said.

"You know what I mean."

"Don't you have, like, school or something?"

"Don't you?" he asked.

Where was I supposed to begin? There were things he probably should know: there was a unicorn—*the* unicorn—somewhere in the vicinity, and as long as it was here, it was in danger. And there were things he probably shouldn't know: the Fells, I was certain, would rather I not talk about them. And there were things I wanted to say but wasn't sure how to put into words.

A story, for example, about a girl who went foraging for mushrooms, and everything that had happened because of her.

"Something needs our help," I said. "It's alone, and it's very precious, and it's in danger, and we might not have a lot of time to find it."

"Well, that sounds urgent and not at all vague," said Sebastian with a smile.

"Sorry," I said. "You deserve to know . . ."

"But?"

But let me tell you what happened when my dad told a guy named Horatio Prendergast that Sturges wasn't the only one.

"It's better for everyone if I don't say anything right now," I said. "Maybe later. I mean, if we find it, you'll see. You'll understand."

"I'm sure I will," he said. He sounded disappointed.

"I'm sorry," I said. "Please don't kick me out of your car?"

He looked like he was considering the idea for a minute. Then he laughed. "If I did that," he said, "I wouldn't have anyone to talk to on this long, lonely drive."

My phone buzzed in my pocket. David Ginn. I silenced the call.

"Everything okay?" asked Sebastian.

"It's fine," I said. "Actually, it's not. I don't know what I'm doing. I'm in way over my head, on everything, and I keep thinking it's all going to fall apart any second. I keep thinking, if I get this one right—this one here in Ithaca—then it's all okay. It's worth it. But then I realize that I don't even know how to find what we're looking for."

Sebastian didn't say anything. His eyes were locked on the road ahead. But it felt like he was listening.

"I'm sorry for whatever this turns out to be," I continued. "I mean, if it turns out badly. Or if it doesn't turn out at all. I'm sorry for dragging you into this. I didn't mean for you to come. But I'm glad you're here, because if you weren't, I'd be saying all these same things, but there wouldn't be anyone else in the car, and I'd look like a crazy person. And I can't even drive, so I'd probably still be standing on the runway."

Sebastian nodded.

"So I guess what I'm saying is thank you," I said. "And also, sorry. Again. That I can't tell you anything. Is that okay?"

Sebastian nodded, eyes forward.

"If you're mad, I don't blame you," I said. "I'd be mad too, probably."

Silence.

"Please don't hold back. I know a lot about being angry. Sometimes you have to just tell people what you're feeling. So, is there anything you want to say?"

Silence at first. Then, a slow clearing of his throat. "There is," he said, "something I would like to say."

"Okay?"

He was quiet and solemn, like he was gathering his thoughts. I braced myself for the fire hose.

"How is it," he said, "that you *mad* Americans can drive

on this side of the road? It's absolute lunacy! Everything is backwards."

Then he smiled a wicked smile, and I smacked him on the shoulder.

"You're a jerk," I said, but I was smiling when I said it, and so was he.

"Kipling's getting treatment, you know," he said after a moment. "Uncle Simon found a vet to administer care, everything you said to do. It's a delicate process, bringing anyone into our family. It takes time. But he's getting care now. So, I suppose I should thank you, too."

I didn't like the thought of Kipling on an IV drip. The image sat funnily in my head, like something I'd seen before, but twisted all around, and too bright. I shook the picture away, pushed it into the back of my mind, tried to forget about it.

"You're welcome," I said.

We rolled into downtown Ithaca ten minutes later. Sebastian parked the car near a bar and grill that looked local enough, then ran around and opened the passenger door. The wind surged around me. Its roar filled my ears like a chorus of animal cries. I got out, and he shut the door, and all of a sudden, completely by accident, we were standing very close to each other.

We stood there on the sidewalk, our bodies nearly touching, for a moment, and then for another. The wind, wild and unpredictable, swirled in my head, scrambled my thoughts. *What are we doing?*

At last Sebastian took a small step back.

"Well," he said. But it was pretty clear he meant something else.

"Yeah, let's go," I said.

And suddenly we both had a purpose again, which was

a relief. I turned my shoulder into the gusts and followed Sebastian into the restaurant.

A bartender handed us menus and nodded at a table in the corner.

"We check IDs," he said.

There were a few other people seated around the place, and a few others at the bar. As we walked to the table, I scanned their faces for anything suspicious. Glenn of the forty-dollar bribe had told me that you could always tell, when someone was looking. Maybe I'd spot the Fells by the looks in their eyes, or by the way they held their shoulders. Maybe I'd recognize someone who'd been touched by the unicorn, just by the curl of their mouth.

But every face I saw looked ordinary. No one stood out.

When we were seated, Sebastian leaned across the table.

"So what do we do now?" he whispered.

"I think we just listen," I said.

"What are we listening for?"

"Anything that sounds unusual," I said.

We sat there for an awkward moment, listening to the murmur of conversation around us.

"This isn't going to get us anywhere, is it?" I asked.

Sebastian breathed a sigh of relief.

"Thank you," he said. "I was afraid we were going to have to sit like that for the next hour."

I felt my stomach sinking. We had no plan, no idea what we were doing here. To my great surprise, I really wished Ezra were here. She would know what to do. I considered calling her for a second, but thought better of it. The last person in the world I wanted knowing about the unicorn was Horatio.

We decided to just focus on eating, and then figure out what to do. I excused myself to go to the bathroom to wash my face. As I did, I caught a look at myself in the mirror. There were bags under my eyes. My skin looked pale. My cheeks were sunken. My hair was doing the thing where it gets stringy and brittle.

I looked hungry. I felt hungry too, but not for food. For something I couldn't name but had wanted for as long as I could remember.

The wind was wailing on the other side of the wall. I opened the bathroom's frosted casement window and listened as it swirled and gusted and swallowed up the everyday sounds of the street. The echo of it thrummed in my head even as I walked back to the table.

"That wind is crazy," I said as I sat down.

Sebastian glanced up at me, a quizzical look on his face.

"What wind?" he asked.

"You didn't hear it when we came in?"

He shook his head.

My heart began to race in my chest. I jumped up and ran outside. Sebastian was following me, but I wasn't paying attention to him. I stood on the sidewalk and listened as it wailed and whooshed around me.

"You don't feel that?" I asked. Sebastian shook his head.

I put my hand out and felt its force, a million billion molecules slamming into my skin, over and over again, pushing against my palm.

No.

Not pushing.

Pulling.

"Sebastian," I said, "get into the car. I know what we need to do."

The wind was howling around us, but the air was perfectly still. My hair wasn't being blown around. Sebastian's clothes weren't fluttering. I felt it on my skin, and heard it in my ears, and sometimes it gusted and took my breath away, but it didn't shake the branches of the trees overhead.

There was a storm over Ithaca, and only I could feel it.

CHAPTER TWENTY-ONE

THE HEART OF THE WIND

Maybe they spotted us outside the restaurant. Maybe they saw me standing there, arms out to catch the secret message hidden in the invisible wind. Or maybe they'd been tailing us since the airport.

There were two of them, a driver and a passenger, in the silver van behind us. I noticed it shortly after we left the bar and grill. Sebastian thought I was being paranoid at first, but after three randomly chosen detours, the van was still a couple of cars behind us.

"Who are they?" asked Sebastian.

"I don't know," I said.

"What do they want?"

"They probably want to know where we're going."

"I'll try to lose them," said Sebastian.

He turned suddenly, then turned again, and for a moment, the van disappeared from view.

"That was easy," he said, guiding us through a warren of residential streets until we were back on the main road.

But a minute later, the van was behind us again, matching our pace.

"Pull over," I said.

"What? No! What if they want to mug us?"

"They don't," I said. "Trust me. Signal, then pull over."

Sebastian glanced in the rearview, then looked at me with concern. But at last he relented, put on the blinker, and pulled the car over into a dirt turnout off the main road.

The van followed. Its wheels crunched over the rocks, sending up a thin cloud of dirt. A few feet behind our car, it came to a stop and stayed there, engine rumbling. No one moved.

"I'm going to talk to them," I said.

"Don't be stupid," said Sebastian. "You have no idea who's in that car, or what they want."

Against Sebastian's protests, I opened the car door. As I stood to leave, I felt his hand on my arm. It was gentle and warm, and for a second, it confused my thoughts.

"I'm keeping the engine running," he said. "Any trouble, you come right back."

I got out and faced the van. Through its grinning grille, the engine growled. The way the light hit the windshield, I could only see the silhouettes of driver and passenger.

What if they do want to mug us?

I walked to the passenger window and waited. For a long second, nothing happened. Then the window began to roll down, revealing a man with a lean, haunted face and dark eyes that locked on to mine. Behind him, in the driver's seat, a woman who could have easily been his sister watched over his shoulder.

"Why are you following us?" I asked.

Neither one spoke.

"Are you with the Fells?" I said.

The two glanced at each other and said nothing.

"You need to leave me alone," I said.

The faintest smile crossed the man's face, for just a second, then vanished.

"I'm not going to take you there," I said.

Silence. Smirks. I began to lose patience.

"Stop following us!" I shouted.

The man smiled again, a tiny, patient smile that made it clear he wasn't about to listen to me.

"Fine," I said. "I want to talk to Jane Glass."

The two of them looked at each other.

"Call her," I said. "I know she sent you here. You're probably field agents. Middle-content, right? She's high-content. And I want to talk to her. Now."

The man looked at his sister—I was sure they were siblings now—and made a kind of questioning hand gesture. An unspoken thought passed between them, practically a whole conversation in eyes and subtle facial expressions. Then the woman shrugged, reached into a pocket, and pulled out a cell phone. She punched in a number, then handed it to me, ringing.

"Hello?" A familiar voice on the other end of the line.

"Tell your people here to stop following me," I said.

"Marjan," she said. "I can't do that."

"This one doesn't belong to you. It doesn't belong to anyone. It's not like the others."

"None of them belongs to us."

"This one's different. You said you wanted to work with me. So work with me. Trust me. You have to leave it alone."

There was a long silence on the other end of the line.

"Are you sure?" she said at last.

"I know what I felt."

"I'll get in a lot of trouble for this."

"It's the right thing to do," I said.

Another silence. Finally she spoke again.

"I'm going to give you a phone number," she said. "If you need anything, call me."

As if on cue, the man passed a Sharpie out the window to me, and I wrote the number on the back of my hand.

"I'm trusting you, Marjan," said Jane. "I'm going to buy you some space. Whatever you have to do, do it quickly. Now hand the phone back to Molly."

I passed the phone into the van. The woman listened for a moment, then put it away. The siblings gave me a final, scornful look. Then the window rolled up and the van revved, kicking up dirt and pebbles. It rolled out into the road, joined the passing traffic, and was soon gone from sight.

The wind led us out of town to a lonely county road that wobbled through spiny forests of bare trees, past old farmhouses and other faint signs of civilization. The sun's light came through the spindly branches in brilliant spears that exploded into dazzling fireworks in my eyes. Every few minutes, Sebastian would pull over and stop the car, and I'd put my hand out the window to feel. The gusts were stronger here, more focused. I could tell we were nearer the source. Now the wind came from several directions at once, drawing tighter around us, until at last we were parked at the end of a long gravel driveway with an old farmhouse at the end of it.

The wind had gone silent. We'd reached its center.

The house was covered in a crackling coat of white paint. A broad porch sagged out front. A pair of dusty windows looked out from the upper floor. Cobwebs gathered beneath the porch steps. Behind the house was a battered red barn whose big, tractor-sized door was barred shut from the outside. A pickup truck was parked out front. I was glad I wasn't here alone.

We got out and walked up the driveway. As we got close to the house, something moved in one of the upper windows. I heard the creaking of old stairs. The front door opened.

A man stepped onto the porch. He was in his late thirties, dressed in flannel and thick denim, with a solid beard and a trucker hat and quiet green eyes that never seemed to rest on anything for very long. He wore heavy boots and walked with a slight limp, so that the sound of his footsteps on the floorboards had a stuttered rhythm, like a slow heartbeat.

"Let's go," said Sebastian. "I don't like this."

"Hang on," I whispered.

"Get off my land," said the man.

He brought a shotgun up from behind a porch rail and held it in his hands.

My mouth went dry. I couldn't speak.

"Go on," said the man. He raised the shotgun.

Sebastian stepped between me and the man with the gun, hands open in front of him.

"You don't need that, sir," he said. "We're going." His voice had the waver of fear, but he spoke slowly and carefully.

Sebastian nodded to me and began to back away from the house. I wanted to go with him, but I felt rooted in place.

"W-wait," I stammered.

"Marjan!" Sebastian hissed.

"The hell you want?" said the man on the porch.

Slowly, with great effort, I raised my hands up.

"It's not worth it, Marjan," whispered Sebastian. He glared at me, willing me to move, to do the sane thing and back away from the man with the big gun. But instead I looked up the drive and locked eyes with him, and a single word cracked out of my throat.

"Unicorn."

He glared at me for a moment, then lowered the gun. I heard Sebastian's breath catch in surprise.

"Who are you?" barked the man.

"My name's Marjan," I said. "This is my friend Sebastian."

He squinted at us in distrust.

"Who told you?" he asked.

"No one," I said. "I swear. I can feel it. I know it's here. And we're not the only people looking for it."

"What are you talking about?" His defensiveness and anger were giving way to confusion.

"It's complicated," I said. "But I don't think it's supposed to belong to anyone. I think it's supposed to be free."

The man stepped down off the porch and approached. He scanned the road behind me for signs of danger.

"I don't see anyone," he said. His eyes clicked back to me, wary, almost fearful.

"I just want to help it," I said.

Now he was looking at me like I was crazy.

"You want to help *that* thing?" he asked.

He glanced back at the barn.

"It's in there?" I asked. "Can I see it?"

The barn door was barricaded with a thick piece of wood that had been laid roughly into metal brackets on either side of the door frame.

"It doesn't look much like I woulda thought," said the man. "Not that, you know, I thought much about it before."

His name was Devin Thurston. He was propped up against the side of his truck, watching us. He'd leaned the shotgun up next to him. But he hadn't put it away, and I had the sense from the way he was eyeing the door that it wasn't for us anymore.

Sebastian grasped one side of the wooden barricade. As I took hold of the other, fear, raw and primal, buzzed in my chest. Every instinct in my body was telling me not to open the barn door. Sebastian seemed equally reluctant.

With a heave of our shoulders, we tossed the barricade aside. It thunked on the ground. I felt Devin tense up behind me, maybe put a hand on the shotgun.

The door had a crude wooden latch, which I quietly rotated out of its resting spot in the doorframe. Sebastian leaned on the door just enough to open it a crack. I craned my neck into the crack and peered into the musky darkness inside.

The air within was thick with dust. Light came down in tight shafts, tracing just the faintest outlines of things. The tall, boxy shape edged with a spiky glow resolved after a minute into a stack of hay bales. The dark, rounded shadows in a near corner were plastic drums of something—feed or fertilizer or pesticide. The dim frame of a loft emerged from the gloom opposite me, the upper floor stacked with odd-sized objects that might have been farm tools, or old ski gear, or something else. Beneath it, shadows.

A sour, fetid smell hung in the air, the smell of forest loam and blood and captive fear. Inside the barn was something very wild, very afraid, and very dangerous. A nameless old feeling surged in me, dormant for generations and suddenly familiar again. The birthmark on my chest began to itch, and then to burn.

The rafters shuddered. A roosting sparrow, maybe a bat, fluttered its wings. I jumped. As quickly as the commotion had erupted, all was still again.

A loud snort sent a puff of dirt shimmering through the

air. Something huge and knotted and covered in angry spikes passed for an instant through a blade of light, and then disappeared again into the darkness beneath the loft. A low rumbling whoosh of breath, deep enough to make my bones rattle, shook the boards of the barn. A pair of long, muscular forelegs unfolded. Broad, cloven hooves planted in the dirt. With a great, lurching effort, the unicorn drew itself up to full height, and took a halting step into the light.

It was more deer or elk than horse, with gray-brown fur matted with dirt and dust and hay and blood. It was as big and sturdy as a moose, and it stood on long, muscular legs. The gnarled horn that rose from the crown of its head looked like a pair of prize antlers that had been roughly braided together. The tips of its many points were caked with dried blood.

It took a step toward me, and a pair of ropes tied around its neck pulled taut. It strained at the ropes, which had been wrapped around the barn's sturdy wooden support beams. The unicorn huffed and pawed at the ground, but it didn't struggle, and when I took another step, it didn't try to gore me. Its snout was covered in old scars. The crown of its head, where the horn burst forth, was bare. The fur had been rubbed off, and the pinkish-gray skin beneath was calloused and hard. Its black hooves were chipped and scratched.

Scars, hundreds of them, crisscrossed its ribs and its legs. Round, puckered bullet wounds. Neat little slices that might have been where arrows had gone in. Long gashes—swords, knives, spears. Bite marks. Rippled burn scars. A patch of bare skin with a spiderweb of dark veins—a poison that had failed to take? Near the hindquarters, an old injury seemed to show where some kind of netting had dug into its skin. A snare, maybe? Each one contained a story, and when the unicorn shifted its weight between its powerful legs, they shifted with it, a hypnotic weave of violence and survival. I could have watched it move for hours.

"How'd it get here?" I asked.

"It's been prowling round the woods here awhile," he said. "Few months at least. You ask anyone hunts up in the hills. They seen the tracks. Seen what it did to them coyotes."

It blinked and squinted. Its eyes were black and wet—shining orbs wide with distrust and defiance. The unicorn let out a fierce grunt and waved its horn in my direction. I jumped back, but it was more of a gesture than an actual attempt to clobber me. I stepped forward again. Its eyes narrowed to angry slashes. A low growl rumbled in its throat. Beneath a matting of farm dust, a fresh wound on its chest was dark and shiny, and one of its legs was ragged and bloody.

"It's hurt," I said.

"My dogs did some of that, 'fore it killed them," said Devin, stepping up behind me. His face was pale with anger. "I got a couple cattle dogs. Rex and Trig. They're good dogs. Keep the coyotes away. Couple nights ago, I heard them snarling, and then I heard 'em fighting. He gored one of 'em, kicked the other one's head in. They messed up that leg pretty good, though. I cut him in the ribs with a hunting knife, broke the blade right off. Winged him with a round of bird shot, took his breath away long enough to get him tied up. Don't know why I didn't kill him. They were good dogs. Never did nothing wrong."

His voice had gone ragged, and he stopped talking. I looked away. He hadn't meant to share his grief. The unicorn watched without remorse or pity.

"I'm sorry for your loss," I said.

"I loved those dogs," he said bitterly. "They're 'bout the only things I understand anymore."

Devin Thurston looked mad enough to kill. I doubted even the eternal unicorn would survive a round of buckshot at this range. But beneath Devin's anger and sorrow, there was a strange, helpless look on his face, and I knew he wouldn't do it.

"If it's okay with you," I said, both to Devin and the unicorn, "I'm going to say hello."

I stepped into the dark of the barn and reached my hand out toward the animal. It stood motionless, defiant, unafraid. I felt the bristly, rough fur of its snout beneath my fingertips. The mark on my chest burned warm and true. Its heat radiated all through me. I slid my fingers through the unicorn's fur, touched its skin, and closed my eyes.

Running. Always running. All chases, the same chase.

Trucks rumble, horses clatter, hounds bay. Headlights, searchlights, torchlight. Bullets, arrows, stones.

Seek cover. Seek darkness. Find the dense places, the thickets, the deep forests. Find the water. Lose your scent. Follow the deer tracks. Follow the wolf tracks. Leave no trail of your own. Wounds heal. Scars are tougher to break. Be fierce. Be patient.

They are small, all of them.

They chase because they are running out of time.

It came at me all at once, a single, endless escape, lasting eons. How many miles had the unicorn run? How far beyond exhaustion were its legs, its lungs? It was older than anything. Its memory stretched back to a time before people. And here it was, still standing, its heart still beating. No one had killed it yet. It was beautiful and perfect, even with all its scars. Nothing had ever changed it. And now I understood it. I knew what it was.

It was the source.

Every creature I'd met, every creature in Horatio's collection, had a piece of that feeling, a piece of that endless escaping chase. It was in me, and deeper down, it was in everyone. It was the origin. It was the root. It was the father and the mother and the muscle that pumped life force into everything. The unicorn was the purest and the strongest and the most alien of all the creatures, because it had come to this world before there had been humans to dream it.

Maybe it had given us our dreams.

For just a moment, I saw myself the way the unicorn saw all of us—tiny wisps of desire and hunger, blinking in and out of existence, never to be satisfied. We weren't worth the trouble of remembering. We weren't friends, the unicorn and I. It didn't want friends. What did it recognize in me? The phantom pain of an old scar? The panic of being trapped once, long ago? The dim remnants of its own strange essence, threaded somewhere in my blood?

I doubted it remembered a girl in a clearing, with a basket of mushrooms under her arm.

I took my hand back, and as I did, the unicorn's anger softened into a look of curiosity.

In that instant, I knew she'd been real, that girl. She'd lived, and her story—what I knew of it—was true. And because of her—and a thousand other people, but mostly her—there was me. There was this moment now.

"I'm going to keep you safe," I said.

CHAPTER TWENTY-TWO

WHISKEY, A RAZOR, AND CRAZY GLUE

We left the unicorn in the barn and walked back to Devin's house. All three of us were quiet. The ground felt like it might break under our feet if we stepped too hard. Something larger than any of us had just happened.

"Those wounds have to be cleaned," I said when we got to the house. "It needs stitches."

Outside the front door were two dog bowls, empty. Devin paused and stared at them, then looked up at me, like he was trying to figure something out. Then he nodded, opened the door, and showed us in.

A few empty beer bottles sat on a low coffee table in the house's main room. The floor was a bit dusty. A pair of jeans were draped over a faded leather couch. He rolled them up and tossed them upstairs, took up the bottles in a single clinking handful, and bused them into the kitchen.

"Don't really get visitors here," he said as he returned. "You want coffee or tea or anything? No?"

He leaned his back against the window opposite me and took his hat off. Locks of curly brown hair tumbled out, and he pushed them away from his face with an absent swipe of his hand.

"So how we gonna do it?" he asked. "You got a field kit or something?"

"No," I said. "We don't have anything. I didn't know . . ."

"Well," said Devin, "I've got bandages. Got some whiskey to clean the wounds. A sharp knife, case they've gone rotten. Razor blades, a lighter. Probably got a sewing kit somewhere."

"It'll have to do," I said.

Devin nodded, and then stalked off into another room of the house and started clattering around. As soon as he was gone, Sebastian looked at me like I was crazy.

"Exactly which era of medicine will we be practicing here?" he asked. "This sounds medieval. Isn't there another way?"

"I'm open to suggestions," I said.

"Some kind of magic spell or potion or something?" said Sebastian. "Can't you use your powers or whatever they are?"

"Ha," I said. "No. That's not what they do. And that's not how this works."

"Well, you can't just walk up to that creature and start sewing," he said. "I don't care how injured it is, or how much it likes you. It'll kick your head in, if it doesn't skewer you first."

"You don't know what happened back there," I said. "You have no idea how important that animal is. We have to do whatever it takes to protect it."

"You're going to get yourself killed," he said. "And it's going to be my fault for flying you out here. Please don't put that on my conscience."

"I never asked you to come," I said.

It came out more harshly than I'd meant. Sebastian's face fell.

"I'm sorry," I said. "I didn't mean—"

"You're right," he said. "I'm here because I thought we had something in common. In all my life, I haven't found anyone who understands, and I thought you did."

"I do," I said.

But maybe understanding didn't go both ways. How could I possibly explain the unicorn to him? I might as well have been talking to Carrie or Grace, right then.

"This is my choice," I said. "This is what I have to do. Whatever the consequences. I'm not asking you to understand. But as long as you're here, I am asking you to help."

Sebastian said nothing, a look of confusion and helplessness on his face.

We heard Devin's footfalls returning. He came into the room with a big plastic tub in his hands. Inside it: a bottle of distilled water, towels, a razor, a hunting knife, a handle of whiskey, a sewing kit, and a tube of crazy glue.

"This is what I've got," said Devin. "And I can start some water boiling."

Sebastian shook his head.

"Someone's going to get hurt," he said. "If you don't find a way to restrain and sedate that animal like any reasonable doctor would, someone is going to get hurt badly."

"I got more rope," said Devin. "We can tie it down tighter."

"Ropes break," said Sebastian. "Think about it, Marjan. If you get yourself killed, who's going to help the next animal? Who else can do whatever it is you do?"

Sebastian had a point. And in all my years at the clinic, I'd never seen my dad operate on an animal that wasn't sedated.

"Do you have anything that might calm it down?" I asked Devin. "Anything at all?"

He was quiet a moment. His eyes darted around the room, avoiding mine. He rubbed his forehead and sucked air through his teeth.

"Yeah," he said, after a long time. "Yeah, I've got some morphine."

The room was silent while everyone digested this new information.

"Well, okay," I said. "That'd probably work."

"It's . . . uh . . . good," said Devin. "Hospital grade, I mean. Expensive, too, so . . . I buy it off a nurse at the university. My leg. There's shrapnel from an IED in my knee, never gonna come out. Hurts like a bitch sometimes. Old Morpheus takes the edge off."

"You're a soldier," said Sebastian.

"Iraq and Afghanistan," said Devin. "Been out three years. Got a few scars. Few ghosts. Monkey's good for them, too. So were the dogs, but." He shrugged. "Not the first friends I've buried. Probably not the last. Anyway, let's do this before I change my mind about giving that thing the rest of my good stuff."

We lit the barn with work lights. The unicorn watched us from the center of the room, the ropes taut around its throat. Its eyes narrowed into angry squints every time Devin turned another light on.

It likes the dark better, I thought. *Of course it does.*

When we had enough light to work, Devin filled a syringe from a little brown bottle. After a moment of hesitation, he handed it to me.

"Ain't no one else getting anywhere near a vein," he said.

I held the syringe in my hand, wondering, *Is this enough?*

Is it too much? We'd worked out the dosage with an internet search. I hoped the unicorn was similar enough to a horse that we were at least in the right ballpark.

Sebastian put a hand on my shoulder, holding me back for just a second. Then he let go.

"Be careful," he said. "Please."

I nodded.

The unicorn stamped one of its injured legs and grunted. I approached it with slow steps, until its smell was thick in my nose, and one wild move would have left me flattened or gored. But the unicorn didn't flinch, and it didn't panic. It watched me with those burning black eyes, its nostrils flaring, its face quietly furious.

I slid my fingers along its flank, and its eternal essence echoed through them and into me. I gritted my teeth against the weight of millions of years, the rush of millions of miles, and tried to focus on the one thing I needed to do right then. I tried to put myself back into the procedure room at the clinic, my dad guiding my hand, talking quietly in my ear. My fingers drifted across the unicorn's fur until I found the furrow between the muscles of its leg, where the blood beat. With Devin's straight razor, I shaved off the hair, exposing dark, leathery skin beneath. Once again, I felt for the pulse. And then, with a breath, and something like a prayer, I slipped the needle in.

The unicorn tensed. Its muscles instantly turned as tough as iron beneath my fingers. I pushed the plunger in, and then drew away as quickly as I could, dodging a lazy swipe of the horn. The unicorn bellowed and clapped its hooves on the ground. A moment later, its head drooped. Its body began to sway. One leg buckled, and then another. It steadied itself with a whinny and a huff, but then it bent its knees, lowered itself to the ground, and rolled onto one side, its eyes wild but softening.

"He's getting it," said Devin.

"It's okay," I whispered to the unicorn. "You're going to be safe."

Its eyes locked on me one last time before they lost focus. Its head came to rest on the ground, eyelids loosely closed, breath slow and heavy and even.

"Is it . . . ," said Sebastian, from somewhere a million miles behind me.

I put a hand to its throat and felt its thoughts swimming in warm, empty waters, its heartbeat firm and insistent.

"It's under," I said. "Let's get started."

My dad started letting me into the procedure room when I turned twelve.

It was one of the few places where our relationship made sense. I put on scrubs and a mask like anyone else, and at first I stood in the back of the room, watched my dad work, and tried to stay out of the way. It felt like a normal thing for a twelve-year-old daughter of a veterinarian to do. And then one day, he called my name.

"Take these, Marjan," he said while he was removing a lipoma from the belly of a Labrador. I was thirteen, and he was motioning to a pair of forceps that were clamped around a flap of skin. "Put your fingers into the holes, and hold them steady." His voice was flat and efficient. It was almost casual. But I was the last person my dad ever asked for help, with anything. There was nothing casual about it.

I did what I was told. Those forceps never moved.

I used to think surgery was something elegant and graceful. It's not elegant. It's cautious, and it's patient. There are elegant and graceful parts—watching an expert surgeon suture a wound closed with needle drivers is beautiful. Laparoscopic procedures are full of elegant, precise moments. But skin is tough, and fat and muscle are tough, and bones are hard. And sometimes you snip ragged holes, and sometimes you dig your fingers into those holes. Sometimes surgery is wrestling. Sometimes it's grappling one piece of slippery flesh through another. Sometimes it's just a matter of trying to hang on.

The bird shot had ripped ribbons of skin from the unicorn's shoulder. Here and there, deeper grooves led to dark speckles where pellets had burrowed through and lodged in its fat and muscle. I daubed at the stripped flesh with whiskey-soaked towels. Sebastian followed just behind me, with a large, steaming pitcher of water.

Neither of us spoke. The only sounds were our breaths—mine, Sebastian's, and the deep, wounded exhalations of the unicorn—and the trickle of water as Sebastian poured it to irrigate the exposed flesh. The silence felt almost holy.

I held Devin's knife to the flame of his lighter, sliding the blade slowly through the fire to sterilize it. With the sharp tip, I removed the pellets that I could reach, and cut away flesh that looked like it might be infected. When I was done, the wound was clean. We filled the pellet holes with glue, and duct-taped a bandage over the whole injury. It had taken maybe ten minutes, but it had felt like seconds. After I pressed the last strip of tape over the bandage, I looked up from the wound to Sebastian. He looked like I felt—wired and dazzled with wonder. I nodded to him, and he nodded back, and we moved on to the dog bites.

The punctures went deep into the unicorn's ropy muscles. When I shaved away the fur, I saw purple pressure bruises where the dogs' jaws had clamped down. I worked the knife into the wounds to clear away dead flesh. Dark blood pooled slowly in the tooth-shaped pits as I cut away the exposed tissue. Once I had the bite as clean as it would get, Sebastian and I flushed it again with a mixture of water and whiskey. Then I took the hoof in one hand and squeezed out the glue to fill the wounds. The clear, gummy liquid settled into the holes and depressions in the unicorn's skin. We wrapped the leg in gauze, and then set it gently on the ground.

"One more," I said, my voice barely breaking a whisper.

The knife wound had split the unicorn's skin like curtains, just below the ribs, revealing a layer of fat, and beneath it, lean, stringy muscle. I pushed the wound open as delicately as I could, to see how deep it ran. I was looking for guts, but the cut just stopped, right in the middle of a band of muscle. Almost like something had stopped it there.

Then I noticed something strange, deep in the wound. The dull glint of old metal peeked out through the layers of flesh. As I pushed the skin aside to get a better look, I spotted another bit of hard metal, this one nearer to the surface. It took me a moment to realize what I was looking at. And once I saw what it was, I realized that it was everywhere.

They were bits and pieces of weaponry. Buckshot and bird shot speckled the meat of the unicorn's muscle. A heavy musket ball was embedded in a fat deposit. Something that might have once been a stone hatchet blade lay beneath the scar its impact must have created. Obsidian arrowheads protruded from between the unicorn's ribs.

Of course Devin's knife hadn't reached the unicorn's guts.

You couldn't have cut that deep with a meat cleaver and a running start. These bits of metal weren't just leftover shrapnel. They were armor—a patchwork armor, made up of all the bullets and blades and arrows and stones that had failed to kill the unicorn.

The broken tip of Devin's knife was probably somewhere in there too, one more weapon absorbed, one more tiny chapter in the unicorn's endless story of survival.

With trembling hands, I began to scrape away dead flesh.

We emptied the tube of glue patching the gash, and when we were done, the wound was sealed in a clear, hard bubble. It wasn't pretty, and it wasn't perfect, but it would hold. In time, the wound would close up, the fur would grow back around it, and only a scar would remain. I doubted the unicorn would mind one more scar.

I stepped back to admire what we'd done. The unicorn's wounds were clean, and the bandages would protect them while they healed. I didn't know where the strength had come from, where I'd found the confidence that I could do this. Looking now at the unicorn, its bandages white and crisp, the task seemed like it should have been too big for us. My breath trembled with pride, and at the same moment, my whole body felt weak with exhaustion. I sat down on the dirt floor, overwhelmed with all of it. Sebastian sat down next to me, and I could tell he was feeling the same thing.

"We did it," he said, his voice soft with awe.

"We did," I said.

"Now what?" asked Devin.

"Set it free," I said. "As soon as it tries to leave, let it go."

Sebastian looked at it.

"What, just like that?" he asked.

"It can take care of itself," I said. "It's been taking care of itself for a long time."

"It needed a bit of help today," said Sebastian.

"I guess it did," I said. I turned to Devin. "Do you mind if we stay until it's awake? I'd like to see it one more time."

He nodded. Then he turned and trudged out of the barn, and Sebastian and I were alone with the unicorn.

"I'm sorry for what I said before," I said. "I should be thanking you."

"I'm sorry I doubted you," said Sebastian. "Seems like you do know what you're doing after all."

"I couldn't have done this without you, Sebastian," I said. "It just wouldn't have happened."

"Well, that's something, isn't it," he said.

The unicorn let out a loud whoosh of air and stirred. I found myself wondering how long it had been alone in the world. I wondered if it ever hungered for anything more than its solitary, wandering life, or if its ragged armor protected it from such feelings.

I turned back to Sebastian. He seemed to be waiting for something. I guess I was too.

That's when we heard the motorcycle out front.

Sebastian and I came up behind Devin, just in time to see Ezra Danzig taking her helmet off, a grin of triumph on her face.

"What are you doing here?" I said.

"Wolf work," said Ezra.

"How did you know I was here?"

"I had someone watching you back home. When you got on that charter jet, I made a few calls and found the flight manifest. I figured Ithaca was too much of a coincidence, so here I am." She glanced at all of us, one by one. "Looks like quite the party. I'm guessing this place is yours"—she nodded to Devin, then looked at Sebastian—"but I can't figure out who you are, or what you're doing here."

"He's doing wolf work too," I said, before he could answer. That made Ezra smile. She looked back at the barn.

"So what's behind door number two?" she said. "Something pretty special, I'm guessing."

"That's none of your business," said Devin. "And you're trespassing."

"That's true," said Ezra. "So how about I put it another way, before I show myself out. Let's say I have a blank check with your name on it. What number do I write in, for whatever it is you've got in that barn there?"

"It's not for sale," I said.

"Oh," said Ezra. "Does it belong to you, Marjan? Because as your friend just reminded us all, this is his property."

"It doesn't belong to anyone," I said.

"Meaning it hasn't been claimed yet," said Ezra. "Any takers? I've got millions to play with. Name your price."

Neither Devin nor I said a word.

"It's better this way, Marjan," said Ezra. "You get to leave here with your moral compass intact, and I get to make . . ." She looked at Devin. "What's your name?—an offer he can't refuse."

Devin had the shotgun loose in one hand. "Who the hell are you?" he said.

"Ezra Danzig," said Ezra. "I'd like to make you very rich."

Devin didn't say anything.

"Oh my God," said Sebastian from behind me. "He's actually thinking about it."

"All of you, stay where you are," said Devin. Ezra made an emphatic show of complying, feet planted firmly, hands open and visible.

"It's not for sale," I said.

Ezra gave me a sympathetic look. Then she turned her attention back to Devin, and gestured to the barn. "Is it in there?" Devin didn't say anything. "I understand you've probably got some questions right now," said Ezra. "But I'm going to give you, let's say, twenty million dollars, if you let me take that animal."

"Bullshit," said Devin.

"Serious," said Ezra.

Devin was quiet. I had a sick feeling in my stomach. If the unicorn didn't belong in a barn, it definitely didn't belong in a cage several hundred feet underground.

Devin glanced back at me. "Is she serious?"

"That's the price, sight unseen," said Ezra. "If I get in there and it's sick or hurt or anything, I might have to come down. But right now, this second, twenty is the offer."

Sebastian was right. Devin was clearly considering. Ezra offered me a shrug of apology.

"You can't," said Sebastian, pushing past both of us to confront Ezra. "Whoever you are, you have no right to be here." Then he turned to Devin. "And *you* have no right to be selling something that was never yours in the first place."

Ezra chuckled. Devin was silent for a moment. Then he glared at Sebastian.

"Don't tell me my rights," he said, his voice cold.

"Wait," I said, and Devin looked over. "I know that's a lot of money. I don't know what I'd do if someone offered me that much money. But I know her. I know where she's going to take it. Listen to me. It's not right. It doesn't belong there." Then I looked at Ezra. "It's injured," I said.

She shot me an icy stare, then laughed.

"Marjan, you're a sharp girl," she said. "Maybe you're a wolf after all. You called my bluff. Fine. Even if it's hurt, twenty million's on the table. What do you say, soldier?"

Devin was silent.

"Set it free," I said. "It's supposed to be in the wild. I know it's not your responsibility. It shouldn't be. But it is mine. So I can't let you sell it."

"Who the hell said it was up to you?" said Devin, and my heart dropped.

He looked past me, then turned back to Ezra.

"Thirty," he called out.

Before Ezra could answer, and before Devin or I could stop him, Sebastian raced to the barn and threw open the door. Inside, the unicorn was sprawled where we'd left it, its eyes groggy and unfocused.

"Get up!" Sebastian shouted. He began working at the knots that held it. "Get up, you stupid animal! Get out of here!"

Ezra and Devin watched in quiet bafflement. The unicorn, still hazy from the morphine, blinked and shifted its head. But it didn't stand up.

"Help me, Marjan!" he said. "Get the other knots! Set it free! He can't sell it if he doesn't have it!" Then, to the unicorn, "Wake up! Get on your feet!"

But the unicorn didn't move.

"Stop standing there, help me!" cried Sebastian, his voice getting more and more desperate with every word. "We need to set it free!"

But the knots weren't coming loose. Sebastian was breathing

hard. He pulled once more at the rope, then gave the unicorn a shove of frustration and collapsed in a corner of the barn. I ran to him. His face was flushed and there were tears in his eyes.

"Don't let her do it," he said through clenched teeth. "It's not right."

"It's business," said Ezra, coming up behind us. "Right or wrong, it keeps on happening."

Devin came into the barn and inspected the knots, one by one. Ezra stayed with us. I refused to look her in the eye.

"Walk with me, Marjan," she said.

"Not a chance," I said.

"You're going to want to hear what I have to tell you." She glanced down at Sebastian. "Your friend needs a minute anyway."

I looked down at Sebastian. His eyes, full of helpless rage, met mine. I saw a boy who was hurting and scared, and the eels started swimming in my stomach. I looked away, ashamed, and turned to follow Ezra out of the barn.

"You should be asking for a finder's fee," she said as we walked down the driveway.

"I don't want his money," I said.

"You might," she said. "From what I've heard."

"What's that supposed to mean?"

Ezra shrugged. "Running a clinic," she said. "Gets expensive, doesn't it."

"You're spying on my accountant, too?"

"I'm in the information business," she said. "Speaking of which, I looked up our friend Vance Cogland—he of the suspiciously similar murder circumstances."

Was this all a game to Ezra? Did she think I was just going to forget about the unicorn if she brought up my dad?

"So?"

"He's a ghost," said Ezra. "The only record of him in this world is his criminal record. Social Security, birth certificate, driver's license . . . all fake. No family. No next of kin. No friends, even. He's buried in an unmarked grave in a potter's field. There's nothing in his name. If I didn't know that he'd died, I'd never believe he existed in the first place."

"So what?"

"I believe someone has done their very best to erase him from the memory of the world," said Ezra. "And seeing how they've done a pretty good job of it, I'd say our someone is kind of powerful."

"Where's that leave us?" I asked.

"Look at your dad's finances," said Ezra. "See what doesn't make sense. Murder's almost always personal. Money, or jealousy, or fear. Your dad wasn't very scary, and unless I've got him all wrong, he wasn't messing around with someone else's girlfriend. So, follow the money."

"You're making a mistake," I said. "The unicorn—it doesn't belong down there."

"Not my problem," said Ezra.

"It could be," I said. "I mean, what if it matters—like, really matters—that it's free? What if the world goes to hell because it's not?"

"Sounds like you've been talking to the Fells," said Ezra. "I wouldn't trust them. They only make things more expensive."

"Is that all they do?" I asked.

"I'd better head back and close this deal," said Ezra. "I'll set a little something aside for you. Just in case."

She smiled, then turned and walked back up the drive, her steps crunching on the gravel.

"You do that," I said quietly. "You try to close that deal."

I was about to make things more expensive.

I don't know what Jane Glass promised Devin. He didn't say much during the call. When it was done, he handed me the phone back with a wordless nod and limped over to the porch. Sebastian, leaning on the wall of the barn, watched, a curious look on his weary, tear-streaked face.

"I'll match whatever they're offering," said Ezra. "I'll beat it. You tell me what you want."

Devin set his weight on his good leg, and held up the shotgun in two hands.

"I think my friend told you before," he said. "It's not for sale."

Ezra laughed out loud.

"I was trying to protect you," she said to me. "I was trying to save you from making a choice you might regret for the rest of your life. I don't know why I bothered."

"I'm sure you had my feelings in mind," I said.

"You should be grateful anyone cares how you feel."

"What's that supposed to mean?"

"You ever wonder why your dad never told you anything about this?" said Ezra. "Why he kept it from you? Because I've been wondering. And I think it's because he didn't trust you. And you know what? I don't blame him. I wouldn't trust you either. Something's missing with you. Something's not there, that's supposed to be, and you're the only one who can't see it."

No one spoke for a moment. I could feel Devin's eyes on me too, judging me, seeing exactly what Ezra saw. And now even Sebastian was peering right through me to that hollow place. Everyone saw it, when they looked close enough. For a second,

I wished I could see myself too. Wished I could see where the emptiness lay, where the piece was missing. But of course, even wanting that would mean that Ezra was right. So I stopped wanting it and glared at her.

"Well," I said, "I think you're a terrible investigator."

She laughed, because of course I was wrong, and she was right, and somehow I'd just proven it.

"Good luck, Marjan," she said. "With everything."

Ezra was long gone when the Fells arrived fifteen minutes later: the silver van I'd seen before, followed by a pale blue hybrid. They came up the drive, one after the other, and stopped in front of Devin's house. The siblings got out of the van and didn't say a word to anyone, just stood there, taking in Devin, me, Sebastian, and the farm, with quick, hungry flicks of their eyes.

The driver of the hybrid got out. It was the same driver who'd taken me to meet Jane Glass. Even though he was kind of terrifying, I felt a sense of relief at seeing another familiar face. He glanced at me and broke character long enough to give me a nod that seemed genuinely respectful. I was sure I didn't deserve it, but I returned it as best I could. Then the passenger door opened, and Jane stepped out.

"You must be Devin," she said with a warm, friendly smile. She walked right up to him and gave him a big, earnest hug. "We're so honored to meet you."

Other than her, the Fells didn't seem particularly honored. The siblings were watching the road, and Jane's driver was standing away from everyone else, a wary look on his face.

"Who are they?" said Devin, motioning to the siblings.

"They're going to help you," said Jane, releasing Devin from her arms. "Until this is settled in the way that we settle these kinds of arrangements, they're going to keep an eye on things here." When she saw Devin's uncertainty, she lowered her voice. "They look feral. But they're okay. Most of the time, you won't even know they're here."

The woman smiled a wan, shallow smile that vanished as quickly as it had appeared. I raised a feeble hand in reply.

"I'd love to see it," said Jane. "May I?"

Devin glanced at me, and I nodded. He opened the door to the barn. The dusty darkness yawned out. The unicorn wrenched itself up to stand, proud and pitiful in its bindings. Jane gasped.

"It's beautiful," she whispered.

"It's injured," I said. "But the wounds are clean."

"I'm sure they are," said Jane. "We'll see that it gets the care it needs." The siblings both nodded—simple, competent nods that told me they knew exactly how to handle these kinds of things.

Devin pushed the door shut. "What happens now?" he asked.

"For the time being, keep on doing exactly what you've been doing," said Jane. "Don't change anything. When we're ready, we'll let you know. And then we'll take it off your hands. In the meantime, Molly and Luke are here to help. You're very lucky. You've been given an incredible gift. You've seen something almost no one ever gets to see. Your work now, and maybe for the rest of your life, is to understand why."

She gave him another hug, and then turned and walked back toward her car. She motioned for me to join her.

"Is it always like this?" I asked.

"It never feels quite right until it's all done," she said. "And then it does. You'll see."

"What did you tell him?" I said.

"Some people are afraid of the responsibility," she said. "They're looking for someone to make it go away. Some people only want the money." She paused. "For most people, though, this is a moment that defines their whole lives. They just want to know that there's a reason for it. They want it to mean something."

I looked back at Devin. He was leaning against the wall of the barn.

"Will he be okay?"

"He'll be confused for a while," she said, "but he'll find his bearings. He did the right thing, and now he's part of something bigger than himself. Some people need that in their lives. Just a guess, but I think he's one of those people."

She opened the door to the car, and got in.

"Jane?"

"Yes?"

"Did I do the right thing?"

She smiled.

"I'll see you at the auction," she said.

CHAPTER TWENTY-THREE

LUBBOCK

Sebastian drove us back to the airport. Those final minutes— the traffic lights, the stop signs, the road ahead growing ever shorter—felt precious, a treasure that was slipping away with every moment. But neither of us really knew what to say. When I looked at him, all I wanted was to reel back time, to the moment when it was just him and me and the sleeping unicorn, and I hadn't seen his pain, and he hadn't seen my emptiness. Those few seconds felt left behind and unfinished. Something had been starting to happen. Something had been coming alive, before Ezra showed up.

"I was a bit mad, wasn't I?" he said. "Running in there like that."

"You were brave," I said.

"Foolish, more like."

"If you hadn't done that," I said, "I wouldn't have been able to stop her."

"That's very generous," he said.

We were quiet for a moment, both of us lost in the things that had just happened.

"What she said about you," said Sebastian at last.

"Don't," I said. "You don't need to say anything."

He didn't protest, and so I knew he believed her.

"And now there's to be an auction," said Sebastian.

"It was the best I could do."

"Maybe Uncle Simon could place a bid."

"Maybe," I said. "I have no idea how it works."

At the airport, we arranged flights for both of us to our respective destinations, and when Sebastian's plane was ready to leave, he gave me a big, clumsy hug goodbye.

"You really were brave," I said.

The words felt small. I wished I hadn't said them. I wished I'd told him how I really felt: like for a few moments, the air around us had shimmered with gold; like we'd breathed something priceless and rare and warm into our chests; and, like breath, we hadn't been able to hold on to it.

Instead I kissed him on the cheek, which was warm and smooth, and for a second I wanted more, and for another second that wanting battled with shame and regret, for how far I'd brought this boy, for how much trouble I'd caused him, for how strangely things had gone. By the third second, all I could feel was awful.

Sebastian smiled and touched my hand.

"Somehow," he said, "I feel like I've ruined everything."

"You haven't," I said. Not a lie.

On the way home, I scrolled through messages I'd missed or ignored. Another text from Grace. Another message from David. A call from the clinic. And a note from Ezra:

Follow the money.

I still couldn't bring myself to hate Ezra. At least she was honest about her treachery. At least she didn't apologize.

• • •

I went to school the next day, which felt like a mistake.

Grace and Carrie peppered me with questions I didn't have good answers to—where had I been? Was anything wrong? Was I okay? I told them I'd been sick, which I don't think either one of them believed. Carrie was too polite to admit it, but as soon as she was gone (swim rally—the team was still undefeated), Grace grabbed my sleeve and glared at me.

"You're full of crap, Mar," she said. "I don't know why you're lying, but you're not fooling me. What's going on?"

I didn't have a good answer to that, either. I jerked my arm away and glared back, and then stormed off.

After school, I took a bus to David Ginn's office. I spotted him in the hallway, fussing with his door. He didn't see me, and for a moment I watched him. His shoulders hunched wearily, and he gave a frustrated sigh as he tried to get a sticky lock to turn. After a minute or so, he noticed me, so I waved and pretended I'd just gotten there. His face brightened, and the slump in his shoulders relaxed.

"Marjan!" he exclaimed. "I was worried. Is everything okay?" I nodded and smiled as best I could. Everything wasn't okay, but I wasn't about to try to explain. He sighed in relief. "It's good you came. We have work to do."

"I know," I said. "I actually came for something else, but we can talk about the payroll thing, too. I wanted to take a look at some of my dad's old records."

"The 'payroll thing' is pretty important." With a comical heave, he opened the door.

Twenty minutes later, we'd canceled some inventory orders and decided to let the next installment on the X-ray machine go unpaid until business equalized. If it equalized.

"Is it always like this?" I asked. "Like, for my dad. Has it always been like this?"

"There are always hard choices, if that's what you mean," he said.

"How did he get through all the hard choices?" I asked.

"Well," said David, "running a business—any business, but especially a small business—you have to believe in it. You have to believe in it so much that other people believe in it too, even if there's really nothing there. Even if it's just an illusion. It's a bit like magic."

"That's it?" I said. "That's how he avoided going bankrupt? He *believed*?"

David sighed. "Sometimes we moved things around," he said. "A little misdirection. Let a few payments slide so we could make others, and held on tight. And sometimes even magic wasn't enough, and Jim put his own money in."

"His own money?"

"A few times," said David.

"Where'd it come from? His money?"

"I never asked," said David, "and he never told me."

"I want to see," I said. "I want to see everything you have from him. Everything you have from the clinic, as far back as you can go."

David exhaled heavily, shaking his head.

"That'll take a little time, Marjan," he said. "And I don't know what you'll learn from it that you don't already know."

Half an hour later, David and I emerged from his building with three legal boxes stuffed full of receipts, and a stack of ledger books.

"Slow day here," he said. "How about I drive you home?"

We loaded the boxes into the back of his car, and then I got into the passenger seat.

"David," I said, once we were driving, "can I ask you something?"

"Of course," he said.

"How did you manage to stay friends with my dad for so long? I think . . . I think maybe when he died, you were the only friend he had left. He drove everyone else away, but not you."

"He needed me," he said. "If I hadn't been there, the clinic would have gone under, six or seven different times. But also, I'd say we found each other at exactly the right time. Sometimes people come along, and they're exactly who you need."

"But what did you get out of it?" I asked.

David considered this for a moment.

"Other than a friend?" he said finally. "It's something, knowing that you're useful, that you're making a difference in a person's life. Most clients, eleven months of the year, they just forget you're there. But with your dad, I could always help. And I guess that's what I got out of it." He paused, like he was considering whether to say what was on his mind. "You know, one of the last times I talked to Jim, he said he was going to make things right."

"What do you mean?" I asked.

"Look," said David. "It's not my business, but I know things weren't always smooth between you two. I assumed that's what he meant. I guess he never got the chance . . ."

"No," I said, "he never did."

"I'm sorry to hear that," said David.

"David," I said, "do you know why my dad left Iran?"

"He never told you?"

"I never asked," I said. "I just kind of assumed he came here for school. But it's a long way to go, just for school. And I don't think he ever went back."

"It must have been hard," said David, "learning to live in a place that was so different. I can't imagine what it would be like, changing everything that much, that quickly."

"Did he ever talk to you about it?"

"He kept a lot of things to himself," said David. "I think he didn't want to be seen as 'too Iranian,' whatever that might mean. And maybe he just closed off that part of himself to everyone he knew here. Sometimes people do that. Just put a whole part of themselves into a box and try to forget about it. I wish he'd shared more, with all of us."

I hesitated before asking my next question.

"Did he ever say anything about Ithaca?" I asked.

David shook his head, doubtful. "That doesn't sound familiar."

"And what about . . ." I paused again. I had the unnerving sensation of two worlds drifting together before my eyes. "Vance Cogland? Does that name mean anything to you?"

Again, a moment of frowning and searching, followed by the sad shake of the head. "I don't think so. I'm pretty sure I'd remember that name."

When we got to my house, he pulled into the driveway and we unloaded the boxes. After they were stacked on the front doorstep, he clapped the trunk of the car shut, a kind of closing punctuation, then opened his arms and gave me a hug.

"Come by our place sometime, okay?" he said into my shoulder. "Dinner."

I started with the ledger books. I went page by page, running my finger down the credit column. Any suspicious amount, I made a note of the date. When I'd gone through them all, I'd found a dozen or so payments into the clinic that were either unidentified or labeled as CASH.

Next I dumped the boxes out onto the floor of the living room. The papers settled into three piles that spread out several feet in each direction. I brewed a pot of coffee and began to sort through them, one by one. Malloryn was at work, but Zorro watched me with interest.

The papers went back to when David had first started with us. They were mostly receipts from the vendors you'd expect to see for a veterinarian's clinic. Prescription orders from pharmaceutical suppliers. Client receipts. Electrical bills. Gas receipts.

It was slow and frustrating work. I wasted a lot of time squinting at words that were too faded to make out. But I was able to cross-reference a few of the suspect credits with perfectly ordinary clinic procedures.

After I'd sifted through one pile of rat-eaten papers, I wanted to give up. It didn't feel like I was any nearer to answers. I wasn't sure I would find anything other than paper cuts and toxic mold. So far, following the money had gotten me nowhere—mainly because there was so little money to follow.

Still, I stuffed all the sorted papers into a big garbage bag and moved on to the next pile. An hour later, I had cleared the second pile and settled into the final stack. If there was any money trail to follow, it would have to start here. I picked up the first receipt and looked at the date, and a wave of nausea rushed over me.

It was a medical bill. These were documents from the year my mom died.

The bill, printed on the hospital's sterile letterhead, unlocked a flood of images. The awful linoleum tiles in the waiting rooms, puke-green and striated like slices of liverwurst. The large-format photos of mountain streams and lush forests that lined the hallways. The patterns of holes in the drop-ceiling panels in the room where my mother lay. The translucent quality of her skin.

I felt a heaviness in my guts, remembering the crushing sameness of her days there. There was no rest, no comfort. The chairs were too hard and narrow. The sheets and blankets were too thin and too rough. Every surface felt vaguely hostile. Always, something was buzzing, or humming, or clicking, or beeping.

Some days we stayed for hours. I did homework in the corner of the room, sometimes hunched in a chair, sometimes sitting on my jacket on the disgusting linoleum floor, and my mom read books that my dad had brought for her. Sometimes we talked, and sometimes my dad went out to the Chinese restaurant down the road from the hospital and brought back chow mein and egg rolls with sweet-and-sour sauce for me to eat outside in the lobby. And some days someone came and picked me up—a friend, one of the techs from the clinic—and my dad stayed behind.

I hadn't thought about any of this in years. I hadn't touched those feelings, and now they felt huge and unfamiliar inside me. I threw the bill away, shoved it down deep into the trash bag, wished I'd never laid eyes on it. I tore into the final pile, my focus sharp and furious and relentless. And halfway through, I found something.

A single, crumpled receipt from the OK Diner on Fiftieth Street in Lubbock, Texas. A cup of coffee, a plate of fries. Time-stamped 3:15 a.m., three months after Mom died, and a day before Vance Cogland's body was discovered in the back of his pawnshop.

I thought a lot that night about my dad, and all the secrets he'd taken with him. What had he meant, when he'd told David that he wanted to make things right? Did it have anything to do with five un-accounted-for payments into the clinic, all coming at times when the business was on the brink of collapse? Was it related to the death of Vance Cogland? Did he really want to somehow reconcile things with me, and if so, what did that even mean? Or was he talking about the restless beast churning the floor inside that barn in Ithaca?

I wondered about the money. Had it come from people like the Stoddards? Or had it come from people like Horatio, or the Fells? I'd always thought he was at least an honorable doctor, but how honorable had he really been? What lay at the end of the money trail, and would it bring me closer to finding his killer?

I wondered what it was that had brought Vance Cogland and my dad together. I wondered if my dad had been there when Cogland had died. I wondered, for a brief moment, if my dad had killed him. I couldn't imagine my dad as a killer, but the more I saw of his world, the more I realized how little I'd ever understood him.

I thought about Malloryn, too, sleeping down the hall, who had never stopped believing that the spirits would smile on her spells. Was that what it would take for me, if I wanted the clinic to survive? Would I have to become someone like her, married to unwavering faith? *Could* I, even if I really wanted to, become that person?

I thought of Sebastian. The feelings I had for him became more complicated as time passed, more confusing. His heart seemed so large, so clear, so vulnerable. I was going to break it—I could feel it coming. I dreaded it.

And I thought of my friends, my teachers, the faces I saw every day. I was aware of how many things I didn't know about them. There were whole lives behind them, full of invisible wonders and struggles, and maybe monsters.

A thought occurred to me. Eight years ago, Jane Glass had told me, something had woken up. Eight years ago, my dad had been in Lubbock. Had Vance Cogland's murder been the signal? Had there been a creature in the room that day, with my dad and Cogland? And if so, what did that mean?

On the hazy border of sleep, I felt the unicorn's wild power echoing: a twitch in my knees, a sudden rush of my heart that made me sit up. It was in me. It had always been there, but it was alive now. It was running.

I wondered, half dreaming, if you could shoot an arrow through time and hit that moment in the clearing, when a girl pried open a hunter's trap. I wondered what that arrow's path would look like, and what other moments it would have to pass through, to get from here to there. I wondered what it meant that I, of all people, was the one firing the arrow.

CHAPTER TWENTY-FOUR

THE TEA SHOP

The next morning, I took a picture of the Lubbock receipt and sent it to Ezra, along with the message:

He was there.

A moment later, the phone rang.

"Looks like your dad witnessed a murder," said Ezra. "At the very least."

"What's that supposed to mean?" I said.

"Do the math, Marjan."

"My dad wasn't a killer," I said.

"Probably not," said Ezra. "But he knew one."

"There's something else," I said. I told her about the five mystery cash infusions.

"Dates and amounts," she said.

I gave her all the information I had. At the other end of the line, silence.

"Ezra?" I said. "Are you still there?"

"Yes," she said.

Even though she was the one who'd had me followed, even though she had almost stolen the unicorn out from under me, I felt a twinge of regret, like I'd somehow betrayed *her* by calling in the Fells.

"I'm . . . ," I started to say.

"Don't be," she said. "All's fair."

"Are you sure?"

"We're not friends," she said. "I'm doing a job. And I'm going to keep doing it. Whether you like it or not."

The line went dead.

The car was idling in front of school when my classes ended that afternoon. There was no telling how long it had been there. When I approached, the driver looked up, and I recognized Sam.

"Hi, Marjan!" he said, flashing a bright, friendly smile.

"Uh, hey, Sam," I said. "What's going on?"

"Here to pick you up."

"Where are we going?" I asked. I checked my phone quickly. There were no messages about incontinent gnomes.

"Horatio wants to see you," he said. "He's in the city today."

Grace and Carrie were talking under a tree nearby. I could feel them watching me.

It's nothing—just a friend of my dad's.

"Hey, Sam?" I said.

"Yep?" Big, easy smile.

"Am I in trouble?"

He looked at me with a puzzled expression. "Why would you be in trouble?" he asked.

After considering screaming for help, I decided that I would be honest about what had happened, and trust that Horatio would understand. He had enough animals already, didn't he? He couldn't possibly care that much about one more.

Sam got out and opened a door for me, and then hopped back into the driver's seat. Grace and Carrie watched me drive off, questions filling their eyes. I waved as we passed. I could feel my life getting more and more different from theirs, by the day.

We drove across the Bay Bridge and into the city. Sam was polite and chatty, but I didn't have much to say. When we arrived at our destination—one of the fancy downtown hotels—I was restless and a little queasy.

"He's waiting at the bar," said Sam as he dropped me off.

The afternoon bar scene at the hotel consisted of overly eager men and women talking shop and trading business cards, all of them wearing the lanyard of some professional confer- ence. I spotted Horatio instantly. He'd secured a booth table in the far corner of the bar, and he was nursing a tall glass of what looked like soda water. The tables on either side of him were empty. He cocked his chin up at me and raised the glass in my direction. Then he motioned for me to sit across from him.

"You've talked to the Fells," he said. He didn't seem too wor- ried about anyone overhearing. "The walls here are a special acoustic design. Conversations don't go anywhere. All you hear is this hum."

He stopped talking so that I could listen.

"They say it makes a constant pitch," he continued. "But I doubt anyone's checking. Sometimes a good story's all you need." He paused. "I'm sure the Fells told you they keep the balance. Is that right?"

"Uh, yeah . . ."

"It gives a noble cast to their true purpose."

"Which is?"

"Control," said Horatio. "They want to control these

animals. All of them. And they have, for a long time. And now they don't, and it terrifies them."

"How do they control them? I mean, they don't *have* them."

"They know where to find them. That's a lot of power, if you know how to use it. And they've been using it for hundreds of years. Did they happen to tell you about the Master Index?"

"What's that?" I said.

"It's a number," said Horatio, "derived from about a thousand different factors. Some are obvious—GDP of this or that nation, total cash in circulation, stock price of this or that company. Some are less intuitive—the average happiness level or health of an average citizen of such and such country. And some—the really fun ones—require an intimate knowledge of these creatures' well-being and whereabouts."

"What's so special about the Index?"

Horatio smiled. "It might be the single best metric of the human condition that's ever been formulated. But that's not why the Fells developed it. And it's not how they use it." He leaned in closer and lowered his voice. "It's an oracle," he said. "If you bet the Index, you get rich." He smiled again, and looked around. "But it only works if you know where they are."

"Then it's not true? The balance?"

"There's some truth, of course. Enough to excuse a lot of bad behavior."

"How do you know all this?"

He grinned proudly. "How do you think the Fells analyze all that data they collect?"

"You've been using your software to spy on them," I said. Horatio put a finger to his lips.

"It's important for you to know that the Fells are not your

friends." He paused. "And despite what's happened the last few days, *I* would still like to be."

"So you're not mad at me."

"I understand what you did," said Horatio. "I'm sure Ezra does too."

I hoped Ezra wasn't in too much trouble over losing the unicorn.

"This wasn't her fault," I said.

"We both underestimated you," said Horatio. He smiled again and held up his glass. "Sam will take you home now. I'm glad we had this little chat."

I left the meeting with a chill on my skin. I had the sense, deep down, that something very important had gone very wrong. And that, somehow, it was all my fault.

But as the days went by, the dread began to fade. Nothing bad happened, and it started to feel like nothing bad would happen. In fact, it almost felt like good things were starting to happen. We had a decent month at the clinic. Zorro took his first dose of Immiticide like a champ. I passed all my finals.

To celebrate the start of winter break, Carrie, Grace, and I piled into the Blue Whale and drove up into the hills to Tilden Park on a chilly afternoon. We had a picnic overlooking the bay as the sun set. As we drove back down, the frigid air howled through the open windows, blasting us from all directions until our faces ached. We cursed the musty smell of the Blue Whale, and laughed.

Malloryn and I had already decided that Christmas would not be a big deal this year. However, no self-respecting witch would let the winter solstice pass unobserved. On Midwinter's Eve, Malloryn made hot cider and sweet buns. I invited

Francesca Wix from next door, and she brought persimmons from the tree in her backyard.

"I read that it's a Persian tradition to enjoy them on the solstice," Francesca said.

"My dad wasn't very traditional," I said. "But he did like persimmons."

As the house filled with the warming smells of cloves and baking bread, the three of us ate and drank to the ending of the season.

Malloryn lit candles around the house and turned off the lights so that we could feel a bit more of the darkness of this darkest of nights. We took turns reading poems about winter—"The Shortest Day" by Susan Cooper, "To Know the Dark" by Wendell Berry, "Spellbound" by Emily Brontë. By candlelight, and by the sounds of our voices in the quiet house, the world seemed much older. The words made the night deeper, the cider warmer, the persimmons sweeter, the air outside colder.

It wasn't magic, but it was a spell.

After we'd each read a poem, and after we'd sat a few minutes with the ancient silence we'd conjured, Francesca said good night and went home to put her dogs to bed. Malloryn excused herself to call her family. And I went upstairs and sat in my father's bedroom.

A mug of cider cupped in my hands, the muffled words of Malloryn talking in gentle tones with her parents, the icy memory of rushing down the hillside with Grace and Carrie—the world was beginning to feel comfortable. I could sit in the flickering darkness with my father's absence and not feel all-consuming rage.

The bright aftertaste of persimmon glowed inside me,

honey-sweet. Did I remember that taste, somewhere in my bones, from another life, somewhere back up the Hyrcanian Line? Or did some moments just exist in a different way: *A girl eats persimmons on the darkest night of the year.*

Maybe the last time, there was tea brewing in the samovar. Maybe a family was huddled around a hearth fire. Maybe the moon was rising over Damavand. Maybe the stars were reflected in the waters of the Caspian.

All those places and moments seemed far away, but now I felt connected to them—to the people who had lived them, up and down the long reach of the Hyrcanian Line.

This is your culture, Marjan.

I didn't know what I was supposed to be. Who my ancestors were. They were ghosts to me—imaginary people without names, without faces, in a land I'd never seen.

But a persimmon tastes the same everywhere.

On the second day of the new year, Jane Glass called.

"Auction's today," she said. She sounded a bit flustered.

"I would have appreciated some advance warning," I said.

Jane didn't respond to that, but I got the feeling from her tone that she would have too.

The driver with the scary tattoos came to pick me up from the office. I thought of Horatio's warning, but I wanted to see this all the way through. And I had some questions for Jane, or whoever would listen. The driver gave the faintest hint of a smirk as he handed me the hood to put over my head.

"We're still doing this?" I asked.

He shrugged and said nothing. I put the hood over my head.

We drove for a while. The driver didn't say anything, and I didn't much feel like talking with a bag on my head. At last the car came to a stop, and the door opened. I felt sunshine, and I heard the sounds of birds. I stepped out onto rough dirt, and the driver lifted the hood from my head.

I stood at the end of a narrow, lonely road that curved away around hills bristling with dry grass and shrubs. Up ahead, in a dirt clearing near the twisting trunk of a dusty oak tree, was a double-wide with vinyl siding and frosted windows, the kind of bland, industrial trailer you'd see at a construction site. The vinyl was faded and cracking in places. A deep dent hadn't been repaired. One of the windows had fallen out or been smashed, and the hole was covered with a piece of plywood. A few assorted cars were parked at odd angles nearby. None of them was remarkable in any way, and none of them had license plates. Other than my driver, there was no one in sight, and not a sound in the air other than the ordinary sounds of nature.

"In there?" I asked. The driver nodded, but he didn't move. "Are you coming?" I asked.

He shook his head.

I took a step toward the trailer, and as I did, the door to the double-wide creaked out from its frame, just an inch. It hung there, an open question wobbling on flimsy hinges.

"Hello?" I said. My voice felt tiny among the hills. The word seemed to sink right into the whispering grass. No one answered.

My heart skipped, but I kept my calm. Whatever happened, I reminded myself, I was here for answers, and one way or another, I'd get them. I took a long breath, then strode across the dirt and tire-flattened grass to the trailer, opened the door, and walked in.

The inside of the trailer was cheap, tacky, and unloved. There were lights in the ceiling, faintly green and a little too bright. The floor was a smooth, plasticky tile with grimy seams. The walls were fake wood panels. A long folding table had been placed in the center of the trailer, and around it several black folding chairs.

At the far end of the table stood Jane Glass, who waved me over. Seated at the table was a small man with dark brown skin and squinty eyes behind round spectacles. Beside him was a woman with thick, curly hair dyed a garish maroon color, and too much blush on her pallid cheeks. On the other side sat another man with a thin beard and a tan complexion. All three of them were dressed in clothes that looked both expensive and shabby. All three were older than my dad. In the center of the table was an ancient-looking teapot made of dull black iron. Stationed near the door, almost crowding it, were two very large men who watched me with cold, expressionless eyes.

"Sit," said Jane.

One of the big men pulled out a chair, and I sat. Jane Glass sat too, beside the man with the beard. Somehow they all seemed to be on the other side of the table from me, like I'd just walked into a particularly sadistic job interview. They were all looking at me.

"So this is the Tea Shop," I said.

The woman with the curly hair laughed out loud, a cold, sharp laugh like the stab of a dagger.

"I hate that name," said Jane. "There hasn't been a tea shop for a long time."

"You can't possibly all be related," I said.

"You understand family as an accident of circumstance," said the dark-skinned man. His voice was deep and severe, every syllable sculpted with ponderous care. "Guided, perhaps, by cultural expectations or personal aspirations, but ultimately, an accident." He paused. "Ours has been most deliberate."

"You're very lucky to be here, young lady," said the bearded man to me. He spoke with an accent I couldn't place. "This isn't something most people get to see."

"Jane was quite insistent," said the woman in a patronizing tone. "She wouldn't take no."

"I told them they wouldn't get the unicorn unless they let you observe," said Jane.

"Who was it again that said the auction committee could use some new blood?" asked the bearded one.

"Don't look at me," said the woman. "I still think she cheated on the test."

"I'll take it again, and I'll ace it again," said Jane, in a voice that made me just a little bit proud to be sitting next to her. "Maybe you should too."

"In any case, here we are," said the small man. "Shall we begin?"

The bearded man reached into the pocket of his old jacket, and when he drew his hand out, he was holding a thin envelope made of leather. A hush fell over the room.

Jane slid her chair down to my side of the table.

"Those are bids," she said. "Buyers submit them at bidding houses. The field-workers collect them, and we decide who wins."

He opened the flap of the envelope. Inside were several plastic baggies, each one containing a scrap of paper. He took them out and laid them on the table in front of the teapot. Each bagged-up piece of paper had a reddish-brown dot on it.

"That's blood," I said.

"Of course it is," said Jane. "How else would we be sure?"

"Sure of what?"

"You'll see."

The small man reached into the envelope and produced a thin pair of silver tweezers. He slid the tweezers into one of the baggies, gripped the scrap of paper, and drew it out. Jane Glass had gone silent. She watched with rapt attention as he grasped the lid of the teapot with his free hand and opened it, just a crack. He slid the tweezers in and dropped the scrap of paper into the pot. Then he drew out the tweezers and shut the lid as quickly as he could.

"Rubicon," he said.

Everyone watched the teapot. It looked as if it had been hammered by hand from a dull, heavy iron. Its surface was battered and scratched, and there was something not exactly right about its dimensions. Its shape had a slight wobble to it, and it was just a bit larger than would be practical for a teapot. It had a worn wooden handle and a curved spout.

A sound, something like a match being struck, seemed to echo from within the teapot. I heard Jane Glass sigh in disappointment, and the old man uttered a swear word under his breath. A moment later, a puff of dark smoke billowed up from the spout of the teapot.

"Not that one," said the old man.

"It'd be easy to just accept the highest bid," said Jane. "Profitable, too. There's no one watching over us. We're the final authority. The only authority. And people are willing to pay . . ." She shook her head in disbelief.

"How much was that bid?" I whispered. "The one you just rejected."

"Four billion dollars," said the woman with the maroon hair. The two men shared a rueful glance.

"Why was it rejected?" I asked. "What just happened?"

"You ask too many questions," said the bearded man without looking up.

"No, she doesn't," said Jane. The old man shot a cautious look across the table. "She's a Hyrcanian," she continued. "She should know." Then she turn
ed to me. "Inside that teapot," she said, "is a dragon."

"A dragon?" I said.

For a moment, no one spoke. A thin, secondary wisp of ash sputtered up from the teapot, as if to emphasize the rejection. The elder Fells shared an uncomfortable look among themselves. Jane sat forward, utterly unruffled.

"Aunt Clara," she said, "you tell it the best."

The woman with maroon hair bristled at the sound of her name. She glanced at the others, who nodded with reluctant resignation. Then she puffed up a bit in pride and cleared her throat.

CHAPTER TWENTY-FIVE

THE YOUNG MAN WHO BOUGHT A DRAGON

Once upon a time, there was a young man who was born to hard times. His mother was his only family, but she died when he was young, and he had to make his way in the world alone.

This young man made a meager living for himself selling rabbit pelts at the town market. His mother had taught him to trap rabbits in the fields outside of town with a box and a stick. Every week, he brought his skins to the market. At best he was able to put bread in his belly and a meager pillow under his head. Many days, he went hungry, and many nights he slept curled up on the cobbles, or against a stone, or nestled in the roots of some old tree.

Before she died, the young man's mother had given him her entire fortune—five pieces of copper—and told him to use it to better his lot in life. Five pieces of copper didn't amount to much, even in those days, but the young man guarded them as if they were the world's greatest riches.

For years he was tempted to spend his tiny treasure. He lingered many times over the rows of juicy sausages in the windows of butcher shops, and the trays of steaming pastries in the windows of bakeries. He lay many nights on the hard ground, dreaming of the sausages and hot pastries that five copper pieces would buy, and wincing at every painful grumble of his empty belly. But even when he hadn't eaten for days and the sausages were whispering his name in sweet, smoky tones from behind the glass, he never gave in to their temptation, nor any other.

And then one market day, an old woman rode into town on a wooden cart drawn by two browbeaten old donkeys. The old woman parked her cart in the town square and set up a little stall of crystals and baubles and other shimmering trinkets. The flash of a silver mirror caught the young man's eye from across the square, and he came across the plaza to gaze at the woman's strange wares.

"A fine sigil for a fine young man?" she said, offering him a pewter necklace with an unfamiliar symbol engraved on it. "To ward off evil spirits?"

"I don't think I can afford such a thing," said the young man. "And anyway, I've never seen any evil spirits."

"A bag, then," said the woman, holding up a sturdy knapsack of stitched leather. "A bag with no bottom. Carry the whole world with you if you so desire."

"I'm sure I can't afford that," said the young man. "And besides, I would have nothing to put in it."

"A watch, then," she said. "If you set it ahead, it will tell you the future."

"The future is of no use to me today," said the young man. "And the sun in the sky is the only watch I need."

"A crystal," she said, offering up a block of translucent quartz. "Its facets will reveal a man's deepest wishes."

"If a man wishes something deeply enough, he will ask," said the young man.

"Perhaps," said the old woman.

At that moment, the young man spied an old iron teapot, hung from a wooden peg on the old woman's wagon. It was a sturdy old pot with a heavy lid. There was nothing fancy or special about it, but the young man couldn't take his eyes from it. The old woman followed his gaze, and without a word, she brought the teapot down and set it before him.

"What is it?" asked the young man.

The old woman glanced left and right, and then leaned in close. "There is a dragon inside this teapot," she whispered. "It is wiser than all the wisest men and women in the kingdom, and it will bring great prosperity and purpose to whoever possesses it."

The young man looked around at the old woman's burdened donkeys and battered wagon, and was doubtful.

"Pardon me for saying so," said the young man, "but you do not seem to have benefited from possessing it."

The old woman smiled. "Well observed," she said. "But I do not possess it. I am merely carrying it until it finds its proper owner."

The young man was still skeptical.

"It seems a very small place to keep a dragon," he said.

"It is a very small dragon," said the old woman.

"Can I see it?" he asked.

"If you open the teapot more than a crack," said the old woman, "then the dragon will escape. But here." She took his hand and placed it against the iron. "You can feel it." Sure enough, the pot felt warm to the touch, like a small flame was burning inside.

"Is it for sale?" asked the young man. He was certain he could not afford such a thing, and he wasn't at all sure what he would do with a dragon in a teapot. But he was captivated by its presence, and he knew from his years at the market that it never hurts to ask if a thing is for sale.

"It could be," said the old woman. "To the right person."

"And who," asked the young man, "is the right person?"

At this the old woman smiled and drew a long silver needle from the folds of her robes. "That is for the dragon to decide," she said. And with her free hand, she reached across her table and grabbed the young man by the wrist. Her grip was surprisingly strong, and try as he might, he couldn't pull free. She pricked his palm with the needle, and caught the blood with a scrap of parchment. Then she released her grip and set the needle down.

"What did you do that for?" demanded the young man.

The old woman didn't answer. Instead she rolled up the scrap of parchment between her fingers. She lifted the lid of the teapot just a tiny crack, slid the blood-dabbed paper into the darkness, and then shut the lid again.

It seemed that nothing happened. The teapot was still. But the young man had the faintest impression that something inside it had stirred.

"Well, well," said the old woman. Then she offered him the teapot for the price of five copper pieces.

The young man hesitated. "Surely a teapot with a tiny dragon inside should be worth much more than five copper pieces," he said.

"It is," said the old woman. "You will pay its true value in ways you cannot yet imagine. But my service is worth five pieces of copper, and I shall take no more, and no less."

"You told me the dragon would bring prosperity," said the young man. "Now you tell me it will cost me. What am I to believe?"

"It will bring you prosperity, and it will cost you," said the old woman. "You will know a great purpose, and you will be richly rewarded. But your work will never end, so long as your blood is quick."

The young man considered this. He hesitated to risk his entire fortune on the old woman's teapot. But he had no fear of hard work, and he craved a purpose to his life. And he had promised his mother that he would use her treasure to better his lot. Perhaps this would be his best chance.

"Very well," he said. "I'll take it."

He handed over his five copper pieces.

"You've made a brave choice," said the old woman. "What is your name, young man?"

"It's Fell," he said. "Lucien Fell."

"Master Fell," she said, "the dragon is yours."

CHAPTER TWENTY-SIX

FULFILLMENT

"So the dragon decides?" I asked.

"The dragon decides," said Jane. She wasn't looking at me, though. She was looking across the table at the elders.

"Let's just say his opinion matters," said the small man.

"That's why you Hyrcanians are so important to us," said Jane. "Nothing can ever happen to the dragon. It's the soul of the Fells. If it suffers, we suffer. If it dies, we're finished."

The small man held up his tweezers and clicked them together twice in the air—*snap, snap.* Then he took the second piece of paper and slipped it into the teapot.

"Declination," he announced.

Again, almost immediately, there came the echoey sound of a match striking, and a puff of smoke from the spout.

The bearded man shook his head. "He's in a foul mood," he said.

"He doesn't have patience for bad buyers." All eyes in the room turned to me. I wasn't sure exactly how I knew this, but I knew it. "I wouldn't either," I added.

Aunt Clara nodded, impressed. "Maybe you should have

been a Fell," she said. "It's not too late. I have a nephew I could introduce you to."

"No thanks," I said.

"At least think about it," she said. "Our families, together. We'd make a good team."

"That's enough, Aunt Clara," said Jane.

The woman snorted. "Your generation is far too precious, my dear," she said. "Marriages were meant to be arranged."

"What happens if the dragon rejects all your bidders?" I asked.

"Then there's no sale," said Jane. "And we keep looking for the right buyer."

"The Index," I said. "It's all about the Index."

The bearded man laughed now, a hollow laugh with no joy.

"You seem to know quite a bit about us," said the small man.

"It's all about finding the right buyer," said Jane.

"She's right, of course," said the small man. "The Index is a happy side effect of our good work. Not the purpose of it."

"We are men and women of honor," said the bearded man. I noticed that he didn't look at anyone when he said it.

The small man glowered at his companion for a moment, then tweezered out another scrap of paper and slid it under the lid.

"Lucent," he said.

Poof!

"Tsk," said the bearded man.

"What's with the funny words?" I asked Jane.

"Code names," said Jane. "The bids are anonymous, to preserve the integrity."

"Zephyr," said the small man. Another scrap. Another wisp of smoke.

A single scrap of paper remained on the table. The elders all looked at each other, and the small man set the tweezers down.

"What are you doing?" asked Jane.

The small man glared at Jane. His good humor and patience were gone. There was a pure, cold darkness in his eyes. With a sigh, he took up the tweezers again.

"Caraval," he said.

And then the match strike.

And then the smoke.

There was a long silence in the room.

"The dragon didn't choose anyone," I said. "What happens now?"

No one answered. The bearded man shifted uncomfortably in his seat and refused to make eye contact with me.

"Perhaps," said the small man, "it's time your friend leaves."

Jane looked from one face to the next. "No," she said. "God damn it, no!"

"There's no need for a scene," said Aunt Clara.

"Your aunt's right," said the bearded man. "The less said, the better."

"It was a pleasure meeting you, Ms. Dastani," said the small man. I felt someone pulling at my chair. One of the big, silent men in the shadows.

"No," snapped Jane, and the big man froze. "She stays. I want her to hear this. I want her to see."

No one spoke. The bearded man looked across the table at Aunt Clara.

"Don't look at me," she said. "I didn't raise her."

"What's going on?" I said to Jane. "What just happened?"

"What happened," said Jane, through clenched teeth, "is that they're taking the money. The dragon didn't decide, so they're going to take the highest price."

"Hang on," I said. "What if there was one more bid?"

All eyes fell on me.

"And what bid would that be?" asked the bearded man.

I glared at him. "Mine," I said.

He drew back, aghast. "You're a Hyrcanian!" he said. "You can't bid!"

"Who says so?" I replied.

"She has just as much right as anyone else," said Jane. "I'll take the bid myself."

Before anyone could object, Jane drew a short knife out of her pocket, grabbed my hand, and sliced open my finger. With a tissue, she dabbed a drop of blood and wadded it up.

"How much?" she demanded. "Quickly! How much for the unicorn?"

"Uh . . ." I tried to remember how much money I had with me. "Fifty bucks?"

"It's official," said Jane in triumph. "Marjan Dastani bids fifty dollars for the unicorn."

Then she stuffed the tissue into the teapot.

"Don't I get a code name?" I asked.

"Pain in the ass," said Aunt Clara.

Then we watched.

The room was suddenly quiet, so quiet that I could hear when the tissue landed at the bottom of the teapot. And if I strained my ears, I was almost certain I could hear something else, something graceful and sleek shifting and scuttling inside that iron pot.

And then silence. No match. No smoke.

"We have a winner," said the bearded man at last. There was no joy in his voice.

Another uncomfortable silence followed.

"So it's mine?" I asked.

"That's what the dragon says," said Aunt Clara.

"Then I want it set free," I said. "Now."

No one replied.

"The dragon's not always right," said the small man.

"Men and women of honor," said Jane.

"Four billion dollars solves a lot of problems," said the bearded man, speaking in Jane's general direction. "You need to take Ms. Dastani away now."

"But . . . I won," I said. "Didn't I?" But even as I said it, I could feel the two large men coming up behind me.

"Don't touch her," said Jane, pounding her palm on the table. She stood up so fast that her chair flew out from under her. "I *knew* you were going to do this."

"Now, Jane, dear," said Aunt Clara. "It's not as if it's the first time."

"This is different," said Jane.

The elders at the table were shamed speechless, but their eyes were clear. The decision had been made, and nothing said in this room would sway it. I felt powerless and sick to my stomach.

With a huff of anger, Jane grabbed my arm and dragged me to my feet.

"Let's get out of here," she snarled.

"The Fells are in trouble, Marjan," said Jane. "We have been for a long time. The Index. It isn't working anymore. Our data isn't good."

"The missing animals."

"We've tried to cover all the gaps in the system, but . . . we've lost . . . a lot," she said. She was stalking in the grass beside the car that had brought me here. The driver was behind the wheel, and the engine was running, but Jane wasn't ready to sit down.

"They're the worst," she said, shaking her head. "Nobody wants to do the right thing when it matters. They're cowards. YOU'RE ALL COWARDS!"

Her fury was beautiful and reassuring. With that much anger, things could be changed.

"What do we do?" I asked, hopeful and ready to do it.

Jane stopped pacing and looked at me. At once, the anger subsided. She sighed and shook her head.

"Nothing," she said. "There isn't anything we can do. We won't be able to get near the unicorn now. And once the sale's final, there's no telling where it will end up. So it's done. I'm sorry, Marjan. I tried. I tried to make it okay."

She glared at the trailer for another moment.

"The worst thing is," she said, "even if the Index were healthy, I think they would still have taken the money. They would have found a reason."

We got into the car: Jane in the front seat, me in the back. The driver reached for the black bag, but Jane waved him off. "Who cares?" she said. "The place'll be cleared out by tonight."

We drove in silence for a little while.

"Can I ask you something?" I said. She looked back over her shoulder. "Did the Fells kill my dad?"

"Ha," said Jane. "No. Why would you think that?"

"Vance Cogland," I said.

"What do you know about Cogland?" asked Jane.

"I know someone killed him, the same way they killed my dad," I said. "And then made him disappear."

"And you think we did that?"

"I think you could, if you wanted to."

Her expression softened, ever so slightly.

"We didn't kill your father," she said. "And we didn't kill Vance Cogland, either." She paused. "But we did make him disappear."

"Why?"

"Because," said Jane, "Vance was one of us."

"He was . . ."

"A Fell," she said. "Not a very good one, though, from what I've heard."

"What do you mean?"

"Lubbock isn't exactly a promotion."

Vance Cogland had been mid-content—Jane called him "middle-blood"—but according to her, he hadn't taken his responsibilities seriously. He was always in trouble, which meant that the high-content leadership—the people back in the trailer, among others—were always bailing him out. He was reckless, and more than anything else, he was greedy. It was decided that he couldn't be trusted in the field. So he was demoted to a bidding room in Lubbock.

"All he had to do was keep his shop running," said Jane, "but instead he started fencing antiques. He even used our networks to move his merchandise. If he'd been caught, it could have done serious damage to our operations."

"So why keep him around?"

"Because he was family," he said. "And you do whatever you can for family. I'm sure you understand that."

"Was Cogland the signal you told me about before?"

"The Index jumped when he died," she said. "We looked all over Texas, but we never found any sign of a creature there. They've never liked Texas."

"So the Fells didn't kill my dad," I said.

"You don't believe me."

"I don't know who to believe."

"Why would we kill your father?"

"Maybe he didn't like the way you use the animals."

At this, Jane laughed out loud. "And I guess you don't either."

"I don't like that there's one family that rules over every single trade," I said.

"You're one to talk about the duties of one family," said Jane. "You'd rather see an open, free market, where literally anyone with the resources can instantly possess a thing that's not only incredibly rare but also incredibly powerful?"

"I'm not so sure these animals want to be bought and sold to begin with," I said. "And I have a feeling my dad felt the same way."

"So you think we killed him? Over a difference of opinion?"

She was right. It didn't make sense. It wasn't enough.

"Ithaca," I said. I thought I saw Jane's shoulders stiffen. Rumbling silence filled the car. Jane glanced at the driver.

"Traditionally," she said, "there hasn't been much trust between our families. Your dad was no exception. And after what just happened back there, I don't blame him."

"You showed him the horn," I said.

"I did," she said.

"And?"

"And he threw me out of his office," she said. "Told me he'd call the cops if I didn't leave. So I left."

"When?"

"A couple of weeks before he died."

"He knew what it was," I said.

"Probably," said Jane.

"So why didn't he go? Why not try to help it?"

"Probably because he knew we were watching," said Jane. "And he didn't want to lead us right to it."

"You mean like I did?"

"It shouldn't have to be this way," said Jane. "Our families, pitted against each other. It could have been different. Maybe it still can be."

Neither of us spoke for the rest of the drive back to the clinic. Watching the highway fly past, I felt a sullen disappointment sinking in. The unicorn was gone from the wild, maybe forever. The consequences of that change felt huge and uncertain. I was no closer to knowing who'd killed my dad or why. And I had the feeling I'd just been swindled.

I decided I'd liked the Fells better when they were still making me wear a bag on my head.

CHAPTER TWENTY-SEVEN

ANOTHER ANIMAL IN THE COLLECTION

You wouldn't have noticed it if you weren't looking.

It ran as a small announcement in a tech blog a week later—barely even a story—buried under leaked photos of smartphone prototypes and puff pieces about that hot new startup. Just a few short sentences reporting the fact that Horatio Prendergast had sold off a third of his company to a foreign fund with a bland and forgettable name, a deal totaling close to four billion dollars.

That was the only official acknowledgment of the sale of the unicorn.

Ezra had been right all along. The Fells had just made everything more expensive. I wasn't sure whether to be relieved that I knew where it was going, or terrified at the prospect of it going there.

I spent the next few days unable to concentrate on anything else. It felt like something huge was shifting all around us. At first it felt like I was the only one who knew. Then, one day, I came home from the clinic to find Malloryn on the couch, cradling a whimpering Zorro in her arms.

"He's freaking out," she said. "I've never seen him like this."

He squirmed in her arms, his little paws scritching at her skin. I stroked his fur. A rush of wild panic shot through me.

"Are we okay?" asked Malloryn. "I mean, is everything okay?"

"I don't know," I said.

I wanted to call Ezra, to find out what she knew. But every time I looked at her number, I was filled with a sick feeling of failure—the one thing I'd been trying to prevent had happened anyway, exactly as promised. The Fells were four billion dollars richer, and the unicorn was in Horatio's possession, and because of those things, I was too embarrassed to call her.

It'll be fine, I told myself. *Just another animal in the collection.* He'd put it in a case and be done with it, until his dream of Wyoming one day came true, or until he died. One way or another, the unicorn would probably be free again sometime. And if any animal could afford to wait, it was that one. At least no one would be hunting it in Horatio's menagerie.

But every day, I woke up feeling like I'd swallowed something heavy and sour and covered in thorns.

Spring semester had started, and Malloryn and I had agreed that she would no longer be invisible at school. Every morning, she rode her bike alongside mine through the residential streets. We said hi in the halls. We even had a class together.

"I don't want to get in your way," she said. "I just want to graduate like a normal person."

Graduating like a normal person sounded nice, but I didn't feel normal. The unicorn's fate haunted me. Sometimes I thought I could feel its rage seething under my skin. Other times I felt nothing, and that terrified me.

My friends made me angry. Carrie was wired from swim practice, and Grace was with Howie half the time. Neither of them could understand what I was feeling. I left classes early, locked myself in bathroom stalls, and waited for the bell to ring. When I looked in the mirror, I could see the dread on my face.

At home, Zorro paced and whined and clawed at the carpet, day and night. He nipped anxiously at Malloryn's heels when she was around, and worried at his tail when she wasn't. Malloryn fussed over him, offering him cuddles and treats, but he bristled and skitched them away. Nothing seemed to make him relax, not even sleep. He whined and twitched and yipped in his dreams. Malloryn even caught him gnawing on his tail once, deep asleep.

One day, between classes, someone knocked on the door to my bathroom stall.

"Occupied," I said.

"We know you're in there, Marjan." It was Carrie.

"We can see your shoes." Grace.

I opened the door to face them.

"Where have you been?" asked Carrie.

"Around," I said. What else could I say?

"What's going on with you?" said Grace. "Are you okay?"

"Nothing's going on," I said. "I'm fine."

Years of practice with that line.

"You're being a bad friend," said Carrie.

"What do you want from me?" I asked. It came out harsh. Carrie was quiet a moment.

"I don't *want* anything from you," she said. "I just thought we were friends. But I'm starting to realize that I don't know anything about you. And I don't think you want me to know anything. I don't think you ever did."

As she pushed past Grace and out of the bathroom, I felt sick to my stomach. Sebastian had been right—there were two versions of me, and right then, the one who knew about captive unicorns and nine-tailed foxes was trapped inside the one who didn't. *The world is falling apart, Carrie. How am I supposed to explain that to you?*

Grace glared at me.

"What's your problem, Marjan?" she asked.

"What's yours?" I said.

"My actual friend just left to find a different bathroom to cry in," she said. "And I want to know why."

"There are things I can't tell you about, G," I said. "And they're not going well."

I had a foolish hope that Grace would understand. That she would recognize something in my voice, in my expression. That she would see that I was speaking for and protecting another version of myself, a version that didn't know how to be in this part of my life. I hoped that she would see this and understand that I couldn't answer her questions, but that in the end, we all wanted the same thing.

But she was angry, and she only saw one version of me. The worst one.

"What the hell does that mean, Marjan?" asked Grace. "What the hell does any of this mean?"

Grace was tough. If she was about to cry, she wasn't going to show me. However much I was hurting her, she would fight for the truth until it didn't matter anymore.

But she was looking for a truth she could handle, a truth that wouldn't reinvent the whole world around her. I just didn't have that. So all I could do was fight back.

"No offense, G," I said, "but it's none of your business."

The world doesn't owe you anything. Least of all an explanation.

"There's something wrong with you," she said. "I used to think you were, like, shy or something. But you're actually not a very nice person. And I don't even think you realize it. I think . . ."

"Something's missing, right?" I said. "Trust me, I already know."

She started to say something, then shook her head. I knew I should be sad. I knew I should be trying to fix things between us. But all I felt was a vague gnawing in the emptiest part of me. I wasn't like Carrie, mourning the loss of a person who'd never really existed. Maybe I was a little like Grace, demanding answers like I deserved them. But really, I wasn't like anyone, and if I didn't react the way a normal person would, should that come as a surprise?

I texted Sebastian that night. The video call came in a moment later. I was filled with relief. Finally—someone who could tell me that what I was feeling was okay. But when his face appeared on my screen, there was no warmth in his eyes.

"You said he would get better," he said. "He's not getting better."

"What do you mean?" I said, every word an eel.

"Kipling." He said the name loud and clear, like he didn't care if the whole world heard it. "I saw him today."

"He's not better?" But I knew he wasn't better, didn't I? If I looked at it the right way, I knew the truth. I imagined a room with an IV drip, a doctor coming in and out, and a floor like liverwurst—*no, paisley.*

"He's a ghost," said Sebastian. "What did you do to him?"

"I don't . . . I didn't," I said. Everything was starting to feel very confused.

"But you know what's wrong with him," he said.

"No . . . ," I said. *Griffons don't die, not like this.* "I tried. I . . . Maybe he just needs more time?"

"Tell the truth, Marjan!" he said.

"That is the truth," I said. Only it wasn't. And I knew that.

Sebastian was quiet for a long time. And when he spoke, his words were soft and wounded. They still fell on me like hammers.

"I don't think I believe you," he said, and then the call ended.

The next morning, I awoke to a scream from Malloryn's room.

Malloryn was sitting up in bed, dressed in an oversized T-shirt and sweats. She was shaking and whimpering, barely coherent. Her frazzled curls hung down in front of her face. When I came in, she lifted a wavering finger to the corner of the room.

Zorro was crouched against the wall, curled up and trembling. He was bleeding. A trail of dried blood led across the carpet from his tense, quivering form to a ragged, coiled ribbon of torn flesh and fox fur.

It took me a moment to realize it was one of his tails.

"Wh-what's wrong with him?" whispered Malloryn. "What is that? What did he do?"

I sat down next to Zorro and stroked his fur. Shock and desperation coursed through him—urgent, frustrated urges cut with spasms of chills and pain. Malloryn sat in horrified stillness. She swallowed and gathered her strength to speak.

"Is he dying?"

Zorro's eyes darted from her to me and back again, quick and sharp. He was hurt and scared, but very much alive.

"I don't think so," I said. "Let's clean this wound, and I'll tell you everything I know."

• • •

Zorro let his tails unbraid as we washed the blood from his fur. While Malloryn held him, I cleaned the stump with alcohol and covered it with bandages and some gauze I'd found in the bathroom. Whenever Zorro flinched, Malloryn cooed in his ear, and that was always enough to settle him down.

"How long have you known?" asked Malloryn, running her fingers gently over each tail with quiet wonder after the bandage was finished.

"Since the first night you brought him in," I said. I didn't have the energy to invent another lie. Malloryn would either hate me or she wouldn't. "I'm sorry. I figured he would show you when he wanted you to know."

"Thank you for that," said Malloryn.

"You're not mad at me?"

She laughed—exhausted and relieved at the same time.

"Of course not, silly," she said. "I told you, magic is very precise. If things happen in the wrong order, it all falls apart. If I'd known what he was, maybe he wouldn't have stayed. Maybe he wouldn't have given me this."

She'd wrapped the tail into a kind of wreath, then tied it with string and hung it from her neck like a pendant. She touched it with one hand.

"It feels powerful," she said. Then, to Zorro, "What did you mean to tell us, Budgins? What's in here?"

Zorro yipped and panted, then dug his snout into Malloryn's elbow.

My phone started ringing.

I excused myself from the bathroom as Malloryn embraced Zorro in a grateful hug, and I walked down the hall and past my dad's room.

For someone trying to make things right, I thought, *you sure left a hell of a mess.*

I didn't recognize the number, but I answered.

"Marjan," said a hushed, furtive voice. "It's Hugo Batiste. You need to come now. It's Horatio."

"What about him?" I asked. "He got what he wanted. I'm not helping him."

"He doesn't want your help."

"What's he want, then?" I asked.

"He wants to kill it."

CHAPTER TWENTY-EIGHT

ANOMALY

The journey to Horatio's compound was a white-hot blur of trains, municipal buses, and an Uber driver who'd never heard of Menagerie. My heart thumped against my ribs. My head raced with panic and dread, and more than anything else, helplessness.

Horatio is going to kill the unicorn.

Dr. Batiste hadn't explained why, and there hadn't been time to ask.

"I'm not going to do it," he'd told me. "If it happens, it won't be me. I will not kill that incredible animal."

By the time the driver had dropped me at the entrance of the complex, it already felt like I was too late. A guard emerged from a sentry box and waved me down.

"Marjan Dastani," I said. "I need to see Horatio."

He muttered something into a radio, and then a moment later waved me through.

I was met at the front steps of the main building by Ava, flanked a few paces back by two very large men in dark suits.

"This way," she said. She turned back toward the building,

and the two men each took a single step toward me. Clearly I was expected to follow her.

She led me down the long hallway and past Horatio's office. The people we passed all greeted us with smiles. I saw champagne bottles lined up on tables, and I heard scattered whoops of excitement coming from the grounds outside. Ava and our silent escorts led me to the elevator. When it arrived, we all stepped inside, and descended into the earth.

For all the activity on the surface, the menagerie was eerily silent. The animals watched us through the glass with wary, somber gazes. Faeries hovered, their bodies motionless except for the flutter of their wings. A fierce-eyed creature with a tortoise shell on its back tracked us with inky black eyes from the waterline of a man-made pond. I felt like I was walking into a funeral.

Standing before one large paddock, Horatio smiled, a calm, saintly smile. Inside, the unicorn glared out with steely, unbroken resolve, strong and very much alive. I breathed a sigh of relief.

Ava gave Horatio a little bow, then nodded to me and retreated into the darkness with her two guards.

"It's an amazing animal, isn't it? The purity, the savagery of it." Horatio had the quietly radiant satisfaction of someone who had achieved something extraordinary.

The unicorn's rage seemed to curdle the air around it.

"I had planned to bring you here," he said. "After . . . well, after the business was done. But you're here now. All the better."

"What's this all about, Horatio?" I asked. "What's going on?"

He turned and began walking down the hall, glancing at his creatures thoughtfully as he passed them.

"I've dreamed of this moment all my life, Marjan," he said. "I've been trying to make the world a better place. It's been my only project, my only true project. I tried first with information, but it turns out not everyone wants to believe in data. Then I tried with money, but there really is only so much money can do. And there are so many problems. So much greed. So much pettiness and evil. So many people who don't have enough of the things we need to survive. Food, shelter, medicine, love. Where to start?"

He stopped to consider a small case in which a golden scarab tended to a tiny, blinding ball of flame with busy, fiddling appendages.

"When your father introduced me to this world," he continued, "he couldn't have known what I would see, what I would discover."

He touched the glass with his palm, and seemed to draw comfort from its warmth. Then he continued walking down the hall.

"They're not just animals, you know," he said. "They're tied to us in ways that transcend reason. When they thrive, we thrive. When they collapse, we fall into darkness. Do you understand what I'm saying?"

"I'm not sure," I said.

Horatio continued. "Our dreams, our hopes, the fires in our hearts—it all comes from them. It exists because of them. And they exist because of it. The Fells saw the connection a long time ago. They've made a fortune off it. But they've never understood it. Not like I do."

We had reached the end of the hallway. Sturges the house gnome crouched on the post of Horatio's childhood bed, sad eyes watching our every move. Horatio smiled at his first creature, but the gnome didn't respond. Horatio shrugged, then turned back to take in the full sweep of his crawling, seething menagerie. He smiled broadly, drunk with wonder.

"They're not just animals, Marjan," he said. His voice dropped to a whisper. "They're our imagination."

I must have had a confused expression on my face, because Horatio laughed. Then he started walking again, back up the long hall. The giant with the huge stony hands pounded away at a boulder, pulverizing it with idle persistence.

"You're a lot like me," he said. "You know something's missing. You've always known it. I see it in your eyes. Do you know what it is? It's them. It's what they hold inside. We are not complete without them. We're not whole without our dreams, our hopes, our fears. Have you ever seen something so clearly that it burns to look at it?"

Kipling among medical machines, wings spreading against the pain, unfurling in impossible brilliance.

"I know this like I've never known anything else in my life," he continued. "And I didn't even need the Fells and their nine hundred years of data to see it. These animals are our most precious treasure. The greatest glory of the world."

He passed the black salamander, churning in its pot of flame. Round, onyx eyes, glimmering with firelight, looked up at me as we passed.

"And I'll tell you something else the Fells don't know," said Horatio, leaning in and lowering his voice to a conspirator's whisper. "Their math isn't as good as they think it is."

He winked. Behind him the darkness of the manticore's enclosure thrummed with malevolent energy.

"Come with me," he said.

* * *

The elevator doors opened on the ground floor of the mansion, and Horatio led me to a lavish conference room. The hallway was quiet and empty, but there was an audible buzz of activity from the grounds. He shut the door behind us and flipped a switch. The lights dimmed. A projector on the ceiling whirred to life, and a graph appeared on the wall.

Two lines crept across the field of the graph, nearly paralleling each other until the lower one leapt up, then dropped steeply before leveling off again. At the same spot, the upper line rose and fell, but neither change was as sharp or as drastic as that of the lower line.

He pointed to the upper line. "This is the Master Index." He smiled, then turned his attention to the bottom line. "This is the population of creatures," he said. "As you can see, the two map pretty well to each other. The connection is undeniable." He traced with an outstretched finger the points where the two lines behaved in a similar way. I nodded. It sure looked like there was a similarity.

"But," he continued. He was pointing at a particular spot on the Master Index. It didn't look like anything special to me.

"What am I looking at?"

"A secret," said Horatio. "A secret, hidden inside a lot of noise."

"So you're saying the Fells can't read a graph?" I asked.

At this, Horatio laughed out loud. He looked at the graph a moment longer and grew thoughtful. "They've been studying this for nine hundred years. The secret has always been there. A constant hum. The same anomaly, over and over, until everyone forgets that it's there."

"What anomaly?" I said.

"The Index never goes as low as it should," said Horatio.

"Theoretically, if we and the creatures feed one another, as I believe is the case, this population drop"—he pointed to a steep trough on the creatures line—"should have been extreme enough to create a negative feedback effect. We should have been decimated. But we weren't. We've never been. We struggle, of course. We suffer. But the Index always seems to correct itself. We always bounce back."

"So?"

"So," he said patiently, "either we humans are made of stronger stuff than the Fells give us credit for. Or . . ." He smiled and waited to see if I would guess where this was going. I couldn't, and after a moment he gave a disappointed shrug and continued. "Or there's something wrong with the model."

He paused, and his smile grew wide with triumph. "I don't believe," he said, "they've ever properly accounted for the unicorn."

He tilted his head to one side, a gesture of apology that would have seemed smug coming from anyone else. Somehow Horatio carried it off with something approximating deference.

"It's not their fault," he said. "It's never been theirs to count. They did the best they could with the data they had."

"So the unicorn, what, saved us?"

"I doubt that animal has any interest in our salvation," said Horatio with a chuckle. I couldn't disagree. "I believe the unicorn exerts an elemental force on the entire ecosystem. It is gravity. A magnet, always drawing us back to safety. Always drawing us away from the extremes."

"What's wrong with that?" I asked. "What's wrong with gravity?"

"Without it," he said, "we could fly."

"Fly off into space," I said.

"The world is fragile," said Horatio. "You can see its frailty here in these lines, if you look closely enough. If the system were orderly, if it followed its own rules, it would collapse. It would fail. And then, perhaps a new system would rise. A sturdier system. A stronger people. Order—the ultimate foundation upon which to build a better world. That's what I want. That's what I've always wanted. And it will never happen, not as long as the unicorn lives."

"So you want to kill it."

"The unicorn is our curse, Marjan," he said. "We are doomed to repeat our mistakes because at the end of the day, there is never a consequence. The same injustices, the same cruelty, the same atrocities, the same carelessness, over and over again, since the dawn of history, and we never learn."

"If we're so awful, why go to all this trouble?"

"Because I believe in humanity," said Horatio. "I believe that we can be better. Buried under all the cruelty and pettiness, in the deepest depths of our hearts, is the kernel of something great, something monumental. I know it exists because I feel it here, among these creatures. But the world has never seen it. And I blame the unicorn."

He switched off the projector, and the graphs disappeared.

"What do you hope to achieve?" I asked.

"Freedom," said Horatio. "Freedom from the endless cycle of history. Freedom from the curse. We're ready, Marjan. We're ready to start again."

"What about the other animals?" I asked.

He smiled, reassuring.

"They will be the seeds of the next great epoch of humanity," he said. "They're our stores of hope against the darkness that has to come first. They're going to unlock the best of us,

Marjan. That's what they do. They make us more than we are. And we will need our dreams, our imagination, more than ever. We can make a new world, a fair and kind world, a world where we share our resources and take care of each other. But first we must set ourselves free."

His face was aglow with wonder.

"You can't," I said. "You can't kill the unicorn."

"It's the only way," said Horatio. "One more awful act, and then we will be better. We're going to cleanse the world of its wickedness, once and for all. And when it's over, the others will live in the open, in peace, free of fear."

"Did my dad know?" I asked. "Did he know what you were doing? What you wanted to do?"

"He couldn't see," said Horatio. "He couldn't see my vision, Marjan. He only saw the suffering. He didn't want to cause pain. He couldn't see that there was something beyond that." He paused. "I know it won't be easy. It's an unbalancing the likes of which the world has never known. There will be dark days. Nations will crumble. There will be war. There will be chaos. It will be terrible. But we'll survive. The animals here, they're going to save us. This place will be our ark. And when the flood's over, we'll be a new people."

"I thought you hated chaos," I said.

"Sometimes, the only choice is chaos," said Horatio. "One must face their fears, if one wants to grow stronger. We—those of us who are left—will be stronger, so much stronger. And the world we'll build will be a better world. A just world. An orderly world."

"What if your math is wrong, and nothing changes?"

Horatio nodded. "Pragmatic," he said. "That's good. So am I. The wheels of destiny might need a little grease. Fortunately, we have a back door into the targeting systems of several hundred missiles." My expression must have changed, because Horatio smiled, comforting and apologetic. "Sometimes the sky has to fall," he said, "before you can see the stars."

"You can't do this," I said.

"Your father said the same thing."

For the first time, Horatio's patient veneer clouded over, and something unstable and dark showed itself in his eyes. There was danger in this moment, like the room itself had teeth. Anything could happen, and no one would know. No one even knew I was here.

"You belong with us, Marjan," he said. "You belong in the new world. Stay."

He was watching me carefully. If I said the wrong thing, I was dead.

"I need some time," I said. "To think about all this."

"That's fair," said Horatio. "Take all night if you need. The new world begins at sunrise."

And with that, he nodded and walked past me to the door. When he opened it, I saw the broad shadow of one of Ava's guards, standing just outside. As Horatio slipped out, he whispered something to the guard, then turned back and gave me a reassuring smile. I didn't even need to hear the door locking to know that I was a prisoner.

CHAPTER TWENTY-NINE

A SONG

There was a phone in the room, but it didn't work. My phone, too, seemed suspiciously unable to find a signal. I tried the windows. They were unlocked, and slid open on silent tracks, and for a tiny moment my heart leapt at the thought of escape. But there were metal bumpers screwed into the tracks, and the windows only opened a couple of inches.

In a fit of anger and frustration, I decided to break the glass, and looked around the room for something sturdy enough for the job. My eyes landed on one of the wheeled chairs pulled up to the conference table. It was heavy and awkward, and I ended up having to sort of run at the window while wrenching my upper body around. The impact made a big noise, but the window, which was made of thick glass, didn't even chip.

A moment later, the door opened. My guard stood there, shaking his head. He walked over and took the chair out of my hands without a word, then carried it with him back out of the room and locked the door again. There were other chairs, but he'd made his point. If I tried again, I'd have nowhere to sit. And it was beginning to look like I would be here a while.

I paced around the room, taking an inventory of anything that might be useful: an antique, ornamental encyclopedia set; a smooth glass paperweight with a curved tooth of uncertain origin embedded in its center; an assortment of office supplies.

There were things that could be weaponized: the paperweight; a pair of scissors; a small, abstract sculpture in marbled black stone that stood as a bookend. I laid the items on the table and looked at them in the hopes that a plan would take shape. But I couldn't see myself stabbing or bludgeoning anyone. And I doubted I would be able to overcome the sentry, even if I somehow managed to manufacture some element of surprise.

The sun disappeared behind a line of low fog. The sky went pink, then pale, then dark. Lights blinked on around the property, chilly pools of peppermint white. A quiet, ordinary night on the Menagerie campus.

A little after dark, there was a knock on the door. I glanced halfheartedly at my array of makeshift weapons, but it seemed pointless to try anything.

The door opened, and Ezra came in. She had a tray in her hands with food on it.

"I'm not hungry," I said.

"You will be," she said.

"So now you're the good cop?" I asked.

Ignoring my question, she walked over and set the tray on the table. It had a bowl of rice on it, a bowl of sautéed greens, and a metal cup full of water. As she put it down, she noticed my array of makeshift weapons, and looked them over, one after the other.

To the paperweight, she shook her head. "Not this one," she said.

To the scissors, she pursed her lips and said, "Nope."

She stopped at the statue, took it in her hand, and tested its weight. "Maybe," she said. "But, no." She set it back down. "Alonzo's got a black belt in jujitsu. He's a former Navy SEAL. And he's definitely expecting you'll try something on him. So, don't."

She collected the weapons one at a time, and put them away.

"What are you doing here, Ezra?" I asked.

She stopped, her back to me. "I brought you dinner," she said, after a long pause.

"That's not what I mean. What are you doing *here*?"

She turned around, and when she did, I could see that her face was troubled. She sat down on the table.

"He's got a way of finding people," she said. "Or getting people to find him. He's there, right when you need him. Right when you need something good to happen. When your investigation gets shut down because the dealer you're chasing is a judge's kid, when you get passed over for promotion for the third time, when you realize you're never going any further, not here, not with any department, this job listing pops up. Nothing fancy . . . maybe twenty words. But . . ." She shook her head. "He doesn't ever hire locally. I bet you didn't know that."

I shook my head.

"You have to want to be somewhere else," she said. "Somewhere other than where you are. So you end up here. And then he shows you what it's all really for. Suddenly there's a purpose. He can make anything happen—that's what it feels like. Anything's possible. Wherever you came from, I guarantee that you never felt anything like that before."

For a moment, I felt sorry for her. It wasn't her fault that

she'd been sucked into this. The Fells were right about the creatures. They changed you.

"Do they know?" I asked. "The families, all the people who
live here. Do they know what he's doing?"

"They believe in him," said Ezra. "They trust him."

"What about you? Do you believe in him?"

She was quiet a moment. "Most of the people here, they've
never seen the animals outside of the menagerie. They don't
know what the creatures are really like, out in the world." She
paused. "I didn't think it would happen like this, all at once."

"So basically, as long as there weren't any consequences, you
were fine doing something you knew was wrong?"

"I never pretended to be a saint," she said. "I'm not much
better or worse than most people. I just happen to be more
effective."

"Oh yeah?" I said. "Have you found my dad's killer yet?"

"Funny you should mention that," she said. "Because I followed the money, and guess where it led?"

She looked around the room meaningfully.

"Here?" I asked.

"Five cash payments," she said, "corresponding to the arrivals here, soon after each, of five animals—a Chinese rain bird,
a mer-lion from Singapore, an ignis fatuus from the Great
Dismal Swamp, a wyvern from a village in the Dolomites, and
some kind of dog-tree thing from I'm not sure where."

"So what does that mean?" I asked.

"It's hard to be certain," said Ezra. "But it sure looks like
your dad was selling out his clients."

My stomach lurched. I couldn't speak. For everything I'd
done wrong, I would never have betrayed a client's secret. I
might have lied to the Stoddards, but I'd never sell Kipling.

"Morality's a luxury," said Ezra. "Not everyone can afford it."

"What about you?" I said. "You seem pretty comfortable. Is that why you're here bringing me dinner? Telling me all this? So you can feel better about yourself when the half-assed rapture comes?" Ezra didn't say anything. "If you came here to ease your conscience," I said, "you can leave now. You helped make this happen. You're not less guilty just because you're starting to feel bad."

Ezra looked me in the eye.

"You've got the right to be angry," she said. "Anger's a powerful engine. It might even bring you answers. But it's not going to fix you. It's never going to fix you."

She nodded, turned, walked to the door, and knocked three times. The door opened. Alonzo gave her a nod and then looked back into the room to make sure everything was still in its place. Not sure what else to do, I waved.

Ezra glanced over her shoulder at me. In that moment, for just a second, there was no hunger in her eyes, no hot plasma under her skin. She was just a woman who, more than anything else, looked very tired.

"Eat your rice," she said.

The door shut and locked behind her, and once again I was alone in the room. There wasn't much to do, so after a few minutes I began idly picking at the food. I had a few bites of the greens, and a sip of water. Out of pure spite, I ignored the rice.

I watched as people walked up and down the glowing paths of the Menagerie campus. Men, women, children. They'd all come from somewhere else, every last one. They'd all felt the lack of something essential, and they'd come here looking for it. Something was missing. Something's always missing.

I was hungry after all, hungrier than I was proud or spiteful. I took the bowl of rice, dug the fork in, and hit something hard. A screwdriver.

I unscrewed the bumpers, slid the window open, and slipped through, and nobody noticed. The cafeteria was closing up for the night. The last few stragglers from dinner were heading back to their quarters. A man with noise-canceling headphones sat at a gas-powered firepit, drinking tea and writing code by firelight.

Any moment, I was sure, someone would notice I was gone, and the peaceful night would shatter into shouts and flashlight beams. Any moment, I would be caught. All I could do was crawl along the side of the building, keeping to the shadows, avoiding the light.

At last, I found a pocket of darkness, and crept through it into the pasture at the edge of the compound. As I felt my way through the tall grass, my arm caught on a hook of the barbed wire that surrounded the hills where the cattle grazed. Gritting my teeth against the shock and pain, I followed the fence until I came to a slab of granite big enough to hide me, and then I curled up behind it, cold and bleeding and terrified.

All chases, the same chase.

The last time I'd felt this helpless, I was eleven years old, shivering in an unfamiliar park beneath a cold moon. Just like then, my plans had all unraveled. Just like then, the result had been failure and danger and chaos. Just like then, nothing was better, and everything was worse.

But this time, I was still angry.

All of this was my dad's fault. He'd told Horatio about the other creatures. He'd even helped Horatio to get his hands on some of them. And he hadn't told me anything except a few stories that didn't do me any good now.

My blood boiled at the realization—*my father had trusted Horatio Prendergast more than he'd trusted me.*

And look where that had gotten him. I now believed Horatio was more than capable of murder. And if my dad had tried to stop Horatio's plans, because he'd been trying to "make things right"—whatever that meant—I wouldn't be surprised if Horatio had responded by killing him.

But had I really been so much better than my dad? In the last few months, I'd lied. I'd snuck around and disappeared as much as he had. And in the end, I was the one who had let the unicorn fall into the wrong hands.

Maybe the Hyrcanian Line was just as broken and lost as the Fells. Maybe whatever it was that made us special was drying up. Maybe I was just unlucky. It wasn't my fault, or anyone's fault, that I happened to be the last living vestige of something that had once been magical.

They chase because they are running out of time.

The sting of the cut on my arm distracted me from my thoughts. I was still here. The unicorn was still alive, and the world hadn't ended yet. I wasn't my dad, and I didn't have to make the same mistakes he'd made.

I took out my phone and found that I had a signal again. I took a deep breath and made a call.

The phone rang once, twice. If it went to voice mail, well, that would be what I deserved. But it didn't, and on the third ring, Grace picked up.

"What do you want?" she said. I heard another voice mumble in the background. Howie.

"I need your help, G," I said.

I told Grace what I needed, and then I told her where to find me. She was quiet at first, quiet enough that I could hear Howie in the background. Howie was not a fan of mine.

Fortunately, though, Grace still was.

An hour later, after trudging along grassy slopes littered with cow pies, I was standing at the side of a lonely two-lane road, watching as a pair of squinty headlights appeared out of the darkness, and then Grace, followed by Malloryn, got out of the Blue Whale.

"I'm sorry," I said to Grace. "And thank you."

She shook her head. "He's a dumb boy," she said. "And you're still my friend."

"Do you have his tail?" I asked Malloryn.

She fished into her shirt and pulled it out, a stiff, tightly coiled little ring of fox fur tied with hemp twine.

"Let's go," I said.

Grace didn't move. "You need to tell me what this is all about."

"I'm sorry I've lied to you, Grace," I said. "I'm sorry I kept all this from you. I didn't know how to talk about it, and I still don't. But I'm ready to show you."

"What do you mean?" she asked.

For the first time in hours, I felt something other than fear and anger. I think it was confidence.

"Grace," I said, "we're going to save the world."

The three of us picked our way through the cow pies and the darkness, and on the way, I tried my best to explain what we needed to do. Grace was understandably skeptical. But she didn't turn around and walk away. Malloryn, of course, didn't need any convincing.

There were several large trucks lined up at the compound when we got there, a knot of headlights illuminating clouds of dust. I saw something that looked like a large satellite dish on the back of one of them, and another seemed to be full of food supplies. The three of us crouched behind the granite slab and watched.

I nodded to Zorro's tail.

"Do you know how it works?" I asked Malloryn.

"Not exactly," she said. "But I think I will, when it's time."

"But it's not time yet?"

"Nope," she said.

"So, not an invisibility spell."

"Probably not," she said.

For just a second, I felt like I'd made yet another mistake by bringing these girls here and involving them in this. Now it wasn't just my life on the line. And we didn't even have a plan for getting into the building.

So it came as a great surprise to me when Malloryn suddenly jumped up and began marching down the hill with a bright and unflappable stride.

"Come on," she called out as she stepped out of the darkness, and what else were we supposed to do? It was actually a relief to have an order to follow, even if it seemed absurdly dangerous.

"What are you doing, Malloryn?" I whispered.

"This is how you do it," she said, without looking back, without breaking stride. "You walk like you belong. You look at people like you know them. You don't stop for anything."

"And that works?" I said.

"Sometimes," said Malloryn, nodding at a group of workers as we passed.

Grace and I exchanged glances. There wasn't really much choice now. We were both committed to the momentum Malloryn had created. And her conviction was infectious. After a few purposeful steps, I could feel my posture getting straighter. A smile spread itself easily across my face. We were marching into the most uncertain future, and I could almost feel the twinkle in my eye.

As we neared the main building, Malloryn scooped up a tablet that someone had left unattended. She slipped it under her arm and kept going.

"A little something extra to help the illusion along," she said over her shoulder.

We marched past workers pushing pallets of food into the cellar. No one stopped us. We swept in the front door of Horatio's mansion, and the guards stationed at the entrance let us through. Now I took the lead, down the main hallway, past another knot of workers, a detachment of wandering guards, and an assortment of Horatio's fan club.

We walked with swift, desperate purpose toward the elevator that led down to the menagerie, ducking out of the main hall only when we started to get close to Horatio's study. If Alonzo spotted me, we'd be caught. From two rooms away, I peered in the direction of the room where I'd been held captive. Alonzo was still standing guard, looking drowsy and bored. In all this time, no one had noticed I was missing.

"Does no one think it's weird that I haven't asked to use the bathroom yet?" I whispered. Grace shushed me, and we continued on.

The next room over was another meeting room. The door was open. Inside, Ava glanced up from what looked like an important meeting with several security guards. I looked away quickly, but she'd seen me.

"Crap," I whispered.

I heard her coming out of the office, heading down the hall after us.

"Walk faster," I said.

We were walking like stick figures, legs straight, arms locked and swinging hard. Nothing subtle about it. Ava called after us, and when we didn't respond, she began shouting. We rounded a corner, and I could see the elevator door up ahead.

Grace snatched the tablet from Malloryn's arm and planted herself in the middle of the hall as the clatter of mustering guards echoed around us.

"Run," she said.

"What are you doing?" I asked.

Grace looked at me with fierce eyes. "I'm trusting you, Marjan," she said. "Trust me."

I sprinted to the elevator and pushed the button. Malloryn was right behind me. I glanced back.

Down the hall, Grace looked over her shoulder at me and nodded. Then she took a long, deep breath, grasped the tablet in both hands, and marched right toward the sound of the oncoming guards.

When they came around the corner, the first thing they saw was a girl who looked like she not only belonged there but was in fact in charge of a very important job.

"This is a restricted area!" said Grace in a sharp and commanding voice,. "You're not supposed to be here."

For just a moment, it didn't matter whether you were a highly trained private security professional or a coldly efficient executive assistant. You were pretty sure you weren't supposed to be there. Horatio's best and most capable minions were learning what Carrie Finch and I had known since the first day of sixth grade.

It was impossible to argue with Grace Yee.

Behind us, the elevator door opened. While the guards stood frozen in their tracks, wondering if they had in fact wandered into a restricted area, Malloryn jumped in and pulled me after her.

"Grace!" I yelled. "Let's go!"

Grace tossed the tablet aside and rushed for the elevator door. Just like that, the spell broke. The guards came to their senses and clattered after her. She dove inside, and as she did I punched the DOOR CLOSE button with the bottom of my fist. Footsteps pounded toward us.

The doors slid slowly together, like a priest bringing his palms to touch in prayer. As the last sliver of the hallway disappeared, I saw the face of a guard, peering in, reaching to stop us, and failing. The doors shut, the elevator began to descend, and the sounds of the hallway faded into the silence of stone.

"Okay, *that* was pretty cool," said Malloryn.

"Thanks," said Grace.

Then, suddenly, we all ran out of things to say. The small moment of triumph—escaping the first rush of guards—went sour in my gut. There was nowhere to go. We were in the middle of an elevator shaft with two exits.

"There'll be more of them waiting for us at the bottom, won't there?" asked Grace.

"Probably," I said.

I sank to the floor and rested my back against the wall. We didn't even have a tablet anymore.

"So that's it?" said Grace.

"We tried," I said. "We got really close. Thank you, Grace. Thank you for believing me. Thank you for coming. Thank you for . . . that."

She shrugged. "It *was* pretty cool," she said. "Did you see their faces?" She smiled, then laughed. I laughed too.

"I'm sorry," I said when the laughing had stopped. "This is all my fault."

"Shut up, Mar," said Grace.

Then, softly, Malloryn stood up off the wall. She took off her foxtail necklace and looked at it for a second. She closed her fist around Zorro's tail and held it tight. A baffled smile spread across her face, like she'd just realized something surprising and amazing.

"You guys," she said in a quiet voice. "I think we might be a coven."

From between her fingers, a soft pink light began to glow. She shut her eyes and began whispering to herself, like she was memorizing something. Then she stopped, and the glow faded, and she opened her hand. The tail was gone.

Then she took a slow, deep breath in, and began humming to herself.

It was a strange tune. It wasn't familiar, but for some reason I knew exactly how it went, and I couldn't help but hum along. It had an intoxicating melody, and once it got into my head, it made my whole body feel light and floaty. Malloryn made a gesture like a conductor, and I realized that Grace was humming along also.

And when the doors opened, that's what the guards saw. Three unarmed intruders, tapping our toes and humming like idiots. Malloryn raised her arms, and our voices all got louder, and pretty soon, the guards were all humming along too.

Malloryn led the way out of the elevator, disarming the sentries with blithe flourishes, tossing their guns aside gleefully, and skipping along to the rhythm. With a wave of her hand, she dismissed the guards, except for one. We watched them skip and twirl away, and then Malloryn turned to the last one.

"How do we free the unicorn?" she sang.

"You need to get to the operations room," sang the guard. "That's where the cages are controlled." It was an odd-sounding rejoinder that missed the beat and almost derailed the whole song. But Malloryn recovered the melody after a tense, fumbling moment.

"Show us," she sang, taking the guard's hand.

The guard leapt and spun with joy, and when he came down, he fell into a shuffle-step dance past the paddocks, pulling Malloryn along with him. Grace and I followed, the song carrying us as well.

As we passed the rows of enclosures, the creatures inside all pressed their faces to the glass to watch us. It was hard to tell, because my head was spinning with the song, but it seemed they, too, had joined in the dance. Birds wreathed in flames traced retina-burning shapes against the windows. The giant with boulder fists pounded out a crude rhythm on the floor of his cage. A majestic, snow-white ruminant with three curved horns swayed its massive head from side to side, its patient brown eyes following us as we waltzed by.

"What is this?" I asked, my words coming out in song. "What's happening?"

"No stupid questions," said Malloryn, her words rising and falling with the music's refrain. "We don't have a lot of time. I can't keep this up very long."

Down the hall, I heard shouts and cries that dissolved into harmonies as we got near. Guards and medical staff danced past us, following their own baffled muses. Somewhere far away, sirens began to blare. But here in the hall, there was only the song, and it held all in its sway.

All except one.

The yawning darkness of the manticore's enclosure swallowed up the music, and I knew as soon as I saw it that the thing inside had no interest in dancing.

"Come on," cried Malloryn, trailing behind the guard soft-shoeing his way down the hall. But the manticore's power held me rooted in place. The darkness sucked me in, even as the dance sped up around me. "Come on!" shouted Malloryn again, so loud that the music skipped a beat. But I couldn't move. I wouldn't. And as I stood there, the song began to fade from my ears and my bones, and all I could feel was the hunger pulsating from inside the manticore's enclosure.

A horrible feeling stirred in me. A sickening blackness curdled in my bones. I took a breath, and the air felt thick and evil in my chest. My legs felt weak. I thought I might pass out.

"Marjan," said Malloryn's voice, from very far away. "We don't have time!"

I was aware, faintly, of the song coming to a moment of inflection. The music was about to end. But still, I couldn't draw myself away from the manticore's cage.

Then hands were grabbing me, spinning me around. The song seemed to find an extra coda, and lingered on longer than it should have as I was twirled round and round, farther and farther away from the manticore. Up ahead, the guard was turning right. Grace had me by one arm, her fingers digging into my skin. Malloryn had the other arm, and she was pulling us both toward the end of the hall. Her voice was straining. I heard it crack and falter. Tears were running from her eyes. Her face was pale. But still the song continued as we reached the end of the hall, and turned right, following our guide to a simple, nondescript door.

He nodded, and then threw it open. Half a dozen guards sprang from their chairs as we entered, but the song's finale caught them up too, and Malloryn, letting me go, sent them spinning into the hall, one at a time, then slammed the door shut and locked it, bringing the song to a crashing halt. In the dizzying silence, Malloryn looked at me for a second. Then her face went blank, and she collapsed onto the floor.

My head was pounding. It was difficult to focus anywhere for long. But after a few moments, I was able to put together an idea of where we were.

We were in a dim room filled with buttons and switches and flat-screen TVs, each one monitoring a different area of the silo. There were cameras in the hall of creatures. There were cameras in the infirmary. On all of the screens, guards and creatures were slowly coming to, shaking off the effects of the song.

Grace sat down in a corner. Her body was clearly worn out from the song, but her eyes were wide with awe. Malloryn was lying on the floor, eyes glassy, breath shallow. The dim sound of an alarm echoed through the door, but no one seemed to be coming just yet.

I ran to Malloryn and shook her by the shoulders.

"Hey," I said. "Are you there?"

Malloryn nodded weakly. I stood, and my head spun so hard that I nearly fell over. After I'd steadied myself, I staggered toward what looked like a control panel, and tried to match the row of switches with anything on the screens. It was no use. My circuits were too fried, and I couldn't seem to make the connections that needed to be made.

Shouts and cries came from the hall. Footsteps. On the cameras I saw a platoon of reinforcements entering the creature hall, guns drawn.

I stared at the switches, but they still made no sense.

"Which one?" I said out loud.

Grace stumbled across the room and squinted up at the screens. The guards were getting close. I could hear them reaching the end of the hallway.

"Come on!" I said. Grace looked at another screen, then at the row of switches.

"Thirty-four," she said.

"Are you sure?"

The guards had reached the door. It shuddered in its frame as something heavy pounded against it.

"Thirty-four," she repeated. I found the switch marked thirty-four in the row. The door shook again. Malloryn groaned in fear and pain.

I rested my fingertip against the switch, and as I did, my thoughts aligned in one pure, complete realization, a slot machine hitting the world's worst jackpot.

Freeing the unicorn like this would do no good. It would be caught again, here in the silo. The guards—armed, and in full possession of their senses and faculties—might even shoot it themselves. We'd failed, and soon we'd all be dead, including the unicorn.

There was only one chance, one act that could possibly save the unicorn, that might save all of us.

I am a girl in a forest clearing. I am a falconer to the shah.

I am Marjan Dastani, five hundred feet underground, in the menagerie of Horatio Prendergast. I am the living expression of the Hyrcanian Line, and there are things that will happen over and over again, not because of destiny, or a unicorn's curse, but because people just don't change.

And sometimes, the only choice is chaos.

I opened all the cages.

| CHAPTER THIRTY |

FREEDOM

For a moment, nothing happened. The animals—the ones we could see on the screens, anyway, stood at the thresholds of their paddocks in stunned silence. The guards, the doctors, everyone froze where they were.

A single gunshot rang out, somewhere down the hall. Then more. The security feeds winked out, one at a time. A sound began to swell on the other side of the door, a cacophony of whines and roars and snarls that bled together into a single, vengeful note. The banging on the door went from angry to desperate. The air began to smell like smoke. The guards pleaded, then cried out, and then there was no more banging on the door.

The animal sounds continued, though. They rolled past us in thundering waves. The flapping of wings; the shuffling and stomping of feet, small and large; the shattering of glass; the rending of metal. They passed us by, and we didn't move, and we didn't speak. We barely even breathed.

At last, the hallway was silent again. No animal noises, no human noises. Grace sighed in relief. Malloryn groaned, and then sat up, clutching her head in her hands.

"What happened?" she asked.

"Things went a little sideways," said Grace.

"We're still alive," I said.

"For now," said Grace. "We have to get out of here, though."

She inched open the door and peered out, then waved for us to follow. I helped Malloryn to her feet, and we left the control room together.

The menagerie was a ruin of shattered glass, broken tiles, and flickering lights hanging from the walls by their wiring. Thick smoke filled the air, and tongues of fire crackled here and there amid the rubble. An alarm sounded somewhere down the hall. There was no sign of the guards who'd been banging on the door.

My head was still throbbing from Malloryn's song, and the blare of the alarm and the choking taste of smoke in my lungs did nothing to help.

"Elevator," said Grace, coughing every other syllable. The three of us staggered down the hall, past the empty enclosures, Malloryn leaning on both of us for support.

As we got near to the elevator, I began to taste clean, fresh air, and when we reached it, I could see why. The door had been pried open, and the elevator had been torn from the shaft and heaved down the hall. It lay on its side amid a pile of debris. I peered into the empty shaft. At the top, the metal door had been wrenched open.

"Well, that sucks," said Grace.

We looked back down the way we'd just come, through the haze of smoke. The hallway was quiet, still. But far away, I could hear the echoes of strange noises.

"There's gotta be another way out," I said.

"Let's try the other end of the hall," said Grace.

I turned to Malloryn.

"Can you walk?" I asked.

She nodded weakly.

"Then let's go," I said.

I'd only gone a few paces when something grabbed my arm and drew me into one of the paddocks.

"Help me," whispered a familiar voice. It took a moment for the smoke to clear, but when it did, I saw the face of Dr. Batiste, bloodied and terrified.

I slid an arm under his shoulder.

"We're getting out of here," I said. "Which way?"

He pointed down the hall. Just then, something shifted in the dark at the back of the enclosure, and we both jumped. Together we ran from the paddock and whatever was still inside it.

We caught up to Malloryn and Grace, and the four of us shuffled back through the smoke and the rubble and the wicking fires to the other end of the hall. We turned left and passed through an infirmary. The room had been trashed. Procedure tables had been wrenched from the floor and turned upside down. Fluorescent tubes hung naked from their gutted fixtures, flickering. A sink had been torn from its plumbing, and water flowed freely from the ravaged pipes. But for all the chaos, the room was quiet, except for the soft, round beeps and clicks of medical equipment. Those eerie sounds tugged at me, stung me in places I rarely visited. I paused and listened. I wanted, irrationally, to stop and sit with them, like they were beacons guiding me toward something I'd lost.

"Marjan!" Grace. "What are you doing?"

She and Malloryn were already at the far door. Dr. Batiste was close behind. I shook off the longing and pressed on with them into a room big enough to drive a tractor trailer into.

The remnants of scattered skirmishes lay here and there. A patch of white, downy feathers that fluttered in an invisible breeze. Spent shell casings. Broken weapons. A single black boot, empty, roughly unlaced.

A path of light from industrial lamps installed amid the high ceiling rafters snaked across the wide, flat floor to a tunnel lit with red emergency lamps that curved up and out of sight. On either side and above us, the room dipped into a darkness deep enough to contain all the monsters I could imagine. I wasn't the only one seeing monsters either. The other three had stopped at the entrance. Everyone was watching the shadows.

"This is the intake bay," said Dr. Batiste. "That tunnel leads to the surface."

"Are you sure there isn't another way?" asked Malloryn, looking with apprehension down the lighted pathway.

"The other way out is the elevator," said the doctor.

No one moved. No one wanted to go first.

"You don't have another one of those spells, do you?" Grace asked Malloryn. Malloryn shot her a weak, exhausted glare.

Dr. Batiste looked at me. "You're the whisperer. You should go first. They won't hurt you."

"You don't know that," I said.

"You're the reason we're all here," he said. "I'd say you owe us."

Malloryn and Grace both looked over at me. He had a point. Everyone here had sacrificed something, except for me. Malloryn was as pale as a ghost. Grace had risked her life. Dr. Batiste was bleeding, and was probably out of a job. What had I given up?

"Fine," I said.

I stepped out onto the floor, alone, while Malloryn, Grace, and Dr. Batiste watched from the safety of the infirmary doorway. If anything came out of the shadows, they could easily duck back in and slam the doors shut. Those doors would hold for at least a little while. But I was fully exposed, and there would be nowhere for me to run.

The huge room deadened the sound of my footsteps. The world was reduced to just a few colors and textures. The tunnel, red and sinister before me. The floor, pale gray reflecting the white lights above. And the darkness, which was alive. It moved like troubled water, just at the corners of my vision. It breathed. It made sounds that might have been real or might have been imagined.

Halfway across the room, I looked back. Grace, Malloryn, and Dr. Batiste were watching from the doorway, which seemed very far away. It was reassuring that I'd gone this far without being eaten. At the same time, I felt like an astronaut floating out in space, at the very end of my tether, or maybe off it completely.

"I think it might be okay," I said, into the emptiness between us. They came slowly out of the doorway, first Malloryn, then Grace, and finally Dr. Batiste. They walked with cautious steps, like there were landmines beneath the concrete.

They were close enough that I saw their faces change, all at once. I saw their eyes all lock on the same thing, over my shoulder and off in the distance. I turned slowly around.

A lurching shadow was lumbering down the tunnel toward us on heavy feet. At the entrance to the tunnel, it stopped, its dark bulk blocking the path. A pair of beady black eyes flashed in the darkness. Two massive hands emerged from the shadows, closed into fists, and pounded together so hard that sparks flew off their stony knuckles.

"I say we all run in different directions," said Grace, her voice low. "Try to confuse it."

"What if it doesn't move?" said Dr. Batiste. "It's blocking the only exit. If we scatter, it could pick us off one by one. We should all run back to the infirmary. Shut the door, barricade it, try to find something to fight it with."

"I can't run," said Malloryn.

No one said anything to that.

The giant knocked its fists together again. The crack of its knuckles rattled my bones. Its features knotted into a stony grimace, revealing a row of crooked yellow teeth. Its mouth made the hissing, grating sound of rock sliding against rock.

Dr. Batiste was the first to blink.

"Nope," he said. "Not this." Then he jumped and bolted back toward the infirmary.

I fully expected the giant to charge, but it didn't. The opposite—it seemed to hunker down right where it was. In fact, I almost thought I saw a look of dismay ripple across its face.

"Guys?"

Dr. Batiste's voice came from just a few steps away. He sounded troubled. Still, I didn't really feel like taking my eyes off the giant, and neither did anyone else.

"GUYS?"

Behind us, something huge let out an angry snort.

I turned around to see a long, thick lance of black, thorny spikes advancing lazily toward Dr. Batiste on four powerful legs. A pair of dark eyes found mine and locked on to them.

"Is that . . . ," said Malloryn, her voice soft with awe.

"Yeah," I said. "That's it."

The unicorn lumbered heavily toward us, blocking any hope of returning to the infirmary. It bore new wounds—cuts and scrapes, a bite, a ripped ear. And it bore a new weariness, like a soldier stalking off a battlefield.

It could have killed all four of us with a single swipe of its braided horn. It looked like it had already done its share of killing. The thorny tips were dripping with fresh blood.

The unicorn backed Dr. Batiste right up into us, and then it stopped. It looked at me a moment longer, and then it turned its ageless eyes to the giant. It let out a deep bellow and tossed its head in the air, waving its horn in a fierce, ragged circle.

In reply, the giant stomped its feet, cracking the concrete beneath them. Then it straightened its sloped shoulders, opened its mouth, and let out a grinding hiss.

The unicorn shouldered its way between us, pushing us all aside to make room for its massive frame. It lowered its horn again and took several deliberate, fearless steps toward the tunnel.

At this the giant pounded on the ground in a rage, roaring and smashing the concrete underfoot so that it rose up in a fine mist. Its tiny black eyes never left the unicorn.

The unicorn took another step toward it, then stopped and pawed at the ground with one heavy hoof. It bowed its head so that its horn scraped across the ground, drawing pale blue sparks. Then it let out a stubborn grunt and stood up tall and proud.

For a moment, the giant was as still as rock. Then it growled once more, turned, and thundered back up the tunnel and out of sight.

The unicorn stayed exactly where it was a few moments longer, watching the giant go. When the giant had disappeared, the unicorn glanced once back at me, pawed at the ground again, and lumbered on toward the tunnel, its bearing weary and defiant.

No one spoke. For a while, no one moved. At last, we followed it, across the room, up the red tunnel, and finally out into the night, through doors that had been torn and beaten open by hands much bigger and stranger than ours.

Horatio's mansion was on fire. Part of it, anyway—the part near the elevator. Columns of smoke issued out of several windows. Fire alarms blared like angry calliopes, but no one seemed to be doing anything about it.

Probably because there were other things to worry about.

The trucks had been smashed and gutted. Their windshields were spiderwebbed from the force of heavy impacts. One cab had been flipped onto its side. Trailers had been ripped open, their contents spilled everywhere. I saw a few guards and workers wandering the grounds, unarmed, dazed, bloodied. Here and there, people tended to the injured. Everyone seemed only half-conscious. But they were helping each other. They were trying to save each other.

The unicorn stalked among them, ignored, forgotten. No one here had the will anymore to chase it, to run it down with one of those big trucks, to try to shoot it. The creature walked out the front gate, and seemed to grow more powerful with each step. It crossed the highway, and vanished into the trees.

"We did it," said Malloryn. "We saved it, didn't we?"

"Yeah," I said. "We did."

A tired, satisfied smile drifted across Malloryn's face. "We did it," she intoned again.

Except I didn't feel satisfied.

Something's missing.

Somewhere on the compound was the man who'd killed my

father. I needed to face him. I needed to hear it from him, and I needed to know why.

I started toward the house.

"Hey," called Grace. "Where are you going?"

"I need to find someone," I said. "You don't have to come."

I didn't look back. I didn't expect anyone would follow me, and I was right. When I got to the main entrance to the mansion, I was alone.

The front door had been pulled from its hinges. The lights were out. The air smelled of smoke, and the foyer had been ransacked. Claw marks on the floor and the walls. Windows smashed out. The creatures had come through with fury.

A person emerged from the shadows of the hall, staggering on uncertain legs. It took me a moment to recognize Ava. Her hair had come loose. There were bruises on her face and blood on her clothes.

She stumbled toward me, her eyes fixed on the door. She hardly seemed to notice me. As she teetered past, I grabbed her shoulder.

"Horatio," I said.

She looked at me with eyes that swam with confusion. She cocked her head slightly toward the hallway, the gesture almost imperceptible. Then she drew away from me and staggered on toward the door and out.

The hallway was dark, except for the flickering amber glow of a flame in a distant room. The air was warm, and hazy with smoke. I heard a scuffling sound, and the crack of a rifle, once, twice. More scuffling. Another rifle blast. Then a familiar voice cursing as the scuffling resumed.

Distance was a strange thing in the darkened hall. Behind me was the moonlit foyer. Ahead of me, around a corner, maybe farther, was the light of the fire. The space between felt interminable, unfamiliar. I trailed my fingers along one wall and followed the flickering light and the sounds up ahead. I rounded one corner, and the foyer vanished from view.

It was then that I became aware of a presence moving alongside me, silent and steady. Its breath was soft and even. Without its claws, its footfalls on the marble were as gentle as whispers. I couldn't see it, and I could barely hear it, but I knew it by the feeling in my gut, a black, churning sickness, a terrible hunger.

There was nothing to do, though, but keep walking. It seemed we were headed for the same place.

CHAPTER THIRTY-ONE

REBORN AS ANGELS

Horatio was in his office, a hunting rifle tucked under his arm. The smoke was thicker here. An ominous warmth hung in the air. A terrified bird with radiant golden plumage flapped madly around the ceiling. As I came in, a step or two ahead of my silent companion, Horatio fired off another shot, and missed the frantic bird by inches. He swore aloud and then, seeing me in the doorway, turned and leveled the barrel at me.

"Was this you?" he said, his voice tight with rage.

"I . . . ," I began, but the manticore had entered, and Horatio wasn't looking at me anymore.

The bird, sensing its chance, dove for the door and fluttered out into the hall. The manticore began to stalk the perimeter of the room.

"I see you've made a friend," said Horatio.

He turned the gun on the manticore. Her expression remained flat, empty, betraying nothing.

"I thought you shared our vision," he said, his eyes on the animal pacing the floor with languid steps. "I thought you had it in you, the will to change the world. But you don't. You're ordinary. You're just like all the others. Paralyzed by fear. You think I'm a monster, but you'll stand by while we boil our oceans and poison our land and air. You think this animal here is hungry? The human forces that rule the world are hungrier than a thousand manticores. They'll eat everything that's beautiful and precious, and it won't be enough. We had a chance, Marjan. We could have stopped them. We could have torn down their castles and built a new world. We could have been reborn as angels. We could have changed everything."

The manticore thrust out her tail, a probing strike, testing Horatio's nerves. Horatio cried out and jumped out of the way. He fired off a wild shot that hit the floor, digging up splinters.

"You killed my dad," I said.

Horatio laughed. He chambered another bullet and leveled the gun at the manticore again.

"Is that what you think?" he said in disbelief. "Is that what this is all about?"

The manticore's tail shot out again, prodding, playful. She was toying with him. Horatio dodged with a yip, then brought the gun back level.

"You destroyed everything for this?" he said.

"I think he tried to stop you, and you killed him."

"Your father was in so deep, he couldn't have stopped anything," said Horatio. He and the manticore were locked in a slow, deliberate, sidestepping dance. He shuffled to put his big desk between himself and the creature, but she slid it aside with a powerful sweep of her tail. "He said he hated it, taking my money." He glanced over at me for just a moment. "But he always took it."

The manticore jabbed at him again. He was ready, and jumped aside easily, then locked his sights on her and put his finger to the trigger.

"Why should I believe you?" I asked.

His concentration momentarily broken, he eased his finger off and scowled in annoyance. "I don't give a damn what you believe," he said.

The manticore batted at him again, and this time he raised the gun and fired. The bullet struck the manticore in her flank, leaving a clean, simple hole that began, after a moment, to leak blood. Her body stiffened, and she made a sort of cooing noise, but her face didn't change.

"Look at that," said Horatio with dark delight. "I got her."

Then she lunged at him.

The gun clattered across the room, and the manticore pinned him easily to the floor, her paws holding his arms down. Her tail rose up, and its tip hung over his head.

"Help," he said.

"I'm not sure I can," I replied.

The manticore craned her neck down, so that she and Horatio were eye to eye. From down the hall, the sound of the fire was drawing nearer.

"Please," he said.

His voice had gone loose and watery. His lips quivered, and he tried to cower away, but the manticore's paws held him fast. Her eyes shone with naked hunger. Her tiny, placid mouth glimmered with a sheen of saliva.

"Please," he said again.

The manticore's tail drew back to strike. I felt the emptiness inside me swelling, pushing away horror, disgust, fear. At its center, the pulsing catalyst for every awful thing I'd ever done, the deepest truth of my life.

Something's missing.

"Wait," I said.

And to my surprise, the manticore froze.

Horatio began to laugh, a nervous, grateful, unhinged spasm of laughter that quickly became a hacking cough. The smoke was thicker now. The fire was closer. The manticore still held him fast, still watched him with the same untroubled death mask.

"That's right, Marjan," he said when he'd recovered his breath. "Now tell her to let me go. Tell her to—"

"No," I said.

"No?" he said.

"Tell me why."

"Why what?" he asked.

"Why did you kill him?"

His face fell. "Marjan," he said. "I didn't."

"You're lying."

"I didn't kill your father," said Horatio. "I needed him. I needed him alive. Make her stop."

The manticore, bored, hungry, began to paw at his throat. A thin thread of saliva descended from her mouth.

"I don't believe you," I said.

"It's the truth," he said, his voice now trembling. "I would have kidnapped him if I'd needed to. But I wouldn't have killed him. He was too important. He understood these animals. Just like you do. He could reach them, and no one else could. We needed him. Please let me go. Please tell her to let me go."

A fit of coughing overtook his words. The room was hot, a wrathful, choking heat. It was starting to choke me, too. It was making my eyes burn. I could hear the fire. It sounded like some giant animal breathing in and out, in and out.

"We have to get out of here, Marjan," said Horatio. "You have to tell her to let me go. I swear I didn't kill your father."

He looked pathetic. He looked powerless and small, and I felt monstrous, watching him squirm.

"Let him go," I said. The manticore's eyes narrowed. For a long, stubborn moment, she didn't move. Then, reluctantly, she eased off him, one paw at a time. Last of all, she drew her tail back. Horatio sat up, shook out his arms, and took a deep breath.

"Thank you, Marjan." Then he dove for the gun and pointed it at me. "I didn't kill your father," he said. "But I'll be damned if you're going to walk out of here alive."

The manticore moved like lightning. The gun went off, but the bullet sailed wide, hit the wall with a *chock*. The rifle fell, smashed, to the ground. Horatio was on his knees, stunned, clutching his shoulder. In the hall, the fire roared.

Horatio looked from the manticore to me, a tragic, baffled expression on his face. There was, maybe, still time to save him, throw his arm over my shoulder, and limp us out the door together.

The smoke was streaming in now, thick gouts that swept across the ceiling. The heat was becoming unbearable. My brain screamed at me to get away, get out, find good air, survive.

"Help," said Horatio, a pathetic, feeble plea. I could have swooped in and dragged him to safety. He would have owed me his life. Maybe that would have had some value. But I realized in that moment that I didn't care what happened to Horatio Prendergast. I didn't care if the manticore ate him, bones and all. He would have killed millions of people. He would have killed the unicorn.

The manticore's mouth began to draw wide, her awful death smile slicing across the blank canvas of her face.

Horatio screamed. I knew then that he'd told me the truth. He hadn't killed my dad. And it didn't matter.

Something's missing.

I turned away, and found myself looking down at a small figure standing in the doorway, unperturbed by the approaching fire or the horrors taking place over my shoulder. It was Sturges. I had no idea how long he'd been there.

The manticore's jaw snapped shut, twisting Horatio's scream into something that sounded more like the roaring flames. I was glad to be turned away. I put my hand over Sturges's eyes. As my hand touched him, I saw the little boy Horatio had been—curious, wildly intelligent, and vulnerable. I saw, from the corner of that same bedroom that Horatio had kept in the silo, how he'd been bullied, hurt, taken advantage of. I saw how the room had been moved. How it had been sealed away in the far corner of the cavern. I felt how the world had become suddenly and inexplicably small, and dark. How years and years had passed, alone, as Horatio grew stranger and stranger on the other side of the glass, consumed by the fever-dream of all those creatures as they changed him, warped him. I felt his love turning to pity, to distrust, to disgust. Hope turning to sorrow.

Gently, but firmly, Sturges removed my hand from his eyes. I slipped past him, out into the hall.

"We should go," I said to the gnome. The words crackled in my throat.

Sturges glanced at me once, then turned back to the doorway. His meaning was clear. I left him there, and as I walked, then ran, away down the hall, the bellowing of the fire swallowed up Horatio's cries.

Malloryn and Grace were still waiting outside when I came out. I was grateful for the sight of their faces. At the same time, I felt like a monster. I'd let a man die a terrible death, a death

I probably could have stopped, and all I felt inside was disappointment. I'd been wrong. Horatio hadn't killed my dad. But if he hadn't, and the Fells hadn't, who had? I had nothing. No clues. No ideas.

We stood there, the three of us, watching the fire burn for a moment.

"Dr. Batiste?" I said.

"Left," said Malloryn. "Went to find his car. We told him we were going to wait for you."

It felt like an incredible kindness, that they had waited here, not knowing if I was dead or alive, not knowing if I would walk back out of those flames or not.

"We should get out of here," said Grace.

CHAPTER THIRTY-TWO

AFTERMATH

The phone was ringing at reception. It would be a client, the same as it always was. A regular, ordinary client. Still, I listened, just to make sure.

In Exam One, Dr. P was tending to a cockatiel with some kind of fungal infection on its beak. We'd had more birds than usual, the past week. I wasn't sure if that meant something, but Dr. P was happy.

Back in the procedure room, a young beagle's gonads were being removed. If I put my ear to the wall of the office, I could just hear the familiar sound of Dr. Batiste's clipped, precise surgical voice, urgent but calm, muttering single words in a hushed, staccato rhythm.

I left the office, walked out through the lobby, past Ms. Cochran and her tabby, which was starting to develop some kind of kidney issue. I pushed open the front door and walked out onto the street. A pair of cars rushed past, racing to beat the light at the corner. The sky was a pale, blank blue—the kind of clear sky you don't really notice if you've got other things on your mind.

I checked the news again. It had been almost an hour since the last time I'd looked, which was pretty good. The first few days, I'd been refreshing every couple of minutes. And not just during the day. Late into the night.

I hadn't slept well since the night at Horatio's. When I closed my eyes, I saw the manticore's face, her jaws hinging open. I heard Horatio's screams. I felt the heat of the blaze that would eventually consume the whole house. Sometimes I caught a hint of acrid, smoky scent, in my clothes, in my hair, and my stomach lurched. It was like it was all happening again, like I was witnessing it all over again. My heart would race in my chest. Sometimes I caught myself swinging my hands at the air, trying to disperse the visions as if they were a vapor around me. Sometimes I scolded myself for letting my thoughts return to those images. Sometimes I pleaded with my brain to let them go. Once, waking up from a nightmare, I thought I heard something stalking in the backyard. I turned on a light and looked out the window to see a raccoon slink off into the dark. I didn't go back to sleep.

Still, the sky hadn't fallen, so that was something.

The news story was blandly tragic—fire at remote compound claims life of reclusive billionaire and others. There hadn't been a word about the creatures. They'd left Horatio's prison, and they'd simply vanished into the night. Every quiet moment, I spent half expecting a knock on the door—the police; the press; the Fells; Horatio himself, come to seek payment, or to exact revenge. But no one came, and nothing rose to the level of public newsworthiness other than a spate of missing cats that seemed only slightly higher than average.

To be fair, I'd given Jane Glass and the Fells a heads-up about what had happened. I don't know what they did with the information, but they were certainly better equipped than I was to scrub Horatio's compound of clues to the creatures' existence. And it was at least partly their fault that things had happened the way they had, so it seemed only fair to share the mess with them.

I called Dr. Batiste three days after the night at Menagerie. He took my offer. He needed the money, and I needed someone on staff who understood the special landscape of my world, who could do the work that I couldn't. And anyway, he was an excellent vet.

When we'd returned from the menagerie, late at night, there were two cold falafel sandwiches carefully wrapped and sealed in ziplock bags on the front doorstep. In Francesca's cabin next door, a light was on. When we went inside, the light turned off.

Malloryn had crawled into bed that night and slept for twelve hours. Zorro had curled up next to her and never left her side. The next day, she'd had to beg her boss not to fire her for leaving work early to save the world. It seemed that life would never be quite fair to her, so to balance things out, I told her she could stay with me as long as she wanted.

I went to my first swim meet two weeks later. In the water, Carrie was a different person. She was sleek and powerful and, more than anything else, calm. The team came up a bit short in the end, but Carrie and I made up after that. It wasn't hard. Some friends, you just need to show up for them.

With Grace, things were slower and stranger. I sat with her a lot, helping her process everything she'd witnessed that night. What we'd done, what we'd seen, still didn't make sense to her. She knew it had all happened, but a part of her still didn't believe it. One afternoon, I told her some of my dad's stories. They seemed to help. It felt good to say them out loud, after all those years of carrying them in my head, to finally share with another person some of the forces that had shaped my life, that might shape it forever. This was the culture he'd given me—a culture of things that were and were not. It was where my life had happened, and hadn't happened. And now someone else in the world could begin to understand that.

I realized something then too. There was a whole side of my heritage that I barely knew. A language I didn't speak, customs I didn't understand, a country that felt distant and very different. I wanted to be closer to those things. I wanted them to mean something to me, even if I had to work at it. Even if they hadn't been given to me, the way they had been for the kids I used to see at Noruz parties. So I called up my dad's brother Hamid one day, and we talked. He was patient and warm, and funnier than I would have expected from our last meeting. He reminded me a bit of my old memories of my dad, the ones from before Mom died.

"You have family here, Marjan," he said. It felt nice to hear my name spoken in a voice not so different from my father's. "They would very much like to meet you."

"I think I'd like to meet them, too," I said. It was strange to think of all those distant and pixelated faces as family, but for the first time, it felt comforting too. The gap between our lives felt smaller. The things I wanted still seemed very far away, but the world felt a bit bigger, and maybe I did too.

Strangely, I didn't hate Horatio. I felt sorry for him. He'd started something, and it had grown bigger than him, bigger than his mind could handle. Bigger, probably, than any mind on earth could handle. He'd just gotten lost in it.

I wondered if that nameless power was changing me, too. The world seemed much more fragile now. The cars I passed on the way to work, the faces of kids at school, even the comfort of my dad's office—everything was made of the most brilliant and delicate crystal. The slightest touch might shatter it forever.

I checked the eaves of the clinic for my old stray cat, but he was nowhere to be seen. Still, I poured a little cat food into his bowl, rattled it around a few times, and set it outside the door. I knew that the next time I checked, the food would be gone.

Back inside, I peeked around to see if there was anything I could do to help anyone. The lobby was quiet. The patients in back were being tended to. The procedure room was already cleaned and prepped for whatever the next operation might be. There was no one who needed me. So I headed back to my office to do homework.

I'd been there only a few minutes when there was a knock on the door. It was Dr. Paulson.

"Is this a good time to talk?" she asked.

"Sit, please," I said. She smiled and sat down across from me.

She had a slim folder under her arm. It didn't look like a patient record. She looked at it, then at me.

"So," she said. "Sometimes you know someone for years, and then all of a sudden one day, you see them in a different way."

She paused, looked away. She seemed uncertain, almost nervous. I don't think I'd ever seen her nervous before. Then she rested her gaze squarely on me.

"Your dad and I," she said. And then she didn't say anything for a long time. And when I didn't say anything, she held out her hands, palms up, and said, "Well. That's it. Jamsheed and I."

She let out a sigh of relief, and everything, all the birdlike watchfulness, seemed to relax and melt away, and I saw for the first time someone who was confused, and lonely, and grieving. I sat there saying nothing, while the world did that warping thing it did every time the basic facts of my life changed.

"There were feelings," she said. "Nothing more than that. But they were . . . strong feelings."

"I had no idea," I said, which felt stupid, but also absolutely true.

"He didn't want to tell you. He wasn't ready. He told me there was something he had to do first. He told me he had to make things right with you. So I waited. I was waiting . . . " She stopped talking.

My mind began playing back all the times I'd seen my dad and Dr. P together, looking for all the clues I'd missed. I felt like a small child, too young to understand events going on around me. I wanted to demand answers, but there didn't seem to be any more answers to demand. Dr. P, in her usual blunt way, had already told me everything I needed to know.

"How long . . .?" I said, because I needed to ask something.

"It depends on when you start counting," she said. "A couple of months, I guess."

"Why?" I said. "I mean, why him? Why now?"

"He was a good man," she said. "He was hurt, and he was guarded, but he was good. And I think he wanted to be happy."

"Why didn't you tell me sooner?" I asked.

"I didn't think you wanted to know."

"So why tell me now?"

She took another breath, and the stalking bird returned.

"Because I want to buy the clinic," she said, "and I want you to trust me."

She set the folder down between us and slid it over to me. I opened it and scanned the few pages inside.

"It's very fair," she said. "I showed it to your accountant, and he agrees."

"You showed this to David?" I said.

"I asked him not to say anything," said Dr. Paulson. "I wanted to tell you myself."

I read over the number, and then I read over it again. It was more than fair.

"Why?" I asked.

"Because I want you to say yes," she said.

"But, why? Why this place?"

She smiled to herself.

"We had birds, growing up. Parakeets and chickens. I took care of them. I always wanted to be a vet. I've always wanted my own clinic, ever since I was little. But when I got out of vet school, the money wasn't there. My parents were schoolteachers. We didn't have a lot. I worked as a relief vet for a while, a few different places. Then your dad hired me. I thought I'd be here a couple of years, long enough to get my credit in order. But then my dad got sick, and after that was done, my mom got sick. There's never been a good time."

"And you really want this place."

"Everything I need is here."

"And you want to make this offer. This offer here."

"I'm already approved for the loan. The paperwork's in there."

I flipped through the pages.

"I have to think about this," I said.

"I'll take good care of it," she said. "I promise."

"I know you will," I said.

Then, delicate and precise, she stood up to leave.

"Dr. P," I said. She stopped in the doorway. "He never made things right, whatever that means. In case you were wondering. But I think he was trying."

She didn't say anything. When she walked out, the silence that took her place was at least as strange and surreal as any one of Horatio's creatures.

Dad and Dr. P . . . I said those words over and over again, and I couldn't make them make sense. Why hadn't he told me? Why hadn't he made things right? Suddenly I was angry.

I was angry at Ellen Paulson for not being who I thought she was supposed to be. She wasn't just Dr. P, seeing patients in Exam Two, and that very fact upset something delicate and safe. She wanted things, just like me. She was tired and hurt and frustrated, just like me. All these months, she'd carried her secrets, her grief and her desires, revealing nothing—a heron stalking in the reeds. Now that she'd told me, I didn't know how to look at her anymore. I didn't know who she was.

I was angry at my dad, for everything. For not doing whatever it was he meant to do, for waiting too long. For never telling me anything. For making me feel like I was broken. For getting himself killed, probably for something stupid.

I was angry at myself, for not seeing what was happening right in front of me. For missing the truth when it was right under my nose, because I wasn't paying enough attention.

And I was angry that I wasn't enough, that I wasn't old enough or good enough to run this place the way it should be run. I was angry that I had to choose, and that either way I would lose something. If I kept the clinic, Dr. P would drift away—maybe not immediately, but soon. One way or another, she'd find her way to her own practice. If I took the offer, I would lose the one constant left in my life.

   But the meanest, smallest indignation was that she was right to buy me out. I didn't belong here. It was my past.

I didn't deserve to be here, and Dr. Paulson did.

The offer was a good one. I didn't need David Ginn to tell me that. But I went to see him anyway. It was late that afternoon, and he was just shutting down for the day. Still, he welcomed me in and pulled up the chair for me to sit.

"How long have you known?" I asked.

"A couple of weeks," said David. "It's a lot to take in, I know."

"Would my dad have taken an offer like this?"

David laughed to himself and shook his head sadly.

"This was his life," he said. "Maybe if he thought he was ready to retire . . . But honestly, I don't think he would have ever retired, Marjan."

"So this is me, selling off his legacy," I said.

"That's one way of looking at it," he said. He clasped his hands together. "But maybe I can give you another one. These last few months, everything you've done, that's you honoring his legacy."

I had to smile a bit at this. David had no idea of all the things I'd done over the last few months. Nevertheless, he took my smile as encouragement, and continued with an emphatic nod.

"You stepped up, and you didn't have to. You could have sold everything and walked away, but you didn't. You ran that shop, and you kept it running. You met every challenge that came your way. And I think if your dad could see you now, he'd be real proud."

David was right. I think my dad would have been proud. He might have done everything differently, but in the end, we'd saved the world. Dads live for that kind of thing.

"Thank you, David," I said. "That means a lot."

He stood and held out his arms for a hug, and when I walked into it, he wrapped them around my shoulders and held me tight. I thought maybe he was crying, just a bit.

After a moment, he released me and set me back at arms' length. His eyes, bright with a thin glaze of tears, were lit up with the spark of an idea. He clapped his hands together, rested his chin on his knuckles, and raised an inquisitive eyebrow.

"Say, what are you doing tomorrow night?" he asked. "Do you have plans? You should come for dinner. It could be a celebration. Your father's legacy, and your future. Liz and the kids would love to see you. What do you say?"

His eyes twinkled with warmth and sadness and hope.

"Of course," I said.

CHAPTER THIRTY-THREE

DINNER

The Ginn home was smaller than the other houses around it, and just a bit shabbier at the edges. There was a fig tree in the yard with dark teardrops of fruit under its broad leaves. The lights were on in the windows, a warm, welcoming glow. Through the branches of the tree, I could just see into the dining room. Elizabeth was setting the table. I hadn't seen her since the memorial.

I walked past the fig tree and parked my bike under the steps that led to the front door. How many times had I walked up these steps, sleeping bag in hand, my dad's car parked right there at the curb? It could have been my dad standing next to me, waiting to pass me off with a handshake to the Ginns for a night or two. I could have been nine years old, still trusting that this was normal.

For a moment, it felt like this had all happened already, like I was walking into my past. The feeling was so convincing that I caught myself lulling into an earlier version of myself, one who knew nothing about hidden creatures or family secrets. It was tempting to pretend, for a night, that my world was normal—as normal as it could be, anyway.

But I wasn't that nine-year-old girl anymore. I wasn't even the same person I'd been right after my dad had died. I felt tougher. My vision felt sharper. My world wasn't normal, and it never would be. There were secrets everywhere. There were dreams and nightmares standing, invisible, in every doorway, behind every face. And some of them, the very strangest of them, might one day need my help. I had a duty now, to pay attention, to see the world clearly, to try to understand as much as I could.

The door opened, and David was standing in the entry, a smile on his face.

"Kids!" he called over his shoulder. "Marjan's here!"

There was a scrambling at the stairs as he showed me in. Ramsey and Cole came down in a tumble of knees and elbows and nut-blond hair. It had been a couple of years since I'd seen either of them.

"Eight and six, right?" I said.

"Nine and seven, can you believe it?" said David.

They were taller, more possessed of distinct energies and spirits—Ramsey, thoughtful, almost brooding; Cole, wild, messy, and exuberant. They were more the people they would eventually become. But they were still kids, and they proved it when they both ran up to me, Cole taking my hand, and Ramsey grabbing a leg.

"You always were their favorite babysitter," said David. "Come inside."

Inside, it was clean, bright, and warm. A bunch of flowers sat in a vase on a table by the door. David took my coat and hung it up.

"Sit, sit," he said as he led us to the sofa in the living room, the one I used to sleep on. "I'll get you something to drink."

"I'll be right out," came Elizabeth's voice from the kitchen.

There were photos on the mantel above the fireplace: David and Elizabeth on their wedding day; Elizabeth, exhausted, wearing a hospital gown, cradling baby Ramsey; David holding baby Cole, while Ramsey sat on Elizabeth's lap. The brothers on a sunny day, crawling on the rocks at the edge of a vast body of water. Beside the photos were a few assorted trinkets: a polished seashell; a scale model of a vintage Porsche; an ornate, stoppered brass flask. Everything was exactly as I remembered it.

David returned with two tall glasses of water and a bowl of nuts.

Ramsey and Cole had settled into a corner, where they were playing some kind of card game with brightly colored art and inscrutable rules.

"You look different, Marjan," said David. "You look confident. You look like someone who's ready for the world."

"I don't know about that," I said. "But I think I'm ready for the next step."

"Which is?"

"It's hard to explain," I said.

I'd mapped it out in my head. I'd keep up the family tradition—I had to, no question. But I couldn't do it my dad's way. It just wasn't possible.

We weren't going to be a veterinary clinic anymore. We'd be something looser, more flexible. I'd ask Dr. Batiste for help. We'd work something out with Dr. P to rent the procedure room if we needed it. I'd hire Malloryn on retainer—you never knew when a witch would come in handy. I might even call Ezra in. She had skills that might be useful.

If the numbers worked out the way I'd planned, Dr. Paulson's offer would be enough to cover a year's worth of expenses. It would be a chaotic year, but chaos didn't scare me—I'd grown up with it. I guess I had my dad to thank for that.

And, of course, I had to finish school.

We settled into our seats, and I watched the boys go back and forth in their card game, unaware of anything else in the world. Just then, Elizabeth marched out of the kitchen in a green apron, her sleeves rolled up to her elbows, her blond hair pulled back in a practical ponytail.

"It's almost dinnertime," she said. Then, to the boys, "Finish the game and get washed up."

The boys made no move to end the game, and after a moment, Elizabeth strode across the room and took the cards away from them. "After dinner," she said over their protests. Then she turned to me and smiled. "I've been hearing all about your adventures."

"You . . . uh . . . you have?" I said.

"I think it's great what you've been doing," she said.

"It is?" I wondered what it was she thought I'd been doing. I wondered, for a long, dizzying moment, what she knew.

"The clinic meant a lot to your dad," she said. "He would have been so proud of you for keeping it going."

Cole walked between us, beautifully oblivious to our conversation, and held up his cards for me to see. There was a dragon breathing fire on one, and a castle with an eerie glow in the windows on another.

"Looks like a pretty good hand," I said. He nodded, satisfied, and tromped off.

"I made a lamb roast," said Elizabeth, heading back into the kitchen. "I hope that's okay for you."

As if on cue, a warm, wondrous smell wafted in from

the kitchen—garlic and herbs and the rich scent of lamb. Something tugged on my shirt. I looked down, and Ramsey was looking up at me with his big brown eyes, eyes like his dad's. He waved at me.

"Hi, Marjan," he said.

"Hi, Ramsey," I said. "What grade are you in now?"

Ramsey held up three fingers. He grinned, showing a missing tooth.

"But he's doing math with the fourth graders," said David. "Smart kid. Isn't that right, buddy?"

Ramsey shrugged, sheepish and suddenly shy, then slunk off to wash his hands for dinner.

"They're so big now," I said.

"They were babies a week ago," said David. "It hardly even feels real." He pushed up from his chair, took his water glass, and guided me to the dining room.

We took our seats around the table, David at the head of it, Ramsey and Cole sitting opposite each other at the far end. The lamb roast sat trussed up and glistening in its juices on a white serving dish. There was a mound of buttery mashed potatoes in a deep bowl, and a casserole of wilted kale studded with flecks of toasted garlic. There was macaroni and cheese for the kids, and garlic toast in a wicker basket.

David took up the carving utensils and began to slice the meat.

A cut of lamb was placed on my plate, and a dollop of mashed potatoes. Elizabeth dished out mac and cheese to the kids, and they dug in with glee. "Cole's favorite," she explained, to which Ramsey proudly added, "Mine's pizza."

The lamb was pink and tender and moist, perfectly cooked. The potatoes were creamy and thick. The kale shimmered on my plate.

"Well," said Elizabeth, "bon appétit."

I sliced into the lamb. For just a second, the blade caught, and the meat felt as tough as old leather. But a moment later, it gave way, and the knife passed through it like it was warm butter. A column of rosemary-scented steam rose up from the cut. The smell made my mouth water.

As I brought the fork to my lips, though, the intoxicating aroma gave way to a very different smell: dank, fetid, and foul.

No sooner had I smelled it than it was gone, but my stomach had already turned. I put the fork down with a loud clatter. Everyone else looked over at me.

"Is everything okay?" asked David.

"I'm sorry," I said.

David and Elizabeth shared a glance, worried and embarrassed.

"Is there something wrong . . . with the food?" ventured Elizabeth in a meek, wounded voice.

"No," I said. "I'm sure it's wonderful."

I forced a smile, cleared my throat a couple of times, and tried to settle my stomach with a deep breath. I looked down at the plate. The food still looked magnificent, better than anything I'd eaten in weeks. It almost looked good enough to forget the bad smell, but not quite.

I pushed away from the table and stood up. "I just need some air," I said. I walked quickly out of the dining room, back into the living room, and stood there, breathing deeply.

David came in a moment later, a glass of water in his hand.

"Are you all right?" asked David.

"I'll be fine, I'm sure," I said. I did feel better, being away from the food. A couple of minutes out here, and maybe the feeling would pass altogether.

I could feel David standing there. His shadow weighed heavily at the corner of my vision. I was too ashamed, and too confused, to want to look him in the eye. I looked around for something to stare at, and my eyes landed on the old metal flask on the mantel.

"Are you having second thoughts?" he asked, from what seemed like very far away. "It's okay if you are. You haven't signed anything yet."

"No second thoughts," I said.

"I know this is a scary time," said David. "Everything's changing. I'm sure it all feels very uncertain. It's hard to know if you're making the right choice."

"Am I?" I asked, still not looking at him.

Is that really what's bothering me?

"You kind of have to force yourself to believe that you are," he said. "That's the trick. You believe it, until it's true."

"Just like running a business," I said.

The smell—like garbage. Like dead things. Was that doubt? Or was it something else? It seemed so . . .

"Just like anything," he said. "Belief, illusion, reality. We make our world, Marjan. It's magic, and we do it every day."

"Is that what we do?" I asked.

Something surfaced in my brain, a minnow of an idea, a question that darted away into the dark before I could ask it.

"Maybe you want some time alone," said David.

I heard him start to retreat back into the dining room. I stared at the bottle and tried to pull that thought back into my head, tried to get it to hold still. But all I got were David's own words, echoing back to me.

Belief, illusion, reality.

We do it every day.

Something's missing.

"David?" I said.

I heard him stop. My heart punched at the walls of my chest.

"How did you meet my dad?" I asked.

He was quiet a second.

"What do you mean?" he said.

"I mean, the first time you met him. How did it happen? Did he look you up? Did you cold-call him? I mean, what was it?"

Again, a long silence, as the world started to cave in around me. I knew what that kind of silence meant. That's the space where the lie happens.

"I think . . . ," he said. "I think we were introduced."

"Who introduced you?" I said, as evenly as I could.

"I don't . . ." He paused. "I don't think I remember." And then, very quickly, "Here—come back to the table. There's a pie in the oven. Apple pie. We were going to surprise you, but—"

"Misdirection," I said.

"I'm sorry?"

"Vance Cogland," I said. "Lubbock, Texas."

Another long, impenetrable silence.

"Marjan, what's up with these questions?"

I spun around to face him, and saw the fear in his eyes.

"What's missing, David?" I said. "Tell me."

"What are you talking about?" His voice came out high-pitched and cornered. He reached out a hand toward me, and I stepped back.

"Who did it?" I said.

"Did what?" asked David. He took another step toward me, and I took another step back.

Elizabeth was in the doorway now.

"What on earth is going on?" she exclaimed.

"Something's wrong with her," said David.

"Tell her," I said. "Tell her the truth. Tell her about Vance Cogland." He kept advancing, and I kept backing up. "You stay away," I said.

"Should I call the police?" asked Elizabeth. She had her cell phone out.

"Don't," he said, both hands out in front of him now, conciliatory, reasonable.

"Who killed Vance Cogland?" I said.

The look on Elizabeth's face was one of horror. I saw Ramsey peer around the corner of the doorway. I felt half-feral. But it didn't matter now. I was here. I'd come this far. I had to go all the way.

"Who killed my father?"

"David?" Elizabeth, her voice small and terrified. "What is she talking about?"

"It's nothing, Liz," said David, his eyes never leaving mine. "She's just having a hard time."

"Daddy?" said Ramsey.

"You stay back, buddy," he said. "Keep your brother back there too. Marjan . . ."

"No!" I said. "Not until you answer my questions."

"Sit down, and we'll talk."

"Was it you, David? Was it you, in Lubbock?"

"Calm down, Marjan," he said. "You don't know what you're saying."

The room felt hot—a dry, baking heat that smelled of burnt cinnamon and cloves. We danced around the room, him advancing, me sidestepping and retreating.

"You did it," I said. "It was you."

"No," said David. I stepped back into the dining room. Ramsey cowered in a corner. Cole was still sitting in his chair. He was crying.

"It was you," I said again. "You killed them both."

"No!" shouted David. "No! No! No!"

I couldn't get my eyes to focus on him. He was a blur. Everything was a blur—a wobbling, warping smear of color and light. My heart was thumping in my chest. I was sure the room was getting hotter. I felt like I was burning up.

"You killed Vance, and you killed my dad."

"You stay away," David roared. "Stay away from this house, stay away from my family."

The food that had been on our plates was gone. In its place, scraps of cardboard, bits of industrial rubber, crumpled-up paper. Dirty water. Trash. The smells of dinner had vanished, and in their place came the musty odor of years of neglect, the smell of rotting garbage. The paint began peeling off the walls. It cracked and blistered before my eyes. Lightbulbs exploded in their sockets, sending sprays of sparks into the air.

"I just want to know why," I said. "Why did you kill my father?"

But he wasn't listening to me anymore. He upended the table sideways, and it flew through the air and smashed against the wall. Elizabeth screamed. Cole and Ramsey were both sobbing now.

David Ginn looked at me. "What did you do?" he asked. He looked at his own hands, felt his face. "What did you do?"

"David?" said Elizabeth, only her voice was much fainter. The cries of the children grew fainter too. I looked for them, but they were not there anymore. In their places, I saw more trash. An old mop clattered to the floor where Elizabeth Ginn had once stood. A length of rusty chain replaced Ramsey. His brother, Cole, was no more than a ball of faded newspaper. They were gone, all of them. They'd never existed.

I felt sick.

"What did you do?" said David. He stood where the head of the table used to be, arms at his sides, sobbing in helpless disgust as his world disintegrated around him.

The room settled at last into its true form. Dark, boarded-up, home to spiders and rats. This was no place for a family, and no family had lived here in many years. David stood across the room from me, his rage and sorrow burning silent and smokeless behind his eyes.

Neither of us said anything for a long time. Between sobs, he took loud, gasping breaths. He shook his head slowly in disbelief. He looked twenty years older. I wondered how much of this he understood.

"This isn't all . . . ," he muttered to himself. "Isn't all there is."

"You're not human, David," I whispered. "You can feel that, right?"

He gave me a blank, hopeless stare.

"Something's . . . ," he said.

"I know," I said. "I know what you're feeling."

His brow knit up into a jagged, angry V. His eyes locked on mine, and gleamed with dark hatred. The air around me felt thick. It began to vibrate and hum. He took a step toward me, and a rush of hot air nearly knocked me off my feet.

"You did this," he said. "This is your fault."

"No," I said. "David, no. You don't have to—"

But my throat had gone dry. I was breathing in heat. The air curdled around David Ginn as he approached me. I stumbled back, but there was nowhere to go now.

"I'm a monster," said David Ginn, "and it's your fault." His voice came from everywhere. It came from the walls, from the floor. I lost my footing and stumbled, and then I was lying on my back, and David Ginn was standing over me.

"Please," I said. "I want to help."

He shook his head. "You can't help," he said.

Then he reached down and took my neck in both hands, and began to squeeze. I struggled, but he was stronger. His fingers were like steel. A throbbing, crashing sound filled my head. My vision got small, and everything started to feel very far away.

I was eight years old, lying in my bed and looking up at the stars on the ceiling. My dad was telling me a story. The very last story he ever told.

CHAPTER THIRTY-FOUR

THE NIGHTMAN'S LAMP

Once was, once wasn't.

One starry night, on a quiet street of one of the great cities of the older days, a poor man found a tin oil lamp that a traveler had left behind. It was battered and dented, but its construction was sturdy. It was decorated with ornate carvings, and the details and flourishes had been executed with the exquisite refinement of a master artisan. Surely it would fetch a fine price at the bazaar, if the poor man could find a fair merchant.

The poor man brought the lamp back to his hut by the river. He was a nightman, and he made his meager living by emptying the chamber pots of the rich into a great vat, and hauling the waste to the black pits to burn. His hut was near those very pits, and though the smoke from their fires crept often into his little room, so did the damp of the river, so that his room was cold most nights. But it was his life, and he had grown accustomed to it.

He fetched some rags and began to polish the lamp. No sooner had he cleaned it than a column of blue fire burst forth from its spout, shot all the way up to the ceiling, and then came to hover before the poor man's eyes. The spinning whirlwind warped the air with its heat. The flames smelled of burnt cinnamon and cloves but gave off no smoke. In the fire's very center, there floated a small, pale figure with its legs crossed, and its eyes as bright and sharp as diamonds.

"I know what you are," said the poor man. "I don't mean you any trouble."

"And you have caused me none," said the djinn, for djinn he was. "A spiteful wizard locked me away in that prison two hundred and forty years ago. You have set me free."

The poor man, no stranger to the horrors of prisons, relaxed. "Would that your first taste of freedom were a more auspicious place," he said. "I am but a poor nightman, and this hut is all I have. But you are welcome to anything you see."

The djinn bowed, and the flames bowed with him. "An offer worthy of a king," said the djinn. "But it is I who owe you. Thrice may you ask of me, and thrice I shall oblige, be it in my power."

"And what is your power?" asked the poor man.

"The fire and the wind are mine," said the djinn. "There are no secrets from me, for once they are spoken, the wind has them, and the wind never forgets. And no work of man is safe from me, for fire will melt even stone."

"I had a son once," said the poor man. "He was young, and he died of the pox. Can you bring him back to me?"

"Time is not mine," said the djinn. "I grieve for your son, and for you, but I cannot undo that which time has made whole."

"I had a wife once," said the poor man. "I loved her. But when the boy died, she turned away from me. Can you bring her back?"

"If she lives," said the djinn, "I can bring her to you. And if she grieves, perhaps I can gather her grief and take it from her, for grief is the wake of the wind and the fire. But I cannot make her love you."

"Then I am not sure what to ask of you," said the poor man.

"Some ask for gold," said the djinn.

"Gold would not bring me happiness," said the poor man.

"Some ask for harems of women," said the djinn. "Though, truth be told, their harems are phantoms made of fire, and their delights are illusions drawn in subtle flame."

"I suffer no illusions," said the poor man. "And I am too old for harems."

"A kingdom could I bring you," said the djinn.

"I am no king," said the poor man.

"Vitality," said the djinn. "A breath of fire in the veins, and a man will walk for days without sleep, and live a hundred years before he gets old."

"Sleep is where I see my boy," said the poor man. "And I have no desire to live a hundred more years."

"Nonetheless," said the djinn, "I am in your debt. Thrice you may ask of me, and thrice I shall oblige."

The poor man considered. "If the wind is yours," he said, "perhaps you could turn the smoke from the black pits away from my home."

"Done," said the djinn. At once, a wind blew off the river, and the smoke from the black pits was carried away in all directions from the poor man's hut.

The poor man considered again. "If the fire is yours," he said, "perhaps you could leave a little bit behind, to warm this humble place."

"Done," said the djinn. He held out his hand and placed a

tiny, flickering tongue of flame upon the floor in the center of the hut. At once, a radiant heat filled the little room, and the poor man felt a pleasant warmth in his bones.

"Once more may you ask of me," said the djinn.

The poor man considered. "Must it be now?" he asked.

The djinn sighed. "No," he said. "But my people will not have me back until I have fulfilled my obligation to you. Until then, I must walk among your kind."

At this, he stepped out of the flame, and as he did, he became a man, slight of frame, with bright, sharp eyes and the very hint of fire just behind his cheeks.

"I am sorry," said the poor man. "I fear I have imprisoned you yet again."

"You are owed three askings, in your time," said the djinn.

"It is an imposition," said the poor man.

"They were given freely," said the djinn. "I will disappear into this man you see, and perhaps dream of fire and wind, but know nothing else of myself, until you speak my name."

"Very well," said the poor man. "Tell me your name, then."

"I shall say it once, and then I shall forget," said the djinn. "It is the way of these things. It will be yours alone, until you speak it aloud. Are you ready?"

"I am," said the poor man.

CHAPTER THIRTY-FIVE

SOMETHING'S MISSING

The name, when I spoke it, came out thin and strangled. But it came out, and when it did, David released his grip and stepped back. The rage was gone, and in its place was a placid, curious expression.

"Your father saved my life," he said, in a quiet, contemplative voice. "And I saved his."

I sat up, still choking and sputtering. The air in the room was calm and as tender as a bruise. David Ginn smiled sadly at me.

"You killed him," I said.

"Yes," he said, "and no." He offered me his hand. Unsure what else to do, I took it, and he helped me up. Then he opened his hand to reveal a tiny fire flickering inside. He set the little flame in the air between us, and now the room was lit with the flame's warm, strange glow.

"It's true that David Ginn killed your father," he said. "But you are no longer speaking to David Ginn. And had I been there, I would not have allowed your father's death."

He didn't look any different. Calmer, maybe. Unburdened.

But somehow, I knew he was telling the truth. He wasn't David Ginn anymore. He looked like David Ginn, but he was something else entirely.

"I don't understand," I said.

"You understand enough," said the djinn. "You spoke my name."

His eyes twinkled in the eerie glimmer of the floating flame. I coughed. My throat still burned.

"Why," I said. "Why did you kill him?"

"As I said," answered the djinn, "in a very real way, I am not his killer. But I believe I can answer your question. And I believe you deserve to hear my answer. However, there are other things I must explain first."

"Vance Cogland," I said.

"Yes. It began with him."

"Any family big enough, and rich enough, will eventually produce someone like Vance Cogland," said David. "An unfortunate certainty of statistics and human nature. I only knew him a short time, but the wind has told me everything I ever needed to know about him."

Cogland was a small-time bully—lazy, mean, cowardly, and not very bright. He believed himself untouchable, and entitled to anything he wanted. Over and over again, his family bailed him out of jail, paid off witnesses to his many outbursts and acts of petty crime, hired expensive lawyers. For all his years as a low-life scumbag, Vance Cogland never served more than a night in jail.

By day, Vance worked for the Fells out of New Orleans. The port was a prime entry point for international transfers. Vance worked his way into the local maritime union, and became a serviceable doorman for animals, money, and barter entering or leaving the country. For a time, at least, he had some value to the Fells. But there were one too many fights, one too many payouts, and eventually Vance was shuttled inland and given a posting that was virtually guaranteed to see no action at all: Lubbock, Texas.

The move had its intended effect. Vance was effectively fired from the Fells. It also had an unintended consequence: Vance got bored.

He used his family stipend to set up a side hustle fencing stolen antiques. He knew enough smugglers and thieves from his New Orleans days that he always had a steady supply of goods to sell. And from his years with the Fells, he knew plenty of shady rich people willing to buy stolen antiques. For a while, he thrived in the shadows of Lubbock, and had nothing to do with the family business.

But when an old woman brought in her antique bottle—a family heirloom that had come over with her grandmother from Ottoman Iraq—Vance's worlds collided. This woman had hoped to get a fair price for the bottle. Guessing at what the bottle contained, Vance still made her an offer that was anything but fair. When she wisely refused, he followed her home, beat her senseless with a tire iron, and stole the bottle.

A true Fell, in possession of such a powerful object, would have enlisted the family's full resources immediately. But Vance had neither the discipline nor the deference to honor his family obligation over his own greed and desires. That night, in the back room of the pawnshop, he tried to draw out the djinn.

"One can only imagine," said the djinn, "that his wishes would have been sordid, dull, and predictable."

Late that night, my dad received a panicked phone call, and

the next morning, he was on a plane to Dallas, and I was standing on the front porch of the home of Sarah Colton-Wong (my best friend in second grade), overnight bag in hand. It was three months after my mom died.

What Vance Cogland didn't know about the vessels that trap djinn is that they are not easy to open. The spells and hexes that seal a djinn inside don't magically undo themselves when you polish the bottle or the lamp. There are complicated and precise movements that are required, and they must be performed in the correct order. It's possible, of course, to chance on the proper sequence of touches, caresses, words, and gestures. But you have to be lucky. It's also possible to crack the code through trial and error. But you have to be patient. Vance Cogland was neither.

Vance had set the bottle into a table vise, twisted the stopper free with a basin wrench, and tried to pry the creature out, first with a coat hanger, then with a pair of needle-nose pliers. He'd succeeded in drawing the djinn halfway out of the bottle, but it had become stuck, and there it had remained for the better part of a day, half in and half out. And that's what my dad walked in on when he got to Vance's store: a half-freed djinn in unimaginable pain, and a freaked-out moron who only wanted the creature for its wishes.

My dad dismissed Vance to another room and got to work. Vance's actions had hopelessly corrupted the magic that would have allowed the djinn a smooth release. So my dad had no choice but to finish what Vance had started, as gently as possible. He used petroleum jelly to lubricate the bottle's mouth, and held the djinn's hands as he slowly eased it, one inch at a time, out of the bottle, stopping anytime the pain got too much.

"The process was arduous," said David. "Every inch came with new crushing pains. But your father was kind and patient. After each little bit of progress, he would stop to let me catch my breath."

Finally, with a great, sucking pop and a little puff of smokeless flame, the djinn slipped out of the bottle and onto the floor of the pawnshop. No sooner had it hit the ground than Vance Cogland was standing there, a shotgun in his hand.

"Now get out," said Vance to my dad. "This one's mine."

And the djinn, alive in the world for the first time in hundreds of years, found itself with a choice to make. To whom did it owe its freedom? The man who had tried to yank it from the bottle, or the one who had successfully and compassionately released it?

So that's how my dad was given three wishes.

"The first wish," said David, "was barely a wish. It was a necessity for survival. Vance Cogland wanted my favors, and he was unwilling to accept anything less. He raised the gun on your father, and your father asked me to protect him."

"So you killed Cogland," I said.

"The world is hardly worse off without him," said David.

"What were the other two wishes?"

David was quiet a moment. He bowed his head into shadow, and for just a second, in silhouette, he seemed almost his old self. Then he looked up, and the strange light caught in his eyes, and once again he was someone else.

"The second wish," he said, "was for you."

"For me?"

"Yes," said David. "Your father asked me to take your sadness away."

His voice was flat, affectless, the voice of someone reading off a recipe for brownies.

"My . . . sadness?"

"Your mother had died," said David. "Some months before."

"No, I get that," I said. "My *sadness*? He told you to take away *my sadness*?"

"I believe it was too much for him to bear," said David. "Your grief, and his own."

"So you just"—I fumbled for better words and found none—"took it away? All of it?"

"I did what was asked," said David.

I had a hundred incredulous questions, but none of them mattered, because I knew that what David was telling me was true. I hadn't grieved for my father because there was nothing in me to grieve. And my grief for my mother had been arrested, and then erased, and all that had been left behind were fragmented memories that felt like they belonged to someone else. It had to be true. It was the only thing that made sense, the only thing that explained how I was.

"H-how?" I stammered at last. "I mean, how do you take someone's sadness away?"

"You were asleep," said David. "I found you in a dream. You were shackled to your sorrow, like an anchor, and I set you free."

"That's a funny way of saying you screwed up my whole life," I said.

David shrugged. He didn't offer any explanation. Maybe there wasn't one. I felt very small, like a tiny chess piece, being lifted through space and moved across the board by large, dispassionate hands. My own feelings didn't even belong to me. They'd been shaped and twisted while I was sleeping. And all these years, my dad had known, and he hadn't said anything.

As I stood there, lost and seething and helpless, a thought occurred to me.

"So," I said in a small, meek voice, "I *was* sad?"

"You were as sad as sad could be," said David. "You cried all day, and all night. You made yourself sick with tears. Oh yes, you were sad, Marjan. You loved her very much. You missed her with all your heart."

"So, what happened to all of that? Is it just . . . gone?"

"You were a child who had lost her mother," said David. "Your sorrow was a mountain. Even if I wanted to, it would take a lifetime to break it down and scatter it upon the wind. No, it isn't gone. It's never been far away."

Every moment of every day, ever since my mother died, I had felt an empty space inside myself. Every night, I'd listened to the voice in my head that told me *Something's missing.* When I ran away, when I blew up, it was because I was looking for that essential, absent fragment of my heart. I would never, never in all my life, have guessed it had been taken from me by a djinn, acting on the wish of my own father.

I didn't know whether to scream or to laugh.

"What about the third wish?" I asked. "Whose life did he wreck with that one?"

"Your father never used it," said the djinn. "He kept it in reserve, and because he did, I could not return to the palaces of the sky where once I lived. I owed a debt to a human, and so I have remained a human until such time as the debt would be paid."

"I don't understand," I said. "You killed my dad. Why did you kill him, if you needed him to make another wish?"

"I didn't kill him," said David. "David Ginn killed him."

"Isn't that the same thing?" I asked.

"Not at all," said David. "I am a spirit of the wind and the fire. I walk on clouds and dance through dreams. David Ginn is—was—an accountant who loved his family more than anything else in the world, and would have done anything necessary to keep them safe."

"But he was you," I said. "And you were him."

"David was human, through and through," said the djinn. "He didn't know what he was."

"So why did he kill my dad?" I asked. "They were friends."

"Your father called David to his house one day," said David. "He was worried. Worried about you. He was worried that he'd made a mistake. He was afraid of losing you. He was afraid he'd already lost you. David listened, as any good friend would. He offered his best advice, which wasn't very good. And then, your father began to say strange things."

"Strange?"

"He began to apologize," said the djinn. "At first he apologized for burdening David with his problems, but then he began to apologize for something that he said would happen very soon. He thanked David for being such a good friend. He told him that everything would be over quickly, and that David wouldn't feel anything. He told him not to worry about Liz or Cole or Ramsey. He told him that he would say a word, a name, and that things would become very odd after that, and that he was sorry for everything.

"I can't say if David knew, in that moment, what he really was," the djinn continued. "But he knew that if he did not stop your father immediately, something terrible would happen. He didn't care what happened to him—he'd never thought himself anything special. But his children were more precious to him than life itself, and so when this terrible foreboding rose in him, he dug deep into himself, and drew forth a power he did not know he possessed. He summoned the wind and the fire, and thus your father died before he could speak my name."

The djinn bowed his head and was quiet.

"Did he know?" I asked. "Did you—David, I mean—know what he'd done?"

"For a moment," said the djinn. "But when he drew on my power, he awoke me. I made him forget. It was the only way to keep him safe. The guilt and confusion would have destroyed him."

"And now I've destroyed him, right?"

"He was never real," said the djinn. "You destroyed an illusion."

"I babysat those kids," I said.

"Yes," said the djinn. "And they were phantoms. They all believed themselves to be human, of course. But they were figments of David's imagination. And he was a figment of mine."

I looked around at the cold, dead house. It was as dark as a tomb except for the floating light.

"What am I supposed to do now?" I asked, mostly to myself.

"I would think," said the djinn, "you'd want to make your final wish."

"My final wish?" I asked.

"I told you your father never used it," he said.

"So, what, it passes from one generation to the next? Is that how wishes go?"

"He left you everything he had," said David. "The wish belongs to you now."

I looked around, at the old broom, at the newspapers scattered across the floor, at the chain lying in a lifeless heap. They'd been real, just a moment before. All of this had been real.

"Could you bring them back?" I asked.

"I could," said David. "It would do them no favor. They would live on for you. But they would not be real. Their lives would only exist in the moments where they intersected with yours."

I picked up the chain, and let it drop to the floor. It landed with a dull clang and thump. There was no life there, and no desire to be alive. Those boys with their bright eyes and nut-blond hair were gone. There wasn't a trace of them. And still, I felt no sorrow.

"Will anyone miss them?" I asked.

"If anyone remembers them, it will only be as if they knew the Ginns a long time ago," said the djinn.

"What about me?" I said. "Will I remember them?"

"Would you like to?"

"Is that my third wish?"

"It's a courtesy," said the djinn. "The wish is still yours."

"Then yes," I said. "I think I would like to remember them."

The djinn nodded.

"You need not tell me your wish now," said the djinn. "It is yours to do with as you please."

"Good," I said. "I think I'd like some time."

"When you're ready," said the djinn, "speak my name. I will be listening."

I didn't know what else to say. Everything in my life had been a misunderstanding, a mistake. And because of it, my dad was dead, and I couldn't grieve for him. I turned away from the djinn and began fumbling through the darkened house toward the door. As I crossed the living room, I saw that the old bottle was still resting on the moldy mantel, unchanged by the transformation that had come over the house. I considered it for a moment, and was about to continue on to the door, when something on the floor caught my eye.

It was the two cards that Cole had shown me. The dragon and the dark castle. They both lay faceup on the floor, a bit worse for wear, but intact. I picked them up, then glanced back at the djinn. Was it a mistake, these two wayward props of the Ginn family fantasy? Were they even real?

The djinn watched me from the darkness of the dining room, a shadow among shadows, and gave no answer.

CHAPTER THIRTY-SIX

LAST WISHES

I signed the papers with Dr. Paulson a week later. We negotiated a fair rental fee for the procedure room, and some strict protocols around our use of it. It was disorienting to not have David's advice in my ear through the process, but I got the deal that I wanted, and Dr. P seemed happy too. Dr. Batiste eagerly agreed to work with me when I needed him.

Malloryn was happy to come on board too.

"Looks like you're starting to get the hang of the confidence thing," she said.

"Learning from the best," I replied.

Malloryn and I had anatomy class together, and I made no secret of being friends with her. Soon she was eating lunch with me and Carrie and Grace. Carrie was a bit suspicious of her at first. But even though we'd agreed to never discuss the events at Menagerie in public, it was clear that Malloryn, Grace, and I had a connection, and finally Carrie relaxed. We were an odd group, and Malloryn made us more odd, but I didn't mind.

She was talking with her parents now, once a week at least.

They wanted her to come home, but she had refused, politely but firmly.

"They love me," she told me one day. "I know they do. I love them, too. But they're still afraid. And until they know that they don't have to be afraid, it's better this way." She sounded, for a moment, defeated. Then the bright spark returned to her eyes. "Maybe they'll change. I hope they do."

I found myself wondering if there was a spell for that.

I hesitated about calling Ezra. A part of me still didn't want anything to do with her. But Ezra knew the dark side of this world, and we'd need that knowledge. When I did call, it occurred to me that I wasn't sure she'd say yes. I couldn't afford the kind of money Horatio had been throwing around. All I had to offer was the occasional hidden thing to be found, and it turned out that was enough.

Dr. P and I closed the deal in my office. It was studious and quiet, like working in a library, each of us reading carefully the words we'd both agreed on, before putting our signatures down while a notary stood in the corner, her stamp pad in hand. After it was done, we hugged while the notary finalized the contract, and then everyone else left, and I remained.

The room felt smaller and older than it had when I'd first taken over. At the same time, it felt emptier and less familiar, even though I hadn't changed anything. I sat in my dad's chair and kicked my feet up onto the desk one last time.

Something's missing, murmured the voice inside my head. I had to smile a bit. At least I knew what it was.

I wondered if my dad would have approved of how I was handling things, but it didn't matter. It wasn't his problem, keeping all these animals alive and healthy. It was mine, and I had to do it my own way.

I felt like I understood the creatures a little bit—better, at least, than the Fells. Horatio had understood them too, I thought. Differently than I did—maybe better than I did. Maybe they *were* our imagination. Maybe our greatest hopes and our darkest fears are strong enough to will a physical form into being. Maybe the manticore was the sum of nightmares, and Kipling the griffon was the embodiment of our most noble instincts. I wasn't sure. I didn't pretend to know why they existed, or how. Maybe I didn't need to know.

I was sure of one thing, though. Horatio had said it. The creatures all took up space in people's lives. When they came, they brought complexity and change, but more than anything else, they brought the weight of their presence. They came to people who had space to give. Malloryn and her loneliness, Kent Hayashi and his tormented talent, even Horatio and his horribly misguided quest, they'd all beckoned—screamed—for the beings that had padded into their lives.

These animals had a special talent for finding the spaces that fit them. There were so many empty places in so many people's lives. I had them too. And maybe they were like magnets. Maybe they were beacons—not for any animal but for exactly one. And maybe each animal was itself a hungry spirit, looking for exactly the space that fit, exactly the place where it belonged.

I imagined the world crisscrossed with the paths of people and creatures, trying to find each other. Chasing the feeling of something that wasn't there, finding themselves alone in places where the language was unfamiliar, where the customs made no sense. Crossing highways in the dark, hiding out in the deepest forests, or the most silent deserts, or on the lonely rooftops of tall buildings. And then finally finding themselves face-to-face in a warm doorway somewhere, fur caked in mud, hearts bruised and hurting, knowing for the first time why they'd both come so far.

Maybe the day you welcomed one of these animals into your life, the day you accepted both its gifts and its trials, the day you chose to shoulder that weight, was the day you understood at last the shape of the thing that was missing.

Jane Glass called me a few days after the sale of the clinic. It was the first I'd heard from her since the night at Horatio's estate. The night I'd helped save the world.

"I need to see you," she said.

We met on a bench near a fenced-off dog run—the sort of faded old bench that makes you just a little bit invisible as soon as you sit down on it. Maybe some old homeless wizard had put a spell on it. I believed in people like that now—people like Malloryn who might get it exactly right once or twice in their lives, but leave a long trail of interesting failures in their wakes. I got there first, so I sat and watched the rough joy of a golden retriever wrestling with a Staffie.

Jane sat down next to me a few minutes later, and set a large canvas shoulder bag between us. It made a heavy, hollow sound on the bench.

"Open it," she said.

Inside was the teapot.

"Jane," I whispered.

"I had to," she said. "I think . . . I think maybe we're not supposed to be doing this anymore."

"How . . ."

"It wasn't hard," she said. "Not too hard, anyway. I don't know if you've heard, but there are about a hundred and fifty animals running wild right now. Makes for a pretty good distraction."

"When they find out . . ."

"Oh, they'll be mad," said Jane. "But after today, there won't be much they can do. Anyway, I thought you'd like to be here. To see it."

Without another word, she put her hand on the lid of the teapot and lifted it off, revealing a rough-hewn hole. Inside was a heavy, cast-iron darkness that smelled of ash and smoke. For a moment, nothing stirred.

After a few seconds, something scuttled in the depths of the pot. A tiny silver dragon flitted up from the darkness on hummingbird wings. It hovered before us, a delicate shimmer of mercury in the afternoon sunlight. Its large, curious eyes regarded us for a moment.

"There you are," said Jane. "I've been wanting to meet you for so long."

The dragon hovered in front of her face.

"You're free now," she said. "I hope we mostly did right by you."

The dragon said nothing. It floated there a moment longer. Then it disappeared into the sky like a streak of quicksilver lightning. Jane watched it go, a look of wistful satisfaction on her face.

"I figured you of all people would appreciate this," said Jane. "Honestly, you were my inspiration. If you could set all those animals free, well . . ." She paused and laughed to herself. "You set the bar pretty damn high."

"How's anyone going to find me now?" I asked.

"They'll find you," said Jane. "Same way they always seem to find us, when they need us. Maybe I can help you with that."

"We could use your help," I said. "You know this world better than any of us."

"Who's we?"

"A few people," I said. "Friends."

"Are we friends now, Marjan?" said Jane.

"I guess we might be," I said.

"Then yes," said Jane. "I accept. Jacob does too."

"Who's Jacob?"

Jane nodded toward the road. A familiar black sedan was parked there. The driver, leaning against the passenger-side door, offered a lazy, tattooed salute in our general direction.

"Can you trust him?" I asked.

"We're not all bad," said Jane.

"We start in a couple of weeks," I said. "There's something I have to take care of first."

The flight to London was long and uncomfortable. Dr. Batiste and I had to sit in the very back of the plane because they were the only seats I could book at short notice and on my budget. But it wasn't my comfort I was concerned about.

Simon Stoddard didn't seem surprised to hear from me, and he didn't seem all that surprised by what I had to say. Kipling's feathers were falling out in patches. His talons were cracking and splitting when he walked, muscles trembling with each step. His eyesight was failing. Simon took in my words, my admission, with quiet, even concern, and then invited me and Dr. Batiste to the manor.

Driving the narrow country roads to the estate, I felt a lightness inside me. The truth, what I understood of it, didn't scare me anymore. It belonged to other people now. They would do with it what they wanted, and I would be there to help them make the right choice.

But the lightness was balanced out by a dread I'd been

carrying since we'd boarded the plane. At some point, I'd have to face Sebastian. I didn't want to lose him. But I didn't deserve his friendship, and it felt selfish of me to think my feelings mattered at all. I'd used him when I needed him, and whether or not I had meant to do it, I had misled him in a terrible way. I wouldn't want someone like me in my life. Especially not at a time like this.

At the manor, Dr. Batiste and I were met by a small delegation of Stoddards, some pleading for Kipling's life, others pleading to end it. Sebastian wasn't with them, which was a relief. We listened to all of them. Then I told them what I knew, and I let Dr. Batiste speak for himself. Despite jet lag and the general strangeness of this meeting, he was quite good. Between the two of us, we managed to convince nearly all of them to sign off on a plan to end Kipling's life.

Dr. Batiste took over for the next two days. With Simon's help, he procured the chemicals he would need. With mine, he prepared the injection site—a prominent vein on Kipling's left foreleg. We shaved a patch of feathers and fur away and marked the spot with a Sharpie. All the while, Kipling looked on with rheumy disinterest.

The mansion began to fill with Stoddards of all ages. They mingled in the halls and wandered the grounds. They sat by the black pond, alone or in small, whispering groups. And one by one, they filed through the room that had become Kipling's den, and paid quiet respects.

Anytime a car rolled up the driveway, I looked for Sebastian. When it wasn't him, I felt a mixture of disappointment and relief. I wondered if he might not come at all. Part of me hoped I wouldn't have to face him. Another part of me wanted so badly to talk to him, to feel the comfort of not being totally alone.

When he did show up, he barely acknowledged me. He walked right by me in the great hall with little more than a cold nod. I felt sick for the rest of the day.

The next time I saw him, in the same sitting room where we'd first met, he gave me a look that was equal parts angry and helpless, and then looked away. He wasn't going to make any effort to talk to me. If I had something to say to him, I would have to earn his attention.

I walked across a room of Stoddard kin to where he was standing, ignoring the occasional stare. He only looked at me again when I had positioned myself directly beside him. When he did, I could see that his eyes were red from crying.

"Hey," I said.

"Hey," he replied.

"Can we talk?" I asked. "Somewhere away from here?"

We left the manor through a side door and walked across the meadow, and then into the woods, not speaking. A light rain had begun to fall. The forest smelled of loam and moss. My boots sank into the damp earth as I walked. Starlings chittered from the trees. Rain pattered on the leaves. We walked until we couldn't see the manor house anymore, and then I stopped.

"Sebastian," I said. "I'm sorry."

He stopped too, a few paces ahead of me. For a few seconds, he just stood there, his back to me.

"You let me hope," he said at last.

"I was confused," I said. "And then I was scared."

He turned around to face me, tears in his eyes.

"What do you want me to say?" he said. "You want me to forgive you?"

"I couldn't have saved him," I said. "Even then. All I could have done was make this happen sooner. I'm sorry I didn't."

He shook his head.

"You're angry," I said. "You have the right to be angry."

"I don't know what I am," he said. "Yes, I'm angry. I'm not sure who, or what, I'm angry at. Everything, I think. Mostly I'm sad." He paused. "Isn't there something more you can do?" he asked. "Some kind of . . . I don't know, magic?"

"Magic is . . . something else," I said. "It might be in me, somewhere, but it's not what I do."

"Can't you find someone who—"

He bit off his thought, then cursed to himself. He nodded, his eyes lost, somewhere else. He thrust his hands into his pockets and sat down on the stump of a fallen tree.

"So that's it," he said. "A griffon. Gone."

I could have said any number of reassuring things about Kipling then—how he'd lived a good life, how he'd gotten to see so many generations of Stoddards, how he'd known so much love in his time. But sadness, maybe, was like anger. You have a right to as much of it as you need. And like anger, sadness doesn't want to be tempered. It wants to be seen.

drop-ceiling patterns, sunlight, and strange silence

I came to sit next to him. I took his hand in both of mine. I didn't know what we were to each other anymore. But I knew he needed comfort. And I wasn't about to let him down again.

"These are his woods," he said. "I want people to remember that."

"Then tell them," I said. "Tell everyone."

The night before Kipling's last day, Simon, Dr. Batiste, and I sat down together in a small, secluded drawing room to go over the details one last time. The injection had already been prepared. We didn't know how much would be enough, so just to be safe, Dr. Batiste had calculated an amount that would have killed ten horses.

"He pulled me out of the pond when I was five," said Simon. "I fell in. I could have drowned. I reckon he's saved a dozen Stoddard children from that water over the years."

"You'd think someone would put a fence around it," said Dr. Batiste.

"We've never needed one before," said Simon. "I suppose we have taken him for granted in many ways. He's always been there."

"I'm sorry I let him suffer," I said. "I'm sorry to all of you."

Simon smiled a sad smile. "I'm not sure we would have been able to let him go, just like that," he said. "Even now, it seems impossible. How does anyone do this?"

In the grand foyer, a small gathering of Stoddards sat with Kipling by the fire. A mother instructed a young child to pet his forehead gently, along the grain of his feathers. I watched them for a moment, and felt the warm, bitter presence of grief. For the first time, I could sense exactly the empty place inside myself, the hollowness in the very center of my heart where sadness should have been.

"He's all of ours," said someone standing beside me—a house steward who'd come bearing mugs of hot chocolate for the children. He paused in the doorway, cocoa steaming on his tray, tears gathering in his eyes. "Or we're all his. We shall miss him terribly."

The morning was brisk and cool. A light frost twinkled on the tips of the grass, and the low sun painted the frost orange. I showered and dressed and met Simon and Dr. Batiste at the bottom of the stairs. The family was already up and dressed in somber finery.

Together we coaxed Kipling up from the floor. The griffon wobbled to his feet, his legs quivering beneath his weight, his wings extending and folding in to try to moderate his balance.

Simon gently guided Kipling into the broad main hallway. The griffon was led out a back door and onto the grounds. At first, he walked with slow, lumbering steps, pausing every few paces to rest. Each time he stopped, the shaking of his muscles was so clear that I was worried he might not even make it to the spot.

But once he got outside, he seemed to liven up a bit. With Simon leading the way, he seemed to gather where we were going. Soon it was Kipling who led the way, and Simon walked alongside him, one hand resting on the creature's mountainous shoulder.

Aloysius Stoddard was buried on a gentle slope under an oak tree. A faded, worn granite stone with a spade-shaped top marked his grave. Beside Aloysius's grave, a heavy white cloth had been laid out, and Kipling quite naturally curled up on it. The family huddled around him, laying their hands on him, stroking his head and his wings. He looked up at them with big, weary eyes. He gave a little click of his beak, then rested his head on the ground.

There were tears all around. Someone, a groundskeeper, I believe, began to sing "Danny Boy." Dr. Batiste and I kept a respectful distance, watching Simon for the right time to approach and begin.

The song ended and Simon glanced at me. It was as much of a signal as he could give. We stepped forward, and the crowd parted to let us through. Dr. Batiste knelt at Kipling's side, set his bag down, and opened it. Kipling watched with quiet unblinking eyes as Dr. Batiste drew out the syringe.

With a breath to steady myself, I rested a hand on Kipling's flank. His weariness flowed into me. Longing and resignation followed. Kipling looked up to the sky, and I felt his heart flutter in delight.

"Soon," I whispered into his ear.

I glanced at Dr. Batiste, nodded. I was ready. He was too.

"You'll only feel this for a second," I said. The griffon clicked his beak. I turned to the people. "This will be very quick," I said. "Ten or twenty seconds, and it'll be done."

Sobs, whispers of goodbye, soft whimpers of grief. Pausing for just a moment to take in the wonder of Kipling one last time, I touched his shoulder. Suddenly I felt him coursing through me again.

Even stronger than before, the sorrow came, like the people gathered around him were reflecting it back onto him, amplifying it, until it tumbled in walloping, disjointed waves. I let its swells roll into every part of me. It was ferocious and incandescent. It burned hot and sweet in my eyes and in my chest, and in places I didn't even know could feel heat or taste sweetness. It was radiant and pure and honest, and for a single exquisite moment, I could hold in my heart everything and everyone I'd lost or let slip away, and in that moment I felt whole and complete.

Then pain crashed in behind it, and the moment shattered. A wall of agony hit every part of me at once. There was lightning and thunder in his bones, the suffocating absence of hunger in his guts, the fiery scrape of breath in his lungs. I shut my eyes and gritted my teeth against it. It was almost too much to bear, but it was the answer I needed. He was ready. I willed my hand to be still against the pain.

Then Dr. Batiste slipped the needle into his vein, and pushed the plunger down.

Almost immediately Kipling's body relaxed. His wings flopped down onto the ground, one of them coming to rest in a sort of A-frame shape. His eyes went soft, and then vacant. He breathed three times, each breath louder and slower than the one before. Then he was still.

I felt the last of him leave, a flame flickering down to embers, and then winking out into cold darkness.

I left Dr. Batiste among the Stoddards, and walked alone down the grass slope, following the smooth curve of the earth until it ended at the edge of the black pond. Even up close, even with the rays of a weak, distant sun falling over it, the water had the color and opacity of obsidian.

Something had blasted through me. A comet had scudded through my guts, blazing into the depths, revealing for just a moment how deep they were. In its wake, those empty spaces were crying out, hungering for light, for love. I gazed into the fathomless water, and wondered if it went down two feet, or two miles.

"The family appreciates your service," said a voice behind me. I turned to see Simon. He held out an envelope to me, and after a moment, I took it. He nodded, then came to stand beside me at the edge of the pond.

The whirring of machinery stirred the air. A yellow excavator hoisted Kipling's trussed-up body and swiveled to lower it into the fresh grave that had been dug for him beside the grave of Aloysius. A Chopin nocturne started to pipe from the manor, and the family shuffled back down the hill toward the house, where canapés and sandwiches were waiting.

"They'll need me in a moment," said Simon.

"You know," I said, "you're really good at what you do."

"And what's that?" said Simon.

"Taking care of your family," I said.

"Thank you," he said. "You are too. One way or another, our talents are what shape our lives, Ms. Dastani."

He smiled a thoughtful smile. Then he glanced back up to the house.

"A driver will be out front for you in ten minutes," he said. "Take as long as you need. You'll find your travel taken care of, with our gratitude."

And with that, he turned and walked up the hill, and I was alone again.

I knew what my last wish would be, and it seemed like the right time to make it. I walked past the pond and into the woods. The dark air was gentle and cool. Among these low, green trees, I could almost imagine coming across a unicorn, snared in a boar trap.

I walked until I couldn't hear the sounds from the manor. In a little clearing, in a sliver of pale sunlight, I whispered the djinn's name. The air seemed to tighten just a bit, like it was suddenly paying more attention.

"I want it back," I said. "Do you hear me? That's the wish."

For a moment, nothing happened. For a moment, I felt the person I'd been since I was seven years old. I felt her—me—fully, missing parts and all. She was all I'd ever known, all I could ever remember being, and she was about to end. All I could do now was breathe, feel the world pass in and out of me, and wait.

A sound in the woods distracted me. The snap of a twig underfoot. I looked up and saw a cat, bedraggled and weary, ribs showing through its mangy fur, slinking toward me from the wood. As it got closer, I recognized the old feral tom from the clinic. Unafraid now, it padded up to me and nuzzled its snout against my leg.

It's never been far away, David had said.

"I'm sorry," I said to the cat, and to my father, and to everyone I'd hurt, ever.

I reached down and ran my fingers softly over its fur, feeling the spiky ends. The cat arched its back. Maybe it sensed the transformation in the space between my fingertips and its skin. Maybe it just wasn't used to being touched.

As gently as I could, I pushed my fingers through the bristle of its fur, until I felt its skin against mine. I spread my hand so that my palm rested against the curve of the old cat's neck, and the sweet, natural warmth of the blood in its veins radiated into me. I felt the light leave its body, pass into the palm of my hand, and spread until it filled my whole being. I heard the chirp of morning birds, sparrows rising up from the trees. I saw my mother's face smiling back at me, clearer than any picture, as real as if I were six years old again. The world felt warm and sweet, and I couldn't help but smile back. Our secret smile.

And then everything crumbled, and her smile faded into a kaleidoscope of liverwurst floors, chemical drips, machines ticking down her time, until there was almost none left, until we moved her into the extra room that we never used for anything, except her bed. And then one day, when the sky through the windows was so bright that my eyes ached from it, in that bed, in that room, the pain ended, and for a moment the universe was so quiet that I could almost hear her leave.

My breath caught in my ribs. A spasm traveled up my spine. My legs gave out, and I was sobbing in the grass.

I didn't hear Sebastian, and I don't know how he found me. But he was there. He didn't say anything, and I didn't either. We didn't have to.

After a moment, he held out his hand to me. And after another moment, I took it, and he helped me to stand. Somewhere, a car horn beeped once. Somewhere, Dr. Batiste was wondering where I had gone.

Sebastian and I stood there in the clearing, our hands clasped tight, both of us different people than we'd been a day ago, an hour ago. Our hearts were broken open, and the love inside them was tender and full. We were grieving. The future was rushing in.

It could wait a minute longer.

ACKNOWLEDGMENTS

This book would not exist without the support, guidance, and patience of a surprisingly large number of immensely talented and wonderful people. It's been my privilege to work with all of them, and it is my great privilege to be able to thank them here.

My amazing literary agent, Katelyn Detweiler, has been a boundless source of inspiration and encouragement. Her patience and care with every draft (there were many!); her gentle creative nudges that opened up huge new possibilities for characters, scenes, and storylines; and her unwavering support throughout this book's long journey have been a true gift. And the support this book has received from everyone at Jill Grinberg Literary Management, including but not limited to Denise Page, Sam Farkas, and Sophia Seidner, has been empowering and humbling. Every writer should be so lucky to have such angels in their corner.

For introducing me to Katelyn, and for many other good works besides, I must also thank my film and TV agent, Matthew Snyder at Creative Artists. Matthew's counsel over the years has been wise, calm, and direct, and my gratitude to him is boundless.

This book found an incredible home at Simon & Schuster

Books for Young Readers, and the enthusiasm and hospitality shown by everyone I've encountered there has overwhelmed me. First and foremost, my wonderful editor, Kendra Levin, embraced this story with her whole heart and then challenged it to be deeper, sharper, warmer, and stranger than I could have ever hoped for. Working with her has been a thrill and an honor, and the book is exponentially better because of her.

There are many others at Simon & Schuster who deserve thanks—some of whom I have had the pleasure to work with, and others whom I have not yet met directly but whose work has been instrumental in making this book a reality. I owe a great debt of gratitude for the leadership and vision of Jonathan Karp, Jon Anderson, and Justin Chanda. I'm also immensely grateful to Krista Vossen and the art department for turning a barely formatted Word document into a beautiful object. Thanks are also due to my keen-eyed copyeditor, Bara MacNeill, whose diligence and thoroughness have made every scene sparkle, and to Amanda Ramirez and Beza Wondie for their invaluable assistance in the editorial process and beyond. The entire Simon & Schuster Children's marketing team has lit a fire under this book, and I couldn't be more grateful. For bringing *Once There Was* to the United Kingdom, Australia, and other English-language audiences, I am thankful to Rachel Denwood and Katie Lawrence and everyone supporting them at Simon & Schuster UK. And thanks to Stephanie Voros and her foreign rights team, this story will have a life in many other languages, a fact that continues to astound me. And lastly, thanks to Jenica Nasworthy for doing the incredibly important work of making sure that everything runs smoothly backstage and that this manuscript in fact becomes a book.

My partners at Imagine Entertainment have been

inspirational, both with their ideas and with their enthusiasm for this story as it has developed. Thanks especially to Bryce Dallas Howard, to Laeta Kalogridis, to Karen Lunder, to Jon Swartz, and to everyone at Imagine who supports them.

Justin Wilkes was the first champion of this story, and almost a decade later, he remains a great champion. It's been the honor of a lifetime to work on something so personal for so long, with such a great friend. Thank you, Cap.

I'd also like to acknowledge a number of friends and fellow travelers who read and supported this story along the way. Matt Dellinger and Laura Hohnhold saw the early potential in the series of loosely linked short stories that eventually became this book. Scott Westerfeld shared his wisdom on film and television dealings. And Andrew Fitzgerald and Robin Sloan, the Moon Yeti writing squad, gave me multiple rounds of valuable feedback on early drafts, as well as general encouragement and creative awesomeness.

My parents, Mike and Paula, worked hard every day when I was growing up and always encouraged me—sometimes at great expense—to follow my passions. They also encouraged me to understand my Iranian heritage. It's because of them that I was able to write this book. Thank you, guys.

My grandmother, my Mamanbozorg, gave me the gift of "Yeki bood, yeki nabood" when I was very young, and many other gifts too. To this day, when I see those words, I hear them in her voice.

My daughters, Tilden and Sibley, have been very patient with Daddy while he fusses over rewrites and copyedits, and in the meantime have somehow grown up from babies into wonderful, creative, curious kids, and it is wild how much I love them.

Lastly, thank you, Jane. You didn't know what you were signing up for when you told me I should write the one about the veterinary clinic for imaginary animals. You let this story take up space in our lives for a long time—space you created by being professionally brilliant and amazing—with no certain outcome. You talked me out of many bad ideas and yet somehow never gave up on me. You're the best mama our kids could ever have and the best person I could ever hope to go through life with. Fiero forever!